A Burning
in
Homeland

RICHARD YANCEY

Simon & Schuster
NEW YORK   LONDON   TORONTO   SYDNEY   SINGAPORE

Fiction
4

SIMON & SCHUSTER
Rockefeller Center
1230 Avenue of the Americas
New York, NY 10020

SIMON & SCHUSTER and colophon are registered trademarks
of Simon & Schuster, Inc.

For information about special discounts for bulk purchases,
please contact Simon & Schuster Special Sales:
1-800-456-6798 or business@simonandschuster.com

Manufactured in the United States of America

10 9 8 7 6 5 4 3 2 1

Library of Congress Cataloging-in-Publication Data
Yancey, Richard.
    A burning in homeland / Richard Yancey.
      p.   cm.
1. Crimes of passion—Fiction. 2. Florida—Fiction.
PS3625.A675 B87 2003
813'.6—dc21   2002070833

ISBN 0-7432-3013-2

To Sandy, my darling, my one, my all: this is for you.

ACKNOWLEDGMENTS

A Burning in Homeland grew in its telling, beginning as a short story in 1987, becoming a screenplay in 1993, and finally evolving into its present form by the end of this past century. Through the years, I have relied upon the wisdom and guidance of many insightful and talented people, whose enthusiasm for this story helped me tend the garden until it finally bore fruit.

Dr. John L. Foster read the original short story and provided invaluable encouragement. The Academy of Motion Picture Arts and Sciences, through its Nicholl Fellowships in Screenwriting program, recognized the merits of the tale. I am also indebted to the folks at the Austin Film Festival.

Doctors Jeffrey and Vickie Wilt generously offered their help when medical questions arose.

My agent, Brian DeFiore, offered enthusiastic support, inspiration, and guidance. I must also thank Mark Roy for his initial read and recommendation of the book.

Chuck Adams, my editor at Simon & Schuster, enabled me to see this story with a fresh eye. I am deeply grateful for his careful and caring reading of the book.

And, finally, *A Burning in Homeland* would not exist had it not been for my wife, to whom this book is dedicated. She has been, and always will be, my confidante, my dear companion, and my best friend. It was as much her will as it was mine that drove the writing of this story. Though my faith in it often faltered, hers never did.

A Burning
in
Homeland

I opened to my beloved; but my beloved had withdrawn himself, and was gone: my soul failed when he spake: I sought him, but I could not find him; I called him, but he gave me no answer.

— THE SONG OF SOLOMON

PROLOGUE

At the end of our dirt road, on the top of a green hill, beside a live-oak tree draped with Spanish moss, there was a little white church, and beside that little white church was a little white house, where the pastor lived. His name was Ned Jeffries, but everybody called him Pastor. He was a small man, and thin, with dark hair and squinty eyes. He wasn't a very friendly man, and some people said he was too sour, even for a Baptist preacher. Momma didn't like him much; she said he was too cold, that he didn't like people. But Daddy said it wasn't that Pastor didn't like people, he just liked God more. "That's terrible," Momma said. "That's a terrible thing to say." Daddy said, "What I mean to say is, he finds God more interesting." Momma said she never heard of such a thing. "Any man who finds God more interesting than people has no business in a church." Daddy didn't say anything after that.

Now Pastor had a wife, who we called Miss Mavis, and she was the prettiest lady in town. Daddy told my brother Bertram she was the prettiest lady in town because all the other pretty ladies in town talked about her, about how her looks were slipping, and that's how you tell who the prettiest lady in town is.

I didn't know much about that, but she sure seemed pretty to me. On Sundays she wore a white dress, and most of the time she wore her hair up, except for some dark strands that would come loose and hang beside her round face, the ends curling under to touch her neck. She *was* a lot prettier than Pastor. Her teeth were small and even; Pastor's were long and yellow. Her eyes were large and blue; his were squinty, like I said, and very dark, almost black. She was a very pretty woman who

3

looked even prettier next to her husband. His homeliness made her shine. They would stand together after the service just outside the main doors, greeting everybody as they came out, her smiling and laughing and him grinning like it hurt, putting his limp hand in yours and giving it a quick shake while he was looking at the next person in line. "It's good to see you," he'd say, and when my turn came he'd put a sweaty hand on my head and say, "And how good it is to see *you*, Robert Lee." I wouldn't say anything back and Momma would poke me, and later in the car she would turn around in her seat and say, "You must start talking to the pastor, Robert Lee." And Bertram, my brother, would say, "Shiny don't talk to nobody." And Momma would tell Bertram to hush.

They had a daughter together, Pastor and Miss Mavis, their only child. They named her Sharon-Rose. She was a big girl for her age, with long, golden hair and a round face like her momma. She was three years older than me so I didn't know her very well, until that summer came when she moved in with us, because God burned her house to the ground, and me and her became engaged to be married, through no fault of my own.

But it wasn't Sharon-Rose's fault, either, when I think about it. It was more Miss Mavis's fault, for making her take a bath so late. But that wasn't really Miss Mavis's fault, because she wouldn't have been in my house taking a bath if it hadn't been for the fire, which wouldn't have happened if Halley Martin hadn't killed Walter Hughes years and years before I was even born.

So maybe it was Halley Martin's fault I got engaged at the age of seven. Everybody said the fire that night was God's will, but that was hard to think about, God willing Halley Martin to fall in love, so Walter Hughes would die, so Miss Mavis would marry Pastor and have Sharon-Rose, so their house would burn down, so they would have to move in with us, just so I would be engaged to a girl I didn't even like.

God's ways are mysterious indeed. That's what Momma always said. I never knew what she meant by that, but I started to understand, just a little, beginning on that night when the pastor's house burned clear to the ground.

ONE

Bertram?"

"What?"

"Bertram, can you sleep?"

"Uh-huh. I'm in a deep, deep sleep, Shiny."

"Bertram, they ain't really coming to live with us, are they?"

"I don't know. Shut up and go to sleep, Shiny."

But I couldn't sleep. I watched the leaf-shadows dance and twist on the ceiling. I listened to Bertram breathe. I raised my arm in the dark and sniffed it. It smelled like smoke. I sniffed my fingertips. They smelled like smoke too. I threw back the covers and sniffed my knees.

"Shiny, what are you doin'?"

"Sniffing my knees."

"There's something not right about you."

"I smell like smoke. You smell like smoke, Bertram?"

"Well, I don't know. You s'pose I should start pokin' my nose into all my parts, like a dog?" He snorted. "Go to sleep, Shiny."

"I can't sleep."

"Then sniff yourself quieter!"

I watched the leaf-shadows dance some more.

"Momma said they were," I said. "She said it tonight on the way back from the fire. Miss Mavis and Sharon-Rose are coming tomorrow, and Pastor too if he don't die in the hospital."

"So what do you care if they do?"

"Well, where're they going to sleep?"

"Didn't Momma tell you? They're taking your bed. You'll have to sniff yourself on the sofa."

5

"But Bertram, why do they have to stay with *us*?"

"I told you I don't know! Now, shut up. Shut up! Shut up, shut up, shut up!"

"But Bertram . . ."

"If you don't shut up I'm coming over there and shutting you up!"

I didn't want him to come over and shut me up, so I shut up. I tried to sleep. It's hard to sleep when you know it's almost morning and soon the sun will be shining through your window and all the wide world will be awake, except the crickets, which I didn't even know where crickets went during the day. I never saw a cricket in the sun. Where did crickets sleep? They must go underground. I never dug up a cricket, though. Worms and roly-poleys and tiny snails, but never a cricket. Did they sleep in holes like rabbits? Were there cricket holes? Did they live in hollow logs or under dry leaves? I could hear them now, chirping under my window. Momma said crickets sing because they're lonely. Come to think of it, I never saw two crickets together, though I could hear whole choirs of them, singing. I couldn't figure out how there could be so many of them and still all of them so lonely. But here I was with Bertram in the bed right next to mine, and I felt lonely. I didn't want the Jeffries to come live with us. There was something strange and sad about Miss Mavis, and Sharon-Rose was a girl. I didn't know much about girls, but I knew enough to stay clear of them. I didn't understand half the things they talked about, and they smelled funny. Sharon-Rose smelled like burnt oranges, but I had only caught a whiff of it this night, and she had just come from a fire so I wasn't sure if it was her natural smell or if she picked it up inside her burning house before she ran out.

She saw me and Bertram standing beneath the arms of the live-oak tree. I saw her standing with Miss Mavis and Momma by the big red fire truck at the edge of the dirt road. Bertram had taken me halfway up the hill to get a better look at the fire. I had never seen a house-fire before. Even halfway up it was hot on my face, and I could see it reflected in my brother's eyes, dancing.

It was a hot night, made all the hotter by the fire. I saw Daddy with the other volunteer firemen trudging up the hill, dragging the fire hose. Daddy held the nozzle on his shoulder while the man behind him gave the signal to start the pump. Just a trickle came out at first, then a huge stream shot out, and I heard Daddy grunt and saw him go to his knees. The man behind him helped him up. They aimed the hose at Pastor's house, but it was mostly gone, though the front was still burning pretty good.

Beside me, Bertram laughed. "Like spittin' on the fires of hell," he said.

Just then a man came out of the house. He was burning. His whole body was on fire. He walked onto the front porch, his arms spread out, and he was burning; he was burning alive. The man with Daddy gave a shout and tried to aim the hose at the burning man, but Daddy shouted, "No!" and dropped the hose and ran toward the house. The man on fire didn't move; he just stood on the front steps with his arms flung out and his head back, and I don't know if it was the wind or the crackle of the fire, but it sounded to me like he laughed, like he was laughing at the smoke-filled sky.

Daddy grabbed him by the shoulders and flung him to the ground. He rolled him like a log back and forth till the flames were out. Then a lady came running up the hill, her white robe flying behind her, her dark hair loose and flowing. The man with Daddy tried to stop her, but she just reared back her fist and smashed it into the middle of his face. Daddy was coming back down the hill, yelling for the stretcher-men to come up. The lady fell to her knees before the burnt-up man, and lifted her face to the sky. It was Miss Mavis.

"Oh, God! Oh, dear God!" she screamed. "I have given up my husband to the fire!" She pulled Pastor up. He was limp as a rag doll. "Don't die!" she yelled at him, slapping at his face. "Don't you dare die on me, Ned Jeffries!"

She was popping him pretty good by the time Daddy and the stretcher-men reached them. It took all four men to pull her off. Daddy held her as the other men loaded Pastor onto the stretcher, and Miss Mavis leaned on him as they all came back off the hill. The man she punched, whose nose was now the size of a sweet potato, said, "What about the house, Bertram?"

"Forget it, Pete," Daddy said. "Let it burn."

I said, "Let's go, Bertram."

"No. I want to watch the rest of it burn."

"I'm scared," I said.

"Then go and wait on the road with the other women. I'm gonna watch it burn."

I looked down the hill to the dirt road. They were putting Pastor into the ambulance. I could see Momma standing with Miss Mavis, her robe now black with soot, as dark as her hair, which fell forward like a curtain over her face. Coming up the hill toward us was Sharon-Rose, wrapped in an old yellow blanket, her gold hair all knotted and teased around her wide, round face. She was barefoot, and when she got close I could see her bare legs poking through a crack in the blanket. Her legs were plump and slightly pink, the color of the sky just before sunset.

I looked away. Bertram saw her coming and hissed between his teeth.

"Hey, Bertram Parker," Sharon-Rose said. "Hey, Robert Lee Parker."

Bertram didn't say anything. He was watching the fire. I slid around him, till I had him between me and her. She was watching the fire too.

"It's all gone now," she said. "Everything. Even my shoes. Gone, gone, gone."

The ambulance sirens screamed to life, and I must have jumped a little, because she looked over at me and said to Bertram, "What's the matter with your little brother, Bertram?"

Bertram looked at her for a long time. It was the first time he looked at her. Then he bared his teeth and said, "We got to go."

He started down the hill so quick I had to trot after him to catch up. Sharon-Rose followed us.

"Hey! Hey, you boys. You little Parker boys! Wait up! Wait up for me!"

"Don't look back, Shiny, hear?" Bertram said. "Just keep walking."

"It's God's will, this fire," Sharon-Rose said, catching up. "My daddy says everything that happens under the sun is God's will."

"Then what did your daddy do to make God mad enough to burn him up?" Bertram asked.

"My daddy is a hero, Bertram Parker. He saved me and Momma's life."

It seemed like the whole town of Homeland had turned out to watch this fire. There were cars up and down the road and people standing around in their robes and pajamas. Momma and Miss Mavis were standing inside a ring of people. I heard Miss Mavis say, "It's my fault. It's all my fault."

And Momma said, "Hush, Mavis. Everything's going to be all right."

And Miss Mavis said, "No. His blood is on my hands now."

Sharon-Rose stepped up, pushing people out of the way, and they parted when they saw who it was. Miss Mavis looked down at her like she had never seen Sharon-Rose before.

Sharon-Rose said, "Don't worry, Momma. Daddy's gonna be all right. Didn't you hear him, Momma? Didn't you hear him when they put him in the ambulance? He said, 'Jesus.' He said, 'Jesus,' plain as day. 'Jesus, Jesus, Jesus,' he said."

They moved in with us the next night. Miss Mavis took Momma's sewing room and Sharon-Rose got our sofa, so now we had a sofa that smelled like a girl, and I didn't think that was a smell you could get out. At noon the next day a bunch of old ladies came over with covered dishes. Momma pushed back the furniture in the living room and set up a long table in the middle. The table was nearly the length of the whole room but still didn't seem big enough to hold all the food. There was meat loaf and chicken and barbecue pork and sausage. There was green bean casserole and squash casserole and spinach casserole and black-eyed pea casserole and some I didn't even know what kind of casseroles they were. There was cucumber salad and tossed salad and potato salad and egg salad. There was oranges and strawberries and watermelon. There were pies and cakes, and Momma baked her oatmeal cookies. The whole house smelled of food and old lady smell, which smelled like medicine and perfume and hair spray, and all the old ladies went around talking about the fire and what were poor Pastor and Miss Mavis going to do now? Me and Bertram walked around the table filling our plates, and I heard old ladies saying that Pastor was dead; that he was burned so bad he didn't even look human, but like one of those Egyptian mummies after they're unwrapped after five thousand years in a sunless tomb, their faces all black and caved in; that, no, he wasn't burned bad at all, but the smoke had blinded him and addled his brain; that his brain wasn't addled, but both his lungs had collapsed and he was breathing with a pump; and that he was all these things, burned and addled and blind and crying for Jesus to take him home. I sat with my plate on my knees in the corner by the window so I wouldn't have to listen to any more. Whatever he was now, I sure didn't want him in my house. It'd be worse than having a ghost. Bertram sat beside me and said he guessed this was better than Christmas and Thanksgiving dinners put together, and he wished a house burned down every day.

"Where's Sharon-Rose?" I asked.

"Who cares?"

After we ate, Miss Willifred Peters stood in the middle of the room, and we all held hands and said a prayer for Pastor and his family. She thanked God for not killing anybody and praised him for his infinite kindness and mercy. When Miss Willifred prayed, her head bobbed up and down like those funny dogs you see in the back of cars. Everybody said, "Amen," then Miss Willifred clapped her hands and announced committees had been formed by the Homeland Baptist Ladies Prayer and Sewing Club to help the Jeffries in their Hour of Need. There was the Clothing and Essentials Committee, the Rebuilding of the Parsonage Committee, the Medical Bills Repayment Committee, and the Food and Entertainment Committee. Then she thanked the volunteers for signing up and led a prayer for all the volunteers and all the committees. Then Miss Rachel Cook suggested they combine all the committees into one big Save the Jeffries Committee since everyone was on all the committees anyway and who had the time for four committees when one would do just as well?

Miss Willifred said, "Well, I should *hope* that one would always have the time to do the Lord's work."

"It's not the work I object to," Miss Rachel said. "It's the time."

"Well, Rachel Cook, I had no idea you had more important things to do than aid our pastor in his most dire need," said Miss Willifred.

"Willie," Miss Rachel said, "my only point was we're all on every committee, and even if we weren't, we can't expect all the folks in Homeland, which I need not remind everyone is a small town with limited resources, to commit their funds four ways instead of into one large pot, which the big committee would then decide how to divvy up."

Miss Willifred didn't say anything, but her face was turning bright red.

Miss Rachel went on. "With four committees after the same pool of money, one, if not all, is going to be short-changed. People are going to say, 'I already gave to the Clothing and Essentials, I can't afford to give to Parsonage Rebuilding too.' It's conceivable the Jeffries could end up with four thousand dollars in Food and Entertainment and nothing in Medical Bills Repayment."

"What's 'Entertainment' mean, anyway?" somebody said. "Is the church sending the Jeffries on a trip to Hawaii?"

Everybody laughed at that except Miss Willifred.

"Perhaps we should all put this to a vote," she said.

There was an awful fuss about whether it should be a voice vote, a show of hands, a secret ballot, or a referral to the Board of Deacons to decide the whole thing so everybody could get back to supper. The whole house was full of the sound of old Baptist ladies chirping and squeaking.

Bertram said, "I can't take it anymore, Shiny. Let's go."

We set our plates on the floor and went outside. The driveway and yard were filled with the old ladies' cars; the noon sun glinted off the chrome and stung our eyes. The heat pressed down on my head. Sometimes in July it got so hot it felt like you were being squeezed by a giant fist. The hot air shimmered over the dirt road and across the road in Mr. Newton's pasture, making the cypress trees twist at the edge of the horizon like they were trying to screw themselves into the cool ground to get away from the sun. I climbed onto the porch swing, and Bertram sat on the bottom step. He took out his pocketknife and found a stick and began to whittle, his back toward me. Bertram had dark hair like Daddy, and a solid, blocky body like his too. In the summer his dark hair got shaved a half inch from his head, to let his scalp breathe, Daddy said. With his hair short like that his head looked too small for his body, so all summer he walked around with a shrunken head. My hair was cut short for the summer too, but I had a small head and a skinny body. And my hair was very light. When it was short I looked like I had no hair at all; in the sunlight it seemed to float above my head like a fine, golden mist. If I stayed out too long in the sun my scalp got burned, and nothing hurts worse than a sunburned head. I wondered what it must feel like to get burned head to toe like the pastor. He must have been burnt pretty bad—his whole body was lit up when he came out of that house. When you pick up a piece of burnt chicken, the skin just cracks and falls off like loose paint. Thinking of that made me a little sick.

"Bertram?"

"Yeah-a."

"How did their house catch fire?"

"I dunno."

"Why can't one of those old Baptist ladies take 'em in? Why's it have to be us?"

"Shiny, you know Momma would take in every stray dog and cat in town if she could."

"Yeah-a. But the Jeffries aren't dogs or cats. And that Sharon-Rose. She makes me nervous, Bertram."

Bertram spat into the ground and said, "You stay away from her. There's something not right about that girl. I see her at school, and all she does all day long is whisper to herself."

"What's she whisper?"

"How should I know? She whispers it, stupid. Sometimes it sounds like she's singing. Sometimes like she's talking to somebody, but nobody's there. She don't have no friends. When we go outside, she stands off by herself or she sits under a tree and reads a book."

"Well," I said, "sometimes I do that. Read a book, I mean."

Bertram said, "Well, there's something not right about you either."

"But they aren't going to stay with us the whole rest of the summer, are they?"

"What makes you think I know anything about anything, Shiny? Jeez! You think Momma and Daddy asked me what I thought before they took 'em in?"

"It's just—we only got one bathroom for the two of us, and that Sharon-Rose—"

"That's right, Shiny," Bertram said. "So you better be careful and keep that door locked or Sharon-Rose might come in there and pee on you."

Just then our car pulled up and Daddy got out. Sharon-Rose hopped out of the back while Daddy walked around to help Miss Mavis out of the car.

"Why, here's that Bertram Parker and his little brother, Robert Lee Parker!" Sharon-Rose yelled, running toward us, like she was surprised to find us at our own home. "Guess where we've been!"

"The hospital," Bertram said, not looking at her.

"The hospital!" Sharon-Rose said. "The hospital, and your daddy bought me a chocolate shake in the cafeteria. I never been to that cafeteria, but it's three times as big as our cafeteria at school, and I swear I had the best chocolate shake I ever had in my life. I never would have thought a hospital would have such delicious chocolate shakes! But I sucked it down too fast and my right eyeball felt like it was going to pop right out of its socket! You ever have that happen to you? Where your very eyeball's going to pop out of its socket?"

Bertram looked at her and said, "No."

Daddy was leading Miss Mavis through the maze of cars parked willy-nilly by the Baptist ladies. Miss Mavis wore a wide-brimmed hat pulled low over her eyes and carried several bags. Daddy had some bags too, in his free hand.

"Oh," Sharon-Rose said. "And after the hospital we went to the store and I got three new outfits. I'll show them to you."

"We don't want to see them," Bertram said. He stood up so Daddy and Miss Mavis could pass.

"I don't think I can do this, Bertram," Miss Mavis said to Daddy.

"You'll be all right," Daddy said.

"No," Miss Mavis said, "I won't."

"They care for you, Mavis. Boys, help us with these bags."

Bertram took Daddy's bags and I took Miss Mavis's. She smiled at me; it was a sad smile, but even sad as she was, she was still pretty.

"Thank you," she whispered, clutching at Daddy's arm. "Thank you."

We followed them inside, and all the old ladies stopped their bickering and set upon Miss Mavis and Sharon-Rose, circling them and kind of herding them toward the table of food. Miss Mavis kept saying, no, no, she wasn't hungry, she really couldn't eat a bite, but Sharon-Rose, who almost lost an eyeball to a chocolate shake, went at that food like she hadn't eaten in a week. "He's wrapped tight as a mummy, only cleaner," she said, meaning Pastor. Daddy told us to put the bags in the sewing room, and when we came out Miss Mavis was nowhere to be seen. Sharon-Rose was sitting on the piano bench, the food stacked like a small mountain on the plate she balanced on her broad knees. She ate quick, like she was afraid someone might come and snatch the food away.

"Looks like they're going to need that Food and Entertainment Committee after all," Bertram said.

We went into the kitchen, where the old ladies were washing dishes, clattering the plates while they chattered about Miss Mavis and how drawn she looked. How *worn* and *drawn*. Momma was there, pulling a fresh batch of oatmeal cookies from the oven.

"Oh, Robert Lee," she said, "I knew if there were oatmeal cookies in the oven you couldn't be far away."

She slid the cookies onto a plate to cool and handed one to me. An old lady I didn't know, with very thick glasses and a pointy nose like a witch, stared down at me and said, "Why, is this your youngest, Annie? How old is he now?"

"How old are you, Robert Lee?" Momma asked.

"Seven," I told the old lady.

"Seven!" the old lady said. "Why, he's small enough to be five! What is he, a runt?"

"I was small for my age, Miss Alice. He'll grow," Momma said.

"I hope so! Small men make for big mistakes, I always say. Napoleon was a very small man, you know."

"So is Harry Truman," Momma said.

"I never liked that man," Miss Alice said. "Eat vegetables!" she shouted at me. "Make you grow! Milk! Give you strong bones! And meat, red meat, lots of red meat, the redder the better. Don't overcook the child's meat, Annie Parker, or you're asking for trouble. My Alfred, rest his soul, never ate red meat his whole life, and he was a small man. A very small man, and he made my life miserable!"

"Come on, Shiny," Bertram said, and we snuck outside through the kitchen door.

We cut through the side yard, down to the dirt road. The air was heavy and we walked as if wet blankets were thrown over our shoulders. I picked up a long stick and trailed it in the dirt. By late afternoon it would rain, but now the sun was hot and fierce against our necks. I wished I'd remembered my hat.

"Bertram, what's a runt?"

"Never mind."

"No, what is it?"

"Like when a dog has puppies. The littlest puppy's called the runt."

"Oh."

I watched Bertram's wide back and big shoulders as he walked in front of me.

"It's just some old lady talking, Shiny," Bertram said. "Don't listen to her."

"I won't."

"You heard Momma."

"But Momma is still pretty little."

He didn't say anything.

The weeds grew tall and thick on the right side of the road where the ditch had been dug to drain the water from the heavy summer rains. Water lay in there now—brown, sludgy water, covered here and there with green slime. On the other side of the ditch was the barbed-wire fence separating Mr. Newton's land from the road. From deep in the pasture, the cypress stands looked cool and inviting.

"Let's go to the fort," I said.

"No. There's something I want to see."

We came around the curve and up ahead I saw the church. All that was left standing of the house was the chimney, pointing up at the sky like a fat, black finger. I dropped my stick.

"I don't think we're supposed to go up there, Bertram."

"You don't have to come if you don't want. Go on back to the house with the other ladies."

He walked on without looking back. I turned and there was my house, dancing in the heat. I could have a slice of cold watermelon on the porch. I could crawl under the house and lay on the cool ground and no one would find me, especially Sharon-Rose. I turned back. Bertram was still walking toward the hill.

"Bertram, wait for me!"

I ran after him.

"What's to see, Bertram? It's just a burnt-up old house."

"You asked me what started the fire."

"Yeah-a."

"Well, maybe we can find out. Look for some clues. You know, like the Hardy boys."

"Why don't we just ask Sharon-Rose?"

"I did ask Sharon-Rose."

"What's she say?"

"She said it was God."

He stopped and looked down at me.

"You think it was God, Shiny?"

"No. I guess not."

"Neither do I."

The road was empty. The air was still. The winds would come in late afternoon, with the rains. We climbed the hill and stopped to rest in the thin shade of the oak tree. We sat with our backs against the tree and watched the empty road. Bertram stuck a piece of grass in his mouth and chewed on the stalk slowly.

"What's the matter, Bertram?" I asked.

"Something's not right about it, Shiny. Last night Sharon-Rose said her daddy saved her and her momma."

"Yeah-a."

"But he was the last to come out. If he got them out, why was he still in there?"

"Maybe he went back to get something."

"I didn't see him come out with anything. Did you?"

"Miss Mavis said it was all her fault," I said.

"That still don't explain why he was still in that house. You heard what else she said. She said his blood was on her hands."

"What are you talking about, Bertram?" I suddenly felt all cold.

"Maybe she's telling the truth. Maybe she hit him over the head with something and then set the house on fire to cover it up."

"No, Bertram."

"But she didn't hit him hard enough to knock him all the way out, so he wakes up . . ."

"No! Stop it, Bertram!"

He looked at me long and cold.

"Miss Mavis would never do something like that," I said.

"How d'you know?"

"I just know."

"Well, I don't just know. People kill each other every day, Shiny."

"What people?"

"All kinds."

"Not around here."

"Oh, you think we got the only town in the whole world where people don't kill each other? The way I look at it, we got one of two things living with us—a murderer or an arsonist, and I'd kinda like to know which it is before I go to bed tonight."

He threw down the chewed-up stalk of grass and headed for the house. I watched him go. I was shivering all over, scared and mad at the same time. I knew Miss Mavis wasn't a murderer, but I didn't know what an arsonist was, and I was too scared to ask. Bertram was kicking around in the charred wood and ashes, raising little clouds of soot. Here and there in the ruins smoke still lingered, rising lazily toward the bright sky. Bertram found a stick and poked at the piles of smoking junk. He gave a little "whoop!" and yelled for me to come and look. I didn't want to. More than anything I wanted to turn and run, run back to the house and find Momma and ask her what an arsonist was and if anyone had ever killed anyone in Homeland.

"Come on, Shiny. Quick!"

I came, but I didn't come quick. I stopped at the edge of the black and gray mess, where the porch used to be, where Pastor came out on fire, his arms raised up to the sky. Bertram held up something long and thick, crusted black.

"What is it?" I asked.

"A candlestick. I think." He rubbed on it with his thumb. "It's heavy enough, Shiny." He swung it around a couple of times. "We gotta figure how to analyze this for blood . . ."

"Hey! Hey, you boys! You Parker boys!"

It was Sharon-Rose. She was huffing up the hill, lifting her big knees high as she ran. She stopped by me, sucking for air, squatting on her haunches, her face covered with red and white blotches.

"What . . . you're doin' . . . is . . . ill-legal, Bertram Parker. And you . . . Robert Lee Parker are . . . his accomplished in crime."

"What crime, Sharon-Rose?" Bertram asked.

"Trespassing!"

She saw the candlestick in his hand.

"And stealing!" she yelled. "Drop that!"

"I will not."

"I told you to drop that!"

"Make me."

She puffed out her cheeks, then swung her head toward me.

"You're staring at me. Why're you always staring at me?"

Bertram said, "Maybe he stares because he can't believe how big and fat and ugly you are."

Sharon-Rose shook her head hard, like a bull shaking off a fly. Then she launched herself at him. I never saw anyone move so fast, and especially not a girl. Ashes and bits of wood flew from behind her feet. It was like something you'd see in a cartoon. Bertram stood still; he never expected her to come for him—you could see it in his face. He'd look the same if she sprouted wings and flew into the sky. He didn't even raise the candlestick to bop her with. She slammed smack into him, and the candlestick flew into the air, turning end over end. She landed on top of him with a puff of boiling soot. I saw her big, soot-black fist raise up and swoosh back down. I heard Bertram go, "Oof!" and another fat fist came up.

I yelled, "Bertram!" but I didn't move. I wanted to move. Bertram was my brother. She was going to beat him to death and I was going to watch her do it. And when we buried him everyone in town would stare at me and they would whisper, "There goes that boy who let his brother get beaten to death by a *girl*." And Momma and Daddy would lock me in our room. And Bertram would come back and haunt me for letting him die. He'd haunt me for the rest of my life. But even though I knew all that would happen if I let her kill him, I still couldn't move. Sharon-Rose was sitting on his chest hitting him with both fists, swinging her arms high before each pop. The more I tried to move, the more frozen I was to the spot. Nothing was going to make me move.

Then Bertram yelled, "Shiny!" and I don't think I moved faster in my whole life; I don't think the bottom of my shoes got dirty. One second I was standing in the grass and the next I was on Sharon-Rose's back.

I grabbed a fistful of that thick blond hair and yanked back, like a bronco rider at the rodeo. Sharon-Rose gave a yell and reached back, sitting up at the same time, trying to throw me off.

"That's it, Shiny!" Bertram yelled, and he rolled quick to his side, throwing her off—and right on top of me. She landed on my stomach, knocking the wind out of me. Bertram yelled, "God damn you, Sharon-Rose!" and picked up the candlestick.

"Well, well, well!" a voice boomed out. "What do we have here?"

I opened my mouth and nothing came out. Air gushed down my throat, air mixed with ash, and I sat up coughing and spitting, and Sharon-Rose sat down beside me, patting my back like she felt real sorry for me. Bertram dropped the candlestick.

Standing against the sun, rising up tall and black, with a big gun on his hip, a man was frowning down at us.

"It's me, Sheriff Trimbul," Sharon-Rose said. "Sharon-Rose Jeffries, and this is Bertram Parker, a criminal, and this is his criminal brother, Robert Lee Parker, who they call Shiny, I don't know why."

"Well, I can't say why either, Miss Sharon-Rose," Sheriff Trimbul said, "seein' he's black as a tar-baby."

"I would like you, Sheriff Trimbul, to place these two criminal boys under arrest."

"On what charges, Miss Sharon-Rose, should I arrest them?"

"Trespassin'! I caught 'em at it red-handed. Stealin' too!"

"Oh, is that so? Well, now. Trespassing *is* a serious crime."

He put his arm around her shoulders. "Come on over here with me and let's talk about it."

He led her away. She leaned against him, sniffing and snuffling and wiping his shirtfront black, like we were the ones beating up on her. I looked over at Bertram. His face was covered with soot caked up from blood and spit. His right eye was swelling up.

"I told you we shouldn't have come here," I whispered. "Now we're gonna go to jail." Talking made my chest hurt.

"Hush," he said. He spat a wad of dirt out of his mouth and wiped his lips with the back of his hand. He was watching Sharon-Rose and Sheriff Trimbul. She stood next to him, her head down, listening while he whispered into her ear. She began to shake her head back and forth, real quick, and then she began to cry, the tears cutting pink trails down her black face.

Bertram sucked in his breath.

"We ain't goin' to jail, Shiny," he said. "Sharon-Rose is."

Sheriff Trimbul didn't take Sharon-Rose to prison. He drove her back to our house in his police car. Bertram and me rode in the back; Sharon-Rose got to ride in the front next to Sheriff Trimbul and the neat radio and the shotgun. Sheriff Trimbul told us the next time he caught us tramping around that burned-down house he *was* going to arrest us because little kids had no business playing with fire. Bertram poked me when he said that and nodded toward Sharon-Rose. His eye was nearly swollen all the way shut, and he whispered to me as we walked up to the house that if I ever told anyone a girl beat him up he would kill me and scatter my dried bones in the cypress swamp.

He tried to make it to our room before Momma and Daddy saw him, but Miss Willifred shouted, "Poor child!" so loud everybody turned to look. Soon we were surrounded by a dozen jabbering old Baptist ladies, poking us and asking questions, and Sheriff Trimbul was saying, "No, no, no, just children tussling," and Daddy came over and took Bertram away. I was glad I didn't have to watch what happened next to Bertram. Momma took me to the bathroom to wash me up. I heard Sheriff Trimbul say,

"Where's Miss Mavis?" and Miss Willifred say, "She's lying down, poor thing," before Momma closed the door and swatted me on the behind.

"It wasn't my idea, Momma!" I cried.

"It doesn't matter whose idea it was, Robert Lee. You should know better."

I was going to tell her I did know better, that it was all Bertram's fault and I tried to stop him the whole time, but it felt like tattling, so I bit my lower lip to keep it shut. Momma told me to stop pouting. She wet a washcloth and scrubbed my face and hands.

"Ow, Momma!"

"Hush. I am very disappointed in you, Robert Lee. I've told you a thousand times you are too small to be fighting with Bertram."

"I wasn't fighting with Bertram. I was fighting with Sharon-Rose."

Momma stared at me for a long, terrible time. "You struck a girl?"

"Yeah-a, I did, but——"

She backhanded me across the mouth. She had never hit me like that before, and I don't know if it was the slap or the fact that she had never hit me like that before, but I busted out into tears. I thought my head would burst from the pressure of all those tears. It hurt a thousand times worse than what Sharon-Rose did to me.

Momma's eyes were small and cold. "A gentleman never strikes a girl. Never. Do you understand me?"

"But she was killing Bertram!"

"Sharon-Rose Jeffries was killing your brother?"

"Yes, ma'am! I swear she was. She was sitting on him and beatin' him, Momma! I couldn't let her do that. I couldn't let her do that to Bertram!"

"Well! She must be one strong little girl, is all I can say."

She ran the washcloth over my cheeks and eyes. I was bawling like a baby. There was the taste of blood in my mouth. Momma said, "Hush now, or those ladies will think I'm murdering you in here." She took me into her arms and hugged me, saying "Hush, baby, shush now, baby," until my crying turned to hiccupping.

"Was I supposed to let her kill him, Momma?"

"No, of course not. But you're never to go to that house again, hear?"

"Yes, ma'am."

"And you must be gentle with Sharon-Rose. She has lost all she had in the world. She may also lose her daddy. Can you imagine such a thing, Robert Lee? Losing all you have in the world and your only daddy?"

I snuffled against her shoulder.

"Bertram says she's crazy. Bertram says—"

"I'm not interested in Bertram's opinion on the matter. I want you to ask yourself how you would feel."

"Momma, does Pastor really look like a mummy?"

Momma laughed. "Did Sharon-Rose say that?"

I nodded.

"Well, I suppose some would say he looks like a mummy. But I would say he looks more like a caterpillar in a cocoon. And you know what a caterpillar turns into."

She kissed my cheek and looked into my eyes.

"Is Pastor going to die, Momma?" I asked.

"I don't know. He's hurt very badly, and the Lord's ways are mysterious and not for us to question."

She dried my face and combed my hair and told me one more time to try to understand Sharon-Rose. Then she said: "And one more thing. My momma always told me, if you can't get along with someone, just stay away from them."

"How can I stay away from her, Momma? She's in our house."

"Well, there's always your room, you know."

We went back into the living room. I looked for Bertram and Daddy, but they weren't there. Daddy probably took him outside to the toolshed. I felt bad for him, but at the same time I was glad it wasn't me. The old ladies were packing up the food. Sheriff Trimbul sat off in a corner with a big plateful. He chewed with his mouth open, and I could hear his teeth clicking together from across the room. He smiled and waved at me, and I gave a little wave back. A couple old ladies made over me and told Momma, "Boys will be boys," and everybody nodded like it was a very smart thing to say. I didn't see Sharon-Rose. She was probably hiding from Sheriff Trimbul.

———————

"Bertram?"

"Yeah-a."

"Did Daddy whip you bad?"

"Pretty bad."

"I'm sorry, Bertram."

"Why're you sorry? You didn't do nothing."

"Well, I'm still sorry."

"Well, you're still stupid."

Our door swung open and Momma's shadow fell across the floor.

"Time for your prayers," she said.

She sat on Bertram's bed and he said his prayer. When he got to the part about dying before he waked, my heart gave a little jump. When he was done, Momma came over to my bed and sat beside me.

"Hi, Momma," I said.

"Hi, Robert Lee," she said. She ran a hand over my forehead.

I folded my hands and closed my eyes and said my prayer.

"Momma," I said.

"Yes, honey?"

"Bertram said people kill each other every day."

"Oh, Shiny," Bertram said.

"Now, why would Bertram say that?" Momma said.

"Do they, Momma?"

"Yes, I suppose somewhere in the world . . ."

"Here, Momma? Do they do it here?"

"In Homeland? Oh, my goodness, no. Not for years and years anyway."

Bertram sat up. "When, Momma?"

"Twenty years ago or more."

"What happened?"

"Oh, you don't need to hear about that."

Bertram said, "Yes, we do!"

Momma sighed. "There was a killing here in Homeland. The only one ever, as far as I know, since the war, anyway."

"What war, Momma?" I asked.

"The Civil War, dear."

"Come on and tell us, Momma!" Bertram said.

Momma closed her eyes and took a deep breath. When she opened them again she didn't look at me, but at some spot over my head.

"Years ago, years before either of you were born, there was a man named Halley Martin, and this Halley Martin killed another man in . . . in a bar fight."

"What'd he do, Momma?" Bertram asked. "Did he shoot him?"

"No. Halley Martin stabbed him. Stabbed him with a hunting knife."

She pulled the covers up close under my chin.

"Now that was twenty years ago, a long, long time, Robert Lee, and Halley Martin is in prison, far, far away." She kissed me on the forehead.

"Did you know him, Momma?" Bertram asked.

"Everyone knew Halley Martin."

"Who did he kill?"

"No. No more tonight."

"But, Momma!—"

"Hush now, Bertram." She smiled at me, running her hand over my stubby head of hair. "There's no more killers running around the streets of Homeland."

"You promise, Momma?"

"Yes, I promise, Robert Lee." She kissed my forehead again.

"Halley," I said. "That's a funny name."

"It's the name of a comet. A very famous comet. He was named after it."

I laid awake for a long time after she left. I laid until Bertram's breathing got heavy and long. I laid and watched the leaf-shadows dancing on the ceiling. When I was real little, something got in my lungs and I woke up not able to breathe. I woke up choking and sucking at the air, but no air would come down my throat. I started kicking at the wall by my bed till Momma heard and came running. I never saw Momma so scared. She grabbed me and shook me and slapped me hard on the back, screaming for Daddy, but by the time he got there the fit was gone, and after the doctor left Momma held me for a long time. I was scared to go back to sleep. I just knew if I went back to sleep my lungs would stop working again, and I would die before I waked. But Momma pointed at my bedpost and told me there was a guardian angel sitting there, and though I couldn't see him, he was always there, watching over me. And if something ever happened to me he would fly up right away to heaven and tell God about it so he could help me. Momma said everyone has a guardian angel, because looking after the whole world and all the people in it was a big job, even for God, which was why we all had angels in the first place. I wondered what Pastor's angel was doing the night of the fire, why he wasn't there to save Pastor from getting burned up. Maybe the angel was asleep or had to go to the bathroom or something. Or maybe if God gets mad at you the angel looks after someone God likes better. Bertram told Sharon-Rose God must be mad at her daddy, but you'd think God would like a preacher most of all. Daddy said Pastor liked God more than people, so why would God be mad at him? It didn't seem right. God might be mad at Pastor, but burning him up and burning his house up hurt Miss Mavis and Sharon-Rose too. It even hurt me and Bertram, since we both had to live with her now. Why didn't God just make the Pastor catch fire walking down the road or off in the woods, so no one else would get hurt? Then I thought maybe he was mad at all of us, and that's why things turned out the way they did. I closed my eyes and prayed: I'm sorry, God, if I made you mad at me. And then I asked my guardian angel to fly up to heaven and tell him, just in case God was too busy with more important prayers than mine.

I still couldn't sleep. Bertram was snoring. Nothing bothered Bertram. He was the bravest person I knew, besides Daddy. Nothing, not even a killer sleeping on the other side of our wall, could keep him awake.

I wondered if my guardian angel had come back from delivering my message to God. What would my angel do if Sharon-Rose snuck into our room and lit my bed on fire? Bertram would sleep right through it, and before Momma or Daddy or even God could do anything about it I would be like the pastor, like a burned drumstick, my black skin breaking off in sheets, my eyeballs melting and dripping out of their sockets . . .

I threw back my covers and sat up. The house was very still. Sometimes when I went to the bathroom late at night the floor would creak, just outside our door. I listened for that creak now, straining my ears, but all I could hear was the crickets singing under the window. Momma had left the door open a crack, but no light shone through. My room never seemed so dark as it did that night. Maybe Sharon-Rose was already in the kitchen, hunting up some matches. Maybe she had no need to hunt them up; maybe she still had some with her, from when she set her own house on fire . . .

If she came in the room I could hit her with one of Bertram's Little League trophies, but they were on a shelf across the room and she moved fast for a big girl. Momma said a gentleman never strikes a girl, but a gentleman might have to if he saw some crazy girl coming at him with a lit match.

I slipped out of the bed and tiptoed to the door. I put my eye to the crack. The hall was empty. I could see the night-light in the bathroom casting a yellow band across the floor. It would only take a second to go down the hall and turn right into the living room. If she was on the sofa, if she was sleeping, then maybe I could go to sleep. I eased open the door and slipped into the hallway. I kept on my tiptoes, but the floor creaked anyway. I stopped, pressing my back against the wall, holding my breath, but I didn't hear anything except the grandfather clock's slow tick-tock, tick-tock. I kept against the wall, moving sideways, until I came to the corner. Just around that corner was the sofa. I eased forward slow as a snail and looked down.

There was a big blue lump on the sofa. In the gray light it didn't look like it was moving. I stared at it for a long time. If she was under that blue blanket, she was sleeping like the dead. I lifted a corner of the blanket. What I saw was long and pale and pink with five blood-red blotches at the end, and it took me a minute to figure out it was her foot. It was her toenails painted blood-red. Then the far corner of the blanket flew up, a hand shot out in the dark, and I saw her wide face rise up like a pale ghost coming out of the grave, and then we were nose to nose, me and her. She had hold of my wrist, squeezing it tight. Her breath smelled like rotten apples. Her long hair was tangled and sticking up every which way.

"What're you doin' here, boy?" Sharon-Rose hissed. "You sneakin' 'round me again? Why you always sneakin' 'round me so? You some kind of nasty boy, is that what you are?"

I didn't say anything; none of her questions had any answers I knew. She was squeezing my wrist so hard the blood pounded in my fingertips.

"You're a strange boy, I always knew that," she said. "You never talk; you just watch things. You're always watching and looking and staring at things. And now you come in here and stare at me. How'd you like me to sneak into your little room in the middle of the night and stare at your naked feet?"

"I'm sorry," I whispered. "Please. Please let me go."

"I think I won't let you go. I think I'll drag you right into Momma's bedroom and you can tell her why you're in here spying on me in the middle of the night."

I yanked my arm back, hard as I could. Her nails scraped across my wrist and she fell back with a little "ooohh!"

I took off, hitting my shoulder on the wall, falling through my doorway, slamming the door closed. Bertram rolled over and opened his eyes.

"What is it, Shiny?"

I couldn't catch my breath. There were four red stripes across my wrist where she scratched me.

"Sharon-Rose," I gasped.

"What? She sneakin' in here?"

"No."

I climbed into my bed. My heart was pounding hard in my chest. I was hot all over. My wrist stung. She was going to tell on me, I knew she was. Then Daddy would take me to the toolshed. I had never been to the toolshed with Daddy before, not for getting into trouble.

Bertram snorted. "She come in here I'll bash her head in with my baseball bat." He flopped around for a bit then lay still. The baseball bat. I forgot about that baseball bat. I got out of bed and dug into the closet till I found the bat. I tucked it under the covers with me and felt better right away. It gave me the same feeling I used to get sleeping with my teddy bear.

Safe.

Daddy never took me to the toolshed. I don't know if Sharon-Rose ever told. She didn't tell me she told; she never said a word about it. Maybe she forgot or thought it was a dream. I don't know, but from that night on I took Momma's advice and stayed as far away from her as I could. That month of July was the longest month of July I ever saw. It was the longest month I ever saw period. It seemed ten months long. The mornings came hot and sticky, and we all would eat breakfast together. Momma scrambled eggs and made fresh biscuits with sausage gravy. There was bacon and grits and fried potatoes, and sometimes, if I begged, waffles. Miss Mavis would come out of the sewing room long enough to nibble on some biscuit and drink some coffee, and then she'd disappear into her room again. She looked pretty as ever, except her eyes, which were red and cupped with black circles, like all she did all day was cry. Sharon-Rose would pile her plate full and eat with her mouth about an inch from the food, her eyes darting back and forth as if looking for more food that might foolishly land on the table in front of her. Bertram and me would wait till she was done and in the bathroom brushing her teeth with a lot of spitting and coughing and slobbery type noises coming through the door, and then we'd slip outside and cut across Mr. Newton's pasture into the cypress swamp, where we'd work on our fort or hunt frogs, or sometimes we'd just lie on our backs on the cool, damp ground and wait for lunchtime.

After lunch Miss Mavis and Sharon-Rose would dress and wait for one of the old ladies on the Daily Drive to See the Pastor Committee to pick them up for their daily drive to see the pastor. This was the best time of the day, when it was just me and Bertram and Momma and you could almost forget they lived with us except for the lingering smell of Miss Mavis's perfume and whatever that strange odor was that Sharon-Rose carried around with her. It was just like the old days of June before God got mad at everybody. Sometimes, if Momma wasn't busy, we'd sit down for a game of Chinese checkers, or work a puzzle, or Momma would read to me on the porch. I would lay my head in her lap, close my eyes, and let the words fall down from her lips, scattering on my face like soft summer rain.

In the afternoons the real rain would come. It rained every afternoon in the summer. The fat black clouds would come rolling in about three every afternoon. They'd come in over the cypresses, tall and black, like great dark ships, till their sails covered the sun. Bertram and me would go outside and sit on the curb and dig our bare toes into the dirt and watch the lightning flicker inside the boiling gray of the clouds. The heavy air would begin to stir, and a wind would come rushing ahead of the clouds, cooling the sweat on our foreheads, making us suddenly grateful for the heat, since the swift wind felt so cool. We'd wait till the first fat drops of rain popped on the dirt road, and then we'd run inside before Momma could call us in. She'd fuss at us, tell us lightning strikes was the leading cause of death in Florida, didn't we know that? And then she'd fix a snack, some cookies or blackberry cobbler or cheese and crackers, and we'd take our little plates onto the porch and eat as the rain came straight down, pinging and popping on the tin roof. Sometimes I'd doze off on the swing, and my dreams would be sweet.

By five or so the clouds moved on and it was almost time for Daddy to get home. Momma would be in the kitchen getting dinner started, and me and Bertram would watch TV until Sharon-Rose and her momma came walking through the door; then it was time for me and Bertram to find someplace else to be. Sharon-Rose would go straight for the TV and stare at cartoons, her mouth hanging open a little, her bare legs crossed under her Indian style.

We ate as soon as Daddy washed up and changed his shirt. He never ate dinner in his work shirt. He said a gentleman never does. After dinner we'd watch some more TV or Daddy would read a book while me and Bertram and Sharon-Rose played a game. We'd play Clue or Old Maid or Go Fish, and once we made the mistake of playing Monopoly. I didn't understand much of that game, except I kept having to pay Bertram a lot of money just to move my metal dog around the board. After an hour I was bored, but Bertram wouldn't let me stop playing, no matter how much I begged. Sharon-Rose and him took it real serious.

"You think you're so smart, Bertram Parker," she said.

"Who's got more money?" Bertram said.

"Money don't have nothing to do with being smart," she said.

"Then you must be the richest girl in the world," Bertram said.

By the second hour, when Bertram had houses and hotels all over the board, Sharon-Rose was losing bad. She was almost out of money and was having to turn her cards over just to pay Bertram the rent. Then she landed her wheelbarrow on Bertram's Park Place for the third time in a row. She turned to me and said, "Give me some money."

"Hey," Bertram said.

"He don't care," Sharon-Rose said. "Do you, Robert Lee?"

"*I* care, Sharon-Rose," Bertram said.

"I don't care, Bertram," I said. "She can have it."

"No," Bertram said, real soft. "She can't."

Sharon-Rose reached over and snatched up my pile of money.

"Hey!" Bertram said. He said, teeth clinched tight, "Put that back."

Sharon-Rose said, "But I'll lose."

"That's the point."

He grabbed her wrist. For a terrible moment they looked at each other. I thought, Oh, no, here we go again.

"Please, Bertram," I whispered. My voice was shaking. "Please, don't."

Bertram let her go. She dropped my money into her pile and gave Bertram a big smile.

"Pay me the rent," he growled, which she did.

"Well," she said brightly, "I guess money does have something to do with being smart."

"Smart rhymes with fart," Bertram said, and I laughed out loud. Sharon-Rose shook her head and muttered, *Boys.*

By the third hour I was so bored and sleepy I dozed off. When I woke up Bertram and Sharon-Rose were gone. So was the game. I never found out who won, and I never saw that game again either, not for the rest of that summer.

On Sundays we got up early and dressed for church. I had a brown suit with a clip-on bow tie. Bertram's suit was blue, with a clip-on long tie. We'd pack ourselves into the car, Daddy and Momma and Miss Mavis up front, me and Bertram and Sharon-Rose in the back, and by the time we reached the top of the hill the warring smells of Daddy's cologne and Miss Mavis's and Momma's perfumes and the Sharon-Rose smell was enough to make me gag. At church either Daddy or one of the other deacons would give the sermon; then, after that, Miss Willifred would give an update on Pastor's condition.

He was getting better, she said, but it was a long, long road ahead. He'd had three operations already, and the doctors were saying there may be more, maybe six or seven more, and when she said that everybody gasped and Momma whispered for the Lord to have mercy. Miss Mavis shut her eyes and took a deep, shuddering breath. I looked over at Sharon-Rose. She was picking her nose.

Then one day, near the end of that endless July, Miss Willifred got up and announced that the day of Jubilee was nigh: Pastor was coming home in two weeks.

Coming to *our* home.

"Bertram?"

"Yeah-a."

"You awake?"

"No, I'm having a dream my stupid little brother is about to ask me a dumb question."

"Will Pastor still look like a mummy?"

"No. They take the wrapping off at the hospital. When he comes in he's going to be black and crinkly, and his skin's gonna be hanging down his cheeks and neck like a turkey's beard."

"Stop it," I said.

"And he don't have hair, y'know. He don't have hair nowhere on his body. Not on his head and not on his eyebrows, or his arms or his legs. His tongue is burned black as a snake's, and his eyeballs hang out and swing on their stalks like—"

"Stop!"

"Well, damn it, Shiny, how'm I s'posed to know what he looks like?"

"It's somebody else's turn to take 'em. It's not fair we got to take 'em the whole time."

"You must be on the Who's Gonna Take 'Em Next Committee."

That gave me an idea. "Why can't Miss Willifred take 'em, she loves 'em all so much."

"Miss Willifred's just an old busybody who likes poking around in other people's business. She don't actually want to help nobody."

It was too much for me all of a sudden. Miss Mavis in her white robe and pale, wide face, flitting around like a ghost, never saying a word to anyone; Sharon-Rose with her loud voice and painted toenails and that funny smell and the way she looked at me sometimes like she could see right through my clothes; Pastor coming back from the hospital burned crisp down to his bones so they must rattle inside his black skin when he moved.

It was all too much.

"Shiny? Shiny, what're you doin' over there?"

He turned on our lamp.

"You cryin' again?"

He sat on the edge of his bed and looked at me. His face glowed in the soft yellow light.

"Why're you so scared all the time, Shiny?"

"I'm not scared," I said, trying to catch my breath. "I just don't want them around no more."

He frowned and nodded. "You tell Momma that?"

"Yeah-ess."

"And it didn't do no good."

I shook my head no. It didn't.

"She just starts in on that Christian duty crap," he said. "And Daddy says he's got to set an example since he's a deacon."

He scrubbed the top of his head. "But I'm like you, Shiny. I can't take it no more. That Sharon-Rose, she's crazy, and that used to be funny, but it ain't so funny when it's under your own roof. I'm thinkin' she's just been biding her time, waiting for her daddy to get home."

"And what's she gonna do then?"

He shook his head. "I don't know. I been thinkin' about this a lot, Shiny. I even thought about leavin'."

"Leaving what?"

"Leaving here, stupid."

"You're running away?" That almost got me started again. He saw my bottom lip go out, and then he got up and sat beside me.

"No. I ain't runnin' away. I meant goin' over to Granma's, at least till school starts back. Maybe by then somebody else will take them in or maybe they'll have a new house for them. I heard Daddy talking on the phone about getting money to buy them a house."

"I'll come with you," I said.

"Momma would never let us go," he said. "Momma would see right through it and tell us we can't run from our problems."

"We could still ask her."

"I ain't gonna ask now."

"Why?"

"Because this is my house. I ain't lettin' no one, especially that crazy girl, chase me out of my own house. So I got an idea."

He put his arm around me and leaned down, so close his lips brushed my ear. He whispered for a long time. When he was done he said, "Now this has got to be our secret, Shiny. You can't tell no one, not even Momma. Especially not Momma."

"I can't lie, Bertram. I tried before. She can always tell."

"It ain't lyin', Shiny. It's just—not telling the whole truth."

"I don't understand."

"You don't have to. Just do like I say, and they'll be out of here 'fore you can say 'shoo.' "

Miss Willifred Peters stood on her front porch and watched me and Bertram walk up the driveway. She was leaning on a cane and squinting at us through her thick glasses, her mouth small and puckered and bright pink. Her nose crinkled and kind of bobbed up and down, like a rabbit's, sniffing at us or using her nose to push up her glasses, I couldn't tell which. We stopped in the cool shade of one of the huge oak trees that grew by the walkway leading to her porch.

"Mornin', Miss Peters!" Bertram called.

"Good morning, Mr. Bertram Parker Junior," Miss Willifred said. "You *are* Mr. Bertram Parker Junior, are you not?"

"Yes, ma'am. And this here is my little brother, Robert Lee."

"I believe I know who your brother is, Bertram Parker," Miss

Willifred said crossly. She was a very old lady, older even than Granma, who was very old, at least sixty or maybe even sixty-one. She didn't have gray hair like Granma; Miss Willifred's hair was bluish gray, leaning more toward blue than gray, and she wore it piled high on her head, like Momma's towel when she comes out of the tub after washing. Bertram poked me in the ribs, and I squeaked, "Mornin', Miss Peters!"

"You boys out for a leisurely stroll this morning, or are you on your way to town on important business?"

"Important business, Miss Peters," Bertram said. "But our business ain't in town. It's with you."

"With me? Now what could your business have to do with me? You aren't selling magazine subscriptions, are you?"

"No, ma'am." Bertram took a deep breath and launched into it. I couldn't look at her while he talked. I looked up and spied a mockingbird watching me from his perch in the oak tree. I know what you're up to, the mockingbird said. I closed my eyes and prayed she wouldn't notice me or ask me a question. If she did I'd probably let out a scream and take off down the road, and I wouldn't stop until I was safe under my bed.

"It's about Pastor Jeffries," Bertram said. "Me and Shi—Robert Lee feel just awful about what happened and all, especially after what we did to Sharon-Rose."

I opened my eyes. The mockingbird was still staring at me, his head cocked sideways. You don't try to stare down a mockingbird when his babies are young. A mockingbird will come right at you and try to peck your eyeballs out. I looked away. I know what you're up to, the mockingbird said.

"So our daddy said we ought to try to help out, all we can and all."

Bertram poked me and I shuffled up the walk, keeping my head down and my hands deep in my pockets. I stopped at the bottom step. My shoes were scuffed and caked with the yellow mud of our dirt road. I was surprised how dirty my shoes were, but there's so much to notice in the world it's hard to get around to noticing it all.

"Go on, Robert Lee," Bertram said.

I dug the wad of bills and change from my pocket and offered it up to Miss Willifred.

Bertram said, "It's for the committees, Miss Peters. Seven dollars and eighty-four cents. We broke open our piggy bank."

"Did you now?"

Her voice had gone soft. I raised my head. She was smiling down at me, her face doubly crinkly.

"My, what sweet Christian boys you are! And you walked all this way just to give it to me! You are a credit to your parents, both of you!"

Bertram gave her a quick bobbing nod. We were a credit.

"But you must be very tired from your mission of mercy," Miss Willifred said. She patted the top of my head with one dried-up hand. "Are you hot and tired, Mr. Robert Lee?"

I nodded.

"Well, what would you boys say to a nice tall glass of lemonade?"

"Oh, we can't stay," Bertram said. "We just come by to give you all our money, every penny we have in the world, Miss Peters."

"No, no, no," Miss Willifred said, "I insist; really, I do insist. Now, Mr. Robert Lee, you just put that money right back in your pocket for now. You keep it safe for me till our little visit is over. You should know, Bertram Parker, that it's a terrible breach of etiquette to refuse."

"Well," Bertram said slowly, like he was thinking about it, "I guess it would be okay, but we can't stay long. Momma's expecting us."

She put that old dry hand back on my head and guided me up the steps to the screen door. That's what happens to you when you're little, people pull you around by the top of your head.

"Now let me do the talking, Shiny," Bertram whispered. "Don't say nothin'."

I didn't plan on saying a word. Miss Willifred's house was dark and hot and close as a closet, full of shadows and that strange old lady smell. It was real quiet, except for the tick-tock of the grandfather clock in the front hall. We followed her into the kitchen.

"Now you boys sit down and rest your tired little feet, and I will make you the most delicious lemonade you've ever tasted."

We rested our tired little feet sitting on metal straight-back chairs at a square table with a cracked top. The top was yellow and white checkerboard. The white squares were faded almost to yellow and the yellow

squares almost to white. Miss Willifred cut six lemons in half and
squeezed the juice into a tall pitcher. Then she dumped in about two
pounds of sugar and filled the pitcher with water and ice. While she
worked, she talked. She said folks had it wrong about the younger gener-
ations and that me and Bertram were living proof of that. She thought
just the world of Momma and Daddy: Not everyone would have taken
the Jeffries in like we did; in fact, no one else had offered. She had such a
small house, hardly enough room for her and her cat, Patches, and had we
ever met Patches? She called for him, but the cat never came. That was
fine with me. Cats stare at you, mean as mockingbirds, and I didn't like
any animal that stared. She poured three tall glasses of lemonade and sat
down with us. She was wearing blue house slippers with red bunnies on
them. Her toenails were long and that dark yellow color of old people's
toenails. Our glasses were decorated with bright yellow smiley suns and
pink and blue flowers that smiled back up at the sun. It was good lemonade. I drank half my glass without taking a breath.

Bertram said, "Thank you, Miss Peters, ma'am, for taking our money
and everything. We didn't think nothin' about it till Sheriff Trimbul
kept coming 'round the house, talking to Miss Mavis and Sharon-Rose
and all. He made Sharon-Rose cry, even. We hated to see that, didn't we,
Shiny?"

I nodded.

"We got pretty close to her," Bertram said. "Why, she's almost like a
sister to us, Miss Peters."

Miss Willifred's big eyes blinked quick behind her thick glasses. She
leaned over and lowered her voice, like she was afraid someone might be
hiding under the table, listening.

"Well, there is what one might call a cloud of suspicion about that
whole fire," she whispered. Her breath smelled sour. "The way Mavis
behaved, of course, and Pastor, laughing the way he did, coming out of
the house. But you know how scandal has always followed that Mavis
Howell."

"Mavis Howell?"

"I say 'Howell.' That's what she was till Ned Jeffries came to town
and married her. You boys wouldn't remember that. 'Trouble will come

of this,' I said at the time, and I suppose it has. I just suppose it has. The word is, you see, the word is that *he* is being paroled."

"Paroled?" Bertram asked.

"Released."

"Pastor?"

"Oh, no, no, no, not Pastor. One isn't paroled from the hospital, after all, though for some of us that can be tragically the case."

Bertram said, "Who was paroled?"

"Why, Halley Martin, of course."

We must have had funny looks on our faces, because she laughed.

"You mean to tell me you never heard the story of Halley Martin and Mavis Howell? Well, my! It's only the biggest scandal ever to happen in our town! Well!" She poured herself another glass of lemonade and filled our glasses till the ice danced just below the rims. My mouth had gone dry when she said Halley Martin, and I was grateful for the drink.

"Halley Martin. Halley Martin. What can I say about Halley Martin? It must be near twenty years since he's been gone. Yes, twenty years now—"

"Paroled," Bertram said. "You mean they're letting him out of prison?"

She nodded. "I don't know for certain, y'see. Not for absolutely certain, but that is the word about town, and my word comes from a very reliable source. So one could say the timing of this fire is very . . . strange. Strange, indeed."

She sipped her lemonade and gave a little smack with her lips. "Needs more sugar," she said. "He was a very handsome man. An extremely handsome man. All the young girls were crazy for him, despite his background. His father named him Halley after the comet, you know. Halley's comet. His daddy claimed he saw the comet streak across the sky at the precise moment of his birth. Well, it wasn't the comet; it was a meteor shower, but Freddy Martin wasn't an educated man, none of the Martins were. He's dead now, Freddy, from the moonshine, rest his soul, but he was a mean man. An extremely mean man. When he discovered his mistake, he legally changed Halley's name to Hyram, but by that time Halley was already thirteen or fourteen and no one bothered to call him Hyram, except his daddy, who would beat him every time he didn't answer to it . . ."

"Our momma says Halley Martin killed a man," Bertram said.

"Oh yes. Halley Martin killed Walter Hughes at the old Charhouse Bar out on old Highway 70. It's not there now. Tore it down years ago. There's a Piggly Wiggly there now. Some say you can hear the poor soul of Walter Hughes wailing in the vegetable aisle. Their prices aren't bad, but I prefer to shop at the A&P on Walnut."

"Why'd he kill him, Miss Peters?" Bertram asked.

"Unrequited love," Miss Willifred said, and laughed out loud at the confused look on our faces. "Halley Martin loved Mavis Howell, you see. And Walter Hughes was her intended. Mr. Walter Hughes was *in the way.* Well, that isn't what Halley said at the trial. He said—" She stopped. Her crinkly face went red. "Well, I suppose that's not fit for you to hear."

"You think he did it, Miss Peters?" Bertram asked. "You think Halley Martin come back and set that fire to kill the pastor?"

"Oh, no, no. Halley's still in prison, up in Starke, far as I know. His parole date isn't till sometime next month. But I will say this," she leaned forward again and I got a face full of that sour breath. It made my stomach flop over. "I will say this: You can bet your stars Mavis Howell Jeffries knows he's getting out, and they always said she loved him more than God himself."

It was late afternoon, and the rains were on their way by the time we got out of there. I had drunk three of those big smiley glasses of lemonade and was feeling kind of sick. My stomach was swollen big, and my lips were fat and puffy from all the sugar. I didn't understand half of what Miss Willifred had talked about, but Bertram acted like he did. He nodded a lot and smiled a lot and sometimes said, "Really!" and "You don't say!" which he must have got from Daddy, because Daddy said that a lot. I didn't say anything. I tried to pretend I was a Hardy boy, but I got bored with that since I didn't know how a Hardy boy was supposed to act. Her kitchen was warm, and once I almost nodded off. Miss Willifred talked on and on about Miss Mavis, how she was the most courted girl in three counties, how every young man wanted to marry her, and how she met Halley Martin when he took a job working for her daddy, who was the richest man in town, who owned most of the orange groves in the county, who lost everything after two years of bad freezes, leaving Miss Mavis and her momma penniless when he died. And she told how after they took Halley Martin to prison, Miss Mavis planted the live-oak tree that stands at the top of the hill by the church. She made Pastor build his church right there, Miss Willifred said, by the tree, so Miss Mavis could look out her window and see that tree. "She loved him then and she loves him still," Miss Willifred said, "sure as that tree's still standing." Bertram told her he didn't understand why Miss Mavis got engaged if she loved Halley so much, or why she married the pastor, and Miss Willifred said her daddy forbade her seeing Halley, as he was *common,* and Walter Hughes was from *good stock.* And as for Pastor, she said, that is a true mystery.

Then Bertram wanted to know how Halley Martin killed Walter Hughes, and Miss Willifred told how Halley just walked up to him and took out a big hunting knife and gutted Walter like he was a pig, from gut to neck, so all his insides spilled onto the floor.

That was when I had started feeling sick.

We started for home. The wind began to pick up, cooling the sweat on the back of our necks. The fat black clouds were moving in, and we were nowhere near our house. I told Bertram I had to pee and he waited while I ducked behind some bushes by the side of the road.

"Zip up your pants," he told me when I came out again.

"How's this goin' to get 'em out of our house, Bertram?"

"Never mind. You just wait till tonight."

"Tonight?"

"Yeah-a. And don't worry about nothin'. All you got to do is be yourself."

"Be myself?"

"Yeah. Act scared. Cry a lot. You know, be yourself."

From far off thunder rolled. Bertram looked at the sky behind us. "We better hurry," he said.

By the time we reached our dirt road the sky was dark and the wind had died to nothing. It was that time right before a storm when the whole world holds its breath, with the clouds low enough to touch, and the birds hunker in the trees with their heads down, and dogs stop their barking and slink beneath porches and parked cars, tongues drooping out of their mouths and ears flat on their heads. Then the ground shakes with the first crack of thunder, a crack so loud it sounds like the sky itself is splitting open and all the stars and planets and moons and the black of space itself will fall through the crack and crash on your head. The dirt of the road begins to pop and explode from the first fat drops of rain, and soon you're slipping in the yellow mud as you run, the rain smashing down on your head like it hates you, the thunder rattling the bones inside your skin. You feel heavy and slow, like you're running in slow motion, and when your brother yells at you to run it sounds like he's talking through a sock; the rain knocks his words to the ground.

"Follow me, Shiny!"

Bertram ran on ahead, his head down, his big arms pumping, and I tried to run faster to catch up. I slipped and fell face down in the mud and laid there, because at first I couldn't figure what happened. One second I was running, the next I had a mouthful of yellow mud. Bertram grabbed my arms and yanked me up. I was blind, gasping, spitting the rain and mud out of my mouth as Bertram pulled me to the grass by the side of the road. I had mud in my teeth and on my tongue, and that made me sick, just thinking about it.

"We're almost there!" Bertram yelled. I wiped the back of my hand over my eyes and saw he wasn't talking about our house; he was talking about the church, just up the hill in front of us.

"No!" I yelled as Bertram dragged me up the hill.

"Shut up!" he shouted back. He kicked open the church door and shoved me into the dimness inside.

It seemed real quiet after being under the naked sky, but the rain drummed like an engine running over our heads. The church was spooky, all empty, it not being Sunday. We stood just inside the door, shivering in our wet clothes, rainwater dripping from our eyelashes. Bertram was watching the storm through the crack in the door. I ran my tongue over my teeth, feeling more mud and those little jagged-edged stones that littered the road. I glanced at the front of the church. The light shone through the stained-glass windows, and patterns of Jesus fell over the big wooden cross at the far wall.

Bertram said, "Somebody's coming."

"Who's coming, Bertram?"

"Hide," he said. "Hide, Shiny."

He turned me around and pushed me toward the back row of pews.

"Who's coming, Bertram?"

"Shut up, Shiny! Get down!"

He yanked me down between the two back pews. He pressed his finger to his lips as the door creaked open and footsteps clicked on the bare wooden floor. A shadow glided past us, going up the aisle. Bertram eased up and peeked over the back of the pew. I took a deep breath and copied him. The shadow had stopped a few steps away from the big cross and was looking up at it. The person was wearing a white poncho that shimmered in the gray rain-light. Then the hood was pulled back, and dark hair fell down. I would have known that dark hair anywhere. It was Miss Mavis.

She sank to her knees. She went down so slow and smooth it looked like she was sinking into the floor. The rain drummed over us, but we could hear her crying. It wasn't a wailing kind of crying; it wasn't the yelling and screaming kind, like she cried the night her husband burned. It was slow and soft like the rain when it's just about to end.

The door behind us creaked again, and Bertram shoved me down. We hunkered low as the wood floor creaked with the weight of heavy feet. I saw a flash of a brown uniform and heard Miss Mavis give a little "oooh!"

"I'm sorry, Miss Mavis," Sheriff Trimbul said. "I didn't mean to startle you."

Neither of them said anything for a long time. Then Miss Mavis said, "You've been following me."

"Well," Sheriff Trimbul said. "Well, yes. A bit. I guess I have."

"No," she said, "not a bit. You've been following me every day since the fire. You follow us to the hospital every day, and then you follow us back to the Parkers'."

"Well," Sheriff Trimbul said slowly, "I s'pose you know the reason for that."

"What do you want from me, Sheriff? I told you what happened that night. I told you everything. If it's a crime, you should arrest me. If it isn't, you need to leave me alone."

She didn't sound angry, just sad, the most terrible sad I ever heard anyone sound.

Bertram and me eased up again. Sheriff Trimbul was next to her now, looking down at her, kind of smiling, but serious about it, like when we do something bad and Daddy has to talk to us about it, but he thinks it's kind of funny only he can't let Momma know that.

"He's coming home tomorrow, Miss Mavis," he said.

"I know that," she said.

"He'll come back here."

"Of course he will," Miss Mavis said. "Where else would he go?"

"That's my point. And kind of the answer to your question. Why I've been following you about, so to speak. My friends up in Starke have let me know . . . well, he hasn't made any secret of his intentions. You've seen the old house, you know all that's goin' on over there—"

"He would never harm me," she said.

"It's not you I'm worried about," he said, "begging your pardon. Now, he's made it clear what he wants when he gets here, and he can't have that unless certain parties are out of the picture."

"He's not a violent man," she said. "He never was."

"All the same, better safe than sorry is my motto, Miss Mavis."

He took a long white envelope from his pocket and held it out to her.

"What's this?" she asked.

"Two tickets to Atlanta, unrestricted. You and your little girl can use them whenever you like."

Miss Mavis laughed. "And what would we do in Atlanta?"

"My cousin Ruth has an extra room. Free to use as long as you like. Her address is in here too, and her number. She'll pick you up at the station—"

Miss Mavis handed the envelope back to him. "Thank you, Sheriff, but my place is here. I will not run away."

"Don't think of it as running away. Twenty years is a long time, Miss Mavis. And twenty years up in Starke is a very long time. You know what happened to him in there. Any man who's been through what he's been through gonna be looking for some—justice. Oh, I don't know if that's what you'd call it, but all the same, I'm a one-man operation down here and I can't be in two places at once. I can't watch over you and Ned, so I—"

"Excuse me, Sheriff, but it isn't my business to do your job. If you fear for me or fear for Ned, then it's your responsibility to protect us."

"Well, dear Jesus, woman, what d'you think I'm tryin' to do!" His voice boomed out in the empty church. His face had gone red; he was mad, you could tell, but Miss Mavis wasn't giving in.

"You cannot bully me, Sheriff Trimbul. I've had my full share of bullies, and I know all their tricks. I will not leave this place. I will not leave. Whatever my fate is, I will face it here."

They stared at each other, neither of them saying anything.

Then Sheriff Trimbul laughed.

"All right," he said, stretching the word into two: rye-ite. "All right, but humor an old man, Miss Mavis. Take the tickets. Throw 'em away if you like, or give 'em away, but if you took them it'd sure help me sleep better at night."

She took her time, but she took the envelope.

"Ned comes home tomorrow?" he asked.

She nodded.

"I just—I'm just getting too old for trouble, Miss Mavis."

She shook her head slowly.

"That won't make any difference," she said.

Momma asked us where'd we been all afternoon, when we came through the door still wet from the rain. Bertram told her we were out on an errand of mercy, which I guess meant giving Miss Willifred the money, but I had been so dizzy from all the talk of gut-spilling and the sugar that I forgot to give her the money back, so I don't know how merciful we were. Momma said, "What errand of mercy, Bertram?"

Bertram said, "We'll have to tell you later, Momma," and she gave him a funny look, but she didn't ask us any more questions.

After we changed into dry clothes, Bertram closed the door, sat me on the bed, and looked me close in the eye.

"Now it's time for Phase Two of the operation," he said.

"What operation?"

"We got to move quick, 'fore she gets back."

"'Fore who gets back, Bertram?"

"Miss Mavis," he hissed. He tiptoed to the door and cracked it open. I came up behind him.

"Don't stand so close, Shiny," he whispered. "You stand so damn close all the time it's like you're tryin' to climb into my clothes." He turned and lowered his face down to mine. "Okay, Sharon-Rose is in the kitchen with Momma. I'll be the lookout . . ."

"Lookout for what?"

He told me what I was going to do for this phase of the operation.

"I'm not going to do that, Bertram."

"You want them out of here?"

"You said all I had to do was wait for tonight, be myself . . ."

"Yeah-a."

"Well, doin' somethin' like that ain't myself. It ain't myself at all."

"Look, you got to do it, Shiny. I'm too big. You're little; you won't make much noise, and if somethin' happens you can get under the bed quicker and quieter than me."

"Maybe we should just let 'em stay, Bertram . . ."

"Either they're goin' or I am, and I ain't goin'. Now come on, Shiny, it's just like spies!"

He stepped out of the doorway and gave me a little shove toward the sewing room door. I looked back at him and he gave me a small wave of his hand. "Go on," he whispered. "I'll whistle if I see somebody comin'!"

I could hear Sharon-Rose and Momma talking in the kitchen, just five or so steps from the sewing room door. Sharon-Rose was saying, "You're a much better cook than my momma, Miss Parker. My momma can't cook worth a lick, 'less it's fried. Daddy says it's 'cause nobody ever taught her, her being rich and spoiled and all. Will you teach me how to cook, Miss Parker?" I didn't hear Momma's answer; I was already in the sewing room. I eased the door halfway shut and then just stood there. I'd played in this room since before I could remember playing here, but now it seemed like I was in a stranger's house. The room smelled like Miss

Mavis's perfume laid over the smell of Sharon-Rose, that smell of burnt oranges. There wasn't much else of the two of them in there. They had lost everything in the fire. Just a few new dresses and Miss Mavis's makeup stuff on the little sitting table in the corner. Momma had put some fresh-cut flowers in a green vase on the table. The air was close, where the wetness of the rain had seeped in through cracks around the window too tiny to see, warm and heavy on my face.

"Check everything," Bertram had told me, " 'specially the closet and under the bed. And stick your hand under the mattress—you know, between the mattress and springs. People hide stuff there all the time." I wondered how he knew that. I made up my mind to check between *his* mattress and springs, to see what he had tucked under there. I didn't feel like a Hardy boy right then, or even much of a spy. I just felt small and scared and kind of dirty, like I was doing something very bad. Lying on the bed was an old comic book, its scorched cover yellow and the top edges curled up crinkly and black. Sharon-Rose or maybe Miss Mavis must have rescued it from the fire. I glanced behind me, then knelt down and looked under the bed. There was nothing under there but a few balls of dust and an old roll of yarn. I felt the air getting closer and closer, and my heart was real high up in my throat. I got up and opened the closet door. It was stuffed to the ceiling with winter clothes and Momma's sewing supplies and old shoes and the bow-and-arrow set that Bertram got last Christmas but that got taken away after Momma caught him hauling me outside to play William Tell.

There were no clues in the closet I could see, but I didn't really know what I was looking for. It all sounds really easy in books, finding clues and catching the bad guys, but I didn't think there was much of either in our house. All at once, more than scared I felt stupid. Stupid and ashamed of myself. I started for the door, then remembered what Bertram said about the mattress. For a second I didn't move. I knew I had a choice now. I could look, like Bertram said. I could not look and tell Bertram I didn't, which might get me beaten up. Or I could not look and tell Bertram I did, which was a lie and a sin, and God seemed pretty mad enough at everybody already. I decided to look.

I didn't actually look with my eyes. What I did was stick my arm as far as it would go under the mattress and kind of sweep my hand around. My fingers touched something under there. It felt like paper. I looked toward the door, then pulled the papers out. They were folded three times each and tied up in a little bundle, and there was a lot of them. There was a whole fistful. I was still squatting there with all these papers in my hand when the floor creaked. It seemed like it took me forever to look up at the person standing there in the doorway, like the heavy air was pressing my head down, and I knew who it was before I saw her—I would know that perfume anywhere.

"Well, good afternoon, Mister Robert Lee," Miss Mavis said.

I hid under my bed until Momma called us to dinner.

"You got to come out now, Shiny," Bertram said.

"You were supposed to whistle!" I yelled at him.

"I did whistle."

"I didn't hear you!"

"That ain't my fault! Tell me what she said."

"She didn't say anything. I told you, I just ran out, Bertram. I just ran out as fast as I could."

"What did you do with the clues?"

"Dropped 'em."

"You could have stuffed 'em down your pants or somethin'."

"Bertram, I ain't spyin' no more. It ain't right."

"There's lots of things not right," he said. I was going to ask him what he meant by that, but Momma came into the room.

"I have been calling you boys for ten minutes!" she said. "Where's Robert Lee?"

"Here I am, Momma," I said, and I crawled out from under the bed.

"What in the world . . . ?" she said.

"I lost a penny," Bertram said.

Momma carried a plate to Miss Mavis, who was holed up in the sewing room. Bertram asked Daddy what she did in there all the time, and

Daddy said she was sewing a shroud for her husband. Bertram asked what a shroud was and Daddy said never mind, we were too young to understand, it was a joke. We were too young, I guess, because I didn't get it.

At dinner Sharon-Rose bent over her plate like always, but somehow managed to talk and shovel at the same time.

"My daddy's coming home tomorrow," she said. She didn't sound happy about it. "That means I won't get no more of that hospital ice cream."

"Maybe you'll have some tragic accident and you can have it twenty-four hours a day," Bertram said.

"Bertram," Daddy said.

"He was talking crazy again today," Sharon-Rose said.

Momma said, "Your father is taking a great deal of pain medication, Sharon-Rose. Sometimes that causes people to say strange things."

"Well," Sharon-Rose said, "he's said strange things long as I can remember. These things now are a lot stranger, though."

"What's he say?" Bertram asked.

"Never mind," Daddy said.

"Says a lot about Jesus," Sharon-Rose said. "And the Judgment. The hordes of heaven."

"What hordes of heaven?" Bertram asked.

Momma gave Daddy a look, but he smiled a little and waved his hand.

"You know. All the angels and saints and dead souls pouring down like rain, heavenly rain, raindrops of heavenly light."

"Oh, what a beautiful way to express it, Sharon-Rose!" Momma said.

Sharon-Rose shrugged. A drop of gravy clung to her chin, quivering while she talked. "Daddy said it. He's saying all kinds of strange things, when he's awake. Most of the time he just lays there, droolin' and opening his mouth like a fish." She made her mouth into an O and puffed her cheeks in and out. Bertram laughed. Momma told him to hush.

"We shall all be very glad to have him home," Momma said.

"Oh, he looks just awful," Sharon-Rose said. "His face is all red and crinkly and puckered, like your hands get when you stay too long in the tub, and—"

"I think we shouldn't discuss this at the dinner table," Daddy said, which shut her up. He was the only person I ever saw who could shut Sharon-Rose up.

After dinner we helped Momma get the house ready for Pastor's big coming-home party, though he had no real home to come home to. Bertram and me dusted the shelves and knickknacks. Then he helped Daddy move the big table in from the toolshed and we pushed the furniture back and set it up. Sharon-Rose disappeared into her momma's room for a while, and when she came out her eyes were big and red, like she'd been crying. Momma showed me a big banner that said WELCOME HOME PASTOR NED. It had blue and yellow and red balloons drawn on it and a single gold cross over the pastor's name. She told me she wouldn't be surprised if the whole town turned out to see him, and that made me nervous, thinking of fitting the whole town into our living room. I was more tired than I ever remember being in my whole life, so I was happy for once when bedtime came. Momma said our prayers, and after she kissed my head, she asked Bertram what our mission of mercy was. She hadn't forgotten. Momma never forgot.

"We gave our money to Miss Willifred."

"Why?"

"For all the committees."

"And why did you do that, Bertram?"

"Ain't we—"

"*Aren't* we," Momma said.

"Aren't we supposed to help them, Momma?"

"You never seemed to care about it before."

"We were hopin' it would help them get their own place soon," Bertram said.

Momma smiled. "How sweet of you! And how thoughtful that you've become so concerned with their welfare, Bertram." She looked down at me. Her face glowed in the soft yellow light, framed by her blond hair, and it looked like the dark of her eyes went on forever, and I thought how wrong I was to ever think Miss Mavis was the prettiest lady I'd ever seen.

"Is that true, Shiny?" she asked.

"I forgot to give it to her, Momma."

"You forgot?"

Bertram said, "You idiot!"

Momma said, "Hush that talk, Bertram."

"I'm sorry, Momma," I said. "It was all the lemonade, and I was scared . . ." My eyes felt hot.

"Scared?" she said.

"Shiny's been awful scared, Momma," Bertram said. "I never seen him so scared in his whole life, and you know I've seen him scared a lot. He was about to pee his pants he was so scared."

"I was not! That was the lemonade!"

"Well," Momma said, "what got you scared?"

"Go on," Bertram said. "Tell her."

"Halley Martin," I said.

"Halley Martin?" Momma said.

"Halley Martin," Bertram said. "Miss Willifred told us all about him."

"Oh, she did, did she?"

"Yes'm. She sure did," Bertram said. "How he killed Walter Hughes with a hunting knife and spilled his guts out all over the floor, and how they sent him to prison for twenty years, and how he's getting out and he's coming back, and now something bad's going to happen, worse than the fire, something really bad because he has intentions, Momma . . ."

"Intentions? What intentions?"

"She don't know," Bertram said.

"She *doesn't* know," Momma said.

"No, she don't," Bertram said. "She said nobody knows, but he's coming back, Momma. They're letting him go, and Miss Willifred said we should hide all the knives in the house . . ."

That was too much for me, after all I heard that day, after getting caught in the loud, crackling storm, after hearing Sharon-Rose talk about her daddy's red, puckered face. It was just too much. I let loose with all I had, and Momma sat me up and held me and ran her smooth hand over the back of my stubbly head. She rocked me back and forth, "hushing" me softly while I pressed my nose into her sweet-smelling neck.

Bertram yelled, "See Momma, see! He can't take it! You can't make him take it anymore! It's messing him up, Momma. There's got to be some other place they can go."

"They are staying with us," Momma said.

"But Momma . . ."

"Your father and I have made a promise and we intend to keep it, Bertram."

"Then send us away!"

She stopped rocking me. "And where do you propose we send you, Bertram?"

"Granma's. We could stay with her until the Jeffries move out."

"Bertram, this is your home."

"But Momma, the mad slasher's coming!"

"Halley Martin is many things," Momma said, "but he is no mad slasher."

"He slashed that Walter Hughes."

"And there are many people in this town who think Walter Hughes got what he deserved. Not that it makes what Halley did right, but . . ."

"Why's that, Momma?"

"Never mind."

"That's what everybody's been saying, Momma, but I do mind."

"Don't," Momma said.

"I got to mind—"

"We will not discuss this."

"But why, Momma?"

"Because there are certain things children have no business knowing about!" Momma's voice was cold and hard, and her eyes shone wet in the soft, yellow light. Bertram flinched just as if she had slapped him. She lowered her voice and kept going.

"I don't know everything that old busybody Willifred Peters told you, but you must remember she is not known for her grasp of all the facts. Halley Martin did kill Walter Hughes. It was a terrible crime that divided this town for many years. He has paid for what he did, paid terribly as I hear it, and now it is our Christian duty to forgive him and trust that everything will be all right."

"I'd have a lot more trust if they weren't in our house, Momma," Bertram said.

"Do you really think, Bertram Parker, in your heart of hearts, that your father and I would ever let anything happen to you or your brother, that we would ever do anything that would place you in danger?"

Bertram bit his bottom lip. In his heart of hearts the answer was no, but if he said no, then we weren't going anywhere, and neither was Sharon-Rose. Momma was rubbing the back of my head again while she watched Bertram wrestle with his heart of hearts.

"No, ma'am," he said.

"Of course not." Momma kissed the top of my head. "And you, Robert Lee Parker, you are much too young to be filling your head with such grown-up business. This is your childhood, Shiny, the only one you're ever going to have, so make the most of it."

She gave me one last hug and Bertram a little pat on the cheek.

"Good night, Bertram," she said.

"Good night, Momma," Bertram said.

"Good night, Momma," I said. "Good night, Bertram."

"Shut up," he said. Momma was gone. She left our door open a crack, so when Bertram snapped off the lamp a band of light leaped across the room and shone on the wall beside Bertram's bed and glinted off the trophies. I heard Bertram breathing heavy in the dark. It wasn't the slow, deep, sleep-breathing kind, but a hard, fast breathing, like he was running up a hill. It was going to bust out of him, and I was waiting. He commenced to flopping around, snapping the sheets, and pounding on his pillow. I closed my eyes and waited for it. Sometimes you had to wait a long time, and sometimes, when he was real excited, you only had to wait a minute or two. It was less than a minute tonight.

"Christian duty!" he said. "Christian duty! I don't think it's my Christian duty to get stabbed in my sleep by a crazy man or set on fire by some fat, weirdo girl. This is my home, she says, well, nobody asked *me* if they could come here. I'll just run off, and then what're they goin' to do about it? I'll hide out in the fort till they're gone or everybody's dead, 'cause it's my Christian duty to save my own butt. I'll go to Granma's; she won't make me come back. Or maybe, that's what I'll do, I'll get those tickets; I'll take those train tickets from Miss Mavis and I'll go to Atlanta and stay with cousin Ruth. There's two tickets so you can come with me, Shiny. We'll enjoy our childhoods far away from this crazy place. I don't know what Walter Hughes done to deserve to be gutted like that, but I bet *he* didn't think he deserved it!"

I didn't know what to say, so I said, "Don't go, Bertram."

"I will go."

"Momma says it's going to be all right."

"Momma don't know that. You think they really can protect us, Shiny? That window over your head, what's Momma and Daddy gonna do if Martin slips in through it in the middle of the night? Why, he'd have us slit wide open before Momma and Daddy could sit up in bed—"

"But Momma said—"

" 'But Momma said, but Momma said,' " Bertram whined, making fun. "I s'pose if Momma said the world was flat you'd believe her."

"Momma wouldn't lie to me, Bertram."

"Oh, no, of course not! No grown-up lies to kids!"

"No," I said, "they don't."

"Jesus, Shiny, sometimes you can be so stupid." He flopped on his bed like a fish. Then he said, "So, are you with me?"

"With you?"

"Are you coming with me?"

"I don't know where you're going."

"I'm running away, you idiot! Are you coming with me?"

I thought about it. "I don't think so, Bertram."

"Okay, then. Fine. Good for you. Only you're going to be sorry when you're choking on your own blood in the middle of the night. Try yellin' for your precious Momma then."

He flopped around some more, then like some switch had been clicked off, he fell asleep. I laid awake and listened to the crickets and watched the leaf-shadows dance. I pressed the flat of my hand against the wall beside my bed. On the other side of that wall Momma and Daddy slept. Bertram was wrong, but I couldn't put into words why he was wrong. You just felt it when she held you or rubbed the back of your head. You felt it when Daddy let you climb on his back and swung you around the room till your head was loose on your neck and blood sang in your ears. You even felt it when she popped you in the mouth or he swatted your butt. It was something that went deeper than the darkness in Momma's eyes, and there was nothing bigger or stronger than it was, not even Halley Martin. Next to it, Halley Martin was no bigger than a flea.

I fell asleep the easiest I'd done since Sharon-Rose had come to live with us.

The next morning the sun woke me up shining through my window, warm and friendly until later that day, when it would turn mean. I went into the kitchen and everybody was there except Bertram and Miss Mavis. I asked where Bertram was, and Momma said he must still be asleep, so I ran back to our room and poked the lump under the sheets. It was Bertram's pillow. I ran back into the kitchen and told them Bertram had run away. Daddy left the room and Momma asked what had happened, and I said Bertram was either going to Granma's or Atlanta, and Momma asked, "Why Atlanta?" and I said I didn't know. I figured Bertram was in enough trouble. Daddy came back in jingling his keys and told Momma he'd be back shortly, like he knew exactly where Bertram would go. He was smiling. Momma said she was glad Daddy found all this so amusing, and Daddy said this was part of being a boy, and Sharon-Rose looked over at me like I was some strange creature that had just popped into the kitchen. I decided it was best to pop out of it and wait for Bertram in our room.

I passed the sewing room and a soft voice called out to me, "Robert Lee."

I stopped. Miss Mavis was sitting on the bed, her hands folded in her lap, and she was smiling at me, that same sad smile I'd seen when she caught me kneeling by the bed, those crinkled, yellowed papers in my sinful hand. Miss Mavis's hair was wet, and a big blue comb lay beside her on the white bedspread. She had no makeup on, and it was the first and only time I saw her that way. She looked the same, but different. Her eyes looked smaller and farther back in her face somehow, and they were darker, not the bright, glowing kind of blue as usual, but the purply blue of the sky when the sun is just about to set. She was wearing one of Daddy's white robes, which made her look shrunk, like a little girl with a grown-up lady's face. Her mouth looked smaller too, without the lipstick. It was like looking at a ghost of Miss Mavis, her pale face and dark hair and white robe, and the way she seemed to float on the white bedspread.

She held out her hand and waved me inside, saying, "Don't be afraid, I'm not angry with you, Robert Lee. Come in; I want to chat."

I came two steps into the room and stopped. I felt like I had just fallen down a deep well.

"I can't, Miss Mavis," I said, my voice shaking. "My brother Bertram's run away."

"Why did he do that?"

I couldn't say, "Because he's afraid you're going to kill us all or Halley Martin is or maybe your daughter's going to burn us all to a crisp," so I didn't say anything.

"I'm sure he'll come back," she said. "Has he ever run away before?"

I shook my head no.

"I suppose all this is a little overwhelming, particularly for you children," she said.

"Miss Mavis, I'm sorry," I blurted out. I couldn't hold it in any longer. "Bertram told me to! He made me come in here and look for clues. I didn't look at them, those papers, I didn't look at one of them, I swear I didn't, Miss Mavis!"

"I know, child," she said softly. "They are all that's left, all I managed to bring out." She laughed. It was not a happy laugh. Even Miss Mavis's laugh had turned sad. "I'm sorry, Robert Lee. I'm sorry. I know our being here is not easy for you, your family. But you see, there was simply nowhere else to go . . ."

I had about fifty places I wanted to go to right then, but I didn't move. I don't know what I was waiting for, but there was something about the way she was looking at me, like her eyes were the pin and I was the bug. All of a sudden I thought of that mockingbird in Miss Willifred's tree, I don't know why.

"Oh, we have relatives in Inverness, but I can't leave Ned here. I—

we are all he has now." She looked around the little room, and I didn't feel so pinned down, but I didn't want to just run away. It was like she was shrinking right before my eyes, getting smaller and smaller inside that white robe of Daddy's.

"Miss Mavis . . ." I said.

She went on like she hadn't heard me. "Do you know, when I was your age, Robert Lee, I lived in a house three times the size of this one, and I slept in a four-poster bed with a white canopy and mosquito netting, and I had everything I wanted. I was the richest little girl in town, and now *my* little girl has the clothes on her back and a scorched comic book." She spoke real calm, not crying-like. She spoke like she was talking about someone else. "And I have a collection of old letters." They were lying beside her on the bed. She picked them up and held them on her lap, and she picked at their edges with her fingernails. "Letters never sent. See the old stamps?" She thought I'd be interested in the old-timey stamps, I guess. Miss Mavis was one of those grown-ups who felt they had to entertain you.

"Why not?" I asked. I couldn't help myself. "Why didn't you send them, Miss Mavis?"

"I should have left them to burn." She was looking at me and not looking at me at the same time. "I should have left them to the fire. I left *him.* I left my own husband, but I saved these letters." She laughed that same strange, sad laugh. "Why do you suppose I did that?" She shook her head all at once, as if she was shaking herself out of a dream. "I know you didn't read them, Robert Lee. They were never meant to be read. I really don't know what their purpose is, but the Lord will show the way. I have always believed that. The Lord *will* show the way. If we stop believing that, then we are lost." She put the packet of unmailed letters down and folded her hands in her lap again and smiled at me, and for a moment her eyes sparkled, and I caught the faintest peek of the old Miss Mavis, more sparkly and alive than most people are, and all of a sudden there seemed to be less air in the room and I was working hard just to breathe. "All things, in the end, are delivered, Shiny Parker. Perhaps it is his will that these letters be finally delivered."

"Delivered where, Miss Mavis?" I asked. My voice sounded like it was coming from another room. I don't know why, but it felt like the space between us was as wide as the space between the stars. She was shining like a faraway star, all in white like that. Her face glowed with all the sadness in it.

"To the place they came from," she said. "Where they were written, because that's where he is coming, after all this time, after all these many years. Of all places, to that very house, to *my* house. It is his, now, and he is coming home."

And Miss Mavis sounded thrilled and scared and sad and happy all at the same time, and we both knew who she was talking about, and I remembered Miss Willifred saying how Miss Mavis loved him then and loved him still, and then I remembered the tree with its mossy arms growing at the top of the hill, and now her face was shining, and her eyes shone brightest of all, and the light in her eyes glittered like knife blades, turning in the sun.

"If he makes it to the highway a car will smash him for sure," Sharon-Rose said. She had found me standing on the porch, watching the road for Daddy's car. "I'd run away too if I thought it would do any good. My daddy's coming home today and it ain't even like he's my daddy any-more."

She sounded sad, not like Sharon-Rose at all. She looked down at me, her tangled blond hair curling around her wide face. For the first time she looked like her momma. Maybe it was because she was sad. Bertram called her a crazy girl and said he hated her, and I was scared of her, and thought I hated her too, for coming to live with us and taking over our TV and being nasty every chance she got, but right then all I felt was sad; it was like the sadness I saw in her eyes was dribbling out and falling all over me, like she was leaking sadness on me. Momma said all God wanted from us was to love everybody, which didn't make any sense when she said it, because some people are just too hard to love, but right then I saw how maybe you could. Well, maybe not love, exactly. I didn't love Sharon-Rose, I just understood all of a sudden she wasn't any more happy about things than I was.

"If he don't come back," she said, "if he don't come back, maybe your momma and daddy will adopt me and I can be your sister."

"Daddy will bring him back," I said.

"Why'd he run away, Shiny?"

"I don't know." I couldn't tell her he was afraid she'd burn him alive.

"When'd he set out?"

"I don't know."

"There's not much you do know, is there? Well, he's probably half-way to Timbuktu by now."

"Where's that?"

"I don't know exactly. On the other side of the world, in China, I think. Where they got those big fat statues of men in diapers."

Momma came out on the porch and stood beside me. She put a hand on my shoulder. She had just come out when we saw Daddy's car come up the road. He and Bertram got out. Bertram was carrying his blue cardboard suitcase. He went straight to the toolshed and Daddy followed him inside.

"Ooohhh, he's in for it now," Sharon-Rose said. "Gonna get a whoopin' now." She sounded like her old self again.

Momma took us back inside. I felt just miserable, like I always did when Bertram was marched into the toolshed, which seemed to be happening a lot since Sharon-Rose came to live with us. Afterward, he went straight to our room and closed the door, and when I knocked he shouted at me to go away or he'd bash my head in. I went away.

The old ladies were the first to come, two to a car, because old ladies always traveled in pairs. Miss Willifred came with Miss Rachel, and Miss Willifred took charge the minute she hit the door. She told Daddy and Momma where to hang the banner and how to set the table and what table to put the punch bowl on. All the old ladies came in carrying plates and bowls covered with shiny foil, and soon you couldn't see the white tablecloth for all the food. Miss Willifred said nobody needed more proof how badly the church needed a social hall because once everybody arrived we'd all be sitting in each other's laps. Miss Rachel said no one listened to her when she suggested they rent the VFW hall. Nobody said anything to that, so I guess they still weren't listening. Soon the whole house smelled like casserole and talcum. Miss Nadine came in wearing a blue dress with a white ribbon in her gray hair, carrying a folder full of sheet music. She plunked a few times on the piano and frowned. Her lipstick was painted outside her thin lips, and her face was chalky from all the powder, like someone had dumped a sack of flour over her head. She was all white, except for that blue dress; even her hands were white. She looked like a yard statue come to life. She lowered her head over the piano keys and plunked some more. She yelled over at Momma, "How long since you had this piano tuned?" and Momma said she didn't know, and Miss Nadine yelled back, "What good is there in a piano if you won't keep it tuned!" and Momma came over and said nobody ever played it once Bertram quit piano lessons because his teacher said his fingers were too short and fat and he was generally too awkward to ever play it well. Miss Nadine grabbed my hand and told Momma to look at my long, slender fingers, and Momma said I was too young, and Miss Nadine sniffed and said Mozart was writing whole symphonies at my age, and Momma said, "Well, then, it's probably too late to start now." Miss Nadine let me go and I got out of there as fast as I could. She had a hard grip for an old lady, and her hand was freezing cold.

I went outside and crawled under the porch. I laid on my stomach on the cool, hard-packed ground and watched through the latticework as the cars pulled up and parked by the curb. First the old men came, packed five or six to a car; they were the husbands of the old ladies inside who hadn't lost a husband yet. The old men wore white suits and wide-brimmed straw hats. They all had carnations stuck in their lapels, and some leaned on canes and grumbled about the porch steps as they came up. There was Mr. Lattimer and Mr. Talbot and Mr. Crawley. There was Mr. Franks and Mr. Goddard and Mr. Michaels. Mr. Taylor came, and Mr. Shelby and Mr. Carlson, who was a deacon at the church like Daddy.

After the old men, the families came in their wood-paneled station wagons and low-slung cars with big, shiny tail fins. I saw some kids from my Sunday school class. There was Peter Hilliard in a brown jacket with patches on the elbows. There was Justin Lockhart with his little sister Emily pulling on his pants leg and yelling she had to pee. There was Christy Buchanon, who picked her nose when she thought nobody was looking, but I guess everybody does that, so you couldn't fault her for it. There was John Listrom, who everybody called Jugs because of his big ears. I watched them through a big spiderweb that I was scared to pull down since I didn't know how old it was and the spider might be close by and waiting to pounce the minute my hand touched the strands. Momma said I shouldn't lay up under the porch because there might be black widows under there, and one bite from a black widow is the end of you. But I liked it under the porch. It was cool even on the hottest days, and though it was dark, it was a nice kind of dark. Not the kind of dark when the lightning hits at night and knocks out the electricity, but a comfortable kind of dark, like when you wake up having to pee and it's still night, and after you pee you snuggle back down in your covers and you feel that hollow space in your gut where the pee used to be, and it feels so good, empty and warm, and the dark all around you that meant you didn't have to get up yet; there was still a few minutes left to sleep and dream.

The older kids came up the drive next, the boys slouching along two or three to a group, glancing at the girls, who clustered around one another and giggled a lot. The girls wore yellow or pink or orange dresses. The boys wore blue or brown jackets, and their hair was long and slicked back, shining in the sun. Now everywhere I looked I saw cars; I guess the whole congregation had turned out for Pastor's party, and all Homeland besides. Except the black people. There weren't any black people at our church, and once I asked Momma why that was, and she said because they have their own church. Black people were lucky that way. They had their own church and their own school. They had their own private seats at the diner downtown. They even had their own bathrooms and water fountains. Nobody could use them except other black people. Daddy said they had all been slaves once, but there was a war about it, and then they weren't slaves anymore. Maybe that's why they had all those private things now, to make up for it. I was curious about black people. They all seemed friendly enough, but there was something right behind their yellow-looking eyes and bright teeth that was lost and angry, something like the look Miss Mavis had in the church that day with Sheriff Trimbul. There was an old black doorman at the bank where

Daddy worked who said hello when you came in and tipped his hat to
you and held the door open for the old ladies. His name was Jasper
Johnson, and he called me Mr. Robert Lee and he always had a sucker or
a piece of gum for me when I came to visit Daddy. He wore a red jacket
and black pants with a thin stripe down each leg, and his shoes were
shiny enough to comb your hair in. "Now don't you tell your daddy," he
would whisper, bending over to look me eye to eye. "It be our secret, you
an' me." His breath smelled like oranges. He liked to show me tricks too.
He could make a quarter come out of my ear or flip it so it always came
up heads. Jasper Johnson was the only black person I knew to talk to. On
the night of the fire some black people came to watch, but they stood
apart from the white people, and their children played on the dirt road
like they came out every night and played in the light of a house-fire.

There was a bunch of clumping and bumping over my head, and for
a minute I was scared the floor would fall down on me from the weight
of all those people. You think you live in a little town till everybody in it
is inside your house.

I heard Momma calling from right above me, "Robert Lee! Robert
Lee Parker! Shiny!" I scrambled out the side where the latticework was
broken, and she was standing with her hands on her hips. She fussed at
me for crawling under the porch on today of all days. Pastor and Daddy
would be here any minute. She took me by the shoulders and pushed me
back into the house, guiding me through the knots of people standing
around. She took me to the bathroom and washed me up. She was wearing a white apron over her dress. Her hair was up in a bun and she
smelled like vanilla. After I was washed and my face was stinging from
the washcloth, she took me to our room and banged on the door until
Bertram opened it.

"You're not dressed," Momma said.

Bertram said, "And I ain't gettin' dressed either."

She pulled me past him into the room and took my Sunday suit out
of the closet. "You do know how to pick your moments to vex me,
Bertram Parker. Here I have a hundred guests in my home and you
choose this moment to be contentious."

"I ain't doin' nothin' to *you,* Momma."

Momma pulled my pants off. I lost my balance and fell back onto the bed. She said, "You are choosing to vex me, Bertram. You know better than to say 'ain't' and 'nothin' and you're saying it for the same reason you're refusing to get dressed. So before you say anything else, you decide whether I should involve your father when he gets back home. Sit up, Robert Lee."

She buttoned my white shirt.

"You've already been to the toolshed once today," she said. She clipped my bow tie, pulling the ends of the collar down to hide the metal clasps. Her hands moved quick, like they always did when she was mad or in a hurry. Now she was both.

"You will discover in life that we are obliged to do things we find distasteful, Bertram," she said. "Whether we must do it to please others or simply because if we don't, no one else will. Today you are obliged to attend this party. Put on your pants, Robert Lee."

I stood up and pulled on the long brown pants, and right away my legs began to itch.

"Now I'm telling you for the last time. Get dressed, Bertram. You have five minutes. Then I want both of you outside to greet the pastor when he arrives. They'll be here any minute."

She left the room. I sat back down on the bed, just another little kid dressed up like an old man. It didn't feel right being dressed for Sunday on a Saturday. Bertram was standing by the closet, his arms folded across his chest. He saw me watching him and said, "What're you looking at?" I looked down at my bare feet dangling over the edge of the bed. If you stare at your bare feet long enough they start to look strange, like flippers or long, flat hands with stubby, curled-up fingers. It starts to feel like they don't belong to you, or they're so strange-looking you wish they didn't. I wondered if everything was that way, even things you saw a thousand times, since you never had much of a chance to sit around and stare at your own feet.

Bertram said, "What are you doing?"

"Staring at my feet."

"Why?"

"They don't look like they should belong to me."

"My God, you're weird."

I got up and pulled my socks from the sock drawer. Bertram watched me like he had never seen me pull socks from the sock drawer before. I sat down on the bed and slipped on my socks. Bertram kept staring, and it started to feel funny, him watching me, till I felt like I had never done this before. Fresh socks feel good when you first put them on. I went to the closet and Bertram didn't move; I had to step around him to reach my shoes. I walked back to the bed and sat down and worked on a knot in my laces. I kept my head down, but he was still watching me, I could feel it. The more I worked with it, the tighter the knot got. Bertram stared and I fumbled with the laces, and finally it got to be too much for me and I said, "Please, Bertram."

"Please what?"

"Stop staring at me."

"I'll stare if I want. Whatcha gonna do to stop me?"

I didn't know what I'd do, so I didn't say anything.

"You know, Shiny," he said, "sometimes I look at you and I just want to stomp your little fuzzy head into mush."

I gave up on the knot and tried to force my foot into the shoe. It wouldn't go; my heel was hanging out the back. I pulled that one off and slipped on the other one. My fingers felt thick as sausages trying to tie those laces.

"Oh, you're such a good little boy," Bertram said. "You're so sweet and lovable, always doin' what your momma says."

I couldn't see myself walking through our house full of people with one shoe in my hand, and if I asked Bertram to help me he'd probably shove that shoe into my mouth. I held it on my lap and sat still.

"Oh, now you're going to cry, I suppose," Bertram said. "What good has all that crying ever done you, Shiny? You cry and cry and cry. You cry every day. I can't remember a day when you didn't cry. Tell me what it ever got you, Shiny."

I threw the shoe at him. It hit him smack in the middle of the forehead. He couldn't believe I threw it, and *I* couldn't believe I threw it. For a minute we just looked at each other, then he was on me. I guess I screamed, I don't remember, but he wasn't on me long before Momma pulled him off and threw him on his bed.

"He hit me with his shoe!" he screamed.

"He made fun of me!" I yelled.

"Hush now, both of you! What is in you to do this to me today, Bertram Parker?"

"What's in *me*?!" Bertram screamed in her face. She slapped him hard across the cheek, and his face got red and puckered, and now he was crying, an angry, hateful crying while he stared up at her. He said something softly.

"What did you say?" Momma asked.

"I said, Where's Shiny's slap, for hitting me with his shoe?"

She made like she was going to hit him again. I said, "I did, Momma. I threw my shoe at him. It's my fault, Momma. Don't hit him any more, Momma. Please don't hit him any more."

She didn't look at me.

"Get your clothes on, Bertram. Robert Lee, fetch me that shoe."

I handed her the shoe and she had the knot out in two seconds. She handed it back to me and I slipped it on my foot as fast as I could. I decided I'd rather be in a houseful of people than alone in this room with Bertram. Momma put her hands on my shoulders and walked me out.

"You have five minutes, Bertram," she said, and shut the door on him still sitting on his bed with his red screwed-up face and wet, shaking lips.

"I did throw my shoe at him, Momma," I said.

"We'll discuss it later," she said.

We had to jiggle and duck and slide our way down the hall. Momma kept a firm hand on my shoulder or I would have been crushed. In the living room you couldn't see the long table for all the people crowded around it. The air felt warm and heavy and shook from all the babbling. From nowhere big grown-up hands landed on my head and gave it a rub.

"Would you like a plate, Shiny?" Momma asked.

Just then the sewing room door opened and Miss Mavis came out with Sharon-Rose. Miss Mavis was wearing a white dress with lace around the collar and a white bow in her hair. She looked like the old Miss Mavis, before the fire came and made her sad. Sharon-Rose wore a pink dress with a pink bow in her hair. She looked about as comfortable in a dress as I would. Miss Mavis was all alive, smiling and laughing and hugging everybody, and her big eyes danced, and somehow her being so alive and pretty made everybody else seem small and dull, like they were all behind some foggy piece of glass; and you could see the other ladies move away from her after a smile or a hello, dropping their eyes just a little while the men fought with the crowd to get near her. Momma left my side and disappeared into the kitchen. I saw Sharon-Rose eyeing me, so I ducked behind a fat lady's butt. I made my way to the front of the room and crouched by the window so I could watch for Daddy.

I peeked through the blinds. The light outside was angry-bright, glinting off the car chrome and windshields, stabbing my eyes with little darts of light. The earth had rolled to snuggle against the sun, and heat puddles shone on the dirt road. The front door flew open and a girl in a bright orange dress jumped into the room, "They're here! They're here!" she yelled. The old ladies moved around the room, in that quick, jittery way old ladies have, shushing everybody and flapping their thin, spotty hands palms down, like they were patting the air. And the teenaged kids piled in from the porch. I had to snatch my hand back quick before one of them stepped on it. I felt someone beside me. It was Bertram. He was wearing his Sunday suit and had a mark on his forehead like a tiny triangle where my shoe hit him. He looked like a picture I saw in a book of a Hindu. I didn't know what to say, so I didn't say anything. He wasn't looking at me, anyway. He was staring out the window.

The room was quiet now, as quiet as a room full of a hundred people can get. A few old ladies were still shush, shushing, though they were the only ones talking. Momma, Miss Mavis, and Sharon-Rose were standing right in front of the door. Miss Mavis had her hands folded in front of her, like a bride stands at the altar, and Sharon-Rose stood with her head down, kind of pigeon-toed, her face hidden by her falling blond hair.

Beside me, Bertram said, "There they are."

They came slowly up the drive, weaving between the parked cars, a tall man in a black hat and a smaller man with a white robe or poncho hung over his thin shoulders, his face down, his arm through the crooked elbow of the tall man, who was my daddy, and in the white-robed man's other hand was a wooden cane.

It hurt just to watch Pastor walk, he moved so slow. He walked like he was slogging through knee-deep mud. For some reason Bertram started whispering, "God, God, God, oh God," and he must have said it a hundred times by the time Pastor and Daddy reached the front porch. They were out of our sight now, but you could hear the clumps on the stairs and then on the wooden boards. There was the heavy clumps of their feet, and the light clumps of the cane hitting the boards. Clump-clump, clump-clump, clump-clump. Clump. The room now was completely still and perfectly quiet. Even the old ladies had stopped shushing and Bertram had stopped praying. There was only two sounds in the world now: the clumps outside and my own heart, clumping in my chest.

The pastor had finally come home.

TWO

Today I am free. In a few minutes, at exactly nine o'clock, they will take me from my cell, and the door will clang shut behind me for the last time. I will walk with my hands free past the last locked door, and in a room the size of a linen closet, I will change into a cheap cotton suit. They will hand me a package wrapped in brown paper: the clothes I walked in with twenty years ago. Then they will take me to the warden's office. The warden will look me in the eye, and call me Halley, for the first time, as if on this day, I woke up a man. He will recognize my resurrection. He will offer me his hand. Then he will walk me to the door, a hand on my shoulder. He will mutter a platitude on the nobility of suffering, and his parting words will be, "I don't think, if I'd been on that jury, that you would be here today." He will watch from his office door as they escort me down the hallway, the last hallway, toward the door, the last door, to the outside. He will wear that silly half-grin the whole time, and it will feel as comfortable to him as my new shoes do to me. And I will never see him again.

Today I am free. In another month I will turn thirty-eight years of age. I was eighteen when I came here, and now I am thirty-eight. Within the first year of my arrival the Japanese bombed Pearl Harbor. Jasper, my only brother, enlisted the following year and was killed in the Battle of the Bulge. After she buried him, my mother would not visit me again until the war was over. She told me she could hardly bear it, when he died; it was as if she'd lost both her sons. When Truman dropped the bomb on the Japs, Nester, the only decent screw in this whole place, came to my cell and whispered, "Truman's dropped some new kind of

66

bomb on the Japs. Blew up two whole goddamned cities. Can you imagine? They say they'll surrender now. War'll be over in a week." I didn't say anything. Japan and that whole war was a long damn way from me. It might as well have been fought on Mars. I felt bad about Jasper, though. As the oldest boy, it should have been me.

Today I am free. By tonight, if the train runs on time, I will lie down on a real bed. With a down pillow. And over my head, an open window. If I feel like getting up for a drink of water, I will get up for a drink of water. If I feel like turning on the light, I will turn on the light. If I feel like going for a walk under the stars, I will go for a walk under the stars. I will go for a walk, and the night air will be sweet.

Today I am free, Mavis. Today I gain back my name. Today is the day the stone is rolled from the tomb. Today is the day of awakening, the day when all the dark years between my leaving and returning fall away, the day they fall away with a shrug of my shoulders. Today is the last day and today is the first day. Today is for the living, Mavis, and I, Halley Martin, I am among them.

But Walter Hughes is not. I remember his blood flowing hot over my hands, the licorice smell of his breath, the cry caught in his throat, strangled by blood, but most of all I remember his eyes. He had large eyes and long, black lashes. The light from the kerosene lamps shone in those eyes and glanced off those thick lashes. He sank to his knees and I went with him, my knife still hilt-deep in his gut, his blood washing over my hands. We kneeled before each other, and the whole world was in his eyes. I twisted the knife inside him, turning the blade upward. He grunted, and blood spewed from his open mouth, pouring over his teeth, dripping from his chin. I brought the knife up, through the tough muscles of his stomach, till I hit the base of his breastbone. My knees slipped; it was hard keeping my balance in the sloppy pool of his blood. He wasn't the first man to be killed, and I was not the first man to kill, but it felt that way. At that moment, we were the only men in the world.

He died, and then I was alone.

He fell onto my chest. I lost my balance and landed on my back, my legs bent beneath me, the hilt of the knife digging into my chest. His head rested on my shoulder. He was not a big man, but he felt heavy, and the rest of his blood emptied onto me. His blond hair smelled of lilacs. I eased him up to slip from under him. I know this sounds funny, but I felt almost tender toward him; he was like a helpless child lying in my arms. I got to my feet. The crowd pulled back. "Dear Jesus, he killed him," someone said. It didn't seem right leaving him on the floor like that. I rolled him over and pulled the knife from his chest. I threw the knife across the room. It hit the far wall and clattered onto the floor. I kneeled beside Walter. His eyes were open and staring. I slid my arms beneath him and lifted him. I turned around, looking for a spot to lay him. I walked over to the bar. Wiley figured what I wanted and swept the glasses off the bar. The sound of the glass shattering was very loud. I lifted Walter and laid him on the bar. I pressed his eyelids closed. They slowly slid back open, and his eyes were staring at me and not staring at me at the same time. They were blank as fish eyes. I looked into those eyes for a long time, then I turned. The crowd had moved as far as it could from me. I had passed into another country.

"Well, you've done it now, ain't you?" Wiley said.

He led me to the well out back.

"Take off your shirt," he said.

I stripped to the waist. He filled the bucket and poured the water over my head. It was a warm night, but the water felt icy cold, fresh from deep in the earth. I threw back my head and howled. The water ran into my mouth and choked me. Wiley pounded me between the shoulder blades, stinging my bare skin. I bent over and vomited into the wet earth. Wiley held my head. I screamed your name, and he hissed for me to shut up.

He said, "You got to get out of town, Halley. Shit, you got to get out of the whole fucking state."

He pulled me up. I grabbed the bucket from him and drank. I can't recall ever being so thirsty as I was the night I killed Walter Hughes. I emptied the bucket. "Slow down, slow down, for Chrissakes," Wiley said.

"We'll hop the train," I said. "I know the stationmaster."

"I can't come with you, Halley," he said.

"I wasn't asking you to."

"No, Halley, no. Now there ain't no time for that. A couple of 'em in there's already taken off to find the sheriff. You got to go *now.*"

"Not without her."

"Halley, you ain't thinkin' straight—"

"I'm not leaving without Mavis."

"Mavis ain't the point."

"Mavis is the *only* point," I yelled.

"You'll come back for her."

"No."

"Halley, you got to let things settle down—"

I didn't wait for him to finish. He yelled something after me as I plunged through thick grass behind the bar and slipped down the hill toward the cypress stand at the bottom. The palmetto bushes tore at my pants. Spiderweb clung to my bare chest, and fine sticky strands pulled at my cheeks. I splashed through the standing water at the edge of the cypresses. I didn't try to find a path through the thick growth of trees; I slammed the slender trunks aside as I ran, snapping the thinner ones in two. The mud sucked at my heels and the swaying cypresses groaned with the force of my blows. I ran as if a steel cord was pulling me to your door. I pictured you there, the golden light from inside spilling all around you, your shadow long on the sandstone path. And the golden light was all around you. You lift your arms and I fall into them. No one will ever hurt you again, Mavis, never again.

The swamp closed around me. I let my feet find the way through the tangle of cypress knees and falling grapevines and clinging wild blackberry bushes. I could have closed my eyes and still found my way to your door. The night sky disappeared behind the intertwined arms of the cypresses, and the world was full of the roar of blood in my ears. The cypresses thinned, and then I was in an open field. I could see the long line of oak trees that bordered the wide road leading to your house. I don't remember crossing that field or racing up that wide road; the next thing I remember is stepping onto your porch. There was no golden light; the only light came from the two lamps on either side of the door. The rest of the house was dark, even the windows upstairs. I would burst through the front door, race up the stairs, and break into every room until I found the one that held you.

The front hall was dark. A light came on after I stepped inside, and two men entered the hall. One was your father. The other was Sheriff Trimbul. I stood there, my chest heaving, steam rising from my naked torso in the sudden coolness of the hall, sweat dripping from my hair into my eyes. I was too late; I shouldn't have stopped to wash the blood off.

"You knew I'd come," I said to Sheriff Trimbul.

He said, "There's nowhere else you'd go."

My lawyer at the trial was Farley Wells, who happened to be the same lawyer who helped my father change my name to Hyram. Farley didn't want to go to trial. He thought I should plead guilty. When the state has fifty eyewitnesses you don't have much of a choice, he said. He said he could get the sentence reduced to aggravated manslaughter, which would mean fifteen years, paroled in five, if I behaved myself in prison. I told him I wanted a jury trial. Twelve men would understand what I did, if they were true men. Farley hadn't tried a court case in years, and even though he was a lawyer, he was honest enough to recognize his own limited abilities in a courtroom.

"You don't worry about it, Farley," I told him. "Just put me on the stand."

"Oh, Lord, no, we can't put you on the stand, Halley." Even he wouldn't call me Hyram.

"Why?"

"Because then you got to tell the truth."

"That's what I intend to do."

"The truth will get you life."

"Or it'll set me free."

"Halley, the law is pretty clear on this."

"There's a higher law."

"What law would that be, Halley? 'Thou shalt not kill'?"

"Just put me on the stand, Farley. They'll want to give me a medal when I'm done."

"Yeah, but they may give you the chair."

We were talking in the little jail cell just down the hall from Trimbul's desk. The air was close, and sweat poured off both of us. Farley's round, red face shone in the gray afternoon light. He was balding, and with that round face and thick lips he looked like an overgrown baby. Rolls of fat spilled over his starched collar. He glanced around, then he stood up and walked to the door to look down the hall. He moved on the balls of his small feet, light and quick, like a lot of short, fat men. He came back and kneeled on the floor in front of me.

"We got just one thing going for us, Halley," he whispered. "The way you killed Walter. Only a crazy man would butcher someone in front of fifty witnesses."

"It didn't surprise no one," I said. "Not even Walter."

"What I mean is, if you do take the stand, and I still think you shouldn't, but if you do, that's the point, the main point."

"What?"

"You were driven mad! You weren't in your right mind!"

"You're saying I'm crazy."

"No. Crazy ain't the legal way to say it. You were *temporarily insane.*"

"No," I said.

"Oh, yes. Yes!" He stood up and paced the cell on those little feet, moving so smooth and quick it looked like he was gliding over the floor. "When you heard what Walter had done, you lost your head. It was too much for you to bear."

"Well, that much is true."

"So you went out of your head."

"No."

"Oh, yes! Clear out of your head! The thought of what that man did robbed you of all your senses. It addle-pated you. It drove you loo-loo."

"I don't know what loo-loo means, Farley, but I knew what I was doing."

"No, you did not."

"I knew exactly what I was doing."

"And now you are deeply, deeply sorry." He wasn't listening to me.

"Not really," I said.

"Oh, yes. Yes, you are. You can't believe what you've done, and you're filled with horror at your own actions."

"That ain't the truth, Farley."

"Then you're going to decide it's the truth."

"I won't lie."

"Oh, now, don't get hung up on that. It ain't so simple as truth or falsehood, honesty or lies. What is the truth, anyway?"

"The truth is I knew exactly what I was doing and I would do it again."

"Now, Halley, Halley, you're getting bogged down again. Bear with me on this. Hear me out. Let me, let me ask you something. How'd you feel when you heard what he done?"

"I was angry. I was so goddamned angry I couldn't see straight."

"Yes! 'See straight,' that's more like it! You were enraged. You were beside yourself. You were in a state. You flew into the night, your mind blackened with rage—"

"No. Wiley came over the next night and told me Walter wanted to talk."

"To mock you!"

"No, to explain his side of it."

"A pitiful ploy to lull you into complacency."

"I don't know what that means."

"For all you knew he was plotting to kill you."

"Why would Walter kill me?"

"So you couldn't kill him first!"

"I think he just wanted to talk."

"The audacity! The gall of that prissy little dandy! Who did he think he was, committing a horrendous crime, then calling you out to rub it into your face!"

"He told me he didn't do it."

Farley stopped pacing and stared at me with his bright owl eyes. "When?"

"Before I killed him, Farley."

He took a deep breath and then forgot to whisper. "A bold and infuriating lie! You saw right through it! It blackened your mind even . . . blacker. You weren't planning to harm a hair on his head. You just brought the knife along for your own protection—"

"No, I brought the knife along to kill him."

"You're getting ahead of yourself, Halley. You can't tell me you knew beyond all doubt you were going to kill him when you walked into that bar."

"Yes, I can. I meant to gut him like a pig."

"Oh, now . . ."

"And I did."

"Now, Halley, whose side are you on? Help me understand—"

"I been trying to do that, Farley. You just won't listen."

"All right, then. Let's take this one step at a time so we don't get all tangled up. Before that night, that day, Wiley Newsome comes to you and tells you . . . what?"

"It wasn't that night. It was the day before."

"It's better if it's that day."

"It might be better, but that ain't the way it happened. Wiley came to me on Thursday. The meeting was on Friday."

"You got drunk?"

"What?"

"You got drunk, didn't you? Stinkin' drunk."

"No."

"Oh, Jesus!"

"Wiley came on Thursday afternoon. But there was no question for me, meeting or no meeting. I knew what I had to do."

"But you didn't know; no man can know for sure until the moment is upon him. You at least wanted to hear what Walter had to say."

"Not really."

"To hear his side of it."

"No."

"You're not bearing with me now, Halley."

I shrugged.

"So Wiley sets up this meeting, and that night you head out to the bar. And for three days it's been eating at you. You can't help but picture the horrendous deed in your mind. It plays over and over in your mind's eye. You can't eat; you can't sleep—"

"I slept like a baby."

"You are interrupting my train of thought, Halley."

"Sorry."

"You take the knife because you ain't sure what might happen. You don't know Walter that good—"

"I didn't know him at all."

"Good! Now you're adding steam to the train! Who knows what this man's capable of? We do know he's capable of the most terrible crime a man can visit upon a woman. We do know, or you thought you knew, that any man capable of that was capable of anything. For all you knew, you'd need that knife, for your own protection—"

"Well. I don't know about that."

"Because, although you may be crazy, you ain't stupid."

"No."

"So you come to the bar and there he is in his white suit and four-hundred-dollar shoes and mahogany walking stick with the gold duck's-head grip, and he's got this smug little grin on his face; and here he is, deflowerer of innocent flesh, arrogant in his social position, secure in his untouchable status, deigning to come to your level to lord it over you, you despicable piece of white trash, daring to insert yourself into his privileged world—"

"Farley, what the hell are you talking about?"

"How dare you! Who do you think you are, Halley Martin, to think for a single instant that in his world he can't take what he wants. Who are you to judge the lord of the manor? He's going to explain to you how life works in the rarified air of the landed gentry—"

"He didn't explain nothin' to me."

He was getting impatient. "So what did you do, Halley? Walk right up and slit him open without so much as a howdy-do?"

"Wiley said he wanted to talk. That was Thursday. Friday I tried to find Mavis, but she'd gone to Inverness to visit kin. I found a place in the cypresses to sit, and I sat there and sharpened my knife till night came on, and when it was time I went to the bar. I told Walter to come outside; I didn't want to kill him in front of everyone like that. Not 'cause of witnesses; I just didn't want to embarrass him."

"You didn't want to embarrass him?"

"It was between us."

"Oh."

"But he didn't want to come outside."

"I bet!"

"He said he had something to say to me. I said I had nothin' to say to him."

"Where was the knife?"

"In my belt."

"When'd you take it out?"

"I was gettin' to that. Walter says, 'It's not true.'"

"Not true?" Farley asked.

"Yes. 'Not true.' So I pulled out the knife and killed him."

"You didn't believe him."

"If I believed him I wouldn't have killed him."

"Why didn't you believe him, Halley?"

"That would make Mavis a liar."

"Oh. Yes."

Farley sat down next to me and ran his hand over his bald head. He pulled a handkerchief from his breast pocket and wiped his face.

"He gave me no choice after saying that," I said. "That's, that's insult to injury. He raped her and now he calls her a liar. He calls me out to say that to me. You understand, Farley, you understand now, don't you?"

"It don't matter what I understand," Farley said. "What matters is what the jury understands."

"They'll understand."

"They might, Halley, they might. They might understand completely, and then send you to prison for the rest of your life."

Nester came to my cell last night. It was long after lock-down and lights-out. He wasn't the Guard On Duty that night, so I was surprised to see him.

"What you doin', Nester?" I asked. "You're not the G.O.D. tonight."

"I'm off tomorrow," he said. "Wanted to say good-bye."

I rolled off my bunk and went to the bars. Like I said, Mavis, Nester was the only decent guard in the whole prison. He looked on us as men first and cons second, which made him the most unusual guard in the whole state of Florida. He had a hound dog's face, jowly and dark, with black rings under his sad eyes.

"That's kind of you, Nester," I said.

"You want anything, Halley? I would've brought you something, but I didn't know what you'd want."

"That's all right," I said. "What I want's coming tomorrow."

He nodded. "Funny ain't it? Twenty years."

"Yeah," I said. "It's funny."

"We seen some times, ain't we? You and me."

"Yeah."

"Oh, yeah," Nester said. "That we have. That we have."

He lit a cigarette and held it toward me. He held it as I leaned forward and took a deep drag.

"I'm gonna miss you, Halley. Won't have nobody now to read my papers."

Nester couldn't read or write, and after I learned how he was always bringing me papers to read, letters from his children or his work reviews. I offered to teach him, but he just laughed and said you can't teach old dogs new tricks.

"There's plenty 'round here who can read," I said.

"But damn few I can trust," he said.

"It'll be all right."

"Oh, I s'pose. I s'pose."

He drew deep on the cigarette and blew smoke out his nose. He was looking at the ground.

"Well. That's all I come to say, I guess." He turned away.

"Nester."

"Yeah, Halley?"

"There is one thing, if it ain't too much trouble."

"You name it, Halley."

"I want to see the Preacher."

He frowned, dropping his eyes again.

"I won't get a chance tomorrow," I said. "I'd like to say good-bye."

"You know I'd like to, Halley. You know I would. But if somebody caught us—"

"Who's in the tower tonight?"

"That new kid, Walsh."

"He's all right. Call him up and let him know we're comin'. Tell him it's your good-bye present to me."

"I don't know him that good, Halley."

"You said if there's anything I wanted."

He bit his bottom lip. "Okay. I'll be back."

I hadn't been thinking of the Preacher, hadn't thought of him for days. But now it occurred to me the Preacher deserved a good-bye. If anyone deserved a good-bye, it was him.

Nester came back and unlocked my cell. I stepped into the hallway and felt a shiver go up my spine. Nester was right. If they caught us they might charge me with attempted escape. Nester was sweating, his lower lip moist and quivering.

"I hope you appreciate this," he whispered. I followed him down the long hall to the rear guard station. It was empty. He had either paid off the regular G.O.D. or sent him on a fool's errand. Maybe it was a night for fool's errands. Nester unlocked the outer door and we stepped into the yard, under the open sky.

It was a clear night, the stars bright and hard over our heads. Straight ahead the guard tower rose, a lighter gray against the velvet black sky. A breeze rustled in the palm trees ringing the yard, and from the creek bullfrogs carumphed. I stopped in the middle of the yard. It suddenly occurred to me I would never stand here again. I had always hated the yard, but that night it seemed beautiful. I knew every inch of it, from the path that ringed the perimeter to the basketball poles to the benches where men played cards or dealt contraband under the noses of the bought-off guards. The ground was grassless and hard-packed. In the summer there was no shade; trees blocked lines of vision. In the summer, a week in solitary was better than an hour in the yard. In the winter, nothing blocked the wind that howled in from the north, and men would huddle in tight groups to stay warm. Except during rain, you spent two hours in the yard, year-round. And I hated it. The open sky, the vast fields beyond the gates, and the faint smell of the ocean when the wind blew from the east, it was cruel.

"Halley, what is it?" Nester asked.

"Some cons—they can't make it on the outside," I said.

"Yeah. I seen more'n a few come back."

I said, "Let's go."

We walked to the west, to a large padlocked gate. Nester glanced around, pulled out his keys, then looked around again, like he was afraid someone might jump out of the palmetto bushes any second. We passed through the gate. We were standing on the edge of a field ringed by live-oaks. You couldn't see it in the dark, but this field was fenced-in, topped with razor wire. The prison garden. We grew enough vegetables here to feed the population, and then some. Tomatoes, squash, carrots, cucumber, lettuce, watermelon.

We walked along the outer ring of oak trees. Occasionally, Walsh would turn the searchlight into the field, but Nester said not to worry, it was all for show. We were silent as we walked. The night felt cooler some-how out in the field. I could smell the sea. The grass was soft and spongy under the trees and the crickets sang in the deep shadows. We came to a clearing and stopped. Nester hung back as I stepped gingerly between the leaning wooden crosses. There were no tombstones here, just crude crosses cut from cypress wood. There are some men who die here, Mavis, and there is no one on the outside to claim them. They die here, and they are buried here, six in the twenty years since I came to Starke. Not one of the six died of old age. I straightened the cross over Preacher's grave, and heard the wood crack under the earth; cypress wood rots quickly in the wet ground. With Nester's help I found some stones and used them to prop up the cross. It wouldn't last long. A good wind would knock it over, but I had nothing to dig with and no way to do it if I did.

I stood at the foot of the grave. I said good-bye. I had made it. I was free. Preacher had always said I would see this day. Nester said, "We best be getting back now, Halley."

"I didn't bring anything for him," I said.

"He'd understand."

"I've nothing to give him." I turned to him. "Let me see your keys, Nester."

Nester said, "I don't think that'd be such a good idea, Halley."

"I'll give 'em back."

He held up the keys. I couldn't get my fingers around them. Sweat poured off me, and I shivered in the cool air. Nester looked like he was about to bust out into tears. "Oh, just tell me what you want, Halley!" I told him. He said he wouldn't. Then he saw the look on my face, and he said, "Oh, all right, for Chrissakes, hold out your hand."

I held out my right hand. He peeled back my fingers and drove the teeth of the large padlock key into the tender flesh of my palm. I kneeled and pressed my bleeding hand into the bare earth of Preacher's grave and held it there while my blood soaked into the ground.

I stood up and thanked Nester. He nodded, slipping the keys back into his pocket.

And then I began to cry. I cried for the Preacher, who gave his life for mine. I cried for the other men buried here, with no one anywhere to remember their names. I cried for the eighteen-year-old kid who came here twenty years ago, ignorant and cocksure, and for the middle-aged man walking out twenty years later, his broken shadow. But most of all I cried because the night was so beautiful, and it had been twenty years since I had seen the stars.

Farley bought me a suit for the trial. It was the first suit I ever owned. It was also the last suit I ever owned. A barber came in and gave me a shave and haircut. The next day Farley brought me the suit from the tailor's and I changed in my cell. It was Tuesday morning. I had been in jail ten days and already I was going stir-crazy. If he had told me then I would be living in a cell for the next twenty years I would have torn his eyeballs out.

"You look good," he said. "Almost refined."

"I don't know what that means," I said.

Trimbul came in and handcuffed me. The three of us walked across
the hall into the courtroom. The state attorney was there, a pasty-faced
little man called Franks, and a bailiff. We sat down and after a minute
the judge came in. We stood up. The bailiff read the charge. The judge
asked me what my plea was.

"Not guilty," I said.

The judge ordered me held over for trial, bail at ten thousand dollars.
The trial was set to start in two months. The judge left, and Farley talked
to Franks for a few minutes at the other table, their heads bent low, whispering. Then they took me back to my cell, where I changed back into
my old clothes.

"What were you and Franks talking about?" I asked.

"Oh, you know, lawyer stuff."

"I need nine thousand dollars," I said.

"Don't we all," Farley said.

"I can't stay in here two more months, Farley."

"Well, I don't see how you got much of a choice, Halley."

"Loan it to me."

"Ha!"

"Tack it on my bill."

"Two months ain't that long, Halley," he said.

I sat on the cot and put my head in my hands. Farley shook out his
handkerchief and blew his nose. "Drafty goddamned old courthouse," he
muttered.

"Can you get a message to her for me?"

"Who?"

"Mavis."

"Oh, now, Halley—"

"I need to see her."

"That ain't possible. That's just not going to happen, Halley."

"Ain't I allowed visitors?"

He looked away.

"If you tell her I want to see her, she'll come."

"I'll try, Halley, I'll try."

"And I want a knife."

"You want a knife."

"And some wood. Cypress or pine. I got to do something with my hands."

"I can't get you a knife, Halley. A knife is definitely out of the question."

"A pencil and some paper, then."

"Halley, you can't write."

"Not to write, goddamn it, to draw."

"Okay. I'll get you a pencil and some paper."

"Not any kind, now, Farley. Drawing paper, you know, comes in a pad, a sketch pad . . ."

"Sure. Sure."

"And a drawing pencil. You know what a drawing pencil is?"

"I'm sure I can figure it out, given enough time."

"And I want some fruit."

"Fruit."

"Oranges. I want some oranges."

"I ain't in charge of the fruit, Halley."

"Trimbul won't let me have any."

"How come?"

I shrugged.

"All right. Anything else?"

"No. Yeah. Tell my daddy to stop coming here. He won't listen to me."

He laughed for some reason and said he would. We said good-bye.

"Tell Mavis," I said as he walked out.

He gave a little wave with his pudgy hand as he glided down the hall.

"You tell her, Farley!" I shouted after him. "You tell her now!"

You never came. Farley told me he passed the message on, and I believed him. I blamed your father. I figured he had you locked in your room for the duration of the trial; now we were both prisoners. Personally, I preferred my jail-keeper to yours. Trimbul refused to bring me oranges, but in the afternoons when it was too hot to be outside he would pull up a chair and sit by my cell. He'd lean back in that wooden chair and work his teeth with a toothpick. He had bad teeth and complained about them much of the time. "Got to take care of your teeth," he'd say. "Most important thing in the world, your teeth. You got bad teeth and you're a miserable human being." If you thought teeth were the most important thing in the world, I guess you would be miserable. I told him I didn't have a toothbrush, and the next day he brought me one. He gave me detailed instructions on brushing and one morning showed up to observe my technique.

"You're brushing too fast," he said. "You ain't scrubbin' potatoes there. Get the gums. Brush those good. The rot starts in the gums."

If he wasn't satisfied with my effort, he made me do it again. He was rarely satisfied with my effort.

"Sweets!" he'd say. "Sweets is what done me in. Stay away from the sugar."

Later in the afternoons he would leave for patrol. "I'll be back directly!" he'd call from the door. As if I would worry after him. After he left, I would take the toothbrush and scrape the handle against the stone wall until the edge was razor sharp. If Farley wouldn't bring me a knife, I'd make one.

But Farley did bring me a pad and a drawing pencil. Every night Trimbul would take the pencil and return it the next morning with a fresh point. I'd thank him, set the pencil by the pad, and Trimbul would stand there with his hands in his pockets, staring at me like he expected me to turn into a pumpkin.

One morning he asked me, "What're you doing there with that pad?"

I didn't answer right away. The breakfasts were always good: ham and eggs, bacon, biscuits with sausage gravy, cheese grits and blueberry muffins. I ate better in jail than I had my whole life.

"I draw," I said.

"You draw."

"I draw."

"You draw . . . what?"

"I draw what's in my heart."

"And what's that? What's in your heart?"

"I can't explain it, Sheriff. That's why I have to draw it."

He nodded like he understood, which he didn't. I worked on my breakfast and ignored him.

"So you're an artist," he said. He wasn't going to go away. It suddenly occurred to me that Sheriff Trimbul was a lonely man.

"I ain't no artist."

"I never would have took you for one. I never known any, but I always pictured them as little pansy types."

I chewed my bacon and watched him.

"You ain't the little pansy type," he said.

"I been drawin' since I could hold a pencil," I said. "When I was ten my daddy decided no boy of his was going to waste his time drawing pictures, so he threw all my sketches into a trash fire. I pulled my knife and cut off his earlobe, and I told him the next time he touched my things I'd cut off the rest."

Trimbul's face twisted up like he didn't know whether to laugh or not.

"Nobody fools with what's mine," I said.

"No. No, I don't suppose they do."

I got off the cot and handed the sketch pad to him through the bars. He held it like he didn't know what to do with it.

"It's all right?" he asked. I nodded. He flipped open the pad and whistled.

"You drew these?"

It was one of those stupid questions people ask when they think something has to be said.

He said, "Why this is . . . this appears to be . . ."

"Mavis," I said.

"Yes, that's who I—she don't have no clothes on, Halley."

"The face I know. The rest is my imagination."

"Well, you got one hell of an imagination there, Halley."

He flipped through the pages. "You ever draw anything else?"

"There's nothing else in my heart."

"I can see that. Fact is, I can see a lot." He handed the pad back to me. "I ain't sure, but I'm thinkin' some of those might not be exactly legal."

"It don't matter," I said. "Before I saw Mavis, I drew trees."

"Trees?"

"They're one of those things that stay the same but change while you're looking at them. They're growing, only you don't see it, or you do but can't." I tossed the pad onto the cot. "That's how I met her. I showed her a picture I drew."

"Of a tree?"

"A picture of her, Sheriff."

"She have any clothes on in it?" He laughed. I did not.

"Sorry," he said. "She's a beautiful girl, Halley. I ain't had much experience in that department, but I can see how somethin' like that," he nodded toward my sketch pad, "somethin' like that could drive a fella out of his head."

"I'm not out of my head," I said. "I'm all the way in my head. Let me ask you something, Sheriff. What would you have done?"

He didn't answer for a long time.

"I don't think it's in me to love someone that way. Just ask my wife. But you didn't have to carve up poor Walter so bad. You could've just beat the shit out of him."

"That don't fit the crime. I had to take something he could never get back. That's what he took from her."

"Yeah, well." He smiled sadly. "And now that's sort of what's happened to you."

The sheriff had blushed when he saw those pictures, but there was nothing dirty about them. They were the most beautiful pictures I had ever drawn. When I drew you, I didn't think about it first. I didn't plan it; I didn't know how you would appear. I let the white space fill up with you. I allowed you to emerge from the nothingness. A line. A shadow. The curve of your shoulders. The shape of your eyes. The gentle slope of your hips. The sweep of your hair against your back.

In my mind, you arise. Your shade falls upon the whiteness: shadow before form, form before design, effect before cause. My desire animates you and you animate my desire. I am not God, Mavis, but I know how he must feel. I know that longing, the white space that must be filled, the delight in the filling of it. Once finished, it was as if I never started, as if you had always been there and I, the jailor, released you. In return, you release me. Freed, I run my fingertips over the lines of your face. Freed, I brush my lips against the ends of your lashes. Freed, I caress the length of your thigh, touch the delicate rise of your breast.

I am the creator that love makes necessary, for you were not put here for me to draw, but I was put here to draw you.

Your father sent for me not long after I gave you that first drawing. Wiley and I and the rest of our crew were clearing out the dead orange trees. Your daddy lost half his groves that year of the bad freeze, and we wondered if we'd have jobs in the fall. The rumor was he was in bad shape, your daddy, and between the demands of his bankers and this act of God, he was about to be snapped in two by the Depression, after thumbing his nose at it for years.

I had seen him just once before, on the day I was hired. Cousin Wiley brought me to the house, where your daddy was waiting for me. He was leaning on a heavy, gold-handled cane, standing on the front porch, eating an orange. Wiley introduced us and told him I needed a job. He vouched for my good character and told him I was the strongest man in three counties and no one could touch me when it came to handling an ax. Your daddy told me to take off my shirt.

"Why?" I asked.

"You want the job or don't you, boy?" He spat out an orange seed.

Wiley told me it was all right. I pulled off my shirt. Your daddy came to the porch railing and squinted down at me.

"Turn 'round," he said.

I did a slow turn. He slipped a slice of orange into his mouth and chewed in that thoughtful way horses have, as if the whole world was in the taste of that orange. I started to feel uncomfortable, like next he would order me to open my mouth so he could get a look at my teeth.

"You're a specimen, I'll say that, boy. You as strong as you look?"

"I don't know," I said. "How strong do I look?"

He smiled. He dabbed a droplet of orange juice from his chin.

"I once knew this nigger who would break a solid oak cane with his bare hands," he said. He tossed his cane over the rail. I caught it with my right hand. "Now that's solid mahogany, boy. Much harder wood than cypress or pine or even oak. You think you can break that in half?"

"If I do, I got the job?"

"Well, I reckon, since you'll have to work off the cost of that cane." He laughed. Wiley had warned me your daddy could be like this. He liked playing with you, Wiley said, like he's the cat and you're the mouse.

I grabbed the stick in both hands and pulled down. I put all my force into it, but I could tell it wasn't going to give. He watched me. He was smiling. It occurred to me he knew I couldn't break it and he was just having fun with me; he had no intention of giving me the job. I set my jaw and pushed on that stick with everything I had, till my forearms and shoulders sang with the pain. I even tried to imagine it was his stringy neck, but it was no use.

"You may be strong," your daddy laughed. "But you ain't very smart."

He shouldn't have said that. It wasn't the strength I lacked; I hadn't thought it through. I let go of one end and swung the cane around my back, grabbing the free end as it came around. I pulled, pressing the cane against my shoulder blades. It gave with a loud snap, and I tossed the two pieces onto the porch. Wiley smiled and kept his eyes on your daddy.

"Maybe not so dumb after all," your daddy said.

"Maybe not," I said.

He hired me on the spot, and three months would pass before I saw him again. He sent Wiley to find me. I thought he was playing a joke on me at first, but he was acting all jumpy and twitchy.

"He wants to see you inside," Wiley said as we walked to the house. "He never lets any of us inside."

"Good," I said. "I've been meaning to talk to him." I untied my shirt from my waist and used it to wipe the sweat from my face and neck. We struggled through the sandy soil, up the slope toward the house, past row on row of dead, twisted orange trees, each of them looking like some tortured figure from a dream. By that evening the trees would be pulled, cut, and piled, ready for the morning, ready for the burning day. I slipped on my shirt and smoothed my wet hair.

"Now, tell my momma I love her, in case you don't see me again, Wiley."

"Make jokes," Wiley said. "Go on."

"What's he want?"

"He don't discuss what he wants with me, Halley."

"You know what I think it is?" I said. "I think he's going to make me his heir."

"Ha!"

"You're goin' to be workin' for me, Wiley."

"When hell freezes."

I said, "Take a look around you, boy."

We came out from the last row and stood for a minute on the wide, green lawn.

"Well," Wiley said. "I guess this is it." As if he was never going to see me again. "I gotta get back to work."

"I'll see you directly," I said, and started up the path.

I turned back and saw him standing on the edge of the trees, thin and slick with sweat. He gave a little wave and I waved back. He had got me a little jumpy too, because it felt like maybe I *was* seeing him for the last time. My heart was high in my chest and my face was hot. Inside that house was another country, and I didn't know the language.

A black manservant met me at the door. He said, "Yessah, Mistah Halley sah, this way, sah."

I followed him into your father's study.

It smelled of stale cigar smoke and orange peel. The wooden blinds were drawn; it was as if I stepped inside a cave. The trophies of wild game leered down at me in the semidarkness. The black manservant closed the heavy door behind me, and I was alone with your father.

He sat behind his massive mahogany desk in a fat-backed leather chair, smoking a cigar. It was so cold in there I half-expected to see my breath, though a fire crackled in the huge fireplace behind the desk. My damp shirt was icy on my back. Thirty minutes ago I was felling thirty-year-old trees with three swings of my ax. In the groves, no man was my equal; I was a prince in a golden kingdom, under a blazing sky. Now I felt small and strangely hollow. If he touched me, I would shatter into a thousand pieces. His eyes glittered in the orange light of the fire, behind the blue veil of the cigar smoke.

He didn't say anything at first. Neither did I. The first time we met he made me strip off my clothes. Today I had a feeling he had a different kind of stripping in mind.

"Halley, isn't it?" he finally said.

"Yeah-a," I said.

"Sit down, Halley," he said. He motioned to the small chair in front of his desk.

"Thank you," I said. I didn't sit.

"Awful hot, ain't it?" he asked.

I nodded. "Outside," I said.

"Yes. You want anything? Nice glass of lemonade? Something stronger?"

"I'm fine," I said.

He nodded. "How's the job goin', Halley? We gonna be ready for tomorrow?"

I told him I thought we would. He wondered if it might rain.

"Won't make any difference," I said.

"You don't think? No, I don't suppose it will. I tell you, Halley, ever since this winter I can't bear to go outside. Don't even open the window. Can't bear to look at it. I think trees are as individual as people, y'know? Looking at those groves is like looking at a thousand corpses. You understand?"

"I can."

On the wall behind him hung his largest trophy: the head of a male lion, its jaws open in a silent roar, its glassy eyes shiny with rage. He followed my eyes and said, "Hell of a specimen, huh? Bagged him in Kenya. That's in Africa."

I nodded.

"Beautiful place, Africa. Hot too, like Florida. You do much hunting, Halley?"

"Since I could hold a gun."

"Wonderful sport."

"We do it mostly to eat."

"Yeah. Well. Eating a lion is a disgusting thought. But it's thrilling, the kill I mean. No other feeling like it."

"I s'pose."

"God-like," he said. "God-like. Care for a smoke?"

"No."

"Don't drink. Don't smoke. You gamble?"

"No."

"No! Dear God, boy, don't you have any vices?"

"I never thought about it."

"Everybody does, you know."

"Well, then," I said, "I must."

"I'd be interested to know what they are." He leaned forward, resting his forearms on the desk and lacing his fingers together. He stared at me hard, like it would complete his life's ambition to know what my vices were. I didn't say anything. He smiled.

"You want to know what I think it is?" he asked. "Vanity. I look at a boy like you and think it must be vanity. There's no other explanation for it. I look at a boy like you, and it boggles the mind what you might do, with the proper background. There's more to you than meets the eye, I know that, Halley. Such a shame, such a cruel trick of fate you were born into less than ideal circumstances. Why, a man like you, who knows to what heights you may have reached! Tell me something, Halley, where do you see yourself in twenty years?"

I didn't hesitate.

"Sitting in that chair." And I pointed at him. For a minute I wasn't sure whether he was going to laugh or add my head to his trophies on the wall.

He decided to smile. "Vanity," he whispered. "I was right."

He pulled a long envelope from his drawer and stood up. He balanced the stub of his cigar on the marble ashtray and came around the corner of his desk.

"But vanity arrived at honestly. I have known the other kind, and I find yours infinitely more appealing. There's more to you than first meets the eye. For instance, I never knew you were an artist."

He pulled a sheet of paper from the envelope. It was the sketch I had given you the week before.

I must have flinched, because he smiled slightly. He held the paper close to his eyes.

"The technique is a bit . . . primitive, but there is a definite passion to it. A hunger. You are, of course, self-taught and therefore a bit self-indulgent."

He had lost his phoney good ol' boy accent.

I didn't look at the paper, or at him. He wanted me to make a grab at it, but I wasn't going to give him the satisfaction.

"That was a gift," I said. "For Mavis."

"Oh, yes."

"It was for her. A gift."

"Of course."

"I thought she might . . . that she might like it."

"Oh, I believe she does. I believe she does. Very much. She seemed quite upset when I took it from her."

I wished I hadn't left that ax in the grove. Right then I could've taken his head off with it.

"And it's funny," he said. "I don't recall ever introducing the two of you."

"I can draw what I want," I said.

"Surely." He slipped the drawing back into the envelope. "But I'm curious. Who *did* introduce you?"

"No one."

"Ah. A chance encounter."

"I don't know what that means."

He tapped the envelope against his thigh.

"I asked Mavis, of course. She claimed to have never laid eyes upon you. She was taking a stroll in the rose garden one morning, as is her custom, when you appeared. With this. You said something like, 'This is for you,' and disappeared without another word. Hearing this charming little story caused me to wonder how you could have created this remarkably detailed portrait, unless you had been . . . studying her for some time."

I didn't say anything. He didn't act like he was expecting me to say anything.

"In Africa," he said, "the wild lion will hunker in the high grass. If the wind holds, he can lie in this fashion for hours, without his prey having an inkling of his presence."

"I ain't a lion," I said.

"And my daughter is not prey." He smiled. "You've been watching her." It was not a question.

He said, "I suppose a man, if he was very quiet and very deliberate, could spy on someone in that garden. This man could find a nice, shady place in the hedgerow to . . . study his subject."

"I didn't mean no offense," I said.

He laughed. "Of course not! To the contrary, she thought the whole episode rather sweet."

"She did? What else did she say?"

His smile died. "That," he said, "you shall never know."

He sat down in that fat leather chair again and tossed the envelope onto the desk. He studied me over his folded hands. His eyes were hunter-cold.

"Tell me, Hyram . . . that *is* your real name, isn't it? Hyram. What are your thoughts on Darwin?"

"I don't know him."

"Then I will try to express the theory in terms you can understand. In a nutshell, buzzards do not consort with eagles. They do not occupy the same niche. A buzzard does not attempt to rule the sky, and an eagle does not deign to pick the bones of the dead. Buzzards concern themselves with the business of being buzzards. What do you think?"

"I think you just called me a buzzard."

"Icarus strained toward the sun, and fell."

"You're just trying to make a fool of me," I said. "But nothing you can say can make me stupid."

"No," he drawled. "No. Nothing I can *say.*" He picked up the envelope and tossed it into the fire. I moved for the first time, taking a half-step toward the burning envelope before stopping myself.

"*That* makes you stupid."

I watched the edges blacken and turn up before the envelope burst into flames. When the flames sprang up I felt something give in my chest. I sank into the chair across from him.

"I'm in love with her," I said. "I'm in love with Mavis. I'm in love with your daughter."

He didn't say anything. He kept very still, watching me.

"I've been watching her for months. I'm out there every morning in the hedgerow, and I watch her walk in those tall rose bushes, and when the wind moves, the long stems sway and red petals fall at her feet, and it's the most beautiful thing I ever saw; it's so beautiful I want to die; I want to die on that spot because anything I see after that, my whole life, can't touch the beauty of that. Only heaven can touch the beauty of that, so I want to die."

He nodded like he understood. He took a deep breath. "I've been having thoughts along those same lines," he said.

"You should," I said. "Because I know what you're going to do, Mr. Howell. You're going to fire me. You're going to fire me and if you ever find me again on your property you'll have me shot. You'll hunt me down like a dog and shoot me. Well, you should shoot me. Put me out of my misery, Mr. Howell. Have mercy on me. Put a bullet through my head, because even if there ain't heaven, whatever there is has to be better than this. You don't know what it's like. It's like . . . it's like . . . it's like I could *eat* the whole world. I want to pop the world into my mouth and eat it like a grape. I was late for work today because when I woke up the sun was lighting up the dust in the air and I laid there almost out of my head at the beauty of that, those little flecks of dust floating in the air. I never knew there was such beauty in the world until I saw such beauty in the world. You don't got any idea what I mean."

"Do you?" he asked.

"Kill me," I said. I was a little out of my head.

"Kill you? I'm going to reward you."

He pulled a package out of the desk drawer and slid it across the blotter toward me. It was wrapped in brown paper and tied with twine. I didn't touch it.

"What's this?"

"Open it."

I pulled on the string. The paper fell open and hundred-dollar bills spilled out. I had never seen so much money.

"What's this?" I asked again.

"This is one thousand U.S. dollars. Go on. Count it. It's yours."

I didn't move. Just when I thought I had your daddy figured, he did something like this.

"You see, Halley, or Hyram, or whatever your name is, unlike you I have many vices, the chief of which must be gambling. I cannot resist a good wager." He laughed. "My wife used to say I'd bet on a race between houseflies. Houseflies, you see, do not fly in a straight line. Anyway. Anyway."

He got up and commenced to pace behind the desk. "Anyway, I've had my eye on you for some time, as I've said. You have been watching my daughter, and I have been watching you. Yes, you are poor and ignorant, but you are also clever and very strong. You possess a certain passion. An obvious passion. Empires have been built upon less. All you lack to become an American Alexander is . . . a helping hand. A leg up. A little push. A spark of capital in the dry tinder of your ambition."

"You're just gonna give me a thousand dollars?"

"Yes! You've got the idea! No strings attached. I am not extending you credit. This isn't a loan, Halley."

"You said it was a bet."

"Yes. With myself. You see, I'm betting that with this money you might evolve into an eagle."

"Okay," I said, and reached for the money.

"But I misspoke when I said no strings attached. There is one string."

I froze.

"You must leave."

"Leave."

"Homeland. Actually, the state of Florida. You must leave, and you must leave tomorrow." He pulled a long, white envelope from another desk drawer and tossed it next to the pile of cash. "This is your train ticket."

"No," I said.

"Don't be a fool. These are hard times, Halley. Do you realize how long you'd have to work to earn a thousand dollars?"

"I don't care."

"Imagine what you could do with this money, Halley! You're not interested in business, but this could get you into any art school in the world. I teased you before, but you're very gifted. You have a talent, a God-given talent that would be a sin to waste. You could study with the finest artists in the world. Paris, Halley. The finest art schools in the world are in Paris. That ticket is to Atlanta, but I could cancel it and book you on a passage to Europe. Think over your answer carefully, Halley. You may not believe this now, but there are other women in this world. The world is full of women, and a man who looks like you will have your pick of them, many opportunities will come your way, but this opportunity, Halley," he gestured at the money, "this comes only once in a lifetime."

I said, "I don't want your money, Mr. Howell. I'm sorry if that costs you your bet."

"You are mistaken. This is one bet I cannot lose." He opened another drawer. I wondered what all he had in those drawers; he kept pulling things out. This time he pulled out a Colt revolver and set it beside the pile of cash. It lay within easy reach of both of us.

"Most of life turns on a thousand little decisions, Halley, and we hardly realize how truly significant those decisions are, until it is too late. But sometimes, and it is rare, sometimes these life-changing decisions are so large, so obvious, that there is no mistaking them when they are upon us. This is one of those decisions, Halley."

He waited for me to say something. I didn't.

"Understand me," he said quietly. "This is not personal. I like you, Halley. I really do. You possess a naivete, an aboriginal purity that I frankly admire. But I did not break my back for thirty years, building this for my only child, to watch it pass into the hands of some backwoods piece of inbred white trash like you."

He smiled.

"You are going away, Halley Martin. You are going away forever. You can choose to go away with a thousand dollars in your pocket. You can go away with nothing, or you can simply go away."

He picked up the revolver.

"That's all right," I said. "I've made up my mind."

I scooped up the cash and wrapped it in the brown paper. He held the revolver loosely in his hand and watched me as I tied the package with the twine. My fingers felt thick and clumsy, and I noticed the dirt packed tightly under my nails. For a second I saw myself as he must see me, and I was filled with disgust.

"Now I want the rest," I said.

"The rest?"

"My pay. I ain't been paid for today."

He smiled. "See Wiley."

He rang a bell. He slipped the revolver back into his desk drawer. The wide door behind me opened, and the black manservant glided back into the room. When I turned away something gave in my heart. I could hardly hold myself together. I slipped the brown paper package into my pocket.

"Halley," your father called, "you forgot something."

I turned. He was holding the white envelope.

"Your ticket."

I took it from him.

"There's a whole 'nother world out there, boy," he said, returning to his good ol' boy act. "Whole other worlds to conquer."

"That's right," I said.

I left the house.

I was surprised it was still light outside; it felt like I'd been in that room forever. Wiley was sitting on the porch steps when I came out. He jumped up.

"Well?"

"I'm fired," I said.

"Fired? Whatcha gonna do, Halley?"

"I reckon I'll go home."

He followed me down the path.

"You sure seem damned happy about it."

I told him what happened. He begged to see the money, so I took it out of my pocket and peeled back a corner of the paper. He whistled.

"Well, guess I'd be smiling too."

"Oh, that's not why I'm smiling," I said. "Until now, I didn't know how she felt."

"What?"

"Don't you see, Wiley? Why you think he was so desperate to get rid of me?"

" 'Cause he don't like you?"

"No, 'cause somebody else does."

I grabbed him and spun him around and did a crazy dance right there in the path. Over his shoulder I saw that black manservant on the porch, watching me. He was cradling a rifle in his arms.

"You're out of your head, Halley!" Wiley shouted.

"He thinks he's so goddamned smart," I said. "He won't be feeling so smart tomorrow."

"What's tomorrow?" he asked.

"The burning day," I said. I laughed. The late afternoon sun was warm on my back. I was young and I was strong and I was alive and I was in love and, most of all, I was loved.

Wiley gave me my day's wages and I walked home. I made him promise not to tell anyone what happened between me and your daddy, especially the part about the money. There were some men, including some good friends of mine, who would kill for half that much. The money felt heavy in my pocket, and the brown paper crinkled loudly as I walked. We lived less than two miles from your house, but it couldn't have been farther away. It was in another world altogether. My dogs came running from their hiding places under the porch to greet me, jumping and barking and rolling around in that shameless way they have, as if they had never expected you to return.

My father was waiting for me on the porch. His pants were undone and he was bare-chested. He was also stinking drunk.

"Hey, boy," he called.

"Hey," I said. I went to one knee and gave my blue tick a rub on his belly.

"Hear you lost your job today."

"News travels fast, don't it," I said.

"There ain't nothin' that goes on around here I don't know about," he said. "Where is it?"

"Where's what?"

"Don't play the fool with me, boy. This is your daddy talkin' to you. Let me see it."

"I don't know what you're talking about, Daddy," I said. I gave the dog a swat on the haunches and stepped onto the porch. I was a full head taller than he was. I looked down at him. His eyes were small and red and cupped with black bags. He hadn't shaved in four or five days. He reeked of corn mash and sweat, a rotten kind of smell. I thought of your daddy calling us buzzards. Looking at him now reminded me of the dirt under my nails, and I decided to take a bath before I left.

I started into the house. He grabbed my elbow.

"Don't make me for a fool now, boy," he said.

"You don't need my help for that," I said.

I yanked my arm away. He threw his little body into mine, and I stood still as he threw punch after punch into my belly. I let him tire himself out, then grabbed his wrists and held his arms up. His bones felt frail as a bird's.

"I don't want to hurt you," I said.

"You don't want to hurt *me*? You little bastard . . ."

"You ain't seeing a penny of it, Daddy."

"You my boy!" he shouted. "You live in my house!"

"Not anymore," I said. "I just come home to take a bath and get my things."

"You ain't goin' nowhere, boy!"

I swung him around and let him go. He lost his balance and fell backward off the porch, landing on his backside in the muddy ground. The dogs swarmed around him, lapping at him and tugging on his pants, thinking he'd come down to play.

"Hyram! Hyram, you come back here! I ain't done with you yet, boy! Get the hell away from me, you goddamned fleabags!"

I went inside and told Momma I wanted a bath. She sent my sister

Martha for the tub and set the water on to boil. I went to the back room and stripped off my shirt. My stomach was red from Daddy's fists. I ran my hand over my belly and saw again the dirt beneath my nails.

"Hyram."

I reached down and pulled my hunting knife from my boot. "You touch me and I'll cut the rest of your ear off," I said.

"I just want to see it, boy. I ain't never seen that kind of money before. Besides," he wet his lips with the tip of his tongue, "I can't say I actually believe you got it."

"No," I said.

"Hyram, please," he whined.

I said, "My name is Halley."

"Your name is what I say it is! I'm still your daddy, goddamn it!"

"I like my name," I said.

"You just like it 'cause it makes me feel stupid. Now put that knife down. You really think I'd take your money? Hell, all I'd like to know is how much do I get if I loved her twice as much."

"Don't talk about her."

"Don't you tell me what—"

"It makes me sick, you talking about her."

Momma called from the front that the water was ready. "Now I'm going to take my bath," I told him. "And when I finish my bath I'm going to get my things and leave. I'm going away. For a long time. And I don't expect to see you again."

I walked past him. He shouted after me: "And where you think you're going? How far you think you're going to get, and what the hell you gonna do when you get there? Maybe you forgot who you are, boy, but I don't!"

I turned back to him. He froze up, his mouth moving but making no sound.

"All right," I said. "Who am I?"

"You know," he said. "You know. You don't need me to tell you. You think just because you're young and strong and full of piss you can take on the Lester Howells of this world? Well, let me tell you somethin', boy, you in for some hard lessons."

"How do you know?"

"Because I was once just like you!" he screamed.

"Maybe I'll turn out different."

"No, no you won't, because wherever you end up you'll still be what you are right now."

I said, "Fathers don't talk to their sons this way."

"Don't you tell me how to talk, boy!"

I left him in the back room, still screaming. It was time for my bath. I could hear him tearing the room apart, looking for the cash. He wouldn't find it. I had stashed it before I got in sight of the house.

I packed up that night. Momma cried a good deal. Her crying got my brother and sisters to crying, and Daddy got up from the table and stomped outside to smoke and look at the night sky. He fancied himself quite a star-gazer, as you know, and even his colossal mistake regarding the comet didn't deter him. Momma wrapped up some extra cornbread and tried to give me five dollars, but I told her I had plenty of money and she should keep it.

"No," she said. "If you don't take it, *he* will."

"Hide it someplace."

"What you think I been doin'?"

"Keep saving. When you got enough, leave him."

"He'll be dead from drinkin' or fightin' before that happens," she said. She kissed me on the cheek and whispered, "You were always my favorite, Halley."

"I'll come back some day," I told her. "And I'll buy you a nice big house to live in, the biggest house in town, with servants and . . ."

"Oh, hush. When you talk that way you sound like your father."

"Only difference is you can believe it from me," I said. "I promise you, Momma. I'll come back some day." I didn't know then that some day would be twenty years later. We don't understand half the promises we make. I hugged my brother and sisters good-bye and went outside. Daddy was leaning on the porch rail, looking at the sky. I stood next to him. The night was cool; it was still late spring, before the heaviness of the summer rains weighed down the air.

"I stood right here the night you was born, this very spot," Daddy said. " 'Member it same as yesterday. I come out for a smoke. It was a long, hard labor for your momma. A good fourteen hours, I reckon. Don't know what time it was when I came outside, must've been close to sunrise. I was rolling my smoke when something caught the corner of my eye. Right over there. A flash of light, brighter'n the sun. Right over yonder, over those cypresses. And I watched that white light swoop over the edge of the sky, and just as it was ducking under the horizon I heard you cryin'. So I run back inside and there you was, lying on your momma's belly. And after all those hours of wailing and hollerin', there you were, and you were both still and quiet as church mice. I don't recall nothin' more beautiful than your momma was that night, or as perfect as . . . that comet was." His eyes narrowed at me. "And it *was* the comet. It weren't no meteor or shootin' star or the moon or any other goddamned thing. It was the goddamned comet. I know. Maybe it weren't Halley's comet, but it was a comet just the same."

"I believe you, Daddy," I said.

"I don't give a shit what you believe. You're breakin' your mother's heart, boy."

"You come after her again," I said, "and I'll be back for you."

He started to say something, then shut his mouth.

"Well," he finally said, "I ain't goin' to say good-bye, because you'll be back."

"Good-bye, Daddy."

My dogs followed me across the yard, sniffing and scratching at my heels to get my attention. I stopped and loved them up. I stood and looked back one last time at the house, though calling that two-room shack a house was a stretch. Daddy was gone. I checked behind me as I walked down the road; it would've been like him to follow me in hopes of finding the cash, but I didn't see him. Momma was right about him; his heart gave out while I was in prison. Too much corn whiskey. He was thirty-eight when I left him that night. The same age I am today.

I spent the night in the woods. Growing up, when things got bad at the house, I would take off into the cypress stands and find some high mossy ground to spend the night. If the night was clear and there was a moon, I would draw or whittle till my fingers ached, and then I would lie back and study the stars. I suppose there is some of my daddy in me after all.

I was up before dawn the next day and cut through the woods a quarter mile to Wiley's place. I found him outside tinkering on an old John Deere tractor he had bought secondhand. His wife, Lorraine, brought us two mugs of coffee so hot it scorched my tongue. Wiley rolled a cigarette and tucked it into the corner of his mouth. I told him I was gone for good, and what I planned to do. I told him what I needed him to do.

"There ain't no way, Halley," he said. "I'm foreman of the crew. I can't just take off. We'll be settin' the fire 'round that time anyway."

"It won't take you no more'n ten minutes."

"You got fired just talkin' to her. Hell, you didn't even talk. What you think he'll do to me he catches me in that rose garden?"

"Maybe he'll give you a thousand dollars too."

He laughed. "He ain't afraid of me. Like as not he'd take that elephant gun of his and blow my head clean off my shoulders."

"Then you pass her a note. I'll tell you what to say."

"I got an idea," he said. "Why don't you just sneak out there and talk to her?"

"He's lookin' for me, Wiley."

"And what he'll see is me, that's your idea. Not much better'n mine."

Lorraine went inside and came back out with a pencil and a pad of paper.

"You men are so slow," she said. She turned to Wiley.

"You never loved me like this."

"I love you enough," he said.

"Now, what you want to say?" she asked me.

"I need her to meet me at the train station this afternoon. Four o'clock train."

"All right," she said. She scribbled on the pad. "How you want to end it?"

" 'Please.' "

"No, you want to say, 'Love, Halley,' or 'Love always, Halley,' somethin' like that."

"I don't know," I said.

"I'd say, 'Forever yours,'" Wiley said.

"That ain't bad," Lorraine said. "That sound okay to you, Halley?"

"It's the truth," I said.

"It's good," she said. "Here, sign it now."

"Lorraine," Wiley said.

"Oh. Make your mark then."

I took the pencil from her and drew a quick sketch of a rose petal, a drop of water clinging to its tip.

"Oh, my," she said. "That's so good, Halley. I can almost see the water shake as it's about to fall." She folded the note and slipped it into an envelope.

"This still don't solve our problem," Wiley said.

"She walks the garden the same time every day?" Lorraine asked.

"From eight to nine, yes," I said.

"She walk alone?"

"Yes."

"Well, then it ain't no problem at all," she said. "But you'll have to run."

"Run?"

"Run like hell. Give me your knife."

I pulled my hunting knife from my boot.

"No, dear Jesus, a smaller knife."

Wiley handed her his pocketknife. She took the point and poked a hole through the top of the envelope. Then she took some string from her apron pocket and threaded it through the hole.

"Who's got steady fingers? I'm shakin' like a leaf," she said.

Wiley took the envelope and tied the knot. I had the idea now. I grabbed the note from Wiley and took off. Wiley laughed out loud.

"You make me glad I'm alive, Halley Martin!" he shouted after me. "You make me glad I'm alive!"

I ran like hell. With the rising sun fat and red behind the lithe bodies of the cypresses, I ran. Hip-deep in the mist that rose thick about the marshes, flushing coveys of quail exploding into the still air, wings whistling, I ran. I cut across Main Street, through the town square, past the courthouse and Wilson's Drug Store, up the alley between Fulsom's Funeral Home and the bank. The streets were empty, the morning shadows long on the pavement. In the thrill of solitude that comes when the world sleeps and you alone are awake, I ran. I was running as hard as I had ever run, but it took no effort: The earth bore me up. The world itself was my co-conspirator, and the earth bore me up; I crested the hill by the old Freewill Baptist Church and below me, running for as far as the eye could see, was your daddy's dead groves, the trees pulled and cut and stacked, ready to return to the earth. The plantation house shone white facing east beyond the groves, then disappeared from view as I plunged into the dry, sandy ground. The earth that had borne me up now pulled at my feet. My legs burned and the skin felt tight across my forehead. I ran between stacks of dead wood, rising higher than my head, the morning dew glistening on the bleached bones of the trees. I reached the hedgerow bordering the rose garden and fell to my stomach, crawling into that space between the bushes where I had watched you for months, your secret companion. I had outrun exhaustion, but if I rested it would catch up to me; I could feel the muscles in my legs begin to cramp. The garden was empty, and there was no one in the gazebo or by the little gardener's hut. I crept through the other side of the hedge and stood up. I had passed to the other side.

I chose a tall bush with crimson blooms that grew along the main path near the gazebo. I wrapped the string three times around the delicate stem, just below the bloom, and fumbled with the knot. The weight of the envelope pulled the flower down. It bobbed as if nodding at me: yes, yes, yes. For a second I panicked, thinking maybe today you wouldn't take your walk. There had been some mornings when I waited and you never came. Then a calmness came over me. Sometimes you have to trust that everything will be all right, because the alternative is too terrible to think about. I scrambled back to the hedgerow. I could hear the truck engines rumbling in the distance: The crews were moving out to start the fires. Soon the whole town would gather at the edge of the grove to watch. There would be picnics and games and, as the sun set, hymns would be sung and prayers would be said, for you can't have a fire without God being near.

I went directly to the station. I took the back way through the swamp so no one would see me, stopping only to fetch the cash from its hiding place.

The stationmaster, Phillips, was the only other person there. He was a little upset he had to work when everybody else in town would be enjoying the burning.

"They're closing down the bank and Wilson's," he said. "Hell, there ain't even court today." His wife and two boys were already there, with fried chicken and cole slaw and the first watermelon of the season. His lunch at the station was a pimento cheese sandwich and a pickle.

He didn't act surprised to see me, and he seemed grateful for my company. Men hired to watch over things are invariably lonely, like Phillips watching after his station, like Trimbul watching over me. He found a packing crate for me to sit on, and we passed the hours in his cramped office inside the station house. A ceiling fan spun lazily over our heads. He chain-smoked and swatted the flies that popped against the window and complained about his job. The worst part was pulling the hoboes from the freight cars. He felt so sorry for them he would give each a quarter and a cup of hot coffee before threatening to shoot them if they dared hop a car on his watch.

"And it's two bits I can't spare," he said. "But I'm a Christian." He said it with some regret, as if it was an affliction he was born with, like a club foot. He asked if I'd ever been to Atlanta.

"No," I said.

"Nothin' wrong with Atlanta. You stayin' long?"

"Don't know."

"It's hard to find work, 'specially in this little town. Thought you worked for Lester Howell."

"I did. Got fired."

"I s'pose he let more'n a few go after the freeze."

"Some," I said. I was surprised he hadn't heard the full story.

"I don't like that man," he said, and slapped at a fly. It fell dead onto his desk and he flicked it off with his little finger. "Way he acts, like he was the lone white man in a world of niggers."

"I never saw him much," I said.

"Got a pretty daughter, though. They come up here now and then. They got kin in Inverness. Can't recall her name."

"Mavis."

"That's it. Real pretty girl. Has that air some pretty girls got. You know? Some pretty girls you see are all full of their prettiness, carry it around with 'em like an extra handbag. They're all forward with it, like. But this Mavis Howell, now, she's got that kind of prettiness like . . ." he waved around the flyswatter, trying to whack down the right word. "Like a fire burned down to just the embers. Low-type fire but a lot of heat. I ain't bein' disrespectful." He blushed.

"That ain't," I said. "I like the way you put it." I pulled out the stack of one-hundred-dollar bills. "That reminds me. I got to buy a ticket."

"Thought you had a ticket."

"I need another ticket."

"You need another ticket."

I held out one of the bills.

"That's a hundred-dollar bill," he said.

"It's the smallest I got."

"That's the smallest you got?"

"You can't take it?"

"I don't keep that kinda cash. It's lonesome out here, and although I got a shotgun, you don't want to be tempting folks."

"Well," I said, "I got to have a ticket."

I laid the bill on the desk.

"It only costs three dollars to go to Atlanta," he said.

"I don't have three dollars," I said.

"So what am I supposed to do with this?"

"When we get settled I'll let you know where to send the change."

"Oh, now . . . I don't know about that."

"Or you could just let me have the ticket, and I'll send you the correct change when I get to Atlanta. I can't change it at the bank today. It's not open."

"Oh, now, I definitely couldn't do that. Ain't there someplace else in town you can break it?"

"I can't leave."

"You can't leave?"

"I'm waiting for someone."

"You're waiting for someone?"

"That's why I need the second ticket."

"Oh, right. That's right."

"I don't know when she'll get here."

"It's Miss Mavis, ain't it?"

"That's right."

"I'll be damned."

He smiled. "Well, I guess you *are* fired, ain't you?" He laughed out loud. Then he slid the hundred-dollar bill off the desk.

"That's one damned expensive train ride, ain't it?"

"You're going to send me the change."

"Now, didn't I tell you before I was a Christian? Course I'll send it."

"Just don't mistake it for a dollar and give it to a hobo."

At noon precisely he opened his lunch sack and unwrapped his pimento cheese sandwich. He glanced at me.

"I'll split it with you," he said.

"All right." I hadn't eaten all day.

He tore the sandwich in half. "That'll be ninety-seven dollars," he said.

We both laughed. I ate my half of the sandwich in two bites. He took his time. It wasn't until later, when I was in prison, that I'd learn to savor these simple breaks in the tedium of the day.

"Well, I s'pose those fires are goin' pretty good now," he said. "You want my pickle?" He could tell I was still hungry.

I took his pickle. I could tell he wasn't pleased about that. He wanted that pickle; he had been looking forward to that pickle. He must have wondered if God had sent me to test his Christian virtue: first the hundred dollars and now the pickle. I took a bite and offered the rest to him.

"Oh, no, you have it," he said. So I ate it. It was a good pickle, very crisp.

"Yeah, it gets lonesome here," he said, as if I had asked if he was lonely. "But I never been one to hanker for company." He slapped at a fly. I wondered where all the flies were coming from and why he didn't hang some flypaper. Maybe it had something to do with his lonesomeness, like the odd little habits you pick up in prison to fill the hours. Some men make brushing their teeth a thirty-minute ritual or can't rest until their bunks are made just so. You could spend half a day mopping out your cell, till the floor was so clean you could eat off it.

Phillips lit another cigarette.

"I ain't much of a reader, except the newspaper, so I'm stuck here with lots of time." He picked up the dead fly by its legs and dropped it into a coffee can by his chair. I didn't know why he dropped this one in the can and the last one he flicked on the floor. Maybe he kept only the big ones. "When the orange crop comes in there's three, four trains here a day, and I'm hoppin'. Once a week the passenger train comes in on the way to Tampa, that's year-round, but that's only once a week. Off-season, like now, there's lots of time to spare. I got half a mind to go to the fire today with the family, what the hell, but it would be just my luck the boss man would show up. He's been known to do that, surprise inspection. Bastard. Be nice though, day like today, to watch that fire. Not too hot. You don't talk much, do you?"

I shrugged.

"So you're eloping with Mavis Howell," he said.

"Her daddy gave me a thousand dollars to get out of town," I said.

"So you're taking his daughter with you." He laughed. "You got bigger balls than me. I hear he's mean as a rattlesnake and twice as deadly, once crossed."

"You won't tell him where we went."

"Oh, I think he'll figure that out all on his own."

"I meant, when you send me the money."

"Yeah. No, I wouldn't do that. But if you want my advice, I wouldn't stay in Atlanta if I were you. I'd get out of the South. Hell, I'd get out of the whole goddamned country. You know, in Mexico I hear a man with a thousand dollars can live like a king."

"I don't know where we'll end up," I said.

"That's where I'd go. Set up in one of those haciendas, have me some horses, some cattle, some Mex servants to wait on me. A little senorita or two on the side . . . not that I would. I love my wife; she is truly the world to me. I'm just letting my mind go."

"Yeah."

"Or I'd find a villa on the coast. Not the Gulf coast. The Caribbean Sea."

"I've always wanted to see the ocean," I said.

"I've seen it. My wife has kin in Jacksonville and we go up there every summer. That's the Atlantic. Stand on that beach and you look out and there's nothing but water for as far as you can see. You look out at the horizon where the water meets the sky, and you can see the curve of the earth, and you realize that it's round. Oh, everybody knows it's round, but you don't appreciate the, the . . . roundness of it till you see it with your own eyes. Like bein' in love. You can't describe it."

"Yeah."

He leaned back in his chair and closed his eyes. "Yep, that's what I would do. Find a little village down in Mexico, a little village by the sea, and I'd lie on that beach till I was brown as a nut and I'd never wear a pair of goddamned shoes again for the rest of my life." He took a deep breath, shifted his shoulders, and fell asleep. The lit cigarette dropped from his limp fingers. I picked it up and crushed the tip against my boot. It was one o'clock. Three more hours till you'd come, and already I felt like I had sat in that office for three days.

I went outside. A breeze picked up. I could smell the fires. To the east black smoke rose and thinned into a torn gray curtain against the bright blue of the sky. Had you escaped? Your father would be busy with the fire, occupied with the townsfolk, the lord of the manor come down to mingle with the peasants. It would be easy to slip away, with that colored manservant as your escort. Your invalid mother would be in her room; the house would be yours. You'd have to leave by the back gate and take the path that leads into the copse of live-oak and maple, going the long way around the groves to avoid the crowds. You'd come on foot, unless that manservant somehow managed to sneak your daddy's Packard from the garage.

I watched the road and pictured the note lying in the tangle of leaves and thorns at the bottom of the rosebush until I was almost out of my head. What if he had gone out there to beat the bushes and found the note? Or got the note from you somehow, like he got the drawing? Worst of all, what if you had found the note and decided not to come? I should have waited; I should have waited in the bushes and asked you myself. I was a coward. You don't arrange an elopement by note. It was insulting, childish, like little kids passing notes at school. Why, we'd never even spoken about it. It showed you what kind of man I was, immature and timid. I watched the road and imagined you laughing and tossing the paper into your daddy's fire.

And still I waited. I waited to see the sun glinting off the chrome bumper of the Packard, or the dazzling whiteness of your dress against the brown backdrop of the road, and wondered what kind of fool would believe a lady would abandon her home and family and everything she knew and loved, to run off with some backwoods, inbred piece of white trash like me. Who had spoken just once to her. Who had spied on her. Who had dared to love her without ever hearing the sound of her voice. Your daddy was right: I was stupid. I was a stupid, immature, timid fool. My father was right about me, and your father was right about me. I was ready to collapse under the weight of my own idiocy. You would not come with me, not today, not ever. But I would have to go. I would leave no matter what happened; better to run off a laughing-stock than remain the village idiot. But where would I go and what would I do when I got there? Like Daddy said, wherever I went I'd still be what I was when I got there. I'd be like Phillips, sitting in a little room, dreaming of the sea.

The wind shifted to the west, carrying the smell of the fire with it. There was a heaviness to the air, as if rain was coming, but the sky was that cloudless, shimmering blue of springtime. There is no worse kind of despair than the one that comes in broad daylight. I sat on the edge of the platform facing the road. I took out my knife and cleaned my nails. Doing something with my hands always made me feel better. I ran my hand over my chin and realized I hadn't shaved for two days. I scraped my knife over the whiskers until I had a vision of myself lying on the roadside with my throat cut open from my own hand. I put the knife back into my boot and stood up. I decided to go back into the station house and wake Phillips. Listening to him go on was better than listening to myself.

I turned toward the door, and it seemed to me I felt that car coming before I saw it; the hair rose on my arms and the back of my neck, like when you're hunting in the woods and you feel the deer before you see it. The Packard stopped about fifty yards from the platform. I stayed where I was, at the top of the steps. The sun glinted off the windshield, blinding me; I couldn't see who was in the car. The idling engine sounded very loud, the chugging of the muffler like the heartbeat of some black beast.

The manservant stepped out and opened the back door. I came down the steps and waited in the middle of the road as your daddy got out of the car. He adjusted his white linen duster as his manservant waited patiently with the walking stick. Lester took the cane and said something to him. The man nodded and climbed back into the car.

Lester came slowly down the road toward me. He stopped about six feet away, and smiled.

"Afternoon," he said. He waited for me to say something. I didn't.

"I have a message for you," he said. He pulled a sheet of yellow stationery from his pocket and carefully unfolded it. He was enjoying himself.

" 'My dear Mr. Martin,' " he read. " 'I am in receipt of your kind invitation. Though it is not dated, I assume your proposed rendezvous was for this afternoon. I regret that I cannot answer you in person, and hope you will not take offense at the manner of my reply.' " He glanced up from the paper, as if he was afraid I had lost interest. Satisfied I was all ears, he went on. " 'I must also assume your note to be sincere, and not the product of some warped or senseless mind. Having said this, and answering as a lady to a gentleman, I must decline your invitation. Although I am bound in no way to state my reasons, I will give you one. Though it is only one, it is the chief one, the one that will, I believe, answer all doubts in your mind as to my intentions. The truth is, I am bound to another. In fact, this very afternoon my betrothed and I are announcing our engagement. His name is Walter Hughes, and he hails from one of the finest families in Florida—' "

"Stop," I said.

" ' . . . I have known and loved Mr. Hughes since childhood, and so it is with great joy that I proclaim my undying love for him—' "

"Stop," I said again. "That's enough."

" 'Sincerely yours, Mavis Howell.' " He folded the note slowly and slipped it back into his pocket.

"She didn't write that," I said.

He smiled. He shrugged. He cocked his head slightly. He watched me.

"You wrote that," I said. "You found the note or you took it from her, and you wrote that. I want to hear it from her. I'll believe it when I hear it from her."

"That," he said quietly, "is not going to happen."

"Then I'll find her myself."

"You step one foot onto my property and I will have you shot for trespassing."

The train's whistle sounded in the distance. Suddenly there was no lonelier sound in the world.

Lester said, "I believe that is your train, Halley." He tipped his wide-brimmed hat and walked back to the car. I watched the car turn around, and then I watched the car drive off. I waited until the brown dust settled back onto the road. I turned toward the station house and saw Phillips standing outside the office door, blinking in that stupid way you do after waking from a nap.

"Son of a bitch," he said.

I came back up the steps. He picked up my bag and held it out.

"Get on that train, Halley," he said.

I took the bag and walked over to the tracks. I set my bag down by my feet. This is what it came down to: just me and my little bag. The wood quivered beneath my feet. There was a gathering of air, a tugging on my eardrums, and with an inhuman shriek the train roared into the station, belching black smoke, the grind of metal on metal setting my teeth on edge. I rocked back on my heels and was one blink away from hurling myself against the smouldering body of the engine.

The conductor jumped off holding his little stepping stool. He adjusted his little hat and checked his little pocket watch. Behind me, Phillips said, "Get on that train, Halley Martin."

I walked back to the burning fields. I came from the swamp side, so the crowds gathered on the hill couldn't see me. The wind from the west had turned sharp and mean; there was a storm coming. The fire had burned low, and the wind pressed the smoke down so it rolled and turned close to the ground like a gray and black sea, pocked by the glowing embers of the fire. The white plantation house shimmered behind the heated air. I could see him, your father, standing on the upper porch, that long, white duster billowing around him. He was facing toward me, holding very still. He raised a hand. He saw me.

I opened my bag and pulled out the brown paper package tied with twine. I held it high for a long time; I wanted to make sure he saw it and knew what it was. I thought I saw him nod, as if to say, "Yes, I see. I understand."

I tossed the package into the fire. It was Phillips's low-type fire with a lot of heat. The package didn't just catch fire and burn; it exploded from the heat and was gone in seconds.

I looked up at Lester. He nodded. He had seen. He understood.

The rains came hard by sundown. I sat on Wiley's back porch and watched the lightning flash over the cypresses. It was a ferocious rain, a hateful rain, the kind that shreds tender new leaves and crushes the delicate spring growth. It pounded the earth, which would not yield to it, and within ten minutes Wiley had a small pond for a backyard. He came out of the house with a jug of corn mash and sat beside me. He lit a cigarette and uncorked the jug. The rain drummed on the tin roof and fell in a gray curtain over the eaves.

"I don't suppose it'd do any good to point out there's other fish in the sea," he said.

He took a pull from the jug. "You know, that little Annie Walker was always kind of sweet on you . . ."

"Shut up, Wiley."

"All right."

He was quiet for a minute, then he said, "You gonna be all right, Halley?"

"I'm all right."

"No, I mean, you gonna be all right? This kind of thing can drive a fella clean out of his head. It gets bigger than it really is."

"How big you figure it really is, Wiley?"

"Well, it's only a woman, after all."

It was the wrong thing to say and he knew it the minute he said it. "Don't get me wrong. She's beautiful, but really, you don't know her at all, Halley. My momma always said don't go for the pretty ones—it's like catching a butterfly: Now that you got it, what the hell are you supposed to do with it?"

"You don't know what you're talking about."

"Maybe I don't. But I do know there's a difference between wanting something because you need it and wanting it because you can't have it."

"It ain't a matter of what I can or can't have. It's a matter of what I *am*. She has . . . come into me. Like the rain into the ground."

He stared at me. "Well. That's just fucking strange."

"I don't expect you to understand." I pulled the jug from his hand and took a big swallow. I gagged as the liquor burned its way down my throat. I bent over, coughing and spitting, my eyes burning. Wiley slapped me hard on the back.

"Halley," he laughed, "you don't drink!"

"I know," I gasped. "I forgot."

I sat back in the chair. I wiped the tears away. My face felt hot.

"You know what Lorraine says? She says we were meant to be together."

"So?"

"So, if you're meant to be together, then you're going to be together. Don't matter what ol' Lester says."

"I gotta talk to her."

"Halley, I told you. There's a price on your head now. Two hundred dollars to the man who guns you down on the property. You step one foot near that house and you're a dead man."

"You could talk to her."

"Jesus! I told you I ain't the man for this, Halley. The least he'd do is fire me, and I got Lorraine and the kids to think about."

"Wiley, I have to know if she wrote that letter. I got to know about this Walter Hughes . . ."

"Well, there is such a person. I seen him at the house. The old man took him and introduced him around."

"When?"

"Today. This afternoon."

"Was she with him?"

"Word was she's packing."

"Packing?"

"Goin' on some kind of trip. Inverness, I think, to visit some kin. Anyway, he's one fine dandy, this Walter Hughes. Dresses just like her old man. Talks like him too. Probably why he picked him for Mavis."

"When is she leaving?"

"They don't discuss their travel plans with me, Halley."

"We got to find a way to get word to her 'fore she goes."

"Lester'll have her locked up tight after you was fool enough to show yourself to him at the fire."

He took another swig and offered me the jug. I shook my head.

"Did Lester say they was engaged?" I asked.

"Not that I recall."

"What the hell does that mean? Did he say it or didn't he?"

"Oh, you know, he was . . . he was Lester. Just being Lester . . ."

"Goddamn it, Wiley! Tell me what he said!"

"He said nothing, Halley, he said . . ."

I stood up. He shook his head sadly.

"What you gonna do now, Halley? You gonna beat me up? Cut me with your knife? That where we've come, Halley?"

"Tell me what he said."

He sighed, turning his eyes away. He took another pull from the jug. "He called him Mavis's new beau. He said, 'Here's my daughter's latest beau, Walter Hughes.' That was it, that was all, that was all he said, Halley."

I stayed on my feet long enough for the blood to leave my head. I flopped back into the chair and put my head in my hands.

"But he . . . there was nothing said about marriage."

"No. Nothin'. I swear, Halley. I swear to God."

"All right," I said. "All right. All right."

"I'm sorry," Wiley said.

I waved that away.

"It don't change nothin'."

"How you figure her being engaged don't change anything, Halley?"

"I'm gonna find this man, this Walter Hughes, and I'm going to talk to him."

"Oh, Lord. Talk to him . . . about *what?*"

"And if he is her new *beau*," I spat the word out, "he'll just have to ask her about me. And she'll have to tell him, one way or the other." I laughed. "It's perfect! Where's he live, Wiley?"

"How the hell would I know?"

"Ask around. Somebody out there will know. Ask that manservant, that butler of Lester's. He knows everything that goes on around that house."

"He does?"

"Ask him. Ask him where I can find Walter Hughes. Ask him, Wiley."

"All right."

"Ask him tomorrow."

"Okay, okay. I'll ask him. But how you know he's even going to give you the time of day?"

I said, "Oh, I think he already might want to meet me."

The rain tapered off around midnight. The clouds tore apart and the stars shone bright over the cypresses. Wiley fell asleep, cradling his jug. Inside the house the baby, Jeremiah, woke up wailing. The floorboards creaked as Lorraine walked him back and forth. A shooting star fell out of sight behind the swamp, and I wondered if my life would have been different under a different name. On this night it felt like a mark upon my forehead, as if my daddy had cursed me from the minute I was born. Jeremiah was inconsolable; Lorraine carried him onto the porch and wrinkled her nose at Wiley.

"Here," I said. "Give him to me."

She was skeptical, but lowered the child into my arms. I felt suddenly huge and clumsy with this tiny, squalling child in my lap. He burrowed into my chest, turning his little bald head from side to side.

"I hope he ain't looking for something to eat," I said, and Lorraine laughed.

"He ain't hungry," she said. "He's always been a restless one."

"Yeah," I said. I patted his bowed-up back. He pressed his little ear against my chest and got still, listening. I hummed softly, rubbing his back as he relaxed against me.

"You're a natural," Lorraine said.

"I been good at putting people to sleep today," I said. "He's my third one."

She reached for him.

"No, that's all right," I said. "Let him get settled. I'll bring him in directly."

She kissed my cheek. "Halley Martin," she said. She pointed at Wiley. "I'm leaving him. He sleeps out here most of the time anyway."

She went inside and soon the house was still. Now it was me and Jeremiah and the crickets' raucous singing. The night had turned cool after the rain. I unbuttoned my shirt and moved Jeremiah onto my bare chest, covering him the best I could. His breath was warm and sweet against my skin. I leaned over and smelled the top of his head.

Later, in prison, the Preacher told me he was a strong believer in compensation. He talked about it the night before he died, that God offers something else for everything he takes away. I never had a problem with that, except the taking away part. It seemed a kind of madness to take something so you could show how good you were at giving. Preacher said don't try to understand it; just live it. I never did understand what that meant. I just understood that this had been the worst day of my life, and now here was Jeremiah, like the answer to a question I never knew I asked.

I dozed. When I woke it was still dark and Wiley was gone. Jeremiah was fast asleep, his little fist resting on my shoulder.

A twig snapped around the corner of the house. A ripple spread from the edge of Wiley's new pond, erasing the reflections of the stars as it went. I came wide awake.

"I know you're there," I said. "You may as well come out."

The water rippled again, and there was the sound of soft ground squishing beneath someone's feet. He came around the corner of the house and stopped at the concrete blocks Wiley used as steps, his feet completely under water, his white jacket spotless and shining in the moonlight. It was your daddy's manservant.

"You know who I am, Mistah Halley?"

"I know what you do," I said. "I don't know your name."

"My name is Elias Johnson. I weren't sneakin' up on you, Mistah Halley. I just weren't sure you was here. Heard you was stayin' here, so that's why I come."

"That's all right," I said. "Come up out of that water."

"Much obliged, Mistah Halley. I much obliged."

He stepped onto the porch and stood in front of me, holding his hat.

"Sit down," I said.

"Sure. I sure will. Thank you, sir."

"Don't call me that. Don't call me sir."

"Well, all right, then, if'n you don't mind."

He sank into Wiley's chair and set his hat carefully on his knee. He stared at Jeremiah sleeping on my chest.

"My cousin," I said.

"Oh, sure 'nough. He a cutey."

"You out for a midnight stroll, Elias?"

"No, Mistah Halley. I come to see you."

"Kind of late for a social call."

"I was sent to find you."

"Who sent you?"

"Miss Mavis. Miss Mavis sent me, Mistah Halley." He looked away, wincing, as if just saying your name pained him.

"Mavis. She sent you?"

He nodded. "She asked me if I know where you live, and I tol' her I didn't think you lived there no more. I tol' her I heard you moved out here with Mistah Wiley." He grinned. "And I was right too, wasn't I?"

"Why did Mavis send you to me, Elias?"

"She wanted me to give you a message. And the message is she wants you to know it's all right."

"What's all right?"

"She wanted me to say to you that it's all right, everything's all right, and she'll find some way to explain it all later."

I took a deep breath. "What else did she say?"

"That's all, Mistah Halley. That it's all right, and she'll explain it all later." He seemed to enjoy repeating it. "She'll explain it all later," he said.

"She'll explain all what?"

He looked away. "She made me go right off. She tol' me, don't wait till mornin', Elias. You go right now. Right *now,* she says. So I says, 'All right, Miss Mavis, I'll go right now.' So I come up here to Mistah Wiley's. Somebody up at the house said you was stayin' here, so I come. I don't know what I'd do if you wasn't here. The good Lord has his ways, don't he, Mistah Halley?"

"Why did she want you to come tonight, Elias?"

He drummed on the top of his hat slowly, staring into space. Jeremiah whimpered in his sleep.

"I knew he was no good. I could see it in his eyes. The way he looked at her. He got the rovin' eye; it just rove all over her. The way he carried hisself, just like her daddy. Why, when I first saw him, I tol' myself, Elias, this here boy ain't no good, and dear Lord Jesus, I s'pose I was right. I just s'pose I was right."

He brought a hand to his cheek. He was crying. I said, "Walter Hughes."

He nodded. "It was all her daddy's doin'. Mistah Lester. He my boss an' all, don't mistake me, but this was all his doin'."

"Tell me what happened, Elias."

He burst into tears. He threw his hat on the ground and pounded his fist into his knee.

"Oh, she in a bad way, Mistah Halley. She back in her room now. Mistah Lester, he sending her off to Inverness tomorrow to stay with the cousins. Mistah Lester, he sends me up to fetch a glass of water, an' that's when she tol' me to find you. I tol' her, 'He's on a train to Atlanta.' And Miss Mavis, she say, 'No, he's not. He never got on that train.' Now how she knows that I got no idea . . ."

"Lester saw me," I said. "What else did she say?"

He snuffled loudly and blew his nose. The handkerchief was a brilliant white against his skin.

"He kill me if he finds out I come here. An' he in a mood to kill." He leaned forward. "He hit her, Mistah Halley."

"Walter?"

"Mistah Lester. Walter . . . he done much worse." He folded the handkerchief neatly and tucked it back into his breast pocket. "I tol' Miss Mavis, 'I oughtta go to the sheriff.' An' she say, 'No, go to Halley. Find Halley and tell him it's all right, that now everythin's gonna be all right.' So I come."

"What did Walter do, Elias?" I felt calm now, but strangely heavy all over, like I was made of stone. Jeremiah was wriggling against my tightening muscles.

"Mistah Lester made her go. After dinner was cleared Mistah Walter starts goin' on about that Nash of Mistah Lester's, an' Mistah Lester say, 'Why don't you and Mavis go for a spin?' Miss Mavis, she don't want to go, but Mistah Lester, he insist, he say, 'You two got to know one another better.' So off they go in that car an' they gone maybe one, two hours, an' when they come back Mistah Walter is all upset, an' he won't stay the night, though Mistah Lester, he ask him to. So Mistah Walter goes and Mistah Lester sets in on Miss Mavis. He tell her she's got to be nice to Mistah Walter, talkin' 'bout her future and the bizness future, and she say she understands well enough he wants after Mistah Walter's money, an' then he hits her; he smacks her good across the face and that's when she tells him what that Walter Hughes done to her while they was out for their drive."

He leaned toward me, resting his elbows on his knees. His voice was soft and broken from the crying. He spoke as if he were bringing news of someone's death. In a way, he was.

"He had his way with her, Mistah Halley. He forced hisself on that little girl."

A fresh tear sprang from his eye, and he angrily wiped it away. "He don't believe her," he said. "He don't believe her 'cause this marriage to Walter Hughes is everything to him. Most folks don't know this, but Mistah Lester, he damn near broke. Freeze's damn near ruined him. He be countin' on Mistah Walter's money to save him. I know that for a fact. He don't think I listen, an' I around him so much he stops seein' me. I just the house nigger to him. He don't never look at me as a man."

He lowered his head, slowly shaking it back and forth. "But I tell you, Mistah Halley, if I was her daddy, if I was Mistah Lester, there'd be a reckoning. Yessah, upon all that's holy, there'd be a reckoning."

He raised his eyes. We stared at each other for a long time, and the night seemed very still, more still than it should have been in early summer after a rain; even the crickets had stopped singing. Or maybe it wasn't the world that was suddenly still and heavy and thick with silence; maybe it was me. We were alone, Elias and I, in that dead hour between dark and light.

"Well," he said finally, "I guess I best be gettin' on back."

"No. Sit with me a while, Elias," I said.

So he did.

Mr. Franks, that pasty-faced prosecutor, fixed on my talk with Elias, going over and over it, word for word, making Farley object till he was hoarse and his face red as a beet. Franks had a voice three times the size of his little body; when he first spoke some of the jurors flinched, and a few smiled. It was like hearing a chicken bark. After I went through the whole thing for a third time, he stalked back to his table, head down, hands folded behind his back, then he whirled around and brayed out, "The truth is you made up your mind right then to take the life of Walter Hughes. That is the truth, isn't it, Mr. Martin?"

He came toward me, a finger pointed at my nose.

"The truth is you decided Walter Hughes was a dead man! You passed sentence on him that very night, two whole days before you carried it out! This was no crime of passion, this was no fit of rage! Two days before you viciously murdered this poor boy you coldly and with malice—"

"I object!" Farley cried. "He's making speeches, your honor."

The judge said, "Ask a question, Mr. Franks."

Franks said, "The truth is you decided that night to kill Walter, didn't you?"

"I don't know what I decided."

"You don't know what you decided?!"

"No."

"You kept your decision from yourself?"

That caused some snickering. My face was hot.

"I suppose I thought something had to be done," I said.

"Something like murder?"

"Well, what would you have thought of?"

"I will ask the questions, thank you. And my thoughts are not the issue here, Mr. Martin. What I think or do not think has nothing to do with the fact that you slit that boy's guts out like you were gutting a catfish!"

"Objection!" Farley shouted.

"Sustained!" the judge yelled back. Franks's hollering was contagious. "Ask the defendant a question, Mr. Franks. I will not warn you again."

Franks said, "You thought something had to be done?"

"Yes."

"That is your testimony, that on that night, Wednesday night, after you spoke with Elias Johnson and learned of this so-called attack, you thought on that night something had to be done?"

"Yes."

"Could you be more specific, Mr. Martin? What do you mean by 'something'? Do you mean something such as . . . going to the sheriff? Was that the something you considered?"

"I can't say I thought of that."

"All right. What about getting that little girl to a doctor? After such a brutal attack, a doctor might be something you'd consider."

"Elias said she was all right."

"She was all right?"

"That was the message to me."

"So you did not consider taking her to a doctor?"

"No."

"Or bringing the doctor to her?"

"No."

"But you did think something had to be done?"

"Yes."

"Something as a result of this alleged attack?"

"Yes."

"Not something *for* Mavis, but something *to* Walter?"

"Yes."

"Something along the lines of . . . what did Elias call it, a reckoning?"

"Yes."

"And that night, Wednesday night, what did you take that to mean? When you thought something ought to be done to Walter, what sort of reckoning did you consider commensurate with the crime?"

"I don't understand."

"Did you consider seeking Walter out and telling him he was a bad person?"

"No."

"That wouldn't be quite enough, would it? Find Walter and just tell him off."

"No."

"Did you consider seeking him out and perhaps popping him in the nose?"

"Popping him in the nose?"

"Yes. Popping him in the nose. Did you think about that?"

"No."

"Some other way to hurt him?"

"Yes."

"He deserved it, that's what you thought?"

"Any man would."

"I'm not talking about any man. I'm talking about a specific man. You. I'm asking what you, Halley Martin, thought."

"Yes."

"That night you believed he deserved the harshest of punishments. You believed that, didn't you?"

"Yes. I believed that."

"On that night?"

"Yes."

"If he had stepped onto that porch that night, you wouldn't have cussed him out, would you?"

"No."

"You wouldn't have popped him in the nose, would you?"

"No."

"You would have killed him, right? You would have slit him open right then, correct?"

"Yes, that's right."

"He deserved no less."

"Right."

"And on Friday night, when you did kill him, he still deserved no less, in your mind?"

"Yes. That's right."

"Your mind had not changed, from Wednesday to Friday. What you thought on Wednesday you thought on Friday."

"Yes."

"In fact, you think that now."

"Yes."

"And if someone else attacked Miss Mavis Howell, you'd do the same again—if you were able?"

"Yes."

"If, say, the judge here attacked her, hurt her, you'd kill him, wouldn't you?"

Farley said, "Your honor, I must object to this . . ."

"Overruled," the judge said.

"You are to answer my question," Franks said to me.

"Yes. Yes, I would. I'd kill anybody that hurt her like that."

"No doubt in your mind?"

"No."

"There was never any doubt in your mind, was there, Halley?"

"No. Not really."

"Walter's fate was sealed on Wednesday night, not Thursday, not Friday, but Wednesday, when Elias told you what happened?"

"No."

"No? But didn't you just—"

"Walter's fate wasn't sealed when Elias told me what happened. Walter's fate was sealed the minute he did what he did to her."

"I have no further questions," Franks said, and sat down.

Farley stood up slowly. He mopped the top of his head with a handkerchief. He puffed his cheeks and looked up at the ceiling. Then he looked at me.

"Why, Halley?" he asked.

"Why?"

"Why was his fate sealed?"

"He hurt her."

"Yes. He did. He hurt her. Would his fate have been sealed if he hurt, say, your momma?"

"No. Not like you mean."

"You may have beat him up, broken a few bones, something along those lines?"

"Yes."

"But you wouldn't have killed him?"

"No."

Franks bellowed from his seat, "This is leading and irrelevant, your honor!"

"I'll allow it, but let's get to it, Mr. Wells," the judge said.

Farley rested his hand on the railing in front of me.

"You love your momma, Halley?"

"Of course I love her."

"She's sittin' right over there. She's sat there this whole trial, every minute of it."

"Yes."

"You're her boy, her oldest, the apple of her eye. In fact, you are her favorite, of seven, you are the favorite."

"That's what she says."

"And you love her. You love her dearly."

"Yes."

"In fact, with the exception of Miss Mavis Howell, she is the only person on this earth that you do love, heart and soul, body and mind."

"Yes."

"But if someone hurt her, short of taking her life, you wouldn't take that person's life, would you?"

"I don't know. I don't think so."

He slapped his open palm on the wooden rail. It made a retort as loud as a rifle in the quiet courtroom.

"Then why did you take the life of Walter Hughes, a man you never met, for raping a girl you barely knew?!"

I felt a trickle of sweat run down the middle of my back. My new clothes felt tight and the stiff collar was squeezing my neck, cutting off my air. I didn't say anything.

"That's it, ain't it, Halley? That's the whole question, that's what this whole trial comes down to, this is the question that's in the minds of these jurors, on the minds of the victim's grieving family, on the minds of this entire community . . . why? So tell us, Halley, tell us why Walter Hughes is dead."

I couldn't answer. This was worse than anything Franks had thrown at me. We had never practiced this, and I wondered what Farley was up to. Momma lowered her head, and her shoulders shook as she wept.

Farley went on, "You have never been introduced to Miss Mavis Howell, have you?"

"No."

"You've never had a conversation with her?"

"No."

"The only thing you ever said to her was, 'This is for you,' when you handed her that drawing, that day in the rose garden."

"That's right."

"In fact, you've never even heard the sound of her voice, have you?"

"No."

"For all you know, Mavis Howell croaks like a frog."

"Yes."

"You didn't even know she ever gave you a second thought until Elias came by with her message, ain't that right?"

"Yes, that's right."

"So the truth is, this girl is practically a stranger to you."

"Yes. No. That ain't true."

"Well, how would you describe your relationship, Halley? Is she your lover?"

"No."

"Of course not. That's ridiculous. Well, is she your friend? Someone you know well, someone you can confide in? A friend in the way your cousin Wiley is a friend?"

"No."

"An acquaintance, then. Someone you say 'howdy' to, someone you pass the time of day with, like the postman or Mr. Wilson at the general store?"

"No."

"Then what does that leave, Halley? She ain't your lover, she ain't your friend, she ain't your acquaintance, what does that leave? Is she your enemy?"

"Of course not . . ."

"Then what is Mavis Howell to you that you would kill for her?"

I was cold all over. Black spots swam in front of my eyes and I was afraid I was going to pass out. There was a roaring in my ears like that train coming into the station on the burning day, and I remembered Phillips saying, "Get on that train, Halley."

Farley roared: "Father Abraham was willing to sacrifice his beloved son, but that was for *God,* who at least had the decency to speak to him!"

"Objection!" Franks shouted.

"I don't know what she is!" I cried out. The judge held his gavel in midair, frozen just as he was about to slam it down. Farley's mouth hung open. I fell forward; it felt as if I would keep falling forever. I choked it out, but in the silence my voice carried on and on: "I don't know what she is, but I can't think of what she *isn't,* either, and in that way . . . she is like God."

Farley said, "Your honor, the defense rests."

The court recessed for ten minutes, and when it was over Franks stood up for his final argument. I drank three tall glasses of water, watching the jury out of the corner of my eye while the jury watched me. I leaned over and whispered to Farley, "Why'd you do that to me?" He patted my hand and nodded his head as if to say, "Trust me." I didn't.

Franks walked over to the jury box, stopped in front of the rail, and bounced up and down on the balls of his feet. He pinched the tip of his sharp nose and cleared his throat. He shoved his hands into his pockets and shrugged his shoulders.

"There are only three legal defenses for the crime of murder," he said. "The first is . . . innocence. You didn't do it. In the case before you, there is no doubt who murdered Walter Hughes. The state has a dozen witnesses to that effect, and the defendant himself admits to it. So the question before us is, given he has admitted to it, in fact, seems proud of it, the question is, why are we here?" He smiled like he had made a good joke. "We are here because there are two other legal defenses for murder: murder in self-defense and innocence by reason of insanity. In the former, you have no choice to kill in order to save your own life. The defense has not raised this argument, obviously, since Walter Hughes had not made any threats, real or implied, upon the life of the accused. So that leaves us with insanity. Insanity, gentlemen, in the legal sense, means that the defendant is incapable of understanding that the taking of human life is wrong, that it is by its very nature *evil*, contrary to the laws of God and of man. 'He was out of his head! He didn't know what he was doing!' That's the essence of their defense, an argument so laughable, given the facts of this case, that I hesitate to even address it, lest I insult your intelligence. But before we delve into this ludicrous proposition, before we peel back the scalp of Halley Martin and poke about in his brain for his scalded wit, let's review the facts of this case."

He began to pace. Farley was scribbling on his legal pad. I was wondering what the hell "scalded wit" meant.

"Fact," Franks said. "Walter Hughes is dead. Dead as a doornail. There is no mystery to his death—fifty people saw him die, and fifty people saw at whose hand he died. This brings us to our second fact—" he pointed at me. "Right over there sits the man who did it. There is no doubt of this fact, either; we know it from the witnesses who were there that night, and we know it from the accused; from his own lips has come his confession. You heard him, gentlemen, we all heard him. 'I killed him,' he said, sitting right over there in that witness chair. 'I killed Walter Hughes.' Without batting an eye. Without shedding a tear. 'I killed Walter Hughes.' "

He stopped pacing, his head down, bouncing on the balls of his feet. After a moment he went flat-footed and said, still looking at the floor, "Walter Hughes is dead. Halley Martin has confessed to killing him. Halley Martin is guilty of murder." He looked up at the jury and spread his hands. "I should be able to sit down now, don't you think? A young man in the prime of his life, a life full of promise and great expectations, a young man who was in many ways the cream of his crop, the best of his generation, is brutally butchered before fifty eyewitnesses, and the man who butchered him admits to it in open court, without the slightest hint of remorse, no less, and we here today must debate the issue? It's almost too embarrassing to discuss, isn't it? A child could deliver this verdict. But we are not children, so I will not try your patience further by belaboring the obvious. My job as prosecutor, and your job as jurors, is to stick to the facts, so allow me to add just a couple more.

"Fact: This was no crime of passion! This was no act committed in the white heat of the moment! Walter Hughes was murdered by *appointment*! He had sent word the day following this alleged assault—which, by the way, has never been substantiated in this courtroom—that he wished to meet with the accused, a meeting which Halley Martin agreed to consummate. It is also a fact that two days passed between the time Halley Martin learned of this so-called attack and the time he murdered Walter. Two days. That's an awful long time, two days. That's not flying off the handle; that's *crawling* off it. Furthermore, Halley Martin went to the bar that night for no other reason than to kill Walter Hughes! Why, he admitted as much in his testimony today. He didn't meet with Walter Hughes to hear his side of the matter; he had that knife in him before he had a chance to speak. And what was the last thing he said? What were the dying words of Walter Hughes? 'It isn't true.' "

Franks became very still and lowered his voice.

" 'It isn't true.' Now what do you suppose he was talking about? Makes you wonder, doesn't it? But Halley Martin didn't wonder. Halley Martin didn't wonder about it one bit. Now this is very important, the last and most important fact I want you to consider: Walter Hughes told Halley Martin it wasn't true . . . and *Halley Martin killed him anyway.* Fifty men heard Walter say it, and fifty men saw Halley do it. 'It isn't true,' Walter says, and Halley Martin pulls his knife and slits that poor boy open like a hog in the slaughterhouse.

"I submit to you, gentlemen, that this entire so-called attack was nothing more than an excuse, a convenient explanation for what Halley Martin wanted to do to Walter Hughes. I submit to you, gentlemen, that Walter Hughes did not die because he raped Mavis Howell. Walter Hughes died because he was unfortunate enough to be Halley Martin's rival in love! He made it clear to Lester Howell and he's made it clear to all of you that he will stop at nothing to have Miss Mavis Howell. So, it wasn't what Elias told him that night that sealed Walter's fate, and it wasn't this 'attack' that sealed his fate, as he suggests. What sealed Walter Hughes's fate was the letter Lester read to Halley at the train station. The letter that rejected Halley utterly as her paramour. The letter that placed Walter Hughes above him in the hierarchy of her affection. He demanded proof of that letter's veracity but needed no proof of the terrible allegation against Walter. Do you begin to see? It is a truth which I doubt even Halley sees himself."

He walked over to the evidence table and picked up my knife. He carried it toward the jury box.

"But, my dear friends, the *why* here is not as important as the what. No one can truly know what dark behemoths swim in the black depths of the human heart. And the law, thankfully, doesn't require the state to explain the actions of the accused. What I am required to prove, what I have proved, is that Halley Martin plotted the murder of this poor boy, and that on the night of April nineteenth, nineteen hundred and forty, Halley Martin took this knife and plunged it into the heart of Walter Hughes."

He brought the knife down, burying the tip into the wooden rail, where it stuck, quivering, while he walked back to his table and sat down.

"Mr. Wells," the judge said.

Farley didn't move. He sat beside me, with his bald head in his hands, and he didn't move.

"Mr. Wells, your closing argument," the judge said.

Farley took a deep breath, but he still didn't move. "'No one can truly know what dark behemoths swim in the black depths of the human heart,'" he said softly. "That's good. That's very good."

He pushed back his chair and stood up.

"Who can truly know? Certainly not I." He looked at the jury and gave a small smile. "I am no psychologist. I am no artist. I am no poet. I am no philosopher. I am a lawyer. I'm not even a very good lawyer. In the ten years I've been practicing I've never lost a criminal case. This is because I've never tried a criminal case. This," he said, "is my first."

He came around the table. He stood before the jury looking round and small; he seemed to shrink the closer he got to the jury.

"My practice consists of drawing up wills, handling real estate transactions, arranging divorces and adoptions. My life and my practice have done little to prepare me for this moment, and nothing to prepare me to answer that question. As Mr. Franks said, there is no mystery in what happened. The mystery is: Did this *have* to happen? For if this did *have* to happen, then Halley Martin can be no more guilty of murder than you or me."

He pulled the knife from the railing. He held it up and turned it from side to side. The late afternoon sunlight streamed through the windows behind the box and caught on the knife's edge, flashing in the deepening gloom of the courtroom.

"Mr. Franks loves his facts. He adores them. If facts were girls, he'd kiss 'em on the cheek and call them 'honey.' How wonderful it would be to live in that world of Mr. Franks, a world of facts, a world of absolutes, where black is always black and white is always white, a world as comfortable as your favorite pair of slippers, where human beings are reduced to the sum of their actions, as if our lives were some mathematical equation in which the *why* is irrelevant. How nice it would be to live in that world! And we do live in it, don't we? Until we are confronted by something that confounds our comfortable world of facts and figures, until we come face to face with that unanswerable question: Did this *have* to happen?"

Farley played with the knife.

"Now, to decide the question of 'Did this have to happen?' you got to start with the one person who has brought us together today. Not with cold, precise, impersonal facts. To get at the truth, gentlemen, you must first start with the man."

He stepped backward and swept his arm toward me, pointing at me with the knife.

"Behold the man!" he cried. "Behold the man! The state would have you see what he *did* and ignore what he *is*. And what is he? What is in him that made this terrible day necessary? What is in his heart that made this"—he slammed the knife into the table, right in front of me—"unavoidable."

He whirled back to the jury. "Because this is the issue before us today. Not an issue of who did what to whom, and who decided what on this day or that day. This issue before us is *Was there a decision to make at all?* Given the man, what other outcome could there be? Halley asked Mr. Franks, 'What would you have done?' But the proper question is, 'What else could *Halley* have done?' Given the man. Given the man. So don't try to imagine what you would have done. Imagine what Halley could have done, and what, in his mind, he had no choice but to do.

"I want you to imagine you are Halley Martin. You are born the first of seven children to an illiterate alcoholic father who forces you to quit school in the third grade. You are put to work in the fields before you've learned to write your own name. You grow up in a two-room shack where your mother is savagely beaten nearly every night, and every night you lie down with hunger gnawing at your belly, and you know when you get up the next day will be no different than the one before, or the one before that, or the one before that. Day after day of unrelenting toil and terror. Imagine lying on a mat on a bare floor trying to sleep as your momma cries out in pain from the blows of your father; imagine, if you can, losing your childhood at the age of nine; imagine becoming the family's breadwinner, the man of the house when your daddy disappears for weeks at a time; imagine watching the night fall in uneasy peace, wondering if this will be the night when he comes home, drunk and broke and venting his rage upon your defenseless mother; you are nine years old and your mother looks to you, to *you,* a nine-year-old boy, to protect her.

Imagine living in a world where debts are settled with the knife or with the gun, where men kill each other over the smallest slight, the most insignificant disagreement; imagine witnessing your first murder at the age of twelve when your uncle kills a neighbor in a spat over a card game. Imagine you are a nine-year-old boy bent over for ten hours a day in the boiling heat, picking strawberries, until your backbone feels as if it's going to snap in two, until your fingers curl and cramp and your little fingernails split and bleed; imagine now you're fourteen and your father changes your name—your name! The only thing in this world you can truly call your own. Even the poorest of the poor have that, their name, but imagine you don't even have that anymore. You are no longer Halley. You are Hyram. Hyram! Worse than all the beatings, the degradations, worse than the ten-hour days in the fields—to lose your name. Imagine. Imagine! Even your name doesn't belong to you. Even your name can be taken away.

"And then, one day you look up from the pit of your own nothingness, and in the distance you see something so beautiful you have no words to describe it. The only way you can find to express it is through drawing, to try in your own poor way to transcribe it to paper. Understand what the rest of the world might describe as a pretty girl is not that to you. To you it is beyond your imaginings of heaven itself. For in this mortal vision you glimpse the eternal. You never knew there was such beauty in the world until you saw such beauty in the world. You don't know what she is, but you can't say what she isn't either. And in that way, she is like God. Like God! Imagine seeing the face of God! What do you do? What would you do to capture that beauty, to hold it in your hands, to touch it, to possess it, even for an instant? Imagine, above all, the hope it would bring you. Perhaps there is more to life than just these days of toil and sorrow, more than the grubbing and the scraping for every scrap of bread, more than the sleeping and the waking. Perhaps, just perhaps, life could be beautiful. What would you do with that promise? Would you walk away from it? Would you turn your back forever or would you pursue it with every ounce of energy in your body? Would you be willing to sacrifice everything just for a look, a touch, a word? What price would be too high? You labor in the fields and find a pearl of great price—wouldn't you sell all that you had to have it? And once it was within your grasp, wouldn't you stop at nothing to keep it?

"Imagine, then, learning that this indescribable beauty, this message of hope, has been marred, has been found out by the ugliness in which you have been forced to wallow all your life. Imagine learning this delicate flower has been defiled, defiled in blood beyond all hope of retrieval, and you are Halley Martin, and the only answer you've ever known is violence. And imagine further the defiler is proclaiming his own innocence! Not to spin you all 'round too fast, but imagine now you're Walter Hughes, and you have had an earful about Halley Martin. You know his reputation. Are you going to tell him the truth when he comes to you, as surely he will? Are you going to say, 'Yes, I raped her, and I'm glad'? Or are you going to say, 'It isn't true'? Don't bother imagining you're Walter. What would you yourself say to Halley? Here is a man . . . no, barely a man, more a boy still, but here is a man who from the moment of his birth was up to his neck in blood. Who lived for eighteen years under violence or the threat of violence, who looked up one day and saw a brilliant shooting star, a bea-con, leading him out of the darkness—and then one night that light *goes out*. What would you yourself say? Would you tell this man the truth? How in God's name are we to expect such a man to react? Did this have to happen? You're damned right this had to happen!"

He slammed his fist on the table. His round face was flushed and slick with sweat. He looked into my eyes for a second, then swung back toward the jury.

"Behold the man and know it had to happen! He could no more walk away than you or I could fly to the moon! And me and Mr. Franks, and you and your fellow jurors can argue till we're blue in the face whether it was planned or not planned, whether Walter was telling the truth or not telling the truth, whether it came to Halley on Wednesday or on Thursday, and it won't matter one damned bit; if we would open our eyes we would know it was decided the moment he saw her. If you want to find the day Halley Martin damned himself, look to that day, the day he first saw her, for it is written that no man can look at the face of God and live."

He leaned on the rail of the jury box, looking small, beaten, exhausted. His voice was hoarse and quivered as if he was on the verge of tears.

"I hope you can begin to imagine. I hope you begin to understand. This *did* have to happen. I don't pretend to understand *why* it had to happen, but I do understand it did. It did. Mr. Franks calls it obsession. I call it love, but a love which I do not pretend to understand, a love which makes the way I love pale and feeble in comparison. A love of irresistible force, like gravity. I can decide such things don't exist except in fairy tales. But what I have seen with my eyes I must testify with my lips."

He turned and looked at me.

"And, in a way, I envy him. I envy Halley Martin. We all should envy him. Here is a man who took love to its logical conclusion. And when you go home tonight, gentlemen, I want you to look at your wife and your daughters, and I want you to imagine someone hurting them, hurting them in the worst way a man can hurt a woman short of murder, and I want you to ask yourselves, with all the candor you can muster, what you would want to do to that man who hurt them. Not what you would probably do or actually do, in our little world of facts and figures, right and wrong, good and evil, but what you would most like to do, in your heart of hearts, in your deepest desires, and come back here tomorrow and pass judgment on this man, the only man I have ever known who followed his heart to the exact spot it led him."

And with that, Farley Wells sat down and burst into tears.

It was dusk when Farley sat down. The judge recessed court for the day. Trimbul handcuffed me and led me back to my cell.

"I'm fetchin' your dinner," he said, and left me and Farley alone.

Farley sat on my cot and held his head in his hands. He was acting so low and beaten you'd think it was his life at stake.

"He didn't beat me every night," I said.

"What?"

"My daddy. He didn't beat me or Momma every night."

"Oh, well." He waved his hand in the air. "I was tryin' to capture how it felt."

"And I didn't go to bed hungry every night."

"All right."

"Some days we ate pretty good."

"All right, I said. All right!"

"And that part about the strawberry fields—"

"Jesus, Halley, you want me to get up there tomorrow and tell 'em what a big fat bunch of lies I told today?"

I sat beside him. "Will she be there tomorrow?"

"Halley, I don't know."

"Can you find out?"

"No. Yes. I suppose. Halley, I ain't even sure she's in town."

"I need to know if she'll be there."

"Of course. Of course."

"There's one more thing."

"Well, I thought there might be."

I told him what it was. He looked at me, surprised, and acted like he didn't believe me.

"Why would you do something like that?" he asked.

"I might be crazy, but I ain't completely crazy."

He laughed. "All right, but you're an awful trusting soul, Halley Martin."

"I got no choice. If the worst comes."

He nodded. "I'm afraid it's gonna come, Halley. I'm sorry."

I patted him on the back. It seemed funny I was comforting him.

"That's all right," I said. "I'm not afraid."

A man appeared outside my cell that night. I looked up from my cot and there he was. He looked familiar, but I couldn't think of where I'd seen him before. He was alone. I sat up and we looked at each other in the sickly yellow light coming from the naked bulb behind him in the hall.

"Do you know who I am?" he asked.

I didn't say anything.

"My name is Robert Hughes," he said. "You murdered my son."

He took a breath. "You killed my boy, Walter. He was my only boy. I—I just wanted you to know that. He was my son."

He didn't say anything else. He watched me through the bars. I didn't move from my cot. He put on his hat and walked away. I lay back down. I didn't sleep.

The next morning I had breakfast, showered and dressed, and when Farley showed up, Trimbul shackled me and we walked over to the court-house. The little room was packed and buzzing. I looked over the crowd, but I didn't see you.

"Where is she?" I asked. Farley shrugged, and then the jury filed in. The judge read some instructions to them, and then they stood and filed out again. Trimbul took me back to my cell.

Farley said, "It's not too late to make a deal."

"No," I said.

He nodded and said he'd be back directly. He needed a drink. I sat on my cot and pulled the sharpened toothbrush from under the mattress. I slipped it into my sock.

Farley came back an hour later. His mood was better.

"No word yet," he said. "Means at least we gave 'em something to think about."

"I need to know where she is," I said.

"Halley, with all respect, today ain't the day to be worrying where Mavis Howell is."

"Is she here, in Homeland?"

"I think so."

"Lester won't let her come to court."

"A court of law is like a bar, Halley: Respectable ladies don't visit it. You hungry?"

"No."

"I'm starving! Nerves, I guess. I wasn't too bad, was I? I knew I had 'em with that last part. Maybe the tears was a bit much. What do you think?"

"It don't matter now," I said.

He stayed until lunchtime, then left when Trimbul brought me a roast beef sandwich.

"Jury's let out for lunch," Trimbul said.

He stood outside the cell and watched me eat.

"I just want you to know I never told Franks you drew dirty pictures," he said. "I never said they were dirty, just naked pictures, that's all I said."

I nodded. I pushed my plate away and went to the cot and lay down. I threw my arm over my eyes.

"Ain't you gonna brush your teeth?" he asked. I didn't say anything. He took the hint and left. He and Farley were nervous, but I felt all right. I wasn't nervous at all.

Farley came back around three that afternoon. He'd had too much to drink.

"They're hung, they're hung for sure! Jesus, I'd give my left nut to know what the count is. I know we got three on our side at least, including ol' Harvey Bristol, the foreman. You see his face when I was done closing yesterday? I don't know who was crying harder, him or me. I was worried 'bout him at first. He's a goddamned Southern Baptist, sleeps with his wife on one side and the King James Version on the other. I bet he started today with a prayer and a Bible reading. Hopefully the Beatitudes. Hot damn, we got a hung jury for sure ol' Harvey's with us."

"What's a hung jury?" I said, picturing the noose around my neck.

"Means no verdict. Mistrial."

"And I go home?"

"Unless Franks charges you again."

"Which he will."

"Probably. Maybe not. Who knows? He'd have to move the trial to goddamned Miami to get a jury." He laughed. "Maybe I ain't such a bad lawyer after all."

"It ain't over yet," I said.

He stayed with me the rest of the afternoon. It was after six when Trimbul came back with the shackles. The jury had reached a verdict. Farley pulled a comb from his pocket and ran it through my hair. I wondered why a bald man needed a comb. Trimbul locked my wrists together for the walk; he would take the cuffs off right before we stepped into the courtroom. Farley walked ahead of us. Hearing that the verdict had finally come had taken the wind out of his sails some, but he still walked with that funny bounce in his stride, like a overinflated balloon bobbing on a string.

As we came to the courthouse door Sheriff Trimbul leaned over and said, "I know what you're thinking, Halley. And my advice to you is, don't."

"How do you know what I think?" I asked.

"It's what I'd be thinking," he said, and we went inside.

It all happened very fast. The judge came in. The jury came in. The judge asked Harvey Bristol if they'd reached a verdict. Harvey stood up and said they had. He handed a piece of paper to the bailiff, who carried it over to the judge. The judge told me to stand. I rose, and Farley rose with me. His fear hung around him like a fine mist, mixed with the smell of alcohol. I thought of my father. The judge read the verdict and there was no sound at all after he read it, and then Momma cried out behind me, a long wailing cry that felt hard as a slap against my back. Farley deflated, sighing, "Oh, oh," and I was already by him, the toothbrush in my right hand, shoving Farley against the table and leaping across the aisle to where Franks cowered; he had seen me coming but I was on him too fast. I yanked him to his feet and wrapped an arm around his chest and pressed the point of the sharpened handle against his scrawny neck. I pulled him into the open area in front of the judge's bench. Trimbul was coming up the main aisle, his large hand resting on the butt of his gun. The bailiff had drawn his revolver and was pointing it at my head. Trimbul shouted at him, "Put that down!" and the bailiff looked at him with that dumb look of someone who had snapped out of a sound sleep. "Put it down *now*!" Trimbul said. He stopped beside Farley, about six feet from me. The judge growled at the bailiff, "Goddamn it, do what he says." The bailiff lowered his gun.

Trimbul said, "Well, I told you don't and you did anyway."

"I want a car," I said.

"Halley," Farley said. "Halley, she ain't here."

I said to Trimbul, "Then you're going to take me to where she is."

"All right, Halley," he said softly. "And what are you going to do when we get there?"

"I'll worry about that," I said.

"This ain't goin' to work, Halley, you know that," Sheriff Trimbul said. "You know that."

Farley turned and motioned to Momma. She came up the aisle.

"Halley," she said.

"I can't go to jail, Momma," I said.

"They'll shoot you, Halley. These men will shoot you for sure, you don't let that man go."

"Better than prison," I said.

Franks hissed, "For God's sake, will someone please either get him a car or shoot him?"

"You want to see her, Halley?" Farley said. "You do this, and you won't. I guarantee that, Halley. But you let him go and I promise you'll see her. I promise that, Halley."

"You can't promise that," I said.

"I promise," Trimbul said.

"I don't believe you either," I said.

The judge said, "Will you believe me?"

"I want to see her tonight," I said.

"I promise you'll see her tonight."

"You heard him," Franks said. "Now please for the love of God let me go."

I let him go. The bailiff came at me with his gun raised. Trimbul yelled, "No!" The bailiff smashed the gun over the top of my head, and I went down.

I came to in my cell. It was dark. I tried to sit up, and it felt like my head would burst open, as if someone was pounding on my skull from the inside. A voice said, "Shhhhh, lay back down. Rest. Rest." A hand pressed on my shoulder and pushed me gently down. It was Farley. His face looked old and fleshy in the yellow light. Dark circles ringed his eyes.

"What time is it?" I asked.

"Late. Very late." He smiled. "I got some news. Franks ain't pressing charges."

That made me feel a lot better; I had just been found guilty of murder and Franks wasn't pressing charges on the deadly toothbrush.

Farley's smile faded.

"She's not coming," I said.

He looked away. "We tried, Halley. Trimbul drove all the way to Inverness. She's staying there with her cousins. . . ."

"Why ain't she here then?"

"She, um, she sent this."

He pulled a long envelope from his pocket.

"It's sealed. Nobody's read it. I swear that to you, Halley."

I snatched it from his hand and tore it open. Several sheets of stationery fell onto my chest, covered with your large, flowery script. I crushed the paper to my nose, breathing in the smell of you that still lingered on the paper. I shoved the wrinkled paper at Farley.

"Read it," I said.

"I was afraid you'd say that." He fussed with the papers, putting them in order, smoothing them out over his enormous thigh. He placed his reading glasses on his nose and squinted at the first page. He cleared his throat.

"Goddamn it, Farley!"

"All right, here it is." And he read:

" 'Dear Halley, Please forgive me for not coming as you asked. My father has sent me here to Inverness, where I am a virtual prisoner. Even if I wanted to come, I couldn't. I don't think I could bear seeing you, not now. You will think I am weak and cowardly, but seeing you now would be more than I could stand. I fear I am near a nervous breakdown as it is. I spend every day locked in my little room here. I sit in a chair by a window that overlooks the woods, which are lovely this time of year, but the view is anything but lovely to me, not while I think of you in that cell, because of me. My cousin Mary fusses at me. She tells me it's silly to feel this is all my fault. You did nothing wrong, she tells me. You never even talked to the boy (meaning you). How could what he did be your fault?'

" 'I do want you to know I didn't write that note Daddy read to you at the train station. I suppose you already knew that; you knew when you threw Daddy's money into the fire. I knew then nothing Daddy could do would stop you. And I think Daddy knew it too. It was the only time I can recall seeing my daddy frightened. You frighten him, and I must be honest, you frighten me a little too. Oh, this is as strange and tragic as a play! Have you ever read *Romeo and Juliet*? You really must if you haven't. It reminds me of our story. Now we may never know what might have been.' And, um, it's signed, 'Sincerely yours, Mavis.' "

"That's it?"

"Yes."

"There's got to be more."

"I think she was in a hurry—"

"Why's she talking about this, this play? Why didn't she come?"

"I think she says right here, Halley—"

"She still could've come."

"Halley, she's a seventeen-year-old girl. A child, really. You can't expect—"

"I can expect *everything*!" I shouted at him. My head hurt so bad it felt like it was going to fall off my shoulders and roll across the floor.

"And what'd she do?" I murmured. It was hard to think. "What she . . . how'd she sign it?"

" 'Sincerely yours.' "

"Sincerely yours?"

"Yes. Let me check. Yes, 'Sincerely yours.' "

"Shit."

The sentence was twenty years to life. Trimbul and Farley led me back to my cell and I took off that nice suit for the last time.

Momma came by that afternoon and we said good-bye. She brought Jasper with her, and I saw him for the last time, though we didn't know that then. Momma cried and I held her, and I told Jasper he was the man of the family till I came back. I told him to watch after Momma and if Daddy came after her he was to kill him.

"Then get Farley as your lawyer," I said, which made Farley laugh. He laughed too loud and too long. Finally Momma couldn't take it anymore and collapsed into hysterics. Trimbul and Jasper helped her down the hall and out the door, and me and Farley were alone, again.

"You still got the letter?" I asked.

"Yeah, somewhere . . ."

"Hold on to it for me. Some day I'll want it back."

"Sure, Halley." He cleared his throat. "Halley, about that other matter . . ."

"Your fee."

"Oh, no, no. I told you, you pay me if I win. I didn't win. You may have noticed."

"I trust you, Farley."

"No, what I was goin' to say. I got a few ideas about what we can do with it. I know this fella in Texas . . ."

"I told you, I trust you."

He smiled. "That's your problem, Halley Martin. You trust everybody. You truly believe she'll wait for you, don't you?"

"I believe . . ." There weren't enough words for all I believed. "I believe that one day I'll come home."

THREE

Bertram and me stood up.

The front door swung open and Miss Willifred pointed to Miss Nadine on the piano, and she began to play "For He's a Jolly Good Fellow." The door stayed open but nobody came in as everybody sang. They finished the whole song while Miss Mavis looked through the open door, her face wet with the crying, and Sharon-Rose stood with her head down, the blond hair falling straight to one side like a horse's mane. Still nobody had come through the door. Then Daddy stepped inside and turned to the open door, holding out his hand. Momma came up and stood beside him.

Then I heard a clump-clump, and Pastor was in the room, and Miss Willifred did a whirly thing with her finger and Miss Nadine started playing the same song again, and everybody started to sing again, like in a dream when something happens over and over and you can't wake up or make it stop. There was a sharp cry and Daddy stood on his toes and waved his arms, yelling at everybody to hush. I heard a thin, little voice say, "I can't abide it, for the love of God!" And that was the pastor, though he didn't sound like I remembered him sounding. Miss Nadine stopped playing. I couldn't see Pastor, but I could see the back of Miss Mavis's head as she went to him. Everybody took that as a signal, and they moved in on him too. "Don't get too close!" Daddy yelled. "Don't touch him!" And that stopped everybody and quieted them down, and we all just stood around. Nobody knew what to do. Daddy turned to Pastor and said, "Pastor Jeffries, on behalf of the entire community, the community of your church and the community of Homeland, on behalf of all here today who have wept for you and prayed for you and waited for this great day with hope and joy, I bid you welcome."

Now we all knew what to do. We clapped. I was stuck between the window and a couple of old men with that stale old man smell, and I couldn't see a thing. I heard Miss Willifred talking next.

"I second that wholeheartedly, Pastor. And if I may, I think we should give a prayer of thanksgiving for your safe return. If you will do the honors, Pastor."

Everybody bowed their heads. There was a long piece of quiet, broken by the regular shuffling and coughing and clearing throats you get when a bunch of people are told to be quiet.

I heard Pastor's thin voice say: "Thanks, God." And then he didn't say anything else. We all kept our heads down, waiting for the rest. Pastor said, "That's it. I'm done. Now lift up your damn heads and clear a place for me to sit. I'm tired."

Everybody lifted their damn heads and looked at each other. You don't expect to hear your pastor talk like that.

"Come on, now, you heard the pastor," Daddy called out. "He's tired. He needs to rest."

We ate with paper plates balanced on our knees, sitting by the window, and the afternoon sun shining through the window was hot on my neck. Daddy had helped Pastor to the sofa, across the room from us, but I couldn't get more than a peek or two at him, there were so many people wandering between us and going up to Pastor to say hello. Now that he was here I wasn't so afraid, which was funny; I kind of wanted to get a better look at him. As we ate, the rains came and pounded on the roof, and the thunder smashed over our heads, and that, with all the people talking and laughing and children shrieking and chasing each other around the big table, made the room so loud my head started hurting. I told Bertram my head hurt and Bertram said, "So does mine," and I hung my head because he was talking about the shoe I'd thrown at him.

"Look at Sharon-Rose, Shiny. Just look at that."

She was sitting on the piano stool with a huge plate of food beside her, bending her body toward the plate and shoveling fast.

"Cut her and she'd bleed gravy," Bertram said.

We set our plates down and I followed Bertram into the kitchen. It was hot in there from the oven and the bodies of all the big old ladies moving about with the food. We ducked and dodged around their swishing aprons and flapping hands. I never knew an old lady who didn't flap her hand when she talked. But of course I didn't know a lot of old ladies—just Granma and some of the ladies from church, like Miss Willifred, but they were all hand-flappers. We went out the kitchen door to the side yard.

The rains had moved on. They had cooled the earth and even the trees looked relieved. We weaved between the rain-dotted cars and sat on the curb. Across the field on the other side of the road the sun was beginning to set, growing fat and red and lowering into the raised arms of the cypresses. It was the best part of the day, in the best part of the year. Bertram found a stick and commenced to drawing in the mud of the dirt road. I plucked a blade of grass and crushed it in my fingers, breathing in the smell. I loved the smell of crushed grass. We didn't talk. If Momma caught us outside in our good clothes we'd catch it for sure, but neither of us cared. Our bellies were full and the air was fresh and cool and the sun shone upon us in the last golden, slanting rays of a summer day. Halley Martin himself could have come down the road that minute and we would have laughed and thumbed our noses at him.

"Hey!" a voice behind us shouted. "Hey, where are you? You Parker boys, where are you?"

It was Sharon-Rose. I started to stand up, but Bertram grabbed my arm and pulled me down. She came around the bunch of cars and saw us.

"There you are!" she shouted.

She flopped down beside me and fell back onto the grass. She had changed out of her white dress into a T-shirt and shorts. Her feet were bare, her toenails bright red. "I spilled peach cobbler on my dress," she said. When she fell back her shirt pulled up and I could see her bare tummy. She had a big belly button, about the size of a grape. Not a green grape, but one of those big black grapes with the hard seed in the center. I looked away.

"God, I'm full!" She rolled onto her side and rested her head on her hand. She was giving me one of those long Sharon-Rose stares that made me feel like I didn't have any clothes on.

"Shiny," she said. "Shiny, what kind of name is that, Shiny? Why they call you Shiny, anyway?"

I didn't say anything.

"Shiny. I suppose you're just pure as sunshine, is that it? You pure as sunshine?"

"Shut up, Sharon-Rose," Bertram said.

"Shut up yourself. I think I'm going to puke."

She rolled onto her back again and put her hands behind her head. Her shirt pulled up again and her skin shone golden in the dying light.

"I'm bored," she said. "Bored, bored, bored. Don't you two boys ever *do* anything? I swear, you're the two most boringest boys I ever saw. Hey, hey, I know what we could do. You know what we could do? We could have a say-ounce. You want to have a say-ounce, Shiny?"

"What's a say-ounce?" I said.

"It's where you sit in a circle and chant for the dead to come out."

"I don't want to chant for the dead to come out."

"You can talk to dead people. Like your ancestors and such. Don't you want to talk to your ancestors, Shiny?"

"I don't think I got any," I said.

"Everybody has ancestors, stupid."

Bertram said, "Don't you think you ought to be inside the house, Sharon-Rose, with your daddy?"

"My daddy don't care no more about me than the man on the moon," she said. "You know what he said to me in there? He said, 'Stand away from me, my skin's on fire.' "

One time when I was four I touched the hot stove and burned my hand. I remembered how hot my skin felt, and if I touched that burned spot it would feel like a hot match pressing down. I wondered if Pastor felt that way too, only over his whole body, not just his hand.

She stood up. "Well, I'm not just gonna lay around like some stupid boy. I'm gonna make me a fire and have a say-ounce."

She marched across the road to the barbed-wire fence separating Mr. Newton's field from the road. I looked at Bertram. He was stabbing the end of his stick into the mud.

"Bertram, what's she doin'?"

"Gonna make a fire and have a say-ounce; don't you listen?"

He stood up and threw the stick away. "Come on, Shiny."

He started across the road. I stood up and watched him head for the barbed-wire fence. Sharon-Rose was already through, running down the long slope of the cow pasture toward the cypress-stand.

"But Bertram," I called, "we're wearing our good clothes."

He went through the fence and followed Sharon-Rose into the field. I looked back at the house. They had turned on the lights now that the sun was leaving, and the lights inside looked so warm. I crossed the road and ducked between the strands. A barb caught on my sleeve and I heard the material tear. I was in for it now. I ran after Bertram, my feet making little squishy noises in the wet ground.

"What are you doing, Bertram?"

"I'm following Sharon-Rose."

"Why?"

"'Cause she's hunting ghosts and what she's gonna find is snakes. Rain brings 'em out, you know that, Shiny."

He didn't say any more and I didn't ask any more. She had reached the edge of the cypress trees and was bent over, her hands on her knees, gasping for breath.

"You boys are slow," she said.

"Sharon-Rose," Bertram said, "you ever been in this swamp?"

"Maybe I have."

"Ain't no ghosts here, Sharon-Rose. Just snakes and skeeters and maybe an alligator or two."

"You're scared," she sneered at him. "Just like your little brother. I'm a *girl,* and I'm not scared."

And to prove it, she raced into the trees. Bertram looked at me, his lip curling, then went in after her. I took one last look at my house. I knew what would come when me and Bertram came home with our good clothes covered in mud, and me with my sleeve ripped. It was too late now, though. I wasn't going to leave Bertram in a cypress swamp alone with Sharon-Rose Jeffries. I followed them into the trees.

Mr. Newton's cows had worn paths through the swamp, but the gnarled cypress knees poked through the mud of the paths here and there. They were the same brown color as the mud and hard to see in the near dark. Sharon-Rose didn't see a lot of them, and by the time we caught up to her her white shorts were covered in mud and little clumps of it hung in her long blond hair. She smiled as me and Bertram came up; there was mud on her teeth too. She must have gone down face first, smiling.

"It's so still in here!" she yelled, breaking the stillness. "Listen how still it is!"

Bertram gave a loud "whoop-whoop!" and clapped his hands a few times. She asked him why he was whoop-whooping, and he told her it scared the snakes away. The wet cypress knees shone at the top of their knobs and the wet earth clung to our heels. There was a humming, a throbbing kind of sound, all around me. I heard it every time I came into the swamp. One time I asked Bertram what it was and he said he couldn't hear it and there must be something wrong in my head. I heard it now, behind the thrumming of the frogs and the squishing of the mud and the opening chorus of the cicadas' song.

We were following Bertram now. He had found another big stick and was smacking it against the slender bodies of the cypresses on either side of the path. We were heading straight for the fort. I wondered why. It was our fort, and I didn't think he'd want Sharon-Rose to know where it was. She walked just ahead of me, her blond hair swinging.

We came into the clearing where the fort was. It was a good fort. We'd been working on it all summer. It stood twice as tall as me. We had stacked the dead cypress wood and braced it around with rocks. When me and Sharon-Rose got there Bertram was sitting near the entrance, cross-legged like an Indian, holding the stick in front of him. Guarding the fort.

"This is a great spot for a say-ounce!" she said. "We can make the fire right over there," she pointed at a spot on the far end of the clearing. I went and sat beside Bertram. We watched her piling fallen branches into her arms. Bertram made a growling noise deep in his throat.

"That wood's too damp to burn, Sharon-Rose," he called at her.

"It'll burn," she said.

She dumped the wood onto the ground and pulled a box of kitchen matches from her pocket. Bertram poked me and nodded toward Sharon-Rose.

"Hey, Sharon-Rose, your daddy know you play with matches?"

She ignored him, struck the match, and dropped it on the pile of wood. She jumped back like she expected it to explode. The match just hissed and went out. She lit another one and held it against the wood this time. The match burned down to her fingers. She yelled and flung the match away. She walked over to us, sucking on her finger. She flopped beside me. She was always flopping beside me. I scooted a little closer to Bertram.

She sat with her legs pulled to her chest. She rested her chin on her knees and looked glumly at the stack of wood.

"Oh, well," Bertram said.

"The moon's up," she said. Then she grabbed my arm and pointed at the sky.

"See! There it is, Shiny! There it is! You know what that star is, right beside the moon there?"

"No."

"That ain't a star at all," she said.

"It ain't?" I didn't know it was a trick question.

"That's Venus," she said. "It's called the Evening Star, but it ain't a star at all. It's a planet. I know all about the stars and the planets and all. I got this big book my daddy gave me."

"You used to have a big book," Bertram said.

She ignored him. "So anything you want to know about the stars or the planets or the whole wide universe for that matter you just ask me, Shiny. Take Venus, now, they call it the Evening Star, but it isn't, it's a planet. It swings 'round and 'round the shiny sun, because it loves it so."

"That's stupid, Sharon-Rose," Bertram said. "It ain't love; it's gravity."

"Gravity's just another word for love."

"Yeah-a, and your big head is another word for dog shit."

"I'm tellin' you said a dirty word."

"Go ahead. Your own daddy says 'em."

"My daddy's a preacher; he's allowed."

"I always thought it was a star," I said, hoping to stop a big fight.

"You just ask me anything you want, Shiny," she said. "I know all there is to know."

"Sharon-Rose, nobody knows all there is to know," Bertram said.

"I do so, and I'll tell you how. You want to know how?"

He sighed. "Sure. Tell me how."

"It's because I got a bigger than normal brainpan." She looked at me. "Ask me why I got a bigger than normal brainpan."

"Go on, Shiny," Bertram said. "Ask her."

I asked her why she had a bigger than normal brainpan.

"It's because of my tumor. I got a tumor the size of a grapefruit growing on my brain. They discovered it while my daddy was at the hospital. They x-rayed my brain and found it."

"Found your brain?" Bertram asked.

"It started pretty small," she said. "First it was the size of a raisin, then the size of a peach, and now—"

"And now you can make a nice fruit salad?" Bertram said.

"That's just like you, Bertram Parker," she said. "Laughin' at tragedy."

"You are a tragedy, Sharon-Rose," he said. He stood up and walked over to the pile of sticks and started kicking it apart.

"I'm gonna die," she told me. "I don't got much longer to live. And all those people feelin' so sorry for my daddy and throwin' him a party and everything, and here I am dying and nobody knows."

"Ain't they gonna operate or something?" I asked.

"Can't. Rip half my brain out if they do. I'm a goner, Shiny."

She scooted closer to me so her warm arm was pressing against mine, and she said, "You want to feel of it? Huh? You want to feel my tumor?"

"Go on, Shiny," Bertram yelled from the sticks. "Feel her tumor."

"Here," she said. "Put your hand here."

She took my hand and pressed it against her skull, right where the hard part of her head met her neck.

"You feel it?"

"I guess so."

"Feels big, don't it?"

"I guess so." I pulled my hand away.

She leaned forward and kissed me on the cheek. It happened so fast I didn't have time to get out of the way. And Sharon-Rose looked as surprised as I felt. The kiss was wet and hot on my cheek. I wiped it off with my sleeve. Sharon-Rose whispered, "Tell you another secret. I know who set our house on fire."

"We got to go," Bertram said, coming back to us. We both stood up like he'd caught us at something. He saw it on my face, because he said, "What?"

"Nothing," I said.

"Nothing," Sharon-Rose said.

"Tell him you don't have a tumor, Sharon-Rose."

"I will not."

"Tell him."

"Because I do."

"Tell him or I'll tell your momma about your lies."

"My momma's got lies of her own to worry about."

"Lies like what?"

"Never you mind. Ain't none of your business. I don't like you. I never liked you."

"Stop it; you're going to make me cry."

"You don't know half what I know. You don't know what it's like to live a tragedy, you in your big ol' house and little brother all shining around."

"Maybe you do got a tumor on your brain," Bertram said. "'Cause you don't make no sense."

He marched away. He was going to leave us. I jumped up and followed him.

"You will wait for me!" she cried. "You will wait for me because I am a *girl*."

"Bertram," I said as we made our way down the dark path. Away from the clearing the moonlight didn't have much of a chance to reach the wet ground. The cypresses crowded around us, wrapping their thin arms around each other's shoulders, bending and whispering in the wind. "Bertram," I said, "we can't leave her. She'll get lost in the dark and we'll never find her."

"Good."

"Bertram, we're in enough trouble as it is! Look at our clothes. Bertram, I ripped my sleeve, we can't leave her out here too."

"Oh, for the love of Jesus!" he shouted. He turned around and popped me in the mouth. It wasn't hard enough to break the skin, but it was hard enough to bring tears to my eyes. He had never hit me in the face before. He always picked my stomach or my arm. He realized what he'd done and brought his face close to mine.

"Listen to me, Shiny," he whispered. "And you listen good. Stay away from that girl. Stay far away from her, and from her weirdo momma and especially from her crazy daddy. That whole family's looney, and some-thin' terrible's gonna happen from them stayin' with us—"

"Hey, you left me," Sharon-Rose said from behind me. Bertram turned quick and started back up the path. Right behind me now, Sharon-Rose said, "I'm scared, Shiny. Hold my hand."

She grabbed my hand and squeezed it so tight it felt like she was going to pop the bones right out of the skin. The path was too narrow to walk side by side, so she walked a little behind me, hitting my heel every now and then with her shoe. I thought we'd never get out of that swamp, but finally the trees fell away and we were in the field, the stars blue-bright over us and the moon high and full and turning the grass of the field a pale bluish green.

"Let's run, Shiny!" Sharon-Rose yelled, and she pulled me along, past Bertram and up the slope toward the dirt road. She was a head taller than me and had thicker and stronger legs. My dress shoes had slippery bot-toms, and I slid and skipped along the wet grass, hollering at her to slow down, sure I was going to fall flat on my face, probably in a cow patty, and that would mean for sure I'd take my first trip to the toolshed.

I could see my house at the top of the slope, through the barbed-wire fence, across the road, and the lights were shining inside and voices floated from the lawn, and I could hear laughter and somebody was singing, and in the thick dark the house lights shone bright and warm.

No one took us to the toolshed. Momma told us to change and sent us straight to our room, and she said she would be Talking To Us Later.

After we changed and came out again the old ladies were packing up the food. I didn't see Pastor or Miss Mavis or Sharon-Rose, just the old ladies and a couple of ladies Momma's age helping in the kitchen. We found Daddy on the porch swing talking to Mr. Fredericks. Their heads were close together and Mr. Fredericks's face was redder than usual, and usually it was pretty red. His fat, hairy eyebrows were drawn together. They stopped talking when we came out. Mr. Fredericks said we were growing like weeds and Daddy said we were, and twice as wild. I didn't feel wild. I felt tired right down to my toenails. I squeezed beside Daddy and he put his arm behind me and patted my shoulder with his big hand. Bertram sat on the steps and looked out into the dark. He slapped at a mosquito on his neck. We stayed out there until the old ladies were done and coming onto the porch chattering and flapping their hands and Momma behind them with a stack of dishes covered with foil. Mr. Fredericks got up and chased Miss Willifred down the drive to her car, and they stood there for a minute. It looked like they were fighting about something.

"What's the matter, Daddy?" I asked.

"We're just worried about the pastor," he said. "Some folks don't think he should preach tomorrow."

"Why, Daddy?"

"Oh, they're just worried about him, that's all."

The old ladies were calling their good-byes to each other. Momma stood beside Bertram at the top step and waved and said, "See ya'll tomorrow!" And the night air rumbled with the sound of all those old lady cars starting. Old ladies' cars are louder than regular cars, I don't know why. Momma came and sat beside Daddy, and he put his other arm around her. She wiped her forehead with the back of her hand and said, "I never want to go through that again."

Daddy told her it all went fine, and Momma said, "He is going to preach tomorrow, isn't he?"

"I think so," he said. "He says he will."

She nodded. Her lips got thin. It wasn't good when her lips got thin.

"What's the matter with him preachin'?" Bertram asked. "He's a preacher, ain't he?"

"Pastor is not fully recovered from his ordeal," Momma said.

"He looks like a turtle," Bertram said.

"Bertram Parker!"

"Well, he does. And gone crazy as a loon."

"Hush that talk."

"Yes," Daddy said, so Bertram hushed. You hushed when Daddy said so.

"You both need to understand something," Momma said. "While Pastor Ned is staying with us he may say certain things that will, that might . . . upset you. Or confuse you. He will not be like the old Pastor Ned you knew. This terrible accident has had an effect on his mind. He is heavily medicated and I daresay still in a great deal of pain. That kind of pain can have a voice of its own. You need to understand that sometimes it isn't the pastor talking, but the pain—or the medicine. Be polite to him, but don't ask him any questions. Don't go out of your way to talk to him, but don't run from him either. If looking at him makes you uncomfortable, look over his shoulder, right over his shoulder; he won't mind. And if he says anything that upsets you particularly, find me or your father and we'll talk to you about it. And especially, especially cease teasing Sharon-Rose about him."

"She's got a tumor," I said.

Daddy said, "She's got a what?"

"A tumor. In her brainpan."

Daddy said, "How—how do you know that?"

"She told us. Didn't she, Bertram?"

He didn't say anything.

"She didn't say it was a secret," I said.

"That is one troubled little girl," Daddy said.

"Who's taking them next?" Bertram asked.

"What?" Momma said.

"Who's taking them next? We ain't keepin' them the whole time while they're building the house, are we?"

"We shall keep them as long as necessary," Momma said. "It is our duty."

No one said anything after that. A pair of headlights came down the road and a car turned into our drive. The car had lights on top of it. The door opened and Sheriff Trimbul got out.

Momma stood up. "Bertram, you and Robert Lee go in now and wash up for bed."

"But Momma—"

"Go on now."

"Evenin'," Sheriff Trimbul said.

"Sheriff," Daddy said.

Daddy eased me off the swing and patted my butt. "We'll be in directly," he said, and Bertram grabbed my hand. I looked over my shoulder as we went inside. Sheriff Trimbul was standing on the steps, one foot up on the porch. Momma and Daddy were sitting so close together you couldn't have slid a piece of paper between them.

"Hurry," Bertram whispered. The screen door slammed behind us. He ducked down and dived under the window, and I scooted after him. We crouched beneath the open window that faced the porch swing. Bertram put a finger to his lips, and we listened.

"I would've come sooner," Sheriff Trimbul was saying.

"That's all right, Sheriff," Daddy said. "We understand."

"How's Ned?"

Momma said something I couldn't hear, then Daddy said, "Fragile."

"He plannin' to preach tomorrow?"

"Yes," Momma said.

"I hear he's been sayin' some . . . strange things."

Daddy said, "He's still in shock."

"And great pain," Momma said. "Will you be there tomorrow?"

I didn't hear anything else till Daddy said, "Good."

"Been out to the old Howell place," Sheriff Trimbul said.

"Did you talk to him?" Daddy said.

"Oh, yes."

"And?" Daddy asked. There was a long silence after that.

"Hard to tell with Halley," Sheriff Trimbul said. "He did say he ain't been to church in twenty-five years and he had no intention of starting now."

Daddy laughed. His laugh stopped all at once, so Momma must have given him a look.

I missed the first part of what he said, but Daddy said, "Leave him in peace."

"Oh," Sheriff Trimbul said, "I expect folks'll get tired of it, after a spell."

"Did you see—" Momma said, and I couldn't hear the rest.

"See what, Bertram?" I whispered, and he waved his hand at me. He was squatting just below the window, his head turned sideways as he tried to get his ear close to the screen.

"Yes, I saw them," Sheriff Trimbul said. Then after a quiet, he said, "Terrible."

"Yes," Daddy said, "that's what I heard."

"He is not the same," Sheriff Trimbul said.

"Neither's Pastor," Momma said.

"Neither are any of us," Daddy said.

We raced to the kitchen as they called good night to the Sheriff. The countertops were stacked to the cabinets with dirty dishes and cups and pots and pans and casserole dishes.

"Bertram, why'd we come here?"

"Get a drink," he snapped at me, and shoved a big glass of water at me. I was drinking it quick, I don't know why, but it seemed to make Bertram breathe easier, when Momma and Daddy came in.

"You boys should be in bed," Momma said.

"I know, Momma," Bertram said. "But Shiny said he was thirsty."

Momma said, "Lord, look at this kitchen, and I still have to sew Robert Lee's jacket."

"I'll help," Daddy said, and Momma laughed.

She took us to bed and we said our prayers. She kissed my forehead and kissed Bertram's forehead.

"Momma," I said. "I'm scared."

"Now why should you be scared?"

"I don't know," I said, thinking of a bright red, skinned turtle with no eyelids.

She left our door open a crack and the hall light on. The leaf-shadows came out and danced over my head, and the crickets sang.

"Bertram, you awake?"

"Yeah-a."

"They were talkin' about Halley Martin."

"Yeah-a."

"He's gonna kill Pastor Ned for marryin' Miss Mavis, ain't he?"

"How the hell should I know?"

A door closed in the hallway and I heard Sharon-Rose whining.

"But, Momma . . ."

"Stop butting me, Sharon-Rose," Miss Mavis said. "I am weary to my bones tonight."

"I want to sleep with you . . ."

"There's no room, I told you . . ."

"I could sleep on the floor."

I heard the bathroom door close and the water come on. After a minute the door opened and I heard Miss Mavis say, "Now scrub every single inch, Sharon-Rose."

"That'll take a while," Bertram said. He yawned. The sewing room door closed and the house hummed with the sound of running water. It was a good sound, almost as good as rain on the roof when you're just floating off to sleep. The leaf-shadows ducked and bobbed, and presently Bertram was snoring, and between the snoring and the chirping and the dancing and the water I must have drifted off too, but it couldn't have been for long. When my eyes came open the chirping and the snoring was still there, but not the sound of water. I felt that hard pressure in my stomach, and I hopped out of bed looking forward to that nice hollowed-out feeling you get slipping back under the covers after you stand at the pot, shivering as you pee.

I went down the hall and pushed open the bathroom door. A wave of heat and steam hit me in the face, and I blinked for a second, still sleepy and wondering where all the fog had come from.

And there she was, there was Sharon-Rose, a pink shape in the swirling steam, half out of the tub, one hand on the shower curtain and the other by her side, holding a towel, and the steam swam around her in the yellow room, and the steam clung to the mirror beside me, and one big leg was out of the tub and one big leg was inside, and Sharon-Rose Jeffries was naked. She didn't have any clothes on, and her body was wet and pink from the shower and her long blond hair dark and wet and hanging over one shoulder like a thick rope, and drops of water hung on her forehead and the soft blond hair of her arms, and she was naked. She had no clothes on at all, and she looked at me, and I looked at her, and neither one of us said anything. She just stood where she was and I stood where I was and her mouth came open a little and I could see the pink tip of her tongue. I turned and ran. I turned completely around and ran straight into the wall. I fell back on my butt, I got up, and I ran to my room. Sharon-Rose called after me softly, "Shi—," but I slammed the door and didn't hear the "nee."

Bertram shot up and yelled, "What!" as I jumped three feet onto the mattress and yanked the covers over my head.

"What is it?" he said.

"Nothin'," I said.

"What's the matter with you?"

"Nothin'," I said. My head pounded where it had hit the wall. So God had gotten me back for hitting Bertram with a shoe. Momma always said God pays you back for things like that.

"You're so weird," Bertram said, and he began to snore. I waited for a knock on the door. But a knock never came.

It was funny, but now I didn't need to pee at all.

FOUR

A bus took me to Starke. I was the sole passenger. I never saw the driver again after that day, but his name was Albert Flynn and he didn't speak more than three words to me and if I passed him on the street today I wouldn't recognize him, but I'll always remember his name.

I went straight from the bus to the barbershop, where my head was shaved down to the scalp. Then to the showers, where two trusties scrubbed me down and then dumped a sack full of lye over me to kill any vermin I might have carried in with me. They watched me pull on my new clothes: gray prison-issue with my new name stenciled on the breast: 111959. My third name so far. Then I was taken to the warden's office.

His name was MacAffee. He was tall and barrel-chested and looked younger than his forty-some years. He had served in the cavalry in the Great War; there were pictures of him in France on the office walls. There were also pictures of him on horseback; he was an avid horseman. Two years before I came he had the inmates build a stable behind the prison; he kept his horse there, a mare named Marie. It was considered the greatest measure of his trust to be assigned to clean that stable and walk that horse, which was one of the dumbest animals I ever saw. He thought the world of that horse, though, and spoke of it more often and with more affection than he did his wife. The window behind his desk overlooked the exercise yard. On this late afternoon in the summer of 1940, the light painted the bare earth the color of gold. And Warden MacAffee with his squared shoulders and slightly upturned nose was Midas shining in his golden kingdom.

He was sitting behind his desk when I was led in, and said nothing as we were left alone. My hands were free. I could have leaped over that desk and had him by the throat in two seconds, but he either hadn't thought of that, which I doubted, or the possibility was so remote he knew he had nothing to fear. He didn't ask me to sit, so I didn't. He was absorbed in a stack of papers, his thick, sandy-brown eyebrows knotted together in concentration.

"And so here you are," he said without looking up. He squared the stack of papers carefully, his thick fingers surprisingly nimble.

"Do you know what this is?"

I shook my head. I didn't.

"This is the transcript of your trial. Someone suggested I read it, so I have."

He stood up and came around the desk. He folded his large arms across his chest and looked hard at me.

"Do you know who I am?" he asked.

"Well, I s'pose you're the warden."

"You suppose correctly. My name is MacAffee. I would like to see your hands."

I held out my hands. He reached forward suddenly and grabbed me by the wrists, yanking me toward him. He turned my hands over, looking at the palms, then over again, examining the back of my hands.

"Deep calluses," he said. "You have been working since you were nine."

"Seven and a half," I said. "Farley got that part wrong."

He nodded. "And the part about the drawings? The sketches? Is that wrong?"

"No."

He nodded. "Why?"

"Why?"

"Why do you draw? Why would a man like you draw anything?"

"It keeps me in my head."

"Explain."

"I can't."

He nodded again. He had held my hands so long now I was half expecting him to lead me in a square dance.

"I am an admirer of art," he said, as if that was the most natural thing for the warden of the largest prison in the state to say. "I particularly enjoy the Impressionists."

"The what?"

He shook his head and smiled."I would like to see some of your work."

"I don't got any with me."

"The transcript references some sketches of that girl. Her name . . ."

"Mavis."

"Yes. Yes, Mavis." He had a distracted air about him, as if his mind, like mine, tended to wander on him. "That's it. Those sketches—"

"The prosecutor took them from me."

"Tell your attorney to petition for them. They'll return them."

"All right." He was still holding my hands, and I was beginning to wonder if maybe he was a little funny that way. "Can you let go of my hands now?"

"Extraordinary," he said softly, mostly to himself. He let go and leaned back against the desk, folding his arms again over his chest.

"I'd like to see a sample of your work," he said. "Out of curiosity. Do you mind?"

I shook my head.

"I can't allow writing implements in the cells, for obvious reasons. You sketch by pencil, correct?"

I nodded.

"I might be able to arrange for a soft charcoal nib, something suitable for sketch work, but not very functional as anything else."

"I would appreciate that, Warden, but—"

"But you don't understand why I would extend this small kindness."

"I'm grateful."

"Because it moves beyond cruelty to deny an artist his art. And I am not cruel, despite what you might hear of me out there."

"Yes, sir."

"I am a fair man."

"Yes, sir."

"Only understand, I don't care if you are the next Van Gogh, here you are a ruthless, cold-blooded killer without an ounce of humanity in you. And you shall be treated accordingly."

I was taken from his office, shackled, and led from the administration building along a gravel path to Cell Block C, where I would spend the next twenty years of my life. The rocks crunched under our feet and the sound seemed very loud in the early-evening stillness. I looked to my left and saw the tower rising out of the bare earth. A watchman stood on the rampart, a rifle resting in the crook of his arm. The setting sun glinted off his dark glasses as he turned his head to watch us pass. We stopped outside the door to the Block while the guard searched for the right key. There was no sound at all. I looked straight up. The moon had risen, the Evening Star shining beside it. It would be twenty years before I would see a star again.

Darkness came early inside the Block. The cell windows were too small and narrow to let in much light; something deep in us equates light with freedom, and we were not free here. Spaced evenly along the ceiling were bulbs protected by wire cages, and their glow filled the Block with that same sickly yellow light I had come to know during my stay in the Homeland County jail. In here hung the stale pall of human sweat and urine. As we passed the cells, the chains between my ankles clinking on the concrete floor, men pressed their faces against the bars, like figures in a dream, silent and watching. I looked straight ahead and let the guard lead me, his hand on my elbow. We stopped outside the last cell in the Block. He unlocked the cell door, then my shackles, and I stepped inside. He slid the door closed.

In the shadows at the back of the cell a large shape stirred and came forward: my cell-mate. I spun around and yelled after the guard, my voice bouncing off the walls.

"Hey!" I shouted. "Hey, guard!"

He came back to the cell.

"What?"

"I don't think this is the right cell."

"You're in the right cell."

"But this man," I jerked my head toward the shadow behind me. "You know what he is."

"Yeah. He's your bunk-mate."

"No. See, somebody's made a mistake. You got to let the warden know somebody's made a big mistake." I lowered my voice. "He ain't white."

He made a big show of looking over my shoulder.

"Well, boy-howdy, I think you're right! That man is black as a Nubian prince. Hey, you know, maybe he *is* a Nubian prince. Maybe you oughtta get on your knees and beg for his favor." He laughed. "Have a good night. Night, Preacher," he called over my shoulder.

He walked away. I shouted after him, "You can't do this! Hey, you listening to me? Hey, goddamn it, you can't leave me in here like this!"

Someone hooted in the Block, and soon the air shook with shouts and laughter and tin cups dragged across the bars. Behind me the dark shadow laughed softly.

"That's all right, child. We all one color in here."

"I want to talk to the warden! You hear me!?" I screamed as loud as I could against the din. "I still got rights! I still got some rights, goddamn you!"

I waited for the guard to come back, but he didn't. I had managed to hold on to myself up to now. But they had put me in an eight-by-twelve box with a black man, and to me right then that seemed the cruelest punishment of all. I was poor and I was ignorant, a piece of white trash, your daddy called me, but at least I was white. I sank into the bottom bunk and put my head in my hands.

He waited till the noise died down, then he said, "My name is Isaiah. Isaiah Hughes. But everybody calls me Preacher. Though I ain't really a preacher no more. You Halley Martin. They tol' me you was comin'. That the one you want? The bottom? I ain't particular about it."

"Shut up," I said. "Don't talk to me."

"It ain't easy the first night. The two worse nights are the first night and the last night—"

"Shut up!"

"All right."

He moved back into the shadows. A wooden chair creaked. He began to hum. I didn't recognize the tune, but it sounded religious. After a while I looked back there and saw him holding a guitar across his lap. His right hand moved, but no sound came out. It took me a minute to realize the guitar had no strings.

There's no such thing as lights-out in Starke. The lights stayed on, day and night. The lights inside the cells were turned off at midnight; the hall lights were never put out. In here, it's always twilight. I laid on my bunk that first night and thought of my spot in the cypresses, where I slept when Daddy was on one of his rampages. I slept there the night before I killed Walter. It felt that first night as if I had been hurtling through space at a terrific speed and had suddenly stopped, in this bunk, in this cell, in this prison, in this place I didn't know existed a month before. I had stopped here, in a place of everlasting twilight, stopped with enough force to crush me. It was never completely quiet on the Block; men cried out or moaned in their sleep. Some never seemed to sleep, but muttered or sang or whispered to one another in hoarse, dis-embodied voices until the first light eked through the east windows. I had spent a good deal of my time alone while I was in the world; now I would never be alone: I would be surrounded by people every hour of every day, for the remainder of my sentence.

I was here *for life.* That was where it hit me, where it came to rest in me or I in it, in that bunk on that first night. *Life.* For the first time since Elias came to me, I doubted everything would be all right.

The Block became still as my sobs grew louder. I had fallen into a bottomless sea, and it flowed from my eyes, inexhaustible. I would cry till there was nothing liquid left in me; I would cry until I emptied even the blood from my bones. The light from the kerosene lamps had flickered in Walter's eyes and danced the length of his dark lashes, and the world was his eyes; the world was his eyes, as he looked at me and through me. The world was his eyes. He fell onto me and I cradled him in my arms, his head on my shoulder. Do you see me, Walter? Do you see me now? Lying on that bunk I wailed as if my soul was tearing itself out of my body. All those months spying on you in the rose garden I thought I wanted to die, that I was going to die from the *pull,* the longing for you. I told Lester I wanted to die, and when I sank my knife into Walter that night, I think I was really sinking it into me, and we embraced afterward: intimates, companions.

The bunk above me creaked, and a large hand pressed against my shoulder. I grabbed his fingers and squeezed with all the strength I had. Preacher cried out and I flung his hand away.

"Don't touch me," I gasped. "Don't you ever touch me again."

"It's all right now," Preacher said. "It's gonna be all right."

Which was your message to me, through Elias. It wasn't a good sign: Every time somebody said that, it got worse.

That night in a dream you came to me. You wore a white dress. Your arms were bare. You were laughing. You told me you had found it, and you handed me a long cardboard box. It's for you, you said, for you. Open it! I tore off the lid and saw my hunting knife inside. You ripped the front of your dress to the hemline; it fell open like a robe, and you were naked underneath. You pressed the knife into my hand and closed my fist around it. Please, you whispered; you pressed your moist lips against my ear and whispered, *Please.* And you pulled my arm forward until the knife touched your belly, slick with sweat. The tip punctured your perfect skin. No, I said. No. And you said, *Deeper.* Pulling on my arm. *Deeper.*

The next morning we were marched into the yard for the morning head count. It was warm and bright in the shadeless yard, and we stood blinking in the sun. We were counted and our numbers were checked off, then we received our assignments for the week. I got laundry detail, which, I would soon learn, was the worst duty to have, even worse than the machine shop or the field. Except for lunch and the two-hour break in the afternoon, you spent the day in a windowless room over vats of steaming water, stirring heavy denim with a wooden paddle until it felt as if your shoulders would fall from their sockets. That first week I didn't mind it so much. There's a seductiveness to mindless drudgery; for hours my thoughts would dull as I turned the paddle in the hot water. When the trusty gave the signal, I would plunge my hands into the steaming water, up to my elbows, and pull out the clothes. I'd wring them and hang them on one of the lines that ran the length of the room. The floor was concrete and very slick from the dripping water, and I fell five or six times that first week, until I learned how to slide along the floor kind of flat-footed, which was called the "washerwoman walk." By the end of the week the skin on my hands was red and cracking along the lines of my palms from the hot water and the lye.

The warden was true to his word. When I got back to my cell that first day there was a drawing pad and a flat piece of charcoal lying on my bunk. Preacher eyed them but kept his mouth shut. He sat in his chair in the back of the cell and read his Bible. It was old and ragged and falling apart, but he cradled the book in his big hands, holding it like it was a newborn baby. His lips moved as he read. Sometimes he would stop, lean back his head, and close his eyes. I guessed he was praying. I sat cross-legged on my bunk, and drew. Sometimes I could feel his eyes on me and I looked up, but I couldn't catch him watching me.

I drew your face. I was afraid to draw anything else: They might use it as an excuse to take the pad away. I soon forgot my aching shoulders, the stinging of my eyes from the soap, the chafed skin on my hands. I watched your hair fall off the edge of the page, and I was free.

At lights-out I slipped the pad under the mattress and tucked the nib between the mattress and the wall. Preacher crawled into the bunk above me. Presently he began to talk, but I couldn't make out what he was saying. He wasn't talking to me.

"Hey," I said, "I'm trying to sleep."

"All right," he said, and kept on with the soft chatter.

"Shut up," I said.

"I'm talking," he said.

"That's why I told you to shut up!"

"I will, directly."

"Who the hell you talking to, anyway?"

"Jesus."

"You got to talk to him so loud?"

"You should try it."

"I ain't got nothin' to say to him."

"Maybe he got somethin' to say to you."

"Look, boy, I don't need no sermon from you."

"You just a poor ignorant cracker, so I don't take offense at you."

"Well, thank you very much, your fucking highness! I take a lot of goddamned offense at *you*."

"Don't pay him no mind, Lord," he said to Jesus. "He don't know no better."

"Don't pray for me," I said. "Don't you ever pray for me."

"Everybody needs that. Even ignorant crackers like you."

I swung out of the bunk and stood up. I was going to pull him out of the bed and beat the hell out of him.

"You touch me, cracker-boy," he said, without moving, "you touch me and I'll mess you up, mess you up for sure. I don't care how big you are."

"I'm not afraid of you, nigger." I was sounding like my father now. I could even feel my bottom lip coming out, wet and quivering, all hot air like him too. My face was hot with shame.

"You should be. Ask around about me; ask that Billy Henderson, he the trusty at the laundry. Ask him about the Preacher."

He was lying on his back, his head toward me, his eyes yellow as a big cat's in the half-light.

"And 'nother thing," he said softly. "You just called me nigger for the last time. You call me nigger again, and you dead, boy."

"I'm not afraid," I said again, but my voice had lost some of its strength.

"You a liar, is what you are. Everybody afraid. Let me tell you somethin', Halley Martin: One of these days, and it may not be today, and it may not be tomorrow, but one of these days you gonna need me. One of these days you gonna call my name, and you gonna want me to come. Now go on to bed. Go on now, and you remember what I told you."

He rolled onto his side, turning his back to me. I was getting back in my bunk when I heard him say, "Good night, Jesus," as if somewhere in this tiny room, Jesus was bedding down with us.

The next morning I took Henderson aside and asked him about Isaiah Hughes.

"You mean Preacher? He's a good boy, one of the nicest niggers you'd ever want to meet. But don't let him hear you call him that."

"Why?"

"Last one called him nigger was his bunk-mate, 'fore you. Called him nigger and the next morning they found him with a guitar string wrapped around his neck. Damn near cut his head right off with it. They took the string from him and let him keep the guitar. Got another twenty years onto his sentence, but he don't care. He thinks it's God's will he's here, anyway."

He laughed. "He in charge now of your soul, Martin?"

"He ain't in charge of nothin' to do with me."

At noon precisely a bell rang, and we dropped our paddles and marched to the mess hall. I don't know if you ever heard anything about prison food, but anything good you may have heard is not true. You're packed ten to a table, with no elbow room at all, and men lingered over this slop like it was the best food in the world. I have a theory you can always tell the old-timers from the new blood by the size of the bites they took and how fast they chewed it. Old-timers chewed slow and deliberate, like cows on a cud. Anything to make it last.

I found a table and right after I sat down two big men slid in, one on either side of me. The one on my right had a crooked nose and an ugly scar beginning just below his left eye and running all the way down to his collarbone. He was the larger of the two and had maybe twenty or thirty pounds on me. He had a wide, flat face and small black eyes. His buddy was about my size, with bright blue eyes and thin bluish lips. His prison name was Blueboy; I never learned his real name. The big man's name was Jessup.

"Hey," Jessup said.

I didn't answer. I kept my eyes on my tray and swirled my spoon in the watery mashed potatoes.

"Hey, I'm talkin' to you," Jessup said.

"What?" I said.

"You Preacher's new bunk-mate?"

I nodded. Jessup winked at Blueboy.

"How you like that nigger?"

I shrugged.

"He kilt the last boy, snapped his head right off with a guitar string. What you in for?"

I told him. He gave a little nod to Blueboy, as if I had just passed a test.

"Name's Jessup," he said. "I'm a trusty. This here's Blueboy. We come to see what we can do."

"Do about what?"

"To help you, boy. Boy like you, never been in the joint before, you gonna need some help."

"I don't need any help."

"But you gonna need somebody like us to show you the ropes."

"I ain't interested."

He put his huge left arm around my shoulders. "I'm trying to help you, boy."

"I don't want your help, and if you don't take your fucking hand off me I'll take this spoon and dig your brains out."

I spoke softly, still stirring my potatoes, not looking at him. He shook with laughter, moving his hand to my neck and squeezing hard.

"Jesus! You get this fella, Blueboy? This boy got some balls. You don't know who I am, do you, boy?"

"You're Jessup," I said. "Now take your hand off me."

"You're making a mistake here, boy. You don't know who you're talking to, so I'm goin' to let it pass this time. But just this one time."

"Let me go," I said. "This is the last time I'm gonna tell you." My spoon was frozen in the potatoes. Jessup tightened his grip on my neck, squeezing so hard little bands of pain shot into my ears. I shifted the spoon into my left hand.

Jessup leaned over and whispered in my ear. "They told me how pretty you were. Bet you could last all night, huh, pretty boy?" And he stuck his tongue into my ear.

I brought my right arm up, wrapping it over the top of his left. The force of it ripped his hand from my neck, and I let my hand slide to his wrist. I yanked his arm behind his back, bringing it up high until my hand was level with his thick neck. He howled with pain and fell forward over his tray. I swung off the bench, spoon in my left hand. I flipped it into the air, caught it with the handle facing down, and stabbed it as hard as I could into his ear.

"Jesus Christ!" Blueboy squealed, and he lunged over the bench at me. I kicked him in the gut as he came forward, and he dropped to his knees, gulping air. The mess exploded around us, men shouting, shoving one another for a view, and over the bedlam the whistle of the guards as they tried to push their way through the mass of bodies pressing for a look at the blood.

I pressed down with my full weight on the spoon. Jessup screamed as blood spurted in a small fountain from his ear. Somebody grabbed my ankle—Blueboy, I guess—and yanked. I lost my balance and fell on top of him. Several hands grabbed the back of my shirt and pulled me up.

Jessup was already on his feet, blood pouring down the side of his face and soaking his shirt. He had a homemade knife we called a shiv in his hand.

"You're fucked," he said, and swung the knife toward my crotch. Suddenly a name rang in my head, like an echo: *Walter.*

A large dark hand swung out of the crowd, grabbing Jessup's wrist. The hand belonged to Isaiah Hughes. The room went absolutely still. Even the guards froze.

"I ain't got no quarrel with you, Preacher," Jessup said.

"You want him, you come through me," Preacher said.

"He ain't your boy," Jessup sneered.

"No, and I ain't yours, either," Preacher answered. "Drop it in my hand, now."

Jessup was shaking. I don't know if he was shaking from pain or loss of blood or the fact that he was terrified of the Preacher.

"He poked out my fucking eardrum," he whined. But he dropped the knife. It fell toward the Preacher's free hand. Then it was gone. It happened that fast. I saw it falling, then Preacher had it tucked away.

"This ain't done," Jessup said.

"Most things never are," said Preacher.

They handcuffed me and brought me straight to the warden's office. My brother inmates cheered and swatted me as I passed. Some spat in my face, but generally their estimation of me had improved. Jessup was considered one of the most powerful and important cons in the prison. As a trusty he had a great deal of latitude with the guards, more free time, and MacAffee's ear, if not his trust. But he was considered a stool pigeon and a thug by most of the population, trading his influence for booze and dirty books and cigarettes and practically any other kind of contraband you can think of. Most hated and feared him. Me, I was too stupid then to fear him.

"You have disappointed me," MacAffee said. "Less than a month into your sentence."

"I didn't like him touching me."

"So you puncture the man's eardrum?"

I didn't say anything. He sighed.

"I had high hopes for you." He sounded like a concerned father, or what I supposed a concerned father should sound like. "Despite what I read in your file, I did not consider you a violent man. Hopelessly romantic, but not violent. Perhaps the two are not so different. I'm giving you forty days solitary confinement. That may facilitate your self-control if a similar situation presents itself in the future."

The door opened and Nester shuffled in. Even in 1940 he walked like an old man. He was probably in his late thirties then, the same age I am now. He was carrying my sketch pad. He handed it to MacAffee and stepped back, at attention, waiting for orders.

MacAffee said, "Forty days in the Hole."

Nester nodded and took me by the elbow.

"That's my sketch pad," I said.

MacAffee said, "You will get it back when you demonstrate to me you can behave yourself."

"You can't take my sketch pad," I said.

"Oh?" He raised an eyebrow at me. He flipped open the pad and studied the first drawing. You were staring directly at him, your bangs falling over your eyes, a smile playing on the corners of your mouth. He wiped his mouth with the back of his hand.

"Give me sixty days and let me keep the pad," I said. "I swear, no more fights."

"I'm afraid I select the discipline here."

"You can't take that," I said. "It's the only thing that keeps me sane."

"Your sanity," he said, "is none of my concern."

He nodded to Nester, who pulled gently on my arm.

"Come on, now, Martin," he said softly. "Or you'll get the sixty *and* lose the pad."

I left the warden. He was staring at my drawing. He was staring at you.

Nester led me outside. The Hole was not a hole, but a small structure just a little larger than a doghouse. It had a metal door that padlocked. There were no windows and the only ventilation came through a small opening in the roof. Kneeling, the top of my head brushed the ceiling. In the Hole for forty days meant in the Hole for forty days: You did not leave for any reason. There was a metal bucket for your business that was emptied once a day. You didn't leave to eat and you didn't leave to exercise. You got one meal a day, which was passed through a slot in the door. In the summer some men in the Hole would strip off their clothes and wallow like pigs on the dirt floor, coming out at the end looking more like animals than men. Two or three men have died in the Hole at the height of summer, when the temperature reaches over a hundred and twenty degrees. They give you a jug of water to last you two or three days, but men get desperate, especially the first day or two, before their bodies and their minds adjust to the endless night inside, and they end up drinking the water two days before they're due a refill. Most of the guards will not refill it no matter how much they are threatened or begged.

Nester popped the padlock and swung open the door. It smelled as if something had died in there.

"Don't try to think too much," he said kindly. "Worst thing you can do. Sleep. Sleep as much as you can. Anything special you want for dinner? Maybe I can take care of it for you."

"I ain't hungry," I said.

"Don't worry, he'll give you that drawing pad back. He likes you. Don't know why, but he does. You better get in there now. He's watching."

I thanked him and asked him his name.

"Nester," he said, and I ducked into the darkness. I was looking forward to being alone. I wasn't afraid.

I should have been.

I don't have much to say about my stretch in the Hole. I can't remember most of it and can't talk about the rest. When the door came open on the last day the light punched through my eyes and burst inside my skull. But I brought out some of that darkness with me. A part of it is still with me. At lights-out that first night I broke into a cold sweat, and the Preacher commenced to hum, as if he knew I needed the sound, a reminder that another human being was close. He didn't say anything; he just hummed. I told him to shut up, but I didn't really want him to, and he understood that too and continued to hum.

"Thank you," I whispered. The screaming inside the Hole had made my throat raw.

"You welcome," Preacher said.

"My eyes hurt," I said. Tears streamed down either side of my face, pooling in my ears. There was no stopping them. I fell asleep crying, Preacher humming.

"Jessup's comin' after you," he told me the next morning. "All you gotta do is see it comin'. Then you gotta know what you gonna do when it comes."

"What do you mean?"

"I mean, you gotta decide if you gonna kill him."

"Kill him?"

"Only way to stop him. 'Cause if you let him by this time he shore to come again. And again and again until you dead, or wish you was."

"I kill him and I'll never get out of here," I said.

"You won't if you don't, either. He kill you 'fore you can."

"Don't he want out?"

"Why would Jessup want outta Starke? He like a little prince here. Outside he just another poor white cracker."

"I can't kill him," I said.

"You want me to?"

I looked at him. He was serious.

"Why would you—?"

"Don't matter to me. I in for life. Don't mind." He smiled.

"What'd you do, anyway, Preacher?"

"This ol' white boy stole some money from my church. So I tracked him down, broke in his house, tied him up, and tole him he'd stay tied till I got my money back. He don't deny it; he say, 'You ain't never seein' that money again, nigger.' So I beat him up. I beat the living shit out of him. Still wouldn't tell me. So I picked him up, him and the chair he was tied to, and carried him outside, and I tol' him he'd tell me or I light his house. I tell him I want our money or his house burns right down to the ground. He still don't tell me, so I torched his damn house. An' made him sit right there and watch it burn. So I got twenty years for breaking and entering, assault and battery, kidnapping and arson."

"You get the money back?"

"No," he laughed. "Burnt right up with the house. I didn't think that white boy would be so stupid as to sit there and watch all that money go up, but I guess he was. Maybe he figured niggers' money ain't as good as whites'. Dumb-ass cracker."

I didn't see Jessup that day, but I did notice a different attitude toward me. Men steered clear of me, dropping their eyes when I approached. I caught a couple of guards looking at me and talking softly, shaking their heads. Henderson didn't speak to me all day in the wash-house, and that wasn't like him. Preacher told me bets were being laid, most picking Jessup to kill me by the end of the week. Nester advised I go to MacAffee and demand to be put in solitary for my own protection, until Jessup could be transferred to another prison. "Call your lawyer," he said. "He can make a motion in court to have you or Jessup transferred. MacAffee'll have to follow a court order."

They were the only two men who spoke to me that week. Preacher said, "'Cause you dead already. That's why nobody looks at you, talks to you. You a dead man already." He let it be known if Jessup or any of his men touched me, they would have to answer to him, to the Preacher, and though he knew this might buy some time, eventually the code of honor in Starke would demand Jessup repay blood for blood, or his reign was done. No one would respect him, and sooner or later someone, probably one of his own men, would take his place, literally over his dead body. He *had* to kill me.

Preacher asked me again what I was going to do.

"Nothing," I said.

"That's the worse thing you can do," Preacher said. "You gotta do something first. You gotta take it to him. 'Cause even if he don't kill you, you lost all respect. Respect everything in here, Halley. Only thing a man's got. Only thing keep you alive."

"What comes, comes," I said. "I've killed my last man."

"Then you already dead."

I was also wrong.

A month later, I had my first visitor since my coming to Starke. It was the last person I expected to see.

"You remember me," he said.

We were sitting in the west wing of the administration building, where visitations were held. There were six rows of tables, with wooden chairs grouped around the tables. In those days, nothing separated you from your visitors. Whole families would gather, and inmates would bounce their children on their laps or smooch with their girls. Although this kind of fraternization was against the rules, the two or three guards stationed there let it pass for the most part. They only stepped in if the passion threatened to get out of hand.

"Yes, I remember you," I said. "You're Robert Hughes."

He nodded. He sat very still in his chair, looking straight at me, ignoring the raucous shouts of children and the broken-hearted wailing of forlorn lovers.

"I wanted to ask you a question." There was nothing in his voice. It was flat and dead and somehow distant. He studied me the way a man might look at a spot on his shirt, wondering what he had done to put it there. I waited for the question.

"Are you suffering?" he asked.

I didn't answer.

"You took what I loved most in the world," he said. "So I have come here to ask you, are you suffering?"

"I'm in prison for the rest of my life," I said.

He nodded. "But you will be free one day," he said. "You will be eligible for parole."

"I won't last that long," I said, thinking of Jessup.

"What are your plans, if you are free one day?"

"Is that your business?"

"You have made it my business."

"It was nothing personal against you. It wasn't even personal against Walter."

"You believe Walter took something you loved."

"Yes."

"And so you killed him."

"Yes."

"And now you have taken something I loved. What should I do?"

He wasn't expecting an answer. I didn't offer one.

"You are not suffering," he decided. I shrugged. He glanced down at my hands folded on the tabletop. His eyes flicked back up at me. He had hazel eyes, like your daddy's: cat's eyes. Hunter's eyes. He reached into his pocket and brought out a folded sheet of paper. I knew what it was before he opened it.

"Where'd you get that?" I asked.

He ignored me. I moved my hands to my lap. He spread the paper out on the table. It was my drawing of you, from the sketch pad Warden MacAffee had taken from me before sending me to the Hole.

"Lester had told me you were quite good," he said. "In a primitive way." He smoothed the folds on the paper with his thumb. "The warden seems to believe you have a true gift. An eye, he calls it. But I am no judge of art. I am a businessman. I understand ledger books, accounts, the buying and selling of goods. I do not pretend to understand you or this thing you do."

"Then give that back," I said. "It ain't yours."

He tore the picture in half, stacked it neatly, then tore it again into quarters. He slid the pieces across the table, and stood up.

"I will not see you again," he said.

"Good," I said.

"But you will remember me," he said. His lower lip was quivering slightly, the only sign he had any feeling in him at all. He turned stiffly and walked out of the room.

That night I watched Preacher with his Bible. My pad was gone; there was nothing else to do. His lips moved as he read, and the light from the lamp shone golden on his dark skin.

"How many times you read that book?" I asked.

He looked up, startled, as if I had come in unexpectedly. "Don't know exactly," he said.

"You ever read anything else?"

"Ain't nothin' else that matters."

"Why did you do that?" I asked. "Step in between me and Jessup?"

He stared at me for a long moment, then dropped his eyes back to the Bible. "You don't know, there's no way I can explain it to you, Halley."

"Seems kinda funny to me, you read that Bible all the time and don't think twice about killin' a man for calling you names."

"God's forgiven me for that."

"How d'you know?"

He shrugged. "That's what he does."

"So you decide to kill me someday, that'll be all right with God?"

"Why you tryin' to fight with me?"

"I'm not tryin' to fight. Just makin' conversation."

He knitted his brow, shook his head slightly, and put his nose back into the book.

"I never took up much with religion," I said. "My daddy went through this spell. Got saved when one of my cousins came down from Tallahassee and drug him to a revival. Came home spittin' fire and brimstone. Drug us all back with him the next night and they dunked me in a big washtub. Told me I was saved. Daddy said from then on he'd be only drunk on Jesus. That lasted about a week. Guess corn mash was sweeter. All I remember is the water running up my nose when the preacher laid me back. And I still remember the way that preacher said Jesus. Jeeee-zus!" I laughed.

"Momma went to church every Sunday. Brought us young-uns along until I refused to go. Seemed to me you should see God on days other than just Sunday. Momma would go and sing and pray and wave her hands all around, her face all swollen and bruised up from the night before. And nobody would say a word to her about it, just pretend those bruises weren't there. That's the kind of Christians I knew."

"You shoulda just killed him," Preacher said. "Your daddy."

I laughed. "You're the strangest preacher I ever met."

He sighed. "I shore be glad when they bring you back that sketch pad."

He picked up the shiv he had taken from Jessup and closed it inside his Bible: He was using the weapon as a bookmark. He leaned forward, resting his huge forearms on his thighs. He had a way of looking at you that made you feel naked, like nothing in you was hidden from him. It was hard to look back at him when he did it; it was like looking too long at the sun.

"I killed my first man at ten. That man was my uncle. I took a knife to him and carved him up so bad my momma, his own sister, didn't even know who he was when she found him. Never could hold my temper. There was hate enough in me for ten men. I hated everyone and everything; hated the world and all that was in it. I drank and smoked and consorted with the worst type of folk. Took up with a gang of boys and we tore through three counties raisin' hell. Got drunk every night, and whatever I wanted I took: money, cars, women. I didn't care. When you hate the world, you want the world to hate you back. But nobody hated me back more'n me. I'd jump in fights outnumbered three, four to one, 'cause I hoped deep in my heart that would be the end. Wanted to die in the worst way, 'cause that's all hate is. You ain't truly a man till all the hate is gone. But now I'm preachin'."

He bowed his head and ran a hand through his short, crinkly hair.

"So what happened?" I asked.

"Jesus come to me and say, 'Isaiah Hughes, what you doin'?' And I say, 'I want to die.' And Jesus say, 'No, I got work for you. Get up and live.'"

"You had a dream?"

He smiled slightly. "Don't call 'em dreams. Call 'em visions."

"Maybe you were just drunk."

"Was always drunk. But not after that day. Jesus say, 'Isaiah, go forth and start a church.' So I went forth and started a church. Quit the drinkin', the smokin', the women. Made my peace. That's all it about anyway, peace."

"So you got right with God, and you end up here. Sounds to me you shoulda just kept drinkin' and stealin' and killin'."

He laughed. "His purpose ain't for me to figure. Here."

He tossed the Bible at me. I caught it and held it awkwardly in my lap.

"I don't want to read this." I tossed it back.

"Why not?"

"I can't read."

He blinked at me as if I had just admitted to being from the moon.

I changed the subject. "You never told me why you did it. Stepped in on me and Jessup."

"Come a day you'll know. You'll figure it out," he said, and said no more.

It was five minutes till lights-out when Nester and another guard appeared outside the cell.

"The warden wants to see you," Nester said.

The guard with him shackled my hands and led me down the hall. Nester stayed with Preacher.

"She's beautiful, isn't she?"

MacAffee was staring at the painting of his horse, Marie, hanging on the wall beside his desk. The horse was looking dead-on at you from the canvass, its eyes black and deep.

"Do you ride?"

"Used to," I said. "Not anymore."

The smallest of smiles touched the corner of his lips.

"How do you know Robert Hughes?" I asked.

"Your problem," he said, "is your presumptuousness. You forget where you are, who you are."

He sat behind the desk and watched me as I placed the torn paper in front of him. His expression didn't change.

"This is a public office," he said. "And as a public office, every citizen has the right to air their concerns. Present their grievances."

"That was private property," I said.

"You are ward of the state," he answered. "You have no private property. That sketch pad was a gift to you, from me. You abused the privilege of keeping it, and I took it from you. It is my right to do with it as I see fit."

Something passed over his face, a strange look I couldn't read. He dropped his eyes and spread his hands out on the desk, splaying his thick fingers.

"I'm changing your work assignment. Starting tomorrow you will be working at Block H in the west yard. We've finally got the funds from the legislature to build a new one."

"You didn't bring me here to tell me that," I said.

"No." He sighed. "No, I did not."

He pushed himself up from the desk and walked toward the painting of his horse. He crossed his large arms over his chest and spoke at the painting, not at me.

"I spoke this morning with a trusty whom I believe you may know. Arthur Jessup. The man whose eardrum you tore to pieces. I have every confidence after our little talk that there will be no more trouble from him. I have brought you here for similar assurances."

"I just want to be left alone," I said. "That's the whole reason this happened."

He nodded. He still would not look at me. "I know that. And now Jessup knows that. He isn't happy about it, but he understands that, ultimately, he has no power but that which I allow him to have. He understands now that if you die he must answer for it."

"You're too kind to me, Warden," I said.

If he knew I was being sarcastic, he didn't let on. "It has nothing to do with kindness." His voice trailed away. "Nothing at all. I just want you to understand that whatever happens now, I have done all I can. It is out of my hands."

He turned to me. "Understand I did not bring you here. You killed Walter Hughes and that is what brought you here. Understand that what happens here is a direct result of that—that act. You must understand that sometimes what happens is as a result of events far removed from the actual . . . fact. Understand that."

"I don't understand anything you're saying."

"It is out of my hands now."

"What if Jessup just kills me anyway, the hell with you?"

"I have satisfied Jessup."

"How?"

"That is between me and Jessup." He took a deep breath. "That's all," he said. He nodded to the guard.

"There's something going on here," I said. The guard took me by the elbow. "You gonna tell me what it is?"

He scooped the scraps of paper into his hand and dropped them into the trash can. They fluttered down, turning end over end.

"Give me my sketch pad back!" I shouted as the guard pulled me toward the door.

"Not yet," he said. "No."

Preacher was awake, sitting in his rocker at the back of the cell when the
guard locked me in. In the dim light he was no more than a shadow, a
lump of darkness in the lighter dark around us. I sat on my bunk.
Neither of us spoke for a long time.

"They're changing my work assignment," I said finally.

"Tearing down old Block H," he said.

"Nester told you?"

The dark shape in the back of the cell nodded.

"Me too," he said quietly. "I goin' too."

"What's goin' on, Preacher?"

"Nester say they movin' Jessup. Jessup and Blueboy and nine of
Jessup's boys. Thirteen total, countin' you and me. We all be over there,
in the west yard."

"You should've stayed out of it," I said.

"Don't make no difference now."

"MacAffee says Jessup won't be no trouble."

"Yeah-a, no trouble."

There was nothing in his voice to betray him. Nothing I could put
my finger on. He sounded scooped-out hollow.

"What'll we do?" I asked.

"Pray."

When he was done praying that night, Preacher talked about compensation. How God took things sometimes to let better things come.

"That's the most important thing," he said. "God don't close no door
without opening a window. You keep that in mind, Halley Martin, when
tomorrow come. You remember that. You always remember that. No matter what happens to you in this life, there's a land of glory waiting on the
other side." He sang softly: "Gonna take me to your Gloryland / Come a
day, Lord / Gonna take me to your Gloryland / Come a day / Gonna take
me to your Gloryland / Gonna take me by both my hands . . ." He broke
off singing and hummed the tune softly, then suddenly he burst out in a
loud voice, and I had the feeling he wasn't talking to me anymore, "All I
ever wanted was for God to use me, and when he done, to take me home.

All my life's ever been is a march back home. Home to Gloryland. Can't wait to get there. Can't wait till I see my Lord."

He picked up his stringless guitar and hummed, tapping on the wood, his eyes closed, his head back. The Block was absolutely silent as he sang of Gloryland. I listened, and waited for morning.

Later, as Preacher slept, I slipped his bookmark out of the Bible and tucked the eight-inch piece of sharpened steel under my mattress.

Let Preacher pray. I put my faith in what I knew.

In prison, they don't want you to think too much. Any change in routine excites the mind and you don't want excited minds in prison. Dawn comes. You dress. You fall in line. You get counted. You go on detail. You eat. You go to the yard. You work. You eat again. You go back to your cell. You sleep. Every day like the one before it; only the weather changes. Maybe somebody comes to visit. Maybe you get a letter. One day you get to clean out your cell. Saturdays you shower. On Sunday you can go to the chapel. Except for the two hours in the yard you're always in line. In line for head count. In line for lunch. In line for dinner. In line for mail call. In line to use the phone. After a fight there's usually a day of "restricted exercise," where you march in a circle, in line, for two hours. I cannot begin to describe to you, Mavis, what this does to a man's mind and soul.

Most men look forward to a change in their work assignment. It was the only thing that ever changed in this place. Every morning I had dreaded going to that wash-house, wondering when I might go to the fields. I would dream of corn and squash and rutabagas like some men dreamed of freedom.

Dawn came. Preacher and I rolled out of our bunks. While he was getting dressed I slipped the shiv into my sock and dropped my pants leg over it. We fell in line and marched out of the Block. We marched outside under a low, dark sky. A cold drizzle enveloped us as we lined up to be counted. Winter was coming.

A guard I had never seen before marshaled us for the detail at the old cell block. Preacher and I fell in line behind Jessup, Blueboy, and nine other men. We marched past the guard tower, around Cell Block C, along the fence at the south side of the grounds, to a high gate beside which stood the old guard tower. Here, at the southwest corner of the grounds, the view from the tower was cut off. To our left were the gardens and the graveyard, blocked from sight by a row of pine and palm trees.

Lined up against the wall of the building were thirteen sledgehammers, one for each of us. The guard directed six of us to start on the west wall, the other seven to start on the east wall. Preacher stayed right by my side.

The rain began to fall harder as the morning went on. Though much was weighing on my mind, it was good to be outside again, swinging a tool. How long ago was it I was standing in your daddy's orange groves, hewing the trees for the burning? I had lost fifteen pounds since I came here, most of it while inside the Hole, where a man melts away like a stick of butter in the sun. The sledgehammer must have weighed thirty or forty pounds, and by mid-morning my arms felt thin and rubbery and ready to drop from my shoulders. But here was something I understood, that I still remembered, deep in my marrow. I smashed that hammer into the concrete walls with a feeling that approached joy.

We broke for lunch, laying our hammers down and marching in line back to the mess hall. No one spoke. Talking in line wasn't allowed, though most men and most guards knew this was a rule that could be broken. Sometimes men even broke into song, but only if a guard like Nester was along. Jessup was with the crew on the east side that morning, so I didn't see him. When he came around the building for lunch I looked right at him, but he wouldn't lift his head. I was beginning to believe I was wrong about everything, that Warden MacAffee's promise was true, and by the end of lunch Preacher and me were laughing and talking. He was a great storyteller, Mavis, and I would be a lucky man if I could remember half of the tales he told that day.

We marched back to the job. After another hour of pounding all was down but the foundation. Broken glass and shattered mortar crunched beneath our feet as we surveyed our handiwork. There is pride in a man's heart for building something where nothing once stood. There is something else in a man's heart when he tears it down. The guard told us to break up the bigger pieces of concrete, and then we'd be done for the day. He was letting us go early, we'd been so efficient in our destruction.

I was in my own world, standing with my legs spread wide for balance, bringing that sledgehammer high over my head and letting it fall with a satisfying CRACK on the concrete before me, when Preacher touched me on the elbow. It had stopped raining, and to the west the clouds had pulled back. The lowering sun shone along the horizon, fat and red, as they say it will be at the end of days. I looked up at Preacher. In the light of the setting sun, with his skin plastered with gray dust, he looked like some kind of African warrior-god, come to do battle.

"He gone," he said quietly, and nodded to my right. I turned, thinking he was talking about Jessup. But Jessup wasn't gone; the guard was.

It had come.

Someone grabbed me from behind and twisted me away from Preacher. A foot kicked the head of my sledgehammer, sending it skittering away in the rubble. A large forearm slammed against my neck, yanking my head back. I screamed, "Preacher!" And someone laughed. Thick fingers twisted in my hair and pulled my head back, straight back; I was staring at the clouds, their bottoms painted blood-red by the failing sun. I felt hands all over my body, patting me down. They found the shiv and pulled it out of my sock. The edge ran along my leg, drawing blood. I was whipped around again, and the hand loosened on my hair. I lowered my head and saw Jessup standing between me and Preacher, the knife flickering crimson in Jessup's hand. Preacher was being held by four men: two for his upper half and two squatting behind him holding his legs. Preacher was not struggling. He was staring over Jessup's shoulder, at me. There was a familiar look on Preacher's face; I had seen it before but couldn't remember where. Jessup turned his back on me, brought his arm back, and drove the knife with all his force into Preacher's gut. Then I remembered where I'd seen that expression before: Walter. Jessup leaned into him, bringing the blade up through Preacher's middle: He was gutting him.

Preacher went down to his knees. I howled; my gut contracted, as if I was the one being stabbed. The men let Preacher go and he fell face down into the dirt. Jessup stepped away and swung on his heel.

It was my turn.

"What's the matter, pretty-boy?" he whispered. "I ain't gonna kill you. I'm a man of my word."

I spat in his face. He let it stay there. It dripped off his chin onto the wet earth. He nodded to the men holding me, and they flung me on my face. A piece of concrete stabbed just below my right eye; another inch and it would have put it out. They rolled me onto my back. I tried to sit up and they shoved me back down. Two men took my legs and two my arms. Two more took me at my wrists, using both hands to press down, pinning my arms down tight, spread straight out on either side of my body. Blueboy's face hung right over mine as he squatted behind me, pressing his hands on my shoulders.

"You lucky, boy," Jessup said. "Not like that nigger. He didn't never know his place, never would either. But you gonna. You gonna know right where you stand, boy."

He picked up a sledgehammer and strode to one side of me. It was then I realized what he was going to do and I bucked and twisted and rolled my body from side to side, straining against the men who held me down.

"Here's the first part of your lesson," he said. He brought the hammer up and let it fall on my clinched fist. He brought it up again, let it fall, and then, again, a third time. He stepped over my writhing body and brought the sledgehammer high over his head.

"Here's the second part," he said.

I heard someone howling. It sounded like it was coming from very far away. Nothing was close to me then, not even my own voice. Everything was far away and getting farther, and farther, and farther, until there was nothing near me, not one thing.

You were the first thing near me. Your hand first, on my forehead. The smell of you, as you leaned forward, your dark hair loose and falling over my face. Lilacs. Pungent rose, thick with life. A brush of your lips. A kiss. Your voice in my ear, *Halley.*

Rise.

I woke in a room with a white floor, whitewashed walls, white ceiling tile. A fan turned overhead, white-bladed. People in white moved around me. The sheet around my chest was white. I woke crying your name, and a voice hushed me, a man's voice. In my delirium I thought it was the Preacher's. I thought I was dead and had found him again, in Gloryland.

Of course, it wasn't. It was the prison infirmary.

"Hush," the voice beside me said. "Hush now, Halley."

I didn't know that voice. I tried to turn my head, and the room swam out of focus. A tube was hooked to my arm, snaking out of my line of vision. I didn't feel anything; I was numb from the neck down. I tried to lift my head. I wanted to look at my hands, at what might be left of my hands. I couldn't. I fell back onto the pillow, exhausted.

"Lay still now," the voice said. I could make out the dark shape of its owner's head. A white man in a dark suit. I closed my eyes.

When I opened them again the man was gone. I was alone. There was no sound save a lone fly, popping and buzzing against the screened window above my head. The noise seemed terrifically loud to me. I cried out for someone to kill the goddamned fly. No one answered.

Whoever it was was back when I came to again. I felt his hand on my forearm. When he realized I was awake he took his hand away. I turned my head carefully toward him. The morphine made everything seem bloated somehow, especially me. I was a great bloated fish, bobbing in a dense sea. His face came into sharper focus. He was thin, with sallow skin and jet-black hair, slicked back from his high forehead. His skin was drawn tight over his bones. He smiled, exposing large yellow teeth.

"Hello," he said.

"Preacher," I said, my thick tongue fumbling.

"Who? Oh, Mr. Hughes. I'm terribly sorry, but . . ."

I closed my eyes. The sea lifted me and settled with me. I said, "I'm thirsty."

"I'll get you something."

"Wait." I willed my hand to grab his arm, but my arm did not move. "You been in here all the time."

"Most of it, yes."

"Who are you?"

"My name is Ned Jeffries. I'm the chaplain here. And you, Halley Martin, are going to live, praise God."

He brought me a glass of water and a straw. He slid his hand beneath my head and lifted it high enough so I could drink. The water burned my throat. He set the water on the table beside my bed and dabbed my mouth with a cloth. With that pale skin and dark suit it was as if the Angel of Death was ministering to me. He was a young man, about my age. He had a high, tenor voice, not exactly girlish, but clear and trumpet-like, a pure tone. He was chatty as a girl, though.

He had only come to the prison last month, he told me, part of his final year at the seminary. "Like an internship," he said. He may have looked like an undertaker in that dark suit and with that pale, yellowish skin, but he was as cheerful as any self-respecting do-gooder could be. He brought me water and wiped my brow and read some of the Bible to me until I told him where he ought to put it. He closed the book and set it on the table beside me, where it lay like a silent threat. He introduced me to the prison doctor, Corrigan, a little Irishman with a handlebar mustache and a limp from a wound he claimed to have received in the Great War. Corrigan told me he thought my hands could be saved; he had agonized over it, had called a specialist in Tampa, who told him to amputate, but in the end decided to take a wait-and-see approach. He informed me Jessup had smashed every bone in my wrists and hands, but the veins and arteries in my wrists had somehow survived more or less intact. That gave him some hope, he said. Jeffries called it a miracle, and Corrigan had scowled and said he didn't see much of the miraculous in what Jessup had done to me. I asked him about Preacher.

"Dead before they got him here," he said, and shook his head. "Senseless. I don't understand you men."

He had set my hands, tying each finger to a splint and flattening the palms against a piece of plywood, then wrapping everything in padding. He asked me to wriggle my fingers, and I told him that might be hard, seeing how I couldn't feel anything below my neck.

"Shock," he said. "And the morphine, of course. That'll fade soon. Try to move them anyway."

He shook his head after a second. "That's all right. You see, it's not the bones I'm concerned about, it's the nerves."

"No one ever accused me of lacking that," I said, and he laughed, like I had made a decent joke.

"What happened to Jessup?" I asked.

He shook his head. "I don't know."

I waited for Nester to come to ask him. I knew he would come, and he did, later that night. Jeffries was still there, hovering around my bed. I told him to get lost. He looked hurt, like rejection was the last thing he expected from me, his graduate thesis, but he faded toward the door.

Nester took off his hat and sat down in the chair. He didn't look at me. He turned the hat in his hand and stared at the floor. He found a scuff on his shoe and carefully scrubbed at it with his shirtsleeve.

"Brought you something," he said. He placed it on the table by the bed. I didn't look at it.

"Jessup," I said.

"Still in the Hole. Warden gave him sixty days. Goin' to trial next month. Assault with a deadly weapon for you, murder one for Preacher."

"Bet he's scared," I said. Nester shrugged. He looked at the ceiling.

"You know what Preacher would say," he said after taking a deep breath.

"What?"

"Let it go."

"Like hell."

"Halley, you ain't gonna accomplish—"

"Jessup, Blueboy, the rest of those men, that guard, and the warden too. The goddamned warden too."

"You want to get out of this place?"

I didn't say anything.

"You never will, you know. Not if you—"

"Maybe it don't matter now what I do."

"You keep your head down, you be okay. Jessup's done with you. Score's settled. It's over, Halley. Let it go."

"I let it go before and look what it got me."

"That's okay for you to say," he snapped. "That's okay for you. You're in for life. But you make a threat against the warden of this prison and I got to report it. I got to report it, Halley, or it's my job. I got a wife and kids, you know. A wife and kids."

He dug in his shirt pocket and brought out a crumpled pack of Luckys. He tapped one out and tamped down one end before putting it in his mouth. He struck a match on his heel and lit the cigarette. His hands were shaking.

"Whole place has gone crazy," he muttered. "Whole goddamned prison. Now Jessup's in the Hole everybody and their brother's fightin' to take his spot. Warden's cracked down, restricted exercise and visitation. Jessup's done. Nobody trusts him no more without the warden behind him. He's gonna beg to stay in the Hole 'cause if he comes out somebody's gonna kill him for sure."

"For sure."

"That's what I'm trying to tell you, Halley, only you won't listen. You won't have to do a goddamned thing to Jessup. He's done. He's done, I tell you. Besides, what the hell you think you're goin' to do with those."

He gestured at my hands, then dropped his eyes. "Sorry," he said. "What's the doc say?"

"Says he's gonna sew me on some paddles. Make me like a duck. Duckman, they'll call me. Duckie."

He laughed, then doubled over in a coughing fit. When it passed, he said, "You all right, Halley Martin. You are all right."

"No," I said. "Not anymore."

He put on his hat and shuffled away. I glanced at the bedside table. He had returned my sketch pad.

As I lay in that bed, winter came. I knew it had come because they piled two more blankets on me and the room stayed dark longer. Jeffries appeared in the mornings wearing an overcoat and scarf like he was braving a storm somewhere up north. He had long narrow hands and skinny fingers, and his nails were polished and neatly clipped. I was allowed out of bed in the afternoons, so I walked around the room, Jeffries by my side, chattering like an old lady at a social. Doc Corrigan tested my reflexes and seemed pleased with my progress, though I still couldn't feel anything when he poked me. He gradually reduced my dose of morphine, so in addition to Jeffries I had intense pain as my constant companion. Pain is good, Corrigan told me. It means the nerves in your hands aren't completely destroyed.

After a while I got the courage to look at my hands. I chose a time when Jeffries was off chasing other souls, when the ward was quiet, near the end of day. The splints had just come off and my fingers had curled and twisted like thin paper thrown into a fire. Corrigan told me the bones were shattered beyond repair, and he still could not rule out amputation of both hands.

I asked him if I would ever be able to draw again.

He shrugged and said, "There's always finger painting." He told me if he was me he'd worry more about dressing and feeding myself and if I would be able to clean myself after the toilet.

It was on that day I decided to die.

I told no one. Mostly because I knew there was no one to trust. They'd put me on a twenty-four-hour watch. At least under Jeffries I had a few hours to myself every day. To have them watching me like a flock of buzzards was too much to bear. I needed a plan, and some idiot to help me without figuring it out. Luckily, such a dope was never far away, happy to be of service.

"Good morning!" he called cheerfully from the door. He hung his coat and scarf and ran a comb through his slick hair. He patted his coat pockets and stamped his feet. He had explained what poor circulation he had, how even in the summer his hands and feet felt like chunks of ice. The man never failed to fascinate me. He came over and sat by my bedside. He crossed his thin legs and slapped his hands on his knee.

"So! How are we feeling today?"

I gritted my teeth.

"The pain. It's pretty bad."

"Have they given you your morphine?"

I nodded. "Doc's got me down to half a dose. But it ain't cuttin' it, Ned. I'm in awful pain."

"I'll fetch the orderly."

He leapt up and scurried from the room. He came back with the trusty on day duty, a man named Lawson. Lawson had informed me he didn't like sick people, which was probably the sole reason he'd been assigned to the infirmary. He frowned at my chart.

"He already got his pill," he told Jeffries.

"He says he needs more. Look at him."

I grimaced appropriately.

"I gotta clear this with the doc."

"Well, then," Jeffries said. He reminded me of a fussy aunt.

"Won't be in till tomorrow morning."

"I can't wait that long," I groaned.

"He can't wait that long," Jeffries said.

"Well, he's just gonna have to wait that long. Can't give any medicines without the doc's okay."

"Where is he? You could call him."

"I ain't gonna call him."

"And why not, may I ask? You have a man here in severe pain. Or would you prefer that I call him?"

Lawson scowled. "Gimme a minute."

He walked back to the office. Jeffries turned and gave me a self-satisfied grin. He sat back down beside me. He patted my arm. "Don't worry," he said. "Help is on the way."

Lawson came back out. "He can have another dose," he said. He sounded angry; he had been enjoying my pain. He slid his hand under my head and roughly lifted me, dropping a pill on my tongue. I let it fall to the side of my mouth and sipped the water he held to my lips. I gave him a smile and he dropped my head back to the pillow. He left. Jeffries smiled at me. I smiled back, turned my head away, and pretended to have a coughing fit. The pill dropped out of my mouth, onto the pillow. Jeffries pounded me on the back.

"That's okay," I said. "Pill went down the wrong way." I moved my head to one side, hopefully covering the pill. Jeffries was glowing with the triumph of his victory over the mean, nasty orderly.

"So! The splints are gone. I have it on good authority they'll be moving you back to your cell soon."

"When?"

"Oh, another month. Think about it! You'll be free of this wretched place in time for spring!"

"Gosh."

"It is a sign, Halley. As our Lord and Savior did, you will rise as the lilies bloom."

"You ain't from around here, are you?"

"Why, no. Actually, I'm originally from Ohio. My parents moved down here when I was fourteen. My father lost his job in thirty-two and came down here to start his own church. He had definite ideas of God's plans for this great nation in her moment of peril. His church died with him, unfortunately."

"So you're going to take it over?"

"No. No, I don't think so. Want to strike out on my own. You know, the American dream and all."

"Oh, yeah. That."

"Mother's still with me, praise God. Though her health is not what it used to be."

We were quiet for a moment, feeling bad for Mother.

"Well! You must be feeling better, wanting to talk. I don't think you've said three words since we met."

"You're such a good talker, all I wanted to do was listen."

"That's what they say about you," he said, beaming now. Not only was I talking, but I found him interesting! He fairly shook with excitement. "That you're a . . . a watcher. You watch things. You measure everything in your mind. Did you really tear out that man Jessup's eardrum?"

"Yes."

"Goodness. Why?"

"He touched me."

"He touched you?"

"I told him not to."

"Then I shall be certain to do all you ask, within reason."

And he laughed. I did not. He stopped. Then he said, "They say you killed a man."

"Yes. I killed a man."

"Gutted him like a hog, they say. But I hear those stories and I look at you, and I can't imagine you doing such a thing."

"I've changed."

"I see."

"Prison does that."

"Of course."

"I keep running into preachers since I came to prison," I said. "You think that means anything?"

"Everything happens for a reason. There *is* a plan. God is working through you, Halley."

"Got a funny way of working."

"His ways are mysterious."

"First preacher I met here got gutted with a homemade knife. How do you think you'll do?"

It took him a minute to smile, but he finally did. Then he announced he had to conduct a prayer service, and left, walking faster the closer he got to the door.

It is nearly impossible to hide a pill under your pillow without the use of your hands. Nearly impossible, but not altogether. My hands flopped around so much on my wrists I was afraid I'd flip the pill onto the floor, so I used my teeth to slide the pillow over, my nose to nudge the pill onto the mattress, then my teeth again to pick up the pillow and set it down on the pill. I was lying back, congratulating myself on my ingenuity, when I realized that in two days they would change my sheets. I wrestled with this for some time. It taxed me. Without the use of my hands my options for suicide were limited. You never realize how important your hands are for the purpose of suicide. You can't hold a gun. You can't tie a noose. I supposed the only thing you could do was find a high enough place and jump off it. Or take pills, if you could figure a way to get them from wherever they were to your mouth. Even if I could hide them in my gown somehow, I was given a sponge bath every week and rolled about from side to side every few hours to prevent bedsores. The table beside the bed didn't have a drawer, and even if it did there was no way for me to reach it. Maybe I could provoke someone into killing me. Jeffries was out; I didn't think a fly could provoke him. Corrigan was a doctor under oath. Nester would be afraid of losing his job. That left Lawson, the trusty-orderly, who, by the rough way he cleaned me and fed me, led me to believe he might take me up on the offer. Then again, he might report it to Corrigan, and he'd put me on suicide watch, and then I'd never have my chance. I was beginning to understand how a man alone was useless in this world, even when it came to something as lonely as suicide.

Finally it hit me. It wasn't the best-sounding plan, but it was the only one I could come up with: I pushed the pill with my nose until it fell behind the bed. I heard a little pop as it hit the linoleum and bounced. I lay back, feeling more tired by the effort than I should have been, and thought: thirty days. Thirty days.

The next morning, and every morning after that, I tucked the pill under my tongue and spat it out behind the bed after Lawson left. Without the pill, the pain in my hands became almost unbearable, but I comforted myself with the thought that soon the pain would be gone, gone forever. I didn't lie around feeling sorry for myself. I was kind of relieved. I reminded myself how lucky I was, really, just to have found you, to have felt what I felt, to have seen what I've seen. Most men aren't that lucky. Jeffries remarked more than once how cheerful I seemed, and on some days I truly was glad to see him. He was like a daffy relative who's nice to have around because he reminded you how normal you were. I learned a great deal about his hometown in Ohio, a little place called Van Wert, about the big move to Pensacola and the church his daddy started there. Jeffries told me he was "saved" at the age of fourteen, and had never really considered any other business besides that of preacher.

"Though I did have a brief flirtation with astronomy," he said. "As a child I loved looking at the stars. They were so beautiful. So far away. So . . . untouchable."

We were on one of our daily walks around the room. He had gotten into the habit of placing his thin hand on my arm as we walked. I suppose he either forgot about what happened to Jessup for touching me or figured what the hell could I do about it without my hands. It didn't bother me much. It would have, a great deal, if I had known then what was to come.

"That's like my daddy," I said.

"Ah! I was wondering. The name. It's simply charming, very unique."

"My legal name is Hyram."

He tsk-tsked at that. "Bland and uninspired," he said.

"That's what I thought. Bland. Uninspired."

"Halley is a grand name. A romantic name. They tell me you killed that man . . . for love."

"More for honor than love," I said. "Her honor, not mine."

"What does that feel like?"

"Love?"

"Killing a man."

"You wonder about that, Ned?"

"Oh." That's all he said. Just "oh." We stopped in front of the window facing the yard. Men were milling about under an impossibly blue sky. Late February, the beginning of spring. I could almost feel it through the glass.

"What goes through your mind? They say you cut him open from his groin to his chest. What goes through your mind at a moment like that? How do you—I mean, how do you live with that?"

"I couldn't have lived without it," I said.

"Because of her?"

I nodded.

"I don't think I understand. How something like that could be connected to love."

"Maybe you ought to. Being a preacher and all."

He looked shocked. He said, " 'Vengeance is mine, saith the Lord.' "

"Ned, I ain't too concerned with what the Lord saith."

"Maybe if you were you wouldn't be here."

"But I'm already here, so what the hell?"

"It's never too late," he said. "You'll still be a relatively young man when your parole comes up."

"I ain't gettin' religion, Ned. I tried it. I tried prayin' and all that. It just won't go into me, or me into it. Seems like I don't have a choice in it."

"Me, either," he said. He sounded sad. "Do you think I'll make a good preacher, Halley?" He looked so forlorn, so utterly lost, that I almost felt sorry for him. He was like a little kid asking his daddy if he was really good at baseball.

"Why you want to? 'Cause your daddy was?"

He shrugged helplessly. "Seems like the only thing to do."

"That's what I thought too."

"Yes, and look where it landed you." He realized how harsh this sounded. "Still, to love like that, to find something like that," he said quickly. "Mother says it's time I settled down. She says there's no such thing as a single preacher, but I—I'm not that confident around women. They're so—" he gave a little wave of his hand. "Different." It wasn't quite the word he wanted, and he frowned in his frustration. "Will she wait for you, Halley?"

"I don't know," I said. "And it really doesn't matter."

"It doesn't matter?"

"What matters is if *I* wait."

"Well, a man in your position doesn't have much of a choice. Has she promised to?"

"Not to me."

He looked at me. "Well, what does she say?"

"We ain't spoke."

He blinked. "You——?"

"I got one letter from her, right after the trial."

"And nothing since?"

I shook my head no.

"She hasn't written?"

"No."

"Visited?"

"No."

"Called you on the telephone?"

"No."

"You haven't heard from her since you left Homeland?"

"No."

"But that's——that's extraordinary."

"It don't matter."

He was getting more and more confused. "Why doesn't it matter?"

"What matters is right here," I brought a shattered hand to my heart. "That I feel this. That for at least a little while in my life, I had something . . ." Now it was my turn to search for the right word, and fail.

"Something."

"Why, Halley Martin, I think you do believe in God. You just don't know it yet."

He would sit beside me in the afternoons, when the shadows were long on the floor and the weak light turned amber. He gave up on Bible readings and attempts at prayer. He talked of his childhood instead, how lonely he was as a little boy, picked on by the other children, mocked for his lack of physical ability and his penchant for daydreaming. He was an only child, but not doted upon. His daddy did not believe in doting. The family had descended from Puritan stock, and the blood of his black-coated ancestors ran thick in him. When the family moved to Pensacola, Ned's loneliness deepened. He was mocked less, but only because there were fewer mockers around. He did not make friends easily, he said, and there were few families with children in his father's congregation.

"His message didn't appeal to families," he said. "He was the old-fashioned, fire-and-brimstone type preacher. The world was going to end any day. The sinners would fry and the saints would fly. Blah, blah, blah. When you're young and you're struggling to raise a family, that's not the sort of message you want to hear. Religion was never much about comfort with my father. It was about power. God's power. I was kind of scared of God, to tell you the truth."

"Beginning of wisdom," I said.

"Well!" He beamed like a proud teacher.

"My momma read the Bible all the time," I said. "So how 'bout now? You still scared?"

He nodded. "But of people, not of God."

"That's true wisdom," I said.

He laughed. "I think I'm going to miss you, Halley Martin."

"You gonna leave?"

He nodded. "I just need to decide where to go."

"Why not stay here?"

He shook his head but didn't explain. "The call will come," he said.

On the thirtieth day I spat out the last pill, then kicked myself for it. It was a stupid thing to do on the last day. I don't know why I picked thirty; twenty-five, maybe even twenty, would do the trick. Thirty was a nice, round number. There was more drama and pathos in thirty. I waited till Ned left for the afternoon and Lawson was on his dinner break. Corrigan had gone home for the day. Earlier that afternoon he had examined my hands and told me the next week I would be moved back to Cell Block C; there was no reason I couldn't lie in my bunk just as well as in a hospital bed. I thought about telling him I intended to lie about six feet under, but I didn't say anything.

There are more dignified ways to go about killing yourself, but those options were not open to me, and if they were I wouldn't be killing myself. That's called irony.

I rolled off the bed and landed on my belly. I brought my head up at the last second, otherwise I would have broken my nose. I controlled the urge to break my fall with my hands. I scooted on my stomach under the bed, like an inchworm. There wasn't much clearance under there, and it was filthy with dust bunnies and years of accumulated dirt and human detritus. I found the pills scattered near the head of the bed, and touched them with my tongue one by one, hoisting them stuck on my tongue and swallowing them dry. I lost count at eighteen pills. I think I might have gotten as many as twenty-three or twenty-four. I rested after the last one, laying my cheek against the dirty floor, considering whether I should just let death take me right there, but in the end that seemed too pitiful; I decided to die in bed, with some dignity at least.

I hauled myself onto the mattress and lay on top of the covers, breathing hard, my heart high in my chest, blood singing in my ears. I wondered if Walter could see me, if he was happy about the way things turned out. I could picture his eyes more clearly than yours; his face was before me, not yours, as I waited to die. Compensation. I closed my eyes, and willed myself to find you within my mind's sight. Since I killed Walter, I had heard it was not what you were or what I felt for you that had brought me here; it was what I had done to Walter.

I closed my eyes and whispered, "It isn't true." Walter's words to me. If this was not true, then nothing was true. If this was not pure, then nothing was pure. They said I had butchered him, gutted him like a hog, split him open like a catfish, but at the heart of what I had done, there was beauty. There was nothing ugly in it, nothing at the core of it that made it untrue. To say what had happened and what had come because of it was ugly, just wasn't true. It wasn't true. Something holy, untouched by me or Walter, was at the heart of it and, though I had literally bathed in his blood, I was unstained. I was clean.

The smell of the acrid roses. Your hair, falling over your face. White dress among the bobbing rosebuds. A slender hand pulling back the thick, dark strands and tucking them behind your ear. A thousand years ago I had crouched in the hedgerow, my heart breaking, as you soaked into me like rain falling into the parched earth; I never thought I would struggle to remember how you looked, but as I lay dying, you had already left me. It was as if by losing my hands I had lost my ability to conjure you, to bring you forth, and that alone was reason enough to die.

My heart was slamming in my chest. I didn't know if that was caused by the drug or my panic in losing you. Killing Walter hadn't cost me you; landing in prison for life hadn't cost me you; losing my hands had somehow cost me you. I was leaving, but you were already gone.

"It isn't true," I whispered.

The door slammed. My eyes snapped open. How long since I'd taken the pills? I didn't know. My head lolled to the side, and here came Ned Jeffries, his big feet in those shiny, black shoes slap-slapping on the linoleum. For the first time since I had known him his hair was unkempt, falling over his thin face in greasy strings. His cheeks were flushed and his eyes wide. He was carrying something in his hand.

An envelope.

"Halley, Halley, you awake? Wake up, Halley, I got something. I got something for you; you'll never guess; you'll never guess who it's from! It's a sign, Halley. A sign as sure as I'm standing here. I was leaving for the day; I was in my car practically out of the gates when Nester flagged me down. He was leaving too, but he wanted to make sure you got this, and asked me if I could give it to you tomorrow, but when I saw the return address, when I saw who it was from, I knew you'd want it right away, so I jumped out of my car—dear God, I think I left it running—I jumped out of my car and ran straight here, must be two miles, at least, two good miles—"

He was holding the envelope in front of my eyes. I didn't need to read it. I knew the handwriting. I motioned to him to lean in.

"Stick your fingers down my throat," I said.

"What?"

"Stick your fingers down my throat, Ned. Now."

"Why in the world would I—"

"Goddamn it, shut up for a second, you fucking moron, and stick your goddamn fingers down my throat and do it *now.*"

He dropped the letter. It fell on my chest. He stuck two fingers down my open mouth. I gagged, but nothing came. He pulled his fingers from my mouth and held his hand up in the air, not knowing what to do with the spittle on his fingers.

"Do it again!" I yelled, and opened my mouth wide.

A look of utter disgust came over his face, but he did it again, pushing his fingers in to the knuckles. My whole body convulsed, and the stuff in my gut came up. He yelped and pulled his hand back, but not quick enough to avoid being spattered. I rolled to my side, heaving, vomiting for what seemed like an eternity, until nothing came up but air and spit. I rolled onto my back, gasping, wondering if I had brought it up in time. I'd find out soon.

"I'm going to be sick," Jeffries said matter of factly, and bent over, retching. He straightened, white as a sheet, and said, "I'm going to be sick again." And he doubled over, puking beside the bed.

He came up after a minute, took a handkerchief from his pocket and wiped his mouth. I said something.

"What?" He sounded annoyed.

"I said, I'm alive."

He pulled the sheets from the empty bed beside me and mopped up the mess the best he could. He was whimpering, deep in his throat, like a child. He kicked the sheets against the far wall and stumbled back to the chair by my bed. He fell into the chair and rubbed his face hard with both hands. He didn't say anything for a moment, then his hands flew into the air and he shouted, *"Why?"*

"I swallowed some pills," I said.

"You—you . . . Why'd you do that?"

"To kill myself."

"Kill yourself!"

"Yes."

"You called me a—a very bad name." He was more shaken by my brush with death than I was. I think he wanted me to comfort him, but my mouth was dry and sour-tasting, and my head was pounding with sickening thuds.

"Don't tell anyone," I said.

"Why not?"

"They'll put me on suicide watch."

"Oh, well, we wouldn't want that, would we?"

"Read me the letter, Ned."

"I came all this way. I came all this way."

"Maybe God sent you."

He blinked rapidly. The idea startled him.

"You know," I said, "God sent you to save me."

"I did save you, didn't I?"

"Yes, you did, Ned."

"My God," he said, and he began to weep. "Oh, that's all I ever wanted," he said. "To be used."

"You're doing a good job," I said. "Will you read me the letter now, Ned?"

"You want me to read it?"

"I can't read."

"Oh, yes. Yes, of course. I knew that. But—" He wiped the back of his hand under his nose, snuffling. "But what if it's bad news? I mean, that wouldn't be good, would it?"

"No, bad news would not be good. But some news is better than no news, Ned."

He picked up the letter. His hands were shaking.

"This proves it, doesn't it, Halley?" he whispered. "There must be a God."

"Weren't you already pretty sure about that, Ned?"

He seemed panicked. "Oh, no, no, no. That would be silly. I mean, I'm almost a preacher."

"And I was almost dead. Read the letter."

"Okay."

He slit the envelope carefully along the fold, using his fingernail, going slow, the sound of the ripping paper very loud in the gloom. He stopped halfway through the job and turned on the bedside light. If I had use of my hands I would have strangled him. I wanted to scream for him to hurry up, but I held my tongue. He pulled a single sheet of paper from the envelope, cleared his throat, and said: "My."

"What?"

"She has beautiful handwriting!" He brought the paper up to his nose. "Perfumed, too," he murmured.

"Damn it, Ned . . ."

"Okay, here I go—"

And he read the letter. He read it through once, slowly, then he read it again. In the years to come I would read it myself, sometimes two or three times a day, to hear the echo of your voice in my head, like the memory of a voice in a dream, where the sound fades to only the memory of sound. I still can recite it, word for word, by heart:

"Dear Halley,

"This must be the ninth or tenth letter I've begun since you went away. I get halfway through a letter and I tear it into tiny pieces and, so frightened am I of Daddy, flush the little pieces down the commode, lest he find them. I've made up my mind, however, to finish this letter no matter how stupid it sounds or how foolish I feel in writing it. Sometimes one must be a little foolish, if one is alive at all.

"Please forgive me if I sound silly. I have not seen much of the world, and most, if not all, I know of it is from books. I live inside my own imagination, like the majority of people, I suppose.

"I am home again. I came home last month and for the past thirty days I have kept to my room, only leaving it to eat and to walk in the garden. Just walking among the roses reminds me of you, for that is the only place we 'met,' if you could call what happened a meeting. I hope you can forgive me for not speaking to you that day, but you left so quickly! And I was literally speechless. I didn't know what to say. I want you to know, though, that I was not *too* frightened, though you practically leapt out of the bushes at me! You see, I knew who you were. I had seen you before, many times. I even knew your name. To be perfectly honest, *I* had been watching you too. You never knew, I'm sure, but sometimes in the late afternoons when the heat became truly unbearable, I would go up to the second-floor balcony to enjoy the cool breezes, and it was there that I first saw you, walking in the groves. There was something about you, immediately apparent, something untamed yet noble, an animal purity—oh, I hope this doesn't offend you, but even from a distance I knew you were different from the other men who worked for my father, from any man I had ever known. The day he hired you he entertained us at the table with the story of you breaking his walking stick. He meant the story to be mocking, but it had the opposite effect upon me. I can't really describe what effect it had on me. All I know is something fierce and powerful was awakened inside me . . . can you begin to understand? Part of it was you were the first person I ever knew who challenged my father and refused to be cowed by him. I asked some of the servants if they knew you. Elias knew who you were, and told me your name. I remember thinking how unusual and how poetic it was. Halley Martin. How many times I turned that name on my tongue! Halley Martin. But you must forgive a naive and sheltered girl for not speaking to you that day in the garden. I should at least have said thank you! Please, please forgive me.

"It is early evening here, my favorite time of the day, when the heat at last seems to rise from the earth with a great sigh and the wind begins to whisper in the cypress trees below my window. From my desk I can look out the window at the rows and rows of seedlings stretching for as far as the eye can see, and they make me think of beginnings—promises and harvests long planned for, long counted on. 'In twenty years,' I tell myself, 'Halley Martin will be eligible for parole. If he is good in prison, perhaps they will let him go.'

"*Are* you being good? Forgive me, Halley, if that sounds naive and stupid. But you *must* be good, if you ever hope to be free. 'Perhaps he'll escape and come for me,' I think, and then push that awful thought away. If you escape and they catch you, they'll never let you out again.

"Sometimes I picture us on that day, the day you return to Homeland, walking through the garden, and I can have a little peace in my heart.

"You know Daddy found the picture you gave me. What talent you have! He took it from me by force. At last I let go of it, only because I was afraid he would tear it, and I could not bear the thought of it being ruined. Not because it was a picture of me (I'm not a vain girl, no matter what my friends say!), but it was a present from you, the only present I ever received from you, and it broke my heart to part with it, though it would have killed me to have it marred. Daddy asked, Who gave this to you? And I slipped a bit and said, Halley Martin. Halley Martin gave it to me. Daddy asked, And who is this man to you? And I said, Nothing.

I don't even know him. 'But you know his name,' he said. I couldn't deny that, and I believed my eyes betrayed me at that moment: He saw in my eyes the seed of love already planted in my heart.

"Oh, Halley, how I tormented myself in those days, telling myself I was a stupid, foolish, silly, spoiled girl, who knew nothing of love, who thought she was in love with a man she had only seen from an upstairs window, from afar, and then I would think of poor, tragic Juliet, falling for Romeo at first sight. It *can* happen in real life. I know that from *my* life. It does no good to tell Daddy this. He wouldn't believe me and honestly would find some way to kill you if he did. He has flooded me with 'beaus' since you left. Boy after boy he has 'chosen' for me, parading them through our house, and each I turn away. Some are quite attractive and most offer everything I (or Daddy) could hope for, but, although I tell myself to be practical, I cannot see myself with any of them. 'You only long for what you can't have,' my cousin Mary tells me. Well, that may be so. I may long for something I can't have, but that doesn't make it any less of a longing, or any less true. I suppose there are worse things one could live for. Oh! How I wish I had told Elias more that night. How I wish I told him to tell you to come to me in Inverness, to run, run as fast as you could to me. Walter would be alive, and everything would be all right. That's all I ever wanted, was for everything to be all right, and sometimes I'm afraid it won't be.

" 'You will forget this man,' Daddy tells me. 'You will forget all this, in time.' But my father, having never loved, does not understand love. I have been witness to a loveless marriage (my own parents'), and for me, it is the only thing that can make any of this whole: waiting for the right man to come for me. I'm not afraid of my youth slipping away while I wait. Waiting, living by longing—it's the only way I can see of making it all worthwhile. It is my punishment for what I have done to you, and to Walter.

"What torments me is I had my chance. After Daddy found that note you left for me in the roses, he didn't lock me in a tower and throw away the key. I could have sneaked out. I could have gone with Elias when he went to find you . . . oh, Halley, can you ever forgive me? Perhaps these next twenty years will be time well spent; perhaps in that time you can find it in your heart to forgive me, and I, myself.

"Will you come for me, Halley, when your time there is done? Will you come back for me, to redeem the time, to redeem this longing? Being free, will you release me? I pray every night this could be so, but only God knows the true desires of our hearts, and only he can fulfill them.

"The day has faded now almost altogether. Daddy is upstairs; I can hear him clumping about in that snorting, boorish way of his. Oh, how I hate him! I blame him for what's happened, for my being here and your being there and even for Walter. He is the one who will answer for it all, when Eternity comes.

"Now the stars are coming out, and I am reminded of time. Time is nothing to the stars. These same stars burned when Christ walked the earth, and they are still as young and as beautiful. Our hearts are like stars, Halley, forever bright and shining, though our bodies break and fade. Hope never dies, but grows each day, in my heart, my secret heart, which loved you from the moment I saw you, and will, always, until the day I see you again . . ."

When he had finished reading it the second time, I made him read the last part over again:

"Today I took an oak tree, a seedling which Elias had found for me, and I brought it to the highest point in town, and I planted the tree at the top of that hill. I planted it as a promise, Halley, as a promise and a beacon. As long as this tree lives and grows, I will wait for you."

I took a deep breath.

"And how'd she sign it, Ned?"

"She signed it, 'Love, Mavis.' "

" 'Love,' " I said.

"Yes. 'Love.' "

He folded the letter and slipped it back into the envelope.

"Save it for me, Ned."

"Of course I'll save it for you."

"Ned."

"Yes, Halley."

"I want to read. I want you to teach me how."

"Of course I will, Halley."

"Don't tell them about the pills."

"I won't. Halley, you must answer this letter."

"Tomorrow," I said. "Come back tomorrow."

The next morning he brought a pad of paper and a pencil sharpened to a fine point. He had recovered from the shock of the night before and now was practically beside himself with excitement. It was as if he had stumbled upon his mission in life.

"All right!" he cried, settling into the chair. He wet the point of the pencil with the tip of his tongue. " 'Dear Mavis.' "

" 'Dear Mavis,' " I said, and stopped. He tapped the pencil on the pad.

"There probably should be more to it," he said.

"I don't know what to say," I said.

He looked at me, on the edge of panic. He was always teetering on that edge.

"Well, I don't know, Halley. I've never written to a girl before."

We stared at each other for a few minutes.

"When I saw your letter, it was like it brought me back to life," I said slowly. He nodded rapidly.

"That's good. That's good," he said.

"It was like I was dying and your letter came and I wasn't dying anymore," I said. "I was half-alive before I met you and half-alive when I went away from you . . ."

"Oh, yes!"

"I have to see you," I said.

"See you, yes, you have to," he murmured, pencil flying.

"You have to find a way to get here. I'm allowed visitors. Your daddy's a problem, but you could sneak out for a day. Tell Elias. Elias will help you," I said.

"Elias—who's Elias?"

"Write, Ned. Just write."

"All right."

"Elias will help you. I'm laid up in the hospital right now, but next week I'm out, and you can see me any Thursday. Come to me, Mavis, I must see you. I have to see your face again because it's faded from me. It's faded away from me and I must see you. If you can't come I understand, but what I want you to understand is it doesn't matter; it doesn't matter to me anymore whether you come or don't come, write or don't write, remember me or don't remember me. What matters is what's in my heart, my own heart. I will wait, Mavis. I will wait if it takes the rest of my life, until I am an old man, an old dried-up, shriveled-up old man, and when my waiting is over I will come to you. I will come to you, Mavis, and this time I will not hide; I will not watch you from a distance. I will come to you bold. I will come to you on fire. I will come to you. I will come to you. I will come to you."

He kept writing for a long time after I finished. My head was spinning and I was out of breath. I don't know how he kept up. I told him to read it back to me. When he finished, I said, "That too many 'I will come to you's'?"

"Oh, no. It's good, Halley. I'll copy it neatly and send it off today."

"That ain't everything," I said. " 'Love, Halley.' Put that, 'Love, Halley.' "

"I assumed that part."

"How am I goin' to sign it?"

"I'll sign it for you." He stood up. He held himself straighter. He now had the self-assurance of a prophet. "I'm off. This afternoon we'll start on your letters."

"Another one?"

"Letters of the alphabet, Halley. You have to learn to read. You may not want anyone to see how she answers this!"

I'd have to wait a long time for that. On Monday morning Nester appeared with the shackles. Corrigan signed some papers and handed them to Nester. Lawson had already dressed me. I asked him if he was coming with me to the cell block, as my personal manservant. He didn't say anything. Nester locked my wrists.

"What's the point?" I asked.

"Orders," he said. "Hope this don't hurt."

"Don't worry about it," I said.

I went outside for the first time in four months. Thick black clouds hung low in the morning sky, and a soaking drizzle came down. It felt like heaven. We walked across the muddy yard, past the new cell block, almost halfway done now. Something new was rising on the spot where Preacher died.

"They put him in the orphan's plot," Nester told me. "Said he had no kin."

"That's a lie," I said. "He had three ex-wives and about a dozen children."

He shrugged. We stopped outside Cell Block C.

"You hold your head high now, Halley."

"What?"

"No matter what they do. You got nothin' to be ashamed of."

"What're you talking about, Nester?"

"It'll be okay," he said. He let me go first, falling behind me about three steps. As we walked down the hall toward the last cell, men came forward and pressed their faces against the bars. The block was silent, absolutely still, and as I passed they spat at me, soaking my face and shirt with their spit. Nester shouted at them, "Step back, now, step on back, goddamn it!" But no one stepped back and there was nothing Nester could do about it. We reached my cell. My face was dripping, stinking of spit and tobacco juice. He unlocked my shackles inside the cell. He saw the question in my eyes and he whispered, "It's about the Preacher. They blame you, Halley, and nothin' I say can change that. Say it's your fault he's dead."

I nodded. I probably would have felt the same way. Nester wiped my face dry and he patted my shirt.

"Gonna cut you dead," he whispered.

"Who is?"

"The prison. The whole place. Everybody. Not me; I wouldn't cut you dead, Halley."

"What's that mean, cut me dead?"

"Means you dead. You gone. You ain't here. Nobody's gonna talk to you, look at you, even act like you're here. You're just—gone."

I thought about it.

"That's all right with me," I said.

"It never lasts. Don't worry about it. Practically the only thing to do in this place is talk, so sooner or later they will. They won't hurt you, though. Warden's got strict word out on that."

"Jessup heard it?"

"I told you, you won't have no trouble from Jessup no more. Blueboy's stepped up on him. An' Blueboy's yellow to his bones. Sneaky bastard, but he won't hurt you. Think he's scared of you."

"Hard to imagine why," I said.

Nester left. I sat on the bunk. I was alone in the cell. I looked around. Preacher's Bible was gone. His toothbrush was gone. In the back of the cell his guitar leaned against the wall. Bastards. There was only one reason they left it here.

A guitar with no strings. An artist with no hands.

My days in the wash-house were over. I was counted every morning, then returned to my cell, locked in, and forgotten. Forgotten by Florida State Prison, but not by Ned Jeffries. He came every afternoon at two, with a stack of books and a pad of paper. I picked up my letters quickly, and by the end of the second week I was reading primer books without stopping for his help. I held the book in my lap, keeping it open with the back of one hand, turning the pages by licking the knuckle of my middle finger and pushing the page over.

At mess my first day back a trusty named Vickers met me at the door. Nester was with him.

"Halley," Nester said, "this is Joe Vickers. Warden's assigned him your feeding detail."

I looked at Vickers. He was a heavyset man with a bulging brow and small, black eyes. A scar ran from his cheek to his jowl, the result of a fight years ago over, ironically, food. Vickers did not acknowledge my presence. He was staring at some point over my left shoulder.

"I don't need a feeding," I said. "I'm not some goddamned animal in the zoo."

"Well, Halley," Nester said, a little helpless, "how else you gonna eat?"

I fell into line, Vickers behind me. He didn't say a word. No one said a word, not to me. No one looked at me. You've fallen pretty far when you're beneath even a convict's contempt. I slid my tray along the line using my wrists, and nudged it into the crook of my arms with my chin. I found a place to sit, and before I had even planted myself the table was empty. Vickers slid in beside me. Without looking at my face, he tucked a napkin under my chin and scooped up some stew into my spoon.

"Go to hell," I said.

He didn't even blink. He held the spoon to my lips, looking past my face, out the window to the yard.

"Go to hell, you fat, stinking, motherfucking son of a bitch," I said. "You know, you're one of the ugliest bastards I think I've ever seen. Your momma probably puked when she saw you born. Probably thought you were something else and threw you in the toilet."

He let the spoon fall, spilling the hot stew into my lap.

"Put the goddamned spoon into my stew," I hissed at him. He complied, then turned to his own meal. I stared down at my bowl, the familiar rage burning in my gut, but I did nothing. Nothing but stand and walk out. Vickers didn't even look up.

Every day I refused to let Vickers feed me. I compromised, of course: I ate once a day, when Jeffries brought me a plate. He would jam a fork in my twisted fingers and secure it in place with tape. I got good at eating that way after a few frustrating meals. We both knew he'd lose all privileges, probably be barred from the prison, if he was found bringing me food in my cell, not to mention a utensil as potentially deadly as a fork, but Ned had a growing sense of adventure that this breaking of the rules appealed to. I was taking in four or five simple books a day, as fast as he could check them out of the prison library. He gave me your letter, and I practiced my reading with that, until I knew every word by heart. He waited as anxiously as I did for your reply to my letter, but the weeks dragged by and nothing came.

The success with the fork inspired us to try the same with a pencil. But I lacked the control I needed to draw; my hands felt impossibly loose on my wrists—they still do—and I couldn't control the pressure bearing down on the point; the lead would shatter after a few lines. One time I bore down so hard the pencil broke in half. Then I broke too, right in front of Jeffries, and he held me as I sobbed until I told him to get his goddamned hands off me. I never tried to draw again.

As for the rest of my life in Starke, I was cut dead. No one spoke to me save Nester and Jeffries, not even the other guards. In the yard I was ignored, and in the mess, and in the Block. Corrigan checked me out once a month, but even he didn't say much. What he did say was not encouraging. The bones in my hands had fused, the nerves permanently damaged. My fingers would be forever frozen in their tortured positions. Behind my back, Nester confided, the inmates called me Crabs.

The warden summoned me to his office a month after my release from the infirmary.

"I've decided to give you a work assignment," he said. He would not look at me, as if he was determined to honor as much of the code of banishment as he could. "It's not good for a man to sit idle in his cell."

"I'm not idle, Warden," I said. "I'm very busy."

"Understand I am allowing Ned Jeffries to help you as a courtesy to him, not as a favor to you. Although I am pleased to see a man try to better himself."

He placed his hand behind his neck and let his head fall back, wincing as he massaged himself.

"Where're you putting me, Warden? The mess? I could peel potatoes."

"I'm replacing Gunther Milthrop."

"Oh. Who's Gunther Milthrop?"

"A trusty."

"You're making me a trusty?"

"I'm giving you his job. It's up to you whether you become a trusty."

"What's the job?"

"The library."

I couldn't believe my ears. "When?"

"Starting tomorrow. Milthrop will stay on for another week to help you get on your feet. That is all."

I turned at the door and said, "This make you feel better, Warden MacAffee?"

He forgot himself and looked right at me.

"Better?"

"For giving me to Jessup."

"Get him out of here," he snapped at the guard.

"How much did it cost, Warden?" I shouted at him as I was dragged away. "How much did this cost?" I held up my hands. The guard smacked his fist into the back of my head, and I cried out, "Preacher's blood is on your hands, Warden, yours and Robert Hughes's, not mine! Not mine!"

MacAffee slammed the door.

In December the war came. Our brothers, fathers, and sons shipped out, and we remained. The machine shop was converted to produce shell casings. Some men were given releases to work at the nearby foundry, making tank parts. Jeffries got a deferment, based on religious grounds, and helped me clean up and organize the library during that first winter of the war. We divided the books into fiction and nonfiction and arranged the first by author and the second by subject. As with everything, Jeffries threw himself into the project with a gusto that was almost frightening. He began a "must-read" list for me, books like *The Adventures of Huckleberry Finn* and Homer's *Odyssey,* which, miraculously, the library had. I told him to put *Romeo and Juliet* on the list, and he laughed out loud, shouting, "Of course!" and pounding his fist into his palm. I don't know where he found it, but the next day he appeared with a battered volume of the complete works of Shakespeare.

The library had two hundred and ninety-one books, and I made up my mind to read all of them. I had the time. I read from the moment I got to the library—an old storeroom in the back of the administration building about the size of a large closet—until lights-out in the Block, with breaks only to eat and be Jeffried by Ned. He fretted as the winter dragged on, like the war in Europe, becoming more anxious as each day passed without a letter from you.

"How could she *not* reply?"

"We were stupid," I said. I was reading *Huck Finn* at the time, which had made me acutely aware that the world was full of stupid people. "Lester got that letter."

"Who in the world is Lester?"

So I told him the whole story from the beginning. He was a good audience; he didn't interrupt me but let me tell it to the end. When I was done, he said, "We don't know he got it."

"Only reason she wouldn't answer."

"But this is horrible!" he said. "How will we reach her?"

The next day, after a sleepless and tortured night with much earnest prayer, he announced, "I shall go to Homeland."

I was surprised. "Why?"

"I shall go to Homeland and I shall contact that Negro, what's his name?"

"Elias."

"Yes. I shall contact Elias and arrange everything."

"What're you going to arrange, Ned?"

"I don't know why we didn't think of it before," he said. "We shall arrange a post office box. We'll send our letters there. Elias can pick them up and deliver them to her. Can he be trusted?"

"They're my letters, Ned," I said.

"Oh yes. Of course. It's perfect, Halley! I'll leave tomorrow."

He was beside himself. He was in a tizzy. He had cast himself as a spy in this critical battle of love's war.

"I shall pose as myself . . ."

"How's that posing, Ned?"

He wasn't listening to me, barreling on: "I shall let the townspeople know I've come to explore the possibility of establishing a church. Yes! I am come to gauge the spiritual needs of the population. I shall go to Lester Howell to ask for a donation to the building fund, and when I'm there I will buttonhole Elias. It's absolutely perfect!"

He beamed at me. I thought he was going to kiss me. He said, "And
if it is safe—and I promise you I will not if it isn't, but if it's safe, and I
can talk to her alone—is there anything you want me to say to her? To
Mavis?"

I thought about it.

"Yes. Tell her to keep her promise."

He took the train the next morning, and I was surprised that, in a
strange kind of way, I missed him while he was gone. Nester had been
reassigned to the midnight shift, so Jeffries was my only human contact, the only person on earth who spoke to me. When an inmate wan-
dered into the library for a book, which wasn't often, he would pass any
request to me in writing. If he couldn't write, he brought a friend who
could. It wasn't the kind of library you went to for great literature.
Westerns were very popular and dime-store pulp fiction. The rules pro-
hibited any cops-and-robbers books, as well as dirty books, but Jeffries
and I had found a whole box full of them tucked in a closet and covered
with an old blanket. Milthrop had rented these out special for ten cents
a night. Jeffries hauled them out that night and told me later he threw
them away. I hoped so. I didn't know but could guess what Mother
would have thought of them.

He was gone for ten days. It was the longest stretch of time he'd been
away since I had come to Starke. He appeared in the doorway to the
library one morning, dressed in a dark suit and a dramatic black cloak,
though it was April and eighty-five degrees by mid-morning.

"Success!" he cried.

I stood up. "Did you see her?"

"No, but everything's arranged. That Elias is a sharp customer, and
Lester doesn't suspect a thing."

I didn't quite believe him. I knew your daddy better than that. "How
do you know?"

He ignored me. "It's a charming little town. In some ways it reminds me of Van Wert, though much hotter and wetter." He threw off his cloak and collapsed into my chair. He drew a comb through his black hair.

I was hungry for news from home. I asked him if he had seen my mother, and he had. She was coming up for a visit soon but didn't know when. He told me Jasper had joined the Army and was stationed in London. He didn't tell them about my hands. He had tried to look up Farley, but he was out of town, down in Texas somewhere, he'd been told. Lorraine and Wiley had sent some pound cake, but Jeffries had gotten hungry on the train and eaten it.

"Sorry about that," he said. "It was delicious."

"You didn't even see her?"

"No. I spoke only to Lester; the rest of the family was in Inverness for a few days. But I seized the opportunity and told Elias our plans. He is with us, with us fully. He is a very sharp Negro. And he seems very fond of you. He has the key and will check the box every week. Getting the letters to her will be safe and easy for him."

He told me Lester had replanted the groves, but a hard freeze came again that winter, and most of the seedlings were lost. Folks around town told him Lester was in bad shape, mortgaged to the hilt and staving off creditors. He sold off some land but had to cancel his annual pilgrimage to Africa for safari. His health wasn't good. And Mavis's invalid mother had taken to her room permanently, not able to even attend church.

"Elias did say one thing about her," he said, the smile he had worn since coming in slowly fading. "He said she is not the carefree girl she once was. Mopes around, is how he put it. She mopes around all the time. Spends much of the time when she's home in the rose garden."

"Yes," I said. "She would."

"But never says a word about you. But that I think we should interpret as a good sign," he added quickly. "Elias feels badly himself, Halley. He says he prays every day for God to forgive him."

"Forgive him for what?"

"Telling you about Walter—what he did. Telling you there needed to be a reckoning. I think he feels he put you up to it."

"No one put me up to it."

He nodded slowly and dropped his eyes.

"There's one other thing."

"What?"

"Your father is dead."

"Good."

How long ago it seemed, that night Elias came to me, while the rain-water dripped from the eaves and the cypress trees swayed, whispering, in the deep night. And Jeremiah asleep on my chest, wrapped in my shirt, his warm cheek against my skin. No more to blame than Elias, and no memory either of that night. Today he is twenty years old with two babies of his own, with his own memories now to weigh him down. It's what we remember, not what we do, that truly damns us.

The next day Jeffries appeared in the library with a pad of paper and a freshly sharpened pencil.

"Not today," I told him.

He looked like he was going to cry. He was like a child who had been told we weren't going to the zoo.

"But everything's arranged," he said.

"Not today," I said.

His mouth moved soundlessly, then he turned on his heel and stomped out.

I left the library and walked down the hall to the warden's office. Killebrew, the trusty who served as his receptionist, stood up when I came into the room.

"I need to see the warden," I said.

He stared at me for a minute, chewing on his lower lip, then gestured for me to wait. I waited. He came back after a minute and motioned for me to go in.

MacAffee was working on some papers. I noticed a streak of gray in his thinning hair. He did not look up.

"You are interrupting me."

"I need a typewriter," I said.

"Writing your memoirs?"

"I'm putting together a list of all the books in the library."

"You don't need a typewriter for that."

"I've practiced writing with my feet, but my toes are too far apart."

He tapped his pen on the desktop. He still had not looked at me.

"We don't have any typewriters to spare."

"I don't want it forever. I'll return it."

"The answer is no."

"It's the least you could do for me."

"I owe you nothing."

"And you've paid me in full."

I went back to the library and sat down. The place always smelled of mildew and rotting paper. It got in my clothes; the way some men smelled of alcohol or tobacco, I smelled of old books.

My father was dead. Drowned in the big metal washtub, an empty bottle on the floor beside him. The day before my momma had taken my sisters over to Wiley's place, where they stayed the night. Momma found his body the next day. Wouldn't have happened if they had been there. He picked a bad night to get drunk and take a bath. Made you wonder. It was funny; I always thought I got my reckless streak from my father.

Killebrew came in. He was carrying a typewriter. He dumped it in front of me and left. I found some paper in the desk and managed to load it in the machine by holding the top of the paper in my mouth and lowering it down. I used both twisted hands to roll the paper in. I typed with the middle knuckle of my right middle finger. Each stroke sent shocks of pain up my arm. Each letter was agony, every word torture. By that afternoon, when Jeffries returned, recovered from his little hissy fit, I had finished my first real letter to you. I told him to address the envelope and put the letter in it, and made him swear he wouldn't look at one word of it. He nodded without saying anything, his lower lip quivering, and did as I asked.

"I'll mail it tomorrow," was all he said.

In late summer of 1944, Farley came to visit me. He hadn't changed much. He was a little rounder and his eyes seemed to be disappearing into his face behind rolls of skin that drooped beneath his eyebrows. I think I had changed more than he. He would not look at my hands. He didn't have much news for me, except to say Trimbul was still Sheriff and Franks was now a judge, "heaven help us." Lester had fired Wiley and most of his men. He was drinking heavily and stayed locked inside that big house most of the time. You and your momma were sent down to Inverness for months at a time.

"I brought you something," he said. He opened a paper sack and pulled out my old sketch pad, the one that had been used against me in court, the one that had made Trimbul blush. He held it up for an awkward moment, then laid it on the table.

"I don't want it," I said.

"Why the hell not? You know what I had to go through to get that?"

"It's of no use to me."

"Well, it ain't the kind of thing you *use*." He stopped, embarrassed. "I understand," he said, and started to pull it off the table.

"No. I'll take it."

He seemed relieved. "Okay." He sat back in his chair and smiled slightly. "Things are happening in Texas. Can't tell which way it's gonna go yet, but it looks good. It looks damn good, Halley."

"Let me know," I said.

"I been thinkin', you know, for my time and trouble, a small percentage. If it comes out okay. Only if it comes out okay. I ain't out to fleece you, Halley."

"You do whatever you think is fair."

He nodded. He had said what he came to say, and now there was nothing left to say. He wasn't used to having nothing left to say. He picked up his hat.

"You told me once everything was going to be all right," he said. "You still think that?"

"On good days," I said.

I dropped the pad on my desk beside the typewriter. I didn't look in it. I couldn't, not yet. I walked out of the building, into the yard. It was noon.

There was no breeze. In the shadeless yard the air shook with the force of the heat. I didn't know if I could ever look at those drawings of you. It was like racing after a mirage in the desert. There and not there. Present—and gone. The heat made breathing difficult; you had to work harder to get the heavy air into your lungs. I went back to the library. Jeffries was sitting at the desk, the sketch pad open in front of him. He jumped up when I came in, his face going red up to his greasy black hair.

"It's all right," I said.

He pointed at the pad, his finger shaking slightly. "Halley, I—I hope you don't—these are—" he searched for the right word. "Extraordinary."

"I'm glad you like them, Ned."

"Yes. Why, yes, I do. You're quite talented. You—" he stopped and lowered his head. His jaw clenched. "It is a crime before God what they did to you," he said.

"Not much I can do about that now," I said. I flipped the pad closed with the back of my hand. I crushed it between my gnarled fingers and placed it on the shelf behind the desk.

He cleared his throat. "I didn't know she . . . modeled for you."

"She didn't. It's just my imagination, Ned."

"You have a better imagination than I do."

I shrugged. Whatever he was holding in wasn't going to stay in long. His whole body was shaking with the effort to hold it in. Finally it exploded out of him, an anguished cry: "Oh dear God, Halley, how do you bear it?"

I didn't notice until months had passed that the pad was gone. The war ended, and our brothers and fathers and sons came home, some of them, anyway, and the population inside Starke doubled within three months. They had kept the world safe, and now the world needed to be kept safe from them. I saw less and less of Ned. He still held prayer vigils and made visitations in the infirmary, but he was growing restless. I don't know what I would have done if I had realized then the true nature and extent of his restlessness. He would disappear for weeks at a time. He told me he was traveling, scouting a place to put down his spiritual roots. Mother was on him to start his church. When I did see him I would have to endure monologues lasting a good hour or more as he agonized over his calling, if he truly was saved, and if he was, if that's what God wanted him to do.

"My problem is I don't like people very much," he said at one point. "Well, I like people, but I can't get to that place where they *are*. I don't know how to get to where they really are."

"Oh, I don't know," I said. "You've been okay getting to where I am."

He looked away. "I can't stay here forever, can I, Halley?"

"No, that's my job."

His face twisted into a smile. Ned Jeffries did not have a natural-looking smile. It looked more like a facial tic.

"Getting to where you are," he said.

We were in my cell. I was lying on my bunk, naked but for my underwear, as Jeffries gave me my weekly sponge bath. There was no escaping a sponge bath, unless I wanted to smell like roadkill, and the chore fell to Jeffries when Nester wasn't on duty. He knelt beside my bunk, a bucket of warm, soapy water before him, running the cloth over my arms, neck, chest, stomach, and legs. We did not look at each other during these ministrations, and usually there was little conversation, so as to speed up the process. But on this night something was weighing heavily on him, heavier than usual, and usually his chin seemed to drag the ground from the weight of all his burdens.

"Things are very simple for you," he said. "Even the most complicated things."

"What are you talking about, Ned?"

"Sit up," he said. I sat on the edge of the bunk while he washed my back. "There is something I must tell you, Halley. But I don't know how."

I waited. Waiting had become my speciality, my particular field of expertise. He took a deep breath.

"Halley, I believe I have . . . no, I am sure I have . . . there can't be much doubt that . . . Halley, I'm in love." He choked the word out, as if it galled him.

"Well. Ned, you dog."

"No one is more surprised than I. I wasn't looking. As almighty God is my witness, it found me."

"I know what you mean."

"Yes! You do. You know absolutely what I mean!" he said, running the washcloth up my arm and swirling it around my neck. The water cooled my skin and I shivered. Years ago, after I killed Walter, Wiley led me to a well where he washed the blood from my naked torso, the icy water meeting my hot flesh, and steam rose in the close Florida night. "Oh, I have been praying, studying my Bible, but nothing can replace discussing things with a . . . a kindred spirit." He dunked the cloth into the bucket of water and slowly rung it out. He wore an expression I had never seen before, as if he were about to laugh and cry at the same time. I knew that feeling. For the first time—and probably the last—I actually felt sorry for Ned Jeffries.

"You ain't making much sense, Ned."

He threw the cloth into the water, the only gesture of violence I ever saw from him, and cried, "There is no sense! No sense to any of it! That's why I envy you. You—you, Halley Martin, would not hesitate. You *did not* hesitate! You seized what your heart desired, and damn the consequences!"

"What is it, Ned, is she married?"

"Not—precisely. She is . . . pledged to another."

"Does she love you?"

He frowned. Water dripped from his fingertips onto the edge of the mattress. "I confess, Halley, I do not fully know her heart." He laughed bitterly. "Would that stop *you*?"

"It didn't."

"No. You're quite right, it didn't. And you told me once, once you told me, that what *she* felt didn't matter. That what mattered was what was in your heart. That was the one thing you could be sure of."

"Right."

"And now how long has it been since her letter? Four, five years? And still, you cling to hope."

"If that's what you call it."

"I wouldn't. Forgive me, but I wouldn't. I would call it vanity."

"You know, somebody else once accused me of that, a long time ago."

"Well, it *is* vanity!"

"You angry about something, Ned?"

He didn't answer. He wrapped the wet cloth around my head as I bent forward, and the water dripped on my bare feet. I spoke with my head bowed, my forehead almost touching my knees, as he scrubbed my scalp.

"Maybe it is vanity," I said. "And maybe it's stupidity and maybe it's just crazy. Maybe it's closer to faith—"

"Faith!"

"But something I've come to realize is, it don't matter what I decide to call it. You can say it's vanity. But for me, it just *is*."

He wasn't interested in abstractions; he had come to address a very practical problem. He eased my head back, so my face was now tilted toward the ceiling, and ran the washcloth over my closed eyes. "She's a beautiful young woman, men will pursue her, and how can you hope that one might not succeed in the end? You are here with only a slim hope of returning before you are both old and feeble. You are a prisoner, yes, but does that mean she must be one as well? Tell me something, Halley, with all honesty, what would you do if she didn't wait for you?"

I thought about it. He seemed desperate for an honest answer. I opened my eyes and looked at him. "I don't know what I'd do."

"You killed Walter to have her."

"No. That isn't why I killed Walter. You don't know what you're talking about, Ned."

He took a deep, shuddering breath. His face was now very close to mine. He ran his tongue over his long, yellow teeth and hissed, "What is the one thing that matters most, Halley, in all the world?"

"You giving me a test, Ned?"

"Love," he said. "Would you agree?"

"Yes," I said.

"So when love comes within your grasp, the greatest sin . . . the greatest sin of all is to open your hand. I will tell you honestly, she is pledged to another, but I believe that with some . . . persuasion, she might change her mind."

"Then persuade her, Ned."

He became very still, as if the shadows had an iron grip, rooting him to the spot. He pressed his fist against his forehead and gave a little cry, somewhere between a sob and a laugh.

"I can't let her go, Halley. And *it* will not let me go. I am in the grasp of something I do not understand."

He forced himself to look at me, spreading his arms wide, hands turned slightly toward me, as if in supplication. He was straining to tell me the truth with his whole body, but I was blind to it.

A month later, Nester tapped on the bars with his keys and whispered my name. I sat up, and there was Jeffries, holding a white Panama hat and a small black bag. Nester let him in and he stood awkwardly as Nester faded into the shadows.

"Well, Ned."

"I'm leaving, Halley."

"Where're you going?"

He looked away. "Mother and I have built a small house, south of here," he said. He didn't elaborate. I wasn't going to push him, and he knew I wouldn't. That bothered him more than if I had.

"There comes a point," he said.

"Yes. There comes a point."

"You have been . . . a good friend to me, Halley."

"Now don't get mushy on me, Pastor." It was the first time I had called him that. He began to cry. Everything I said seemed to make it worse for him.

"Halley, I have something for you." He pulled the sketch pad from the black bag and set it on the cot beside me. "I shouldn't have taken it."

"No," I said. "You shouldn't have. Knew you did, though."

"You're not angry with me?"

I thought about it. "No. Yes. It doesn't matter now."

"I spoke to some men—here. They're good men, Christian men, they're part of my prayer group. I told them it was wrong, evil, what they're doing to you. I told them they must stop ostracizing you. It goes beyond cruelty, that's what I told them."

"It's not important to me now," I said.

"There's one other thing, something else I should tell you." He paused. "One day you will be free."

"Yes, Ned. One day."

"And you will have a choice to make, when that day comes. I have no doubt that . . . that day will come."

"When that day comes," I said, "I'll look you up."

He whipped his head in a kind of circle, as if he was trying to nod yes and shake his head no at the same time.

"Yes. Yes," he said. "Yes."

He left me. He never told me what the choice was I had to make. The darkness swallowed him up, and that was the last I saw of Ned Jeffries. It was nearly dawn on that sleepless night when I realized I had never thanked him for saving my life.

I set a goal, as I think I told you around September of '49, of one letter per week. I couldn't manage more. I never found a painless way to use the typewriter. No matter which hand I used or how I struck the key, each stroke set off an explosion of pain. Sometimes I would have to stop after a single paragraph. I would collapse back in my chair, sweat pouring off me, the pain like a fog around my head. I had a supply of morphine, but I rarely took it; it brought back a hard memory. Nester would fold the letter and address the envelope for me, and every day he'd check my mail for me, but nothing came. Nothing ever came.

I gave up writing you. At least a hundred times. But then the next week I would roll a piece of paper back into that old Remington and start again, "Dear Mavis . . ." You would think, you must have thought over the years, that one day, eventually, I'd run out of things to say. I certainly thought I would. But I never did.

I rarely saw Nester anymore, and you had become the only person on earth I could "talk" to. I flung my words into a void, that white sheet of paper, and when Nester took it from me to mail, the words were gone, vanished, as if they were never spoken.

It's true what they say, that a man can get used to practically anything. I grew accustomed to the way they treated me. I got used to being a breathing ghost, a nothing in drab blue clothes. So used to it I stopped noticing it. It had become a part of what I was, immutable, like the color of my eyes. I had told Sheriff Trimbul after my arrest I was all the way inside my head, and now I truly was. I can't say that I was never lonely. I was sometimes lonely even to the point of madness, for it is also true when they say you are never lonelier than when you're in a crowd. I've read about the crazy people who live on the street, walking about in their own little world, muttering to themselves or to the demons only they know, and I became a little like that as the years went on. I spoke to you. I would wake in the morning and say, "Looks like another scorcher, Mavis," or in the library, "I need to remember to order that new Zane Gray, Mavis," and I knew there were times when someone must have heard me and snickered at that ol' crazy Halley Martin. Nester was wrong when he told me someday I would rise from the dead, that eventually someone would talk to me. Once in a great while someone fresh from the outside would say something before he was pulled aside and told the score. And nothing ever came of Jeffries's lecture to his prayer group. I was dead to the men I lived with. I was the only one aware of my own life.

On the inside, I mean. It was easy to forget anyone remembered on the outside. Occasionally, an emissary arrived from the land of the living, to remind me.

In the fall of 1950, on a Thursday, Elias Johnson came to Florida State Prison.

"Mistah Halley," he said. "Your hands."

He hadn't changed a bit. He even wore the same uniform, carried the same wide-brimmed hat.

"It's a long story, Elias."

He nodded. He was that rare kind of man who didn't need explanations. Maybe it had something to do with being a servant his whole life.

"Mistah Halley, I would've come sooner than this—" And maybe as a servant he was used to having to provide explanations.

"That's all right, Elias," I said. "My own mother hasn't been here in nine years."

He nodded again, as if that was the most natural thing in the world.

"Mistah Halley, Lester Howell, he dead."

"How?" I asked.

"Shot hisself. Put that elephant gun in his mouth and pulled the trigger with his big toe. Blew his head clean off his shoulders. You never seen such a mess."

"No," I said honestly, all messes being relative. "You came all this way to tell me that, Elias?"

He dropped his eyes and turned the hat over in his hands. He had beautiful hands, black as space, with long slender fingers and nails buffed till they shone.

"Miss Mavis, she put the house up for sale. It's pretty run down, since Mistah Lester took to his bed. Bank's taken everything now but the house. Mistah Lester, he went broke."

"So he blew his head off his shoulders."

He shrugged. "Only thing matter to him was his money. When that gone, what else he gonna do?"

"Did she send you, Elias?"

He slowly shook his head. "No, Mistah Halley. I come on my own."

"To ask if I was interested in buying a house?"

He allowed himself the slightest of smiles.

"I got some news for you, Mistah Halley. It—it ain't good news. Miss Mavis—" he took a deep breath. "Miss Mavis, she married."

When I could talk, I said, "I am a fool, Elias Johnson. Whenever I see you coming I should run like hell."

"I don't know what to say, Mistah Halley."

"Tell me who."

He lowered his eyes again. He spoke so softly I had to ask him again.

"Ned Jeffries," he whispered.

I heard it the second time but made him say it again. "Ned Jeffries. You know who Ned Jeffries is. You was the one who first sent him down there."

"It was more his idea than mine," I said.

"Well, not too much longer after he come down he comes back, and starts talkin' up Mistah Lester. You know, Mistah Halley, how a man can go his whole life not givin' two shakes to God, but when he hit bottom all of a sudden he wants to sign up. He gets real interested in his own soul. Mistah Ned, he feeds all right into that. An' pretty soon there he is, at the house every night, for dinner and all, an' after he sittin' on the porch, talkin' up Miss Mavis. Oh, I ain't no spy; I ain't sayin' I hear all he say, but he plays on her like nothin' I ever seen. Says how he saved your life here, how he nurse you back to health and practically your nanny, feedin' you and bathin' you, which I couldn't figure till right now when I see those hands. Oh, Lordy, Mistah Halley, what they done to your hands?"

"Mavis Howell married Ned Jeffries."

"Miss Mavis, she beside herself. She don't know what to do. There's bills, Mistah Halley, you don't believe all the bills and the ugly men come by to collect on 'em. She got nothin'. She got her momma, who is sick-crazy; she can't take care of her proper. That ol' house fallin' down 'round our ears 'cause there ain't no money to fix it. Then Ned Jeffries come down to start a church, and right off he builds a little house with an extra room and he got a steady job. An' he sweet to her. Sweet *on* her too. Don't get me wrong, Mistah Halley. I do believe Mistah Ned is in love with her."

"Of course," I said. I was thinking of the day I caught him in the library, looking at the drawings of you, naked, and his cry, *How can you bear it?* Of him washing me, flinging the cloth into the water and joining the shadows that lurked in the back of the cell, speaking in a code to which I had no key. "Did she know you were coming here, Elias?"

"No. No, Mistah Halley. I come on my own."

"I don't understand why."

"Why she married him?"

"Why you came to tell me."

"I didn't want you to find out some other way. I owe you that, Mistah Halley. If it hadn't been for me . . ." A tear rolled down his cheek. And now, I thought, *I* must comfort *him.*

"Don't fret, Elias," I said.

"What you gonna do now, Mistah Halley?"

"Only thing I can do," I said. "For now."

———

That night in my cell I looked in the sketch pad for the first time since 1940. Different hands had worked here. Lover's hands. Before he left, Elias asked me if there was any message I wanted him to bring to you. I told him no.

"*I* am the message."

I turned the pages by sliding my knuckles hard against the paper. The man who had drawn this was a stranger to me. I couldn't recognize the work of my own hands.

The hands that had made this were the same hands that rammed a knife into a man's belly. Drawing you had been my only way of touching you; now, touching you, if I ever touched you, would set my hands on fire, would make me cry out in pain.

I wanted rid of you. I was tired. A vow I had never spoken, a promise I had never made, was sealed by Walter's blood. I had offered Walter up on the altar, and I had always believed I never had a choice in any of it. That I had given the answer love demanded. And it was Walter who had paid the price. I had carried you with me now for ten years, carried you with hands stained in Walter's blood, and I was tired. I wanted rid of you. And you, it seemed, wanted rid of me.

I stood up. The pad fell to the floor. I ground my heel into the pages, crumpling and ripping them. I fell to my knees and clawed at the paper, slapping my twisted fingers onto the hard floor and crying out with the pain. Kneeling, I slammed my wasted hands into the floor until blood spurted from my knuckles, staining the yellowed paper; my blood smeared your naked body.

From far away I heard someone shouting. The lights in the Block blazed on, and Nester was outside the door. He rushed in with another guard and they pulled me up. They grabbed my arms, and I flailed at them, spattering their faces with blood. Nester was in my face, screaming my name, while the other guard twisted my arms behind me and managed to get the handcuffs around my wrists.

After that day I fell into a silence rarely broken. I stopped talking to you. The sound of human voices grated on my nerves, and I would spend hours alone in the library, in a silence broken only by the sound of the fan whizzing in the corner. I still wrote to you, and when I was finished I took the letters to the trash barrel and dropped them into the fire. I lived with my books. Occasionally Farley would drop me a line or two about his adventures in Texas or the happenings in town, but he never touched on you or your new husband. I learned you had a baby from a telegram sent by Elias that read, "MISS MAVIS HAD BABY TODAY. NAMED IT SHARON-ROSE."

In the spring of '57 Farley came to visit. He was dressed in a tailored silk suit and wore a burgundy silk tie. He had a full head of hair. "Feel of it, Halley," he told me. "It's made from real hair." His round face was tanned, and a diamond ring shone on his finger. He opened his briefcase and pulled out a sheet of paper. He slid it across the table in front of me.

"Halley Martin, your present net worth."

I looked at the paper, then back up at him. He was grinning like the Cheshire cat. He leaned forward and whispered, like we were planning a crime.

"It just keeps comin' and comin', Halley. Comin' and comin' and comin'. Biggest oil strike in the history of the state. That is just your share from your initial investment of one thousand dollars. You're a lucky man."

I nodded. "Lucky," I said.

"And you're goin' to get it too, every penny of it."

"I always trusted you, Farley."

He shook out his handkerchief and blew his nose. The handkerchief was monogrammed with his initials.

"I ain't told no one, like I promised," he said. "Anyway, shame Lester ain't around to see this. Guess he won his bet. Never did understand why you let him think you burned it."

"That's all right," I said. "He did."

I told him what I wanted done in Homeland. He stared at me, like he had stared at me seventeen years ago when I first gave him the money. He started to argue with me, then he gave up with a little laugh. Even his laugh had changed: The rich don't laugh like the rest of us.

"I'll get to work on it," he said.

"And your fee," I said. "For representing me at the trial."

"You mean what I charged then or what I'm gonna charge now?"

"It doesn't matter."

"I'll be back next month," he promised, patting me on the shoulder. "You behave yourself now. Be a model prisoner and in three years you'll be comin' home."

"I am coming home," I said.

It's nine o'clock. They are here. I rise from my cot.

One of the guards reads from a sheet of paper. I am paroled from Florida State Prison, based upon my twenty years of good behavior, glowing recommendations from the staff (including Warden MacAffee), and particularly my expressions of remorse at the death of my victim. *My victim.* As if Walter belonged to me now. As if my killing him was a way of taking ownership of him.

I follow them into the hall. My cell door clangs shut behind me for the last time. I walk with my hands free past the other cells, where men press forward against the bars and watch, silently, a man come to life. I am taken to the administration building, where I work my way out of my prison clothes and change into a cheap cotton suit. One of the guards hands me a package: the clothes I wore into Starke twenty years ago. I carry it in the crook of my arm. I am escorted to the warden's office. MacAffee comes around his desk and says my name, for the first time, for today I am risen from the dead.

"Halley," he says. He places a hand on my shoulder. Some big men just go to fat as they age; MacAffee seems harder, packed tighter somehow.

"You know," he says, "I don't think, if I'd been on that jury, that you would be here today."

He follows us to the door and leans against the jamb, his arms folded over his chest. I look back, once. He is smiling. I will not see him again.

A bus waits for me at the gates. I climb aboard with the help of the driver, who grabs my wrist and pulls me up. I sit in the back of the empty bus as we rumble down the gravel road, passing beneath the sign that reads "Florida State Prison." Then we make a right turn, and I look out the window at the collection of buildings I had called home for the past twenty years. The prison disappears behind a gathering of pine trees.

The bus takes me to the train station, where the state of Florida has reserved me a ticket. "Good luck," the driver calls to me, and I nod to him before entering the station.

I am disoriented on the train. I see mothers traveling with their children, and I study them with the curiosity of a foreigner. After a while both they and I begin to feel a little creepy. I buy a newspaper from the porter and bury my nose in it.

The train ride takes three hours. I doze. I wake with the name Sharon-Rose on my lips. Two little boys are sitting across from me, and they are giggling and pointing at my hands. I slide them beneath the newspaper on my lap.

When I step onto the platform I look immediately for Phillips, the stationmaster who shouted at me to get aboard a different train a lifetime ago. He is nowhere in sight, and I figure he must be retired now, or dead. Or perhaps he has finally made it to Mexico, and he sits there now, his senorita at his side, sipping cocktails by an emerald sea.

I come off the steps and Elias Johnson steps out of a sparkling new Cadillac, illegally parked against the main building. He opens the back door for me.

"Mistah Halley," he says.

I look out my window as he takes me home. Homeland looks familiar and strange at the same time, like the memory of a dream. I don't see much of it; Elias takes the back roads to avoid the curious.

"Whole town talkin' 'bout you, Mistah Halley," he says.

At last we are there. He parks the car in the garage, opens the door for me, and helps me out. He takes the package from me and places a hand on my elbow.

"Take me through the garden," I say.

He leads me around the corner of the house. We step over the broken gate onto the path overgrown now with honeysuckle, crab grass, and sandspurs.

"Where are the roses?"

"They died long ago, Mistah Halley."

I hardly recognize it. The neat hedges that had been my refuge now grow wild, towering over our heads. Here and there along the path some dead, blackened bushes are frozen in their death throes. My throat goes dry.

"Take me inside, Elias."

The porch railing gleams with a coat of fresh paint. The Doric columns are dazzling white. There is a huge gold knocker on the door in the shape of a lion's head. Elias opens the door for me and stands to one side.

"Welcome home, Mistah Halley," he says, with only the slightest of smiles.

I walk straight past the grand staircase, following the hall back to the study. The wide double doors are closed, and Elias hurries to open them for me. I step into the room shimmering with golden light: Elias has thought to make a fire. I stand for a moment just inside the doorway. The desktop is bare, except for a stack of envelopes, tied in pink and blue ribbon. Behind me, Elias says, "They for you, Mistah Halley."

"What are they?"

"Why, they letters, Mistah Halley. Miss Mavis asked me to give 'em to you. So you can . . . well, read 'em, I s'pose." I am shocked at first, that you would give them back to me. Then I see the handwriting on the envelopes.

Elias asks softly, "Can I get you anything, Mistah Halley?"

"Just some water," I say hoarsely.

I walk onto the Persian rug and stand for a second before the huge mahogany desk. Elias has removed the trophies from the walls and replaced them with watercolor prints of roses. The room still smells faintly of cigar smoke. I go around the desk. I toss the package containing my old clothes into the fire. I watch them burn. I am beside the chair, his chair, where I had prophesied I would sit. I watch the fire. When Elias comes back, I will drink a glass of water. Tonight, I will go upstairs and lie on a real bed. With a down pillow. And over my head, an open window. If I feel like getting up for a drink of water, I will get up for a drink of water. If I feel like turning on the light, I will turn on the light. If I feel like rising, and going for a walk under the stars, I will rise and go for a walk under the stars. I will go for a walk, and the night air will be sweet. But that will wait. For now, I have some reading to do.

I sit in Lester Howell's chair.

I am home.

FIVE

August 23, 1942

Dear Halley,

Please forgive me for not writing sooner. When I received your letter I wanted to answer it right away, that very moment, but Momma was going through another one of her "spells" and she needs my constant attention. I don't know how much you know about my mother, but she has never been in the best of health, and she suffers from terrible bouts of melancholia. She refuses to eat, won't sleep, will not even wash her hair or care for herself like a proper lady, and mine is the only presence she tolerates. "Oh, all the world is gray," she says. "Gray and sorrowful." Daddy avoids her; the servants are terrified of her (she almost took off Vera's head the other day with a butcher knife), but I am her "dear one," her "little sweet pumpkin." My father explains it this way: "She nearly died bringing you into the world, and she hasn't been the same since. She is limited now in the feminine way." I am not altogether sure what he means by this, but the insinuation is there that somehow her ill health is my fault. Vera tells me not to worry. "You pay him no mind, Miss Mavis. He just tryin' to work on your head." Oh, how I adore Vera. She raised me while my father ignored me and my mother fought with demons known only to herself. It was Vera who brought me your letter.

"Elias Johnson says this is for you," she whispered. She had waited until I had retired for the evening; in fact, I had to get out of bed to answer her knock. Oh, Halley, I can't tell you how relieved I was when

I saw the return address. So much time had passed since my letter to you that I feared that you had never received it or, worse, that you had decided to ignore it. I had been feeling the worst sort of shame and embarrassment, and grim satisfaction, thinking I was getting exactly what I deserved, for having caused you—and everyone—so much pain. I started to tear the envelope open when Vera stepped back into the room, dragging Elias inside, a firm grip on his ear.

"Ow, you're tearin' my ear off!" he cried.

"Shush now, you no-account," Vera scolded him. I dropped the letter in my surprise; no man had ever stepped into my room before, with the exception of Daddy—and Elias himself, on that night so long ago when I sent him to find you. I scooped up the letter as Vera checked the hall, then quietly closed the door.

"I am so sorry, Miss Mavis," she said. "I would never drag this no good, shiftless, worthless piece of manhood into your room without good reason, ma'am. But imagine what I thought when he come to me with this here letter and says, 'Got a letter for Miss Mavis. A secret letter.' And I says, 'What you mean, Elias Johnson, secret letter?' And he shows me the letter and he tells me the whole story an' I like to take my sewing needle and poke out his eyes. So I brung him up so he can tell you hisself what he been up to, behind your back and all."

Elias was looking at the floor, brushing the carpet with the tip of his shoe. He turned his white Panama around and around in his dark hands. He would not look at me as he spoke.

"Miss Mavis, it weren't my idea. I was doin' a favor. I was tryin' to do what I could to set things right."

"Child," Vera said to him, "you ain't tellin' no story. You just dance 'round and 'round. You tell her now."

He coughed. I said, "It's all right, Elias."

"Well, Miss Mavis, there's a post office box now, that's where that letter come to. I got the key. Every day I come down there and check the box. That letter was there today, so I brung it here, gave it to Vera to give to you."

He glanced at Vera, to see if this explanation met with her approval. She stood with her arms crossed, frowning at him. He said, "Nobody knows about it, 'cept me. Well, I the only one in Homeland, anyway. Only two others in the whole world know. Mistah Halley and that preacher."

"Preacher?" I asked. Vera popped Elias in the back of the head.

"There was a preacher. He come to town few months back, talkin' up your daddy. Tol' him he wanted to start a church, an' he was lookin' for a little help, maybe some land and some donations, that kind of help, then after he said his piece I'm showin' him to the door and he whispers to me, 'Elias, I have a proposition for you.' An' I say, 'Preacher, I don' go in for no white folks church.' An' he says, 'It concerns a mutual acquaintance; perhaps you remember him, Mistah Halley Martin?' Well, you could've knocked me down with a feather. We step outside and he tells me Mistah Halley got your letter and he want to write back, only he can't, seein' how your daddy gonna check all the mail. So 'fore I can say 'boo' he presses this key into my hand. An' I say, 'What's this key?' An' he tells me it's a box key for box fourteen at the post office. 'Gonna send the letters there,' he says. 'You pick 'em up and bring 'em on to Miss Mavis. Be right sly and sneaky, an' nobody know the difference.' So I said yes right off, right away, Miss Mavis, 'cause I do know how some of this pain, all this trouble belong to me, since I tol' Mistah Halley to reckon with what Walter done . . ."

"Oh!" cried Vera. "First you won't say, then you won't shut up! I'm so sorry, Miss Mavis, for bringing this man into your room and filling up all four corners with his hot air."

"That's all right, Vera," I said, with a laugh. I took Elias's hand and thanked him.

"You don't know how happy you've made me, Elias."

"Oh, now, Miss Mavis," he said, lowering his eyes like a shy schoolboy. "That's all right. That's all right."

"But who was this man, this preacher? I don't remember a preacher coming to the house."

"You was in Inverness at the time, Miss Mavis. An' I didn't tell you after you come back 'cause there weren't no letters. I mean, I checked every day, but no letter come, so I says to myself, 'Elias, won't do no good tellin' her 'bout it, gettin' her hopes up. Wait till a letter get there and then let her know.' " He looked at Vera and said defiantly, "That's why I didn't say nothin' to nobody."

"You've done wonderfully, Elias," I told him. "But I'm afraid I'll have to expand your role in this little conspiracy: You will mail my replies."

He agreed right away. Vera's anger was by now giving way to excitement.

"Miss Mavis, I tell you, an' I never tol' you before, but I tell you, it is beautiful, what that man done for you. Oh, if only I had me a man like Halley Martin!" She glanced at Elias, who ducked his head as if dodging a blow, and it suddenly occurred to me the true nature of their relationship. This night, it seemed, would be one full of revelations.

"But who is this preacher?" I asked Elias again.

"His name is Fred Jefferson, or somethin' like that. Funny little fella. Said he knows Halley Martin, says he his personal spiritual guide or somesuch, and I said, 'Don't think Mistah Halley the type to go in for no spiritual guide.' But he knowed all about Mistah Halley and Homeland and what happened here, so I figured he was bein' square with me. Says Halley doin' okay. He learnin' hisself to read and write and he keepin' out of trouble. Tol' me there was some trouble when he first come, but that over now and he doin' fine. He doin' real fine, Miss Mavis . . ."

"Dear Jesus sittin' on the right side of God, don't you ever shut up?" Vera said. "We be goin' now, Miss Mavis, so you can read your letter." And they left me as they had come, with Vera dragging him by the ear, and he crying, "Owwww!"

I locked my door and read your letter, three times, and I hope it doesn't bother you when I say I cried that night as I have never cried before. Please don't mistake me, I am glad you told me about your hands; you should be able to tell me anything and everything, but Halley, your hands! How do you bear it? Oh, Halley, how do you bear it? Even Daddy admitted how talented you were, "an artist trapped in a rough-hewn frame," is how he put it once. But surely there is something that could be done for them? When you are free we will find the best doctor, the finest specialist in the world, and perhaps you will be able to draw again. I promise.

But I've written pages and pages and still haven't answered your questions.

As to the first, No, this is the only letter I've received. You must be right: Daddy found the other one, and must have destroyed it. He never confronted me with it. In fact, he has not mentioned your name since you went away. It is as if you no longer exist. But he has become almost as bad as Mother, moping about and not taking care of himself. He used to receive important politicians and bankers and businessmen; now his callers consist of debt collectors and doctors. There are days, long, long stretches of time, when the house is so still, but for the moans of Mother, that I feel as if I dwell in a haunted mansion.

But I do take comfort in my garden, my books, my poetry. Oh, don't assume I have any talent in writing it; it's just I adore reading it. My favorite is Emily Dickinson. You simply *must* get a volume of her poetry for your library. I particularly like "There's a certain Slant of light . . ." and "I'll tell you how the Sun rose / a Ribbon at the time . . ." Sometimes I imagine you reading to me, poetry or the Bible—there is some beautiful poetry in the Bible, you know. "Many waters cannot quench love, neither can the floods drown it . . ." Or from Shakespeare's sonnets. "So till the judgment of your self arise, / You live in this, and dwell in lovers' eyes."

But now I've been writing and writing and still haven't addressed all your questions.

Yes, I will send you a picture, as soon as we can find a camera sturdy enough not to shatter when I'm in front of it! I do not think I photograph well, but the subject is never a proper judge of such things. I must admit one of the first things I thought when I saw that drawing of me, the one you handed me in the rose garden, was, "But I'm not that pretty!" We either do not see ourselves as others do, or there are prisms through which we view the world, where the mediocre is made grand, and the grand mediocre.

But I feel like I'm just babbling. I'm not making hardly any sense at all. Looking over these pages, it strikes me as the strangest letter I've ever written, that *anyone* has ever written . . .

———————

December 7, 1943

Dear Halley,

I have just finished your last letter, dated November 10, and I am determined this time not only to finish this letter, but to "screw my courage to the sticking place" and actually mail it to you. I wrote you one letter, many months ago, set it aside, then almost tore it up. Instead I slipped it under my mattress, and that night I tossed and turned like the proverbial princess over the pea. I will enclose it with this letter, so you may see that you are not forgotten here in Homeland, at least not by the person who is clearly never far from your thoughts. No one has "cut you dead" here.

For you are never far from *my* thoughts. I read your letters every night, and you cannot imagine the comfort they bring me. It is as if a dear friend has come into the room, quite unexpectedly, and soon I am lost in your words.

And, I beg you, fear no judgment from me on the quality of your writing. Why would you be afraid of such a thing? I think it is beautiful, so forceful and clear and to the point. It is refreshing to hear a man speak his mind, even if the subject is at times decidedly outside the confines of "mixed company." You should—I want you to—tell me everything. Spare me no detail of what is happening to you, I do want to know everything. Keep nothing from me, Halley. And yes, I can "decipher" your spelling and typing errors. Sometimes I even enjoy it; it's fun, like working a puzzle.

I hope you are not angry with me for not sending you anything. I have no excuse; I don't know why I can't bring myself to respond. There are days when I write from breakfast to dinner, and then throw it away, my heart filled with despair. Time is my enemy, and time is remorseless, brutal, cruel. I have a picture here I am going to send you, and when I look at it I think by the time he sees me the young girl in this picture will be gone. When you come home I will be thirty-seven years old, well past the proper age for an eligible girl, an "old maid." Already there are whispers in town, whispers and snickers and snide comments, and my father is again on the hunt for a husband for me.

Daddy is absolutely desperate on the subject, for reasons that have nothing to do with me. He received pennies on the dollar in the sale of his land, and it's barely enough to meet our necessary expenses. He's gone far and wide, called in every favor, twisted every arm, to find me a suitor. And each I turn away, and afterward cry myself to sleep. And this never fails but to throw Mother into another depression, which overshadows me and the entire house in a kind of gray shroud, and it seems we all are mourning the passing of my youth.

But this is nothing more than self-pity. My suffering is nothing compared to what you have suffered, what you will continue to suffer, for my sake. In every letter, you confess your love, and I have not used the word, except above my signature, which is a convention more than a sentiment.

You ask, "Do you love me, Mavis?" Do I love you? Do I love? I know I love your words, the way they make me feel. There are times when I hear your voice inside my head as I read, and it is as if you are inside me, speaking toward the outside—forgive me, that makes no sense! I am babbling again. But honestly, I speak to no one in the way I speak to you, in these letters. Is that love? In my books, in what I choose to read, there is much talk of love, and sometimes I feel as if I'm reading about some faraway, exotic place that has no relation to me, like a spot on the map of a country I will never visit. And I, too, have had dreams of you (some that make me blush!). But is this love? Is love made of wishes, or does love, real love, require touch, sight, smell, sound . . . I love God, but I have never experienced him in this way . . . is that what you meant at the trial, when you said I was like God to you? Oh, Halley, you shouldn't say such things. You should never say such things. That is perfect love, and no human love can be that perfect. There are some days I wake up and scold myself, as if I had been indulging myself in a foolish daydream. What part of this could be called love? When I lie in my bed at night and feel every part of my being long for your touch, the sound of your voice, the smell of your hair . . . is this love? I have no point of reference, no map for this alien terrain. You always seem so sure of yourself in your letters. So certain in your love, but what is it that you love? Do you love me, or the promise of me . . . ?

June 6, 1946

Dear Halley,

Well, another letter I probably will never send, but I have literally no one else I can confide in, not in the way I am able to confide in you. Yet, is it true confidence if never sent? On my desk sit a dozen other letters, folded, sealed, addressed, stamped . . . and unmailed. When Elias brings your letters to me, he hesitates at the door, not speaking, but waiting silently, patiently, for my reply. Dear Elias, he never questions me. And for the rest of the afternoon I remain in my room, poring over your words.

You must forgive me. I am a little in the dumps today. You see, my cousin, Mary, got married this weekend. Mary is two years younger than I. My aunt and uncle had been concerned about her "waiting too long." Mary, bless her, did not have many suitors. Her dowry was modest, as are, some say, her looks, though she is not unpleasant to look at, and this weekend she was as radiant as a storybook princess. I was her maid of honor (and, no, I did *not* catch the bouquet). It was a lovely, outdoor ceremony. She and her husband, Mr. Reginald Pierce of the Miami Pierces, were married under a white trellis bedecked in red and yellow rose vines. The reception was held outside as well, and the weather was perfect, not too terribly hot, and all danced till dawn, including me, I must admit, not wishing to disappoint Mary or my father, who in earlier days lavished a small fortune on dancing lessons. Oh, Halley, how I love to dance! Will you take me dancing when you come home?

There was a young man there (I will not mention his name) who apparently made inquiries about me, for when he came to my table he knew my name, knew where I was from and my relation to Mary. He was an exceptional dancer and a very witty person, and we soon discovered our mutual love of books and the arts, and it wasn't long before others were noticing his attention toward me. My aunt drew me aside and said, "Oh, what a handsome young man, and quite a catch, Mavis. I do believe he is smitten!" I made no comment—her remark was like a dagger in my heart. And I was having such a wonderful time! Now I felt the entire burden upon me, for I had seen my father talking to this young man earlier, and I knew the same sorry scene would be replayed, the same threats and pleas and breast-beating melodrama. And I in the middle, for as much as my father wants me to marry, my mother does not to the same degree; she cannot bear the thought of my leaving her.

After the reception, I changed and was packing for the trip back to Homeland when I was informed that this same young man was waiting for me downstairs. He wanted to know if he could call on me in a few days; he had already asked and secured my father's blessing. And without thinking I said, "Yes, I would be honored." He placed a delicate kiss on my hand before leaving.

Well, my father was overjoyed. As it turns out, this young man *is* from a wealthy family, cattle ranchers based in Ocala, with interests in Texas and Oklahoma as well. Educated in the finest academies up north, a graduate of Harvard, handsome and erudite, he has ambitions exceeding the family business; he confided in me his desire to run for governor some day, or perhaps senator . . . or President! He certainly possesses the social skills and connections, the easygoing manner, the keen intelligence. A bit of a show-off, perhaps; he kept whispering to me during our dance, in Greek, no less (though he refused to translate for me!).

"Now don't tell your mother," Daddy said on the trip home. We had driven down alone, with only Elias as our driver and valet. Mother had been too ill to attend the wedding.

"This is a very delicate matter," he continued. "We must do nothing to exacerbate her condition." He was remembering, no doubt, the other disastrous courtships since you left, when Mother would lock herself in her room for days, refusing to eat, crying for me not to leave her.

"I am getting older," Daddy said. "My health is not what it used to be. Perhaps, if things work out well, your young man might want to make Homeland his base. Or your mother and I could sell the estate and move to Ocala. Beautiful country up there, Mavis. They raise thoroughbreds, the fastest horses in the world. I have always wanted to breed race horses."

Already, in his mind, this boy whom I had met just hours earlier was my "young man." I caught Elias looking at us in the rearview mirror, and his face was expressionless.

So my "young man" calls at the end of this week. I don't know how my father is going to keep Mother occupied while he visits, but Daddy has always been inventive. The secret of his success is he never found himself in a situation he didn't believe he could lie, cheat, or finagle his way out of.

But as for myself, what shall I do? If he has heard of the Scandal, as it's referred to around here, he gave no clue at the wedding, but I know he can't be five minutes in Homeland before learning all the lurid details. I myself could never tell him; I speak of it to no one, not even to Vera. There is not much I speak to anyone anymore. Like you, I have been "cut dead," though cut perhaps by my own hand. The only one to whom I can speak these secret thoughts is you, Halley, though I never mail these letters and I doubt I shall mail this one. It has become more a diary than letters. More a prayer than a conversation.

October 5, 1946

Dear Halley,

I have not written for some time. Forgive me; I have had neither the will nor the strength. I take up my pen and I am overcome, laughing, crying, a hysterical mess. I know what I am becoming: one of those eccentric unmarried women who indulge in odd little passions. My garden. My books. My letters to you, my most intimate stranger, my absent companion, my Halley Martin.

Forty-nine letters in all I've written; I counted them tonight. Forty-nine. Vera says to me, "Miss Mavis, what you goin' to do with them letters? Pretty soon you'll have to pull the padding from your mattress to fit them all in." She was only half-joking; she is terrified Daddy might find them, and in the mood he has been in lately . . . well, I honestly don't know what he'd do.

Yet . . . there is freedom here, on this blank page. The one place I can be truly free, for I am the sort whose face cannot hide the secrets of the heart. I am released from my prison only when I pick up this pen. And it doesn't matter what I decide to call them—letters, a diary disguised as letters, or mattress-stuffing. They keep me, as you once said, inside my head. Without them, I would go mad.

I'm afraid my mother already has. She is wailing for me now. "Mavis!" she cries. "Maaaavis!" And I will set down my pen in a moment and go to her. She will say, "Oh, I had the most terrible dream," or, "I'm cold, Mavis, three blankets and a quilt on my bed and I'm freezing to death. Be a dear and light a little fire, will you?" or, "My throat is so dry tonight, pumpkin. Could you bring me just a sip of water, and mind you, no ice." I have few happy memories of her. I can remember being quite small, maybe six or seven, and her chasing me through the house, a game of hide-and-seek. There were ladders and tools and all sorts of equipment about. (Daddy was remodeling at the time. He was also away on safari, which makes the memory even better.) When they were younger, my parents fought a vicious war, with nightly screaming matches that usually ended with my mother locked in her room (they have kept separate rooms for as long as I can remember), and the walls would shake as she threw furniture or smashed priceless vases upon the floor. You have written about your parents, and the beatings suffered by your mother at your father's hand. Well, my father rarely used his fists; he didn't need to. He is one of those rare brutes who discovers early in life that the wounds inflicted by words are deeper, more painful, and never heal. He tormented her for years about her infertility, her inability to bear him a son, an heir. It is ironic, given our current circumstances: I, his daughter, am his only hope of rescue.

A hope that is quickly fading. The young man from Mary's wedding has gone his way. I fully expect to pick up the newspaper in years to come and see that he has been elected to the highest office in the land, though my father, who fancies himself an expert in politics (as well as everything else), says no man from Florida could ever be elected to the presidency. "We are too hot-tempered and blunt, too slow to see the connection of things."

He called upon me the following weekend, as promised. My father had arranged a doctor's appointment with Mother's specialist in Tampa, to place her safely out of the way. He was funny and charming and very handsome, the perfect gentleman, and I felt completely at ease with him, as if I had known him for much longer than a week. As Daddy watched from the gazebo, we took a walk through the rose garden, and near the end of the path he reached over and took my hand. I let him hold it, more comforted than thrilled by his touch (oh, when will I be thrilled by a man's touch?). He turned me to face him. I could see Daddy standing in the shade fifty yards away, watching.

"You are lovely," he said. "Perfectly lovely. Wonderfully lovely. You are the loveliest thing I have ever laid eyes on, and I have been to the Louvre in Paris. But there is a sadness in you, Mavis. I can't quite put my finger on it. A great loss or burden you are bearing. I don't presume to ask you to reveal it to me, this burden, at least not yet; I only comment on it because it causes me pain, to see you suffer. Does that bother you, that it hurts me?"

"You won't need me to tell you," I answered. "If you spend any time in Homeland . . ."

He interrupted me. "Would you like me to?"

"I am sure that is your business, Mr. ———" I said.

"I shall take that as a yes." He smiled. His smile was wry and full of innocent mischief, like a little boy's.

For the next two months he called regularly, two or three nights a week, always after my mother retired for the evening, at my father's insistence. We would play cards, the three of us, or billiards, or sit by the fire and read, which I liked best of all. Before the hour grew too late, Daddy would make a great show of how tired he was or how ill he was feeling that particular evening, and excuse himself for an hour, until it was time for the young gentleman to depart. I actually looked forward to these times; he really was an accomplished conversationalist and always a perfect gentleman. He made me feel special without flattery, interesting without condescension. He was a wonderful storyteller and would regale me for hours with stories from his childhood, his adventures in Europe during the war (he was the captain of his regiment), his antics in school. He would ask polite questions but never press for details about my past or what I dreamed for in the future. And he never once referred to the Scandal, which puzzled me at first, until I decided he must know but was too much of a gentleman to mention it, too much "taken" with me, perhaps, to care.

"This boy is goin' to ask for your hand, Miss Mavis," Vera told me one evening, as she combed out my hair.

"Do you think so, Vera?"

"Oh, child, no mistaking the look in that boy's eyes. Seen it a hundred times before, mmmm-mmmm. Well, maybe not a hundred." She laughed. "Oncest or twice. An' don't you go battin' your eyes, playin' coy with me. You forget who you talkin' to. This is your Miss Vera. Weren't so long ago I was changin' your diaper."

"I'm not sure I love him, Vera."

"You don't. Tell you that right now. You not sure, then you don't."

"All right, then, I don't."

"But you like him."

"Yes. Yes, I do like him. I am very . . . comfortable with him."

"Comfortable? Well, I s'pose there could be worse things."

"Yes," I said. "I suppose."

"There some heat, but there ain't no fire."

"No."

"He a good catch, I understand."

"Oh yes. Well, you see how Daddy behaves around him."

"Yes'm. Your daddy shore like him. An' you like him. That's good. Your momma, now . . ."

"I think it's Daddy's plan to introduce them at the wedding."

She laughed. I love to hear her laugh. It is deep and warm and comforting. "*After* the wedding, you mean. She say, 'Now what in the world is Miss Mavis doin' in that long white dress?'"

We both laughed then. For the first time in years, my laughter was rich and genuine.

She became silent abruptly, then said, "Wonder what Halley will think about him, though."

"Halley?"

"Or him of Halley. You goin' to tell him 'bout Halley?"

"Oh, I'm sure he already knows . . . ouch, Vera!"

"Sorry, child. There's a devil of a knot here. I was meanin' what will he think 'bout them letters."

"Well, I . . . I simply won't tell him about them."

"You ain't gonna tell him? What you goin' to do?"

"I don't see . . . well, I don't see that it matters."

"How you happen to see that, Miss Mavis? How you see it don't matter, him settin' up there in prison writin' you love letter after love letter ever' week and you not tell your husband?"

I didn't answer.

"Well, I ain't the one to tell you what to do, but it seem to me there always come a time when a body has to choose, between what you might want and what you can have in this life. Sometime—most of the time—they ain't the same thing." She laid the brush on the dressing table and came around the chair to face me. She squatted before me and took both my hands in hers. "Will you listen to me now, chil', listen to your Miss Vera?"

I nodded. Her eyes were shining with tears. She has a wide, kind mouth and lovely brown eyes, this woman who has always been more than just a servant. She has been confidante, friend, companion, mother.

"Throw them letters away. Throw 'em all away. And stop writin' him. Oh, I know you don't send nothin' you write, but it ain't the sendin' that's the sin. Write him a letter if you want, one to send him for real. Tell him you sorry and all, but you gettin' married and that's the end of it. An' don't be afraid, what is Halley Martin gonna do about it way up there in Starke? Then Elias will close that box at the post office an' you can go on."

"Go on with what?" I was filled again with despair, a crushing hopelessness. I had never considered what I would do about the letters.

"Why your life, child! The only one you ever gonna have. It breaks ol' Vera's heart, you wastin' away in this ol' house. Why, pretty soon you go on this way you be just like your momma, all pale and alone and sick and out of your head . . ."

"It would solve everything, wouldn't it?" I whispered. "No one would have to worry about anything again. Momma would be cared for. Daddy would have his fortune back."

"An' you would have a husband and a future and lil' chillen for Miss

Vera to spoil rotten," she said. "And Miss Vera, she still have a job."
She laughed again, but the richness was gone. The laughter was forced,
hollow. She pulled me into her arms. I clung to her and sobbed against
her shoulder. I closed my eyes and before me was Walter, not you, as I
expected. I closed my eyes and saw Walter.

"Been like in mournin'," she murmured into my hair, smoothing it
with her dear hand. It was as if she too could see who was in my mind's
eye. "Mournin' for Walter and mournin' for Halley. But now come the
dawn, and it time for you to get up."

She pulled away from me and gripped my shoulders tightly with
both strong hands. She looked deeply into my eyes and said with a
ferociousness I had never heard before: "An' you get up, Mavis Howell.
You get up."

That night I re-read your letters, every one, until my vision blurred
and your words shimmered like black stars. I slipped out of bed and
tiptoed down the hallway to Mother's room. It was nearly midnight,
and the creaking of the ancient floorboards sounded very loud in the
stillness.

Mother was awake, sitting by her window, looking out at the
expanse of lawn that ran past acreage we no longer owned, to the road
beyond. The moonlight bathed her face a ghastly white, and the lines
in her face were deep furrows of care and sorrow. She turned her head
toward me when I came in, and for a moment she didn't recognize me.
Then she smiled.

"Oh, Mavis, dear. How good of you. I was just thinking how nice a
hot cup of tea would be."

"It's too late for tea, Mother," I said. I stood beside her. She turned
back to the window. Her hair was thinning; I could see her scalp
through the steel-gray strands.

"Yes, I s'pose."

"Mother . . ." I paused. I had forgotten why I had come, what I had
come to ask. It had seemed terribly important just a few moments
before.

"Yes, my dear?"

"I love you, Momma."

I placed a hand on her shoulder. She patted my hand. Hers was dry and cold.

"Yes, dear. Now could you hurry along and fetch my tea?"

And two days later, it happened. My young man arrived and our coffee had barely begun to cool when he asked to speak to my father— alone. Daddy could hardly contain himself; his face shone like a child's on Christmas morning. They retired to his study, and I was left alone, feeling awkward and exhilarated and nervous.

As I paced in the small parlor just to the right of the study, Vera came in and said, "He here?" I nodded. "He with your daddy?" I nodded again. "Then it's tonight," she said simply, as calmly as if she were remarking on the weather. "You tell him when he asks you, Miss Mavis. You tell him 'bout them letters, an' what you goin' to do 'bout them. Worse foot to start on, secrets and lies." She brushed back a strand of my hair with her fingertip. "God bless you, child. Life *can* begin again, just ask my Savior, praise God."

She left. I waited for the men to emerge from the study. I was alone. The ticking of the clock on the mantel filled the room; it felt as if my very skin was vibrating with the ticking. It was taking too long. It should not be taking this long, I remember thinking. Then it occurred to me they probably were enjoying a toast. Daddy's finest brandy and Cuban cigars. Where would he ask me? Here, in the parlor? Or would he take me for a walk in the rose garden . . . yes, the rose garden; it would have to be the rose garden, where a thousand years ago I walked alone and another man watched me and thought he saw a vision of God. The rose garden, where a thousand years ago another man approached me, appearing out of thin air, as the gods must have to mortals when gods walked the earth. Approached me and said, "This is for you." And in his trembling hand—me.

And I will say . . . "Yes." I tried out the word. "Yes." Seeing how it felt on my tongue, how it sounded against the tick-ticking of the mantel clock. "Yes, I will. I do. I do, Halley." I froze. I had just called him by your name! I was horrified. I decided to tell him everything about us, before he had the opportunity to ask the Question, to give him a chance to change his mind, and to face his decision gracefully.

There should be no secrets, no more secrets, I thought. I had made up
my mind and was heading for the stairs to get the letters when the
study door opened and he emerged, alone. Over his shoulder I saw my
father, caught just a fleeting glimpse of him at his desk, before my
suitor closed the door and came toward me.

"It's such a lovely evening," he said. "Shall we go for a walk, Mavis?"

It *was* a lovely evening, mild and not too humid, and the roses
rustled in the breeze. He offered me his arm. I fought the impulse to
look back at the house, to see if Daddy was watching this, the
consummation of years of planning and hard work. I remembered
Vera's words, that love is not everything in marriage, that life could
begin again, no matter what dark secrets lay in the past. And even as I
reminded myself that "yes" was the easiest and only answer, I realized
that this "yes" was a "no" as well. This door-opening was a closing too.

"Mavis," he said softly. "Mavis, you are—Mavis, you know I have
grown quite . . . fond of you over these past few weeks. In fact, I might
as well just come out and say it . . ."

"Then say it."

"I love you. I have fallen in love with you. There. I said it. I love you."

There was an invitation in his tone. It was my turn to say I loved
him too. I said nothing.

"I have been speaking with your father . . ."

"I know. I was there."

"Yes! Of course, you knew that. Forgive me. This is difficult, more
difficult than I thought it would be."

We came to the gazebo and stopped. He faced me, pulled a small
object from his pocket. Oh, it was perfect. The perfect setting for a
proposal. It could not have been scripted better. He pressed the thing
into my hand. It was wrapped in shiny foil, tied with a ribbon. I tore
open the paper and stared at the contents, absolutely, completely
speechless.

" 'The Collected Poems of Emily Dickinson,' " I read.

"I thought your volume a tad dog-eared," he said. "Look, it's the
perfect size for traveling, for your trips to Inverness . . ."

"You are saying good-bye."

"No, of course not. Not good-bye . . ."

"You will not be calling again."

He looked away. I sank onto the bench. He did not sit beside me.

"My father needs me in Houston," he said.

"Of course. Your father."

"But I'll be coming back to Florida, at least two or three times a year, for holidays anyway, and I would like to see you then, if that's possible . . ."

"Oh, I don't know," I said. "I don't know if I'll be able to fit you into my crowded social calendar. You went to my father tonight."

"Yes . . ."

"Why? No, you don't have to answer. You went to him to apologize."

"What have I to . . . ?"

"You felt he deserved one, I suppose. Well, perhaps he does. He wanted this more than anyone. Certainly more than I."

"Mavis, I have confessed it. I've told you. I love you. But there are— I have obligations. It's not what you're thinking . . ."

"No man can presume to know what I'm thinking," I snapped at him. I stood up and slapped him across the cheek with the book, then let it fall to the ground. I ran into the house, and that was the last I saw of him.

I burst into my father's study. He was sitting behind that huge, ugly desk, smoking a cigar and nursing a gin and tonic. In my rage I did not notice Elias standing in the shadows in the far corner.

"You told him," I said.

"I told him nothing." His voice was flat, emotionless. He looked and spoke as if he had just learned of a dear friend's death. "Why would I tell him? What could I gain?"

"You thought it would be better if he heard it from you!"

"No," he said, in that same strange, flat voice. "It would have been best if he had heard it from *you*." He was, for the first time in my memory, devoid of any bluster, any arrogance. He had just witnessed his last best hope crumble to dust, and now finally spoke aloud what we both had known since the spring of 1940.

"He really had no choice. He is a young man of impeccable credentials. Moreover and most importantly, he is a young man with political ambitions, and young men with political ambitions cannot afford to risk scandal. You see, it is the heart that betrays our aspirations; he could not afford to let his emotions carry the day. That is the immovable object, Mavis. No man worthy of you will have you now, for what Walter Hughes has taken from you no man can restore."

No man worthy of me. "Oh, I hate you!" I cried. I moved toward him; I wanted to kill him at that moment, kill him for what he had done to me, for what he had done to my mother, for what he had done to you. Elias came out of the shadows and pulled me toward the door.

"Now, come on now, Miss Mavis," he murmured. "It gonna be all right. It gonna be all right . . ."

"Goddamn you!" I screamed at my father. "God*damn* you . . . !"

"Yes," he said, as Elias eased me into the hallway and closed the door. "Yes."

I fled upstairs to my room, locked myself inside, threw myself onto the bed. For a long time I lay there, as Vera tapped softly on the door, calling, "Miss Mavis. Miss Mavis, it's your Vera. Open the door, Mavis. Open this door now . . ."

But I didn't open the door. I knelt by the bed and pulled your letters from beneath the mattress, handful upon handful. They spilled from my arms onto the floor, and on my hands and knees I flung the pages right and left, until I was kneeling upon a white paper carpet. I tore at the letters, mine and yours, mixing them, shuffling them, tangling our words together, as Vera cried behind the door, "Mavis! Mavis!"

I wanted rid of you, Halley. I did not ask for you. I did not ask for Walter. I swore I would never tell you this, but I have had dreams of you coming to me, emerging from a thick fog, and you are naked, and you are holding up your hands, and your hands are twisted, hideously contorted and covered in blood; blood drips from your fingers and runs down your wrists and stains your forearms red, and you whisper, "It hurts, Mavis, it hurts," and you run your bloody hands over my face, my breasts, my thighs, and you say, "Don't worry, Mavis, don't cry. It isn't mine. It's Walter's . . ."

Vera burst into the room, followed closely by Elias. He had broken open the lock. She pulled me to my feet and held me. I beat on her back with both my fists. Over her shoulder I could see Elias watching me, and his face had no expression at all.

August 10, 1949

Dear Halley,

I don't know how you can stand being cooped up in that little library all day in this unbearable heat. Even in our house, which is airy and roomy and, until recently, air-conditioned, it's hot enough to roast marshmallows (as Vera would say). I am writing this on the upstairs balcony, on the shadowy side of the house, but even here, out of the sun, it is simply blistering. In the distance, circling and swooping, gliding on enormous black wings, is a flock of buzzards, keeping watch over some poor dying thing deep in the cypresses. In a moment I will venture downstairs and find something cool to drink, perhaps a lemonade—or something stronger. We always keep a cool pitcher of lemonade in the icebox during the summer, and we *always* have something stronger about.

I don't feel like writing much today. In this heat, the slightest motion takes the greatest effort. How I wish for just a little breeze! And there is the constant roar and buzz of bulldozers. They are leveling the old groves to put up apartment houses. Who knows? By the time you come home, perhaps Homeland will be a bustling metropolis, the Miami of middle Florida.

Yes, you must read, Halley. Read all you can. Read every waking moment. And don't stop writing. I see improvement with every letter.

I do have some bit of news—I am looking for a job! Mr. Wilson at the drugstore is getting older (how odd it seems. He seemed so very old to me even when I was a little girl, buying penny licorice after school), and he says he might need just a little help around the store. Daddy, of course, is furious at the thought of a Howell working as a soda-fountain girl, but what choice do we have? There is no money, and every day

another threatening letter arrives from the bank. Daddy has taken
heavily to drink and spends the day locked in his study. Doctors troop
in and out of the house at all hours. Doctors for him, doctors for
Momma. Momma recognizes no one now, except me. I count myself
lucky if I get ten minutes to myself, particularly at night.

Well, I haven't written very long and I am *completely* exhausted.

I hope, despite this abysmal heat, that you are well.

p.s. Have *you* tried talking to someone? I know they refuse to talk to
you, but you sound so lonely in your letters. If you persist, someone
will surely give in and speak to you.

p.p.s. A strange little man came to the house yesterday. He spent
the afternoon with Daddy, shut up in the study. He did not seem like a
bill collector or banker or lawyer, and he spoke like a Yankee. I was
coming down the stairs as Elias was leading him to the study, and they
both stopped, looking up at me. He (the Yankee) had the oddest
expression, as if he were about to burst into tears. Later I asked Elias
who he was. He told me he couldn't recall his name. "You are a terrible
liar, Elias Johnson," I told him, but I didn't press him. He is also
terrible at keeping a secret.

p.p.p.s. Last night I had another one of *those* dreams about us.

November 19, 1949

Dear Halley,

Ned Jeffries came to the house again yesterday afternoon. His fourth or
fifth such visit. Daddy sent Elias to fetch me.

"I'm sorry, Miss Mavis," he said.

"Why?"

"'Cause this is the same man who knowed Mistah Halley in prison.
The post office box preacher. I'm sorry. Should have told you before, but
I . . ."

I didn't wait for him to finish. I ran to the study, straightening my
clothes, patting at my hair; I'm not sure why. I paused at the door,

wondering if I should change first into my blue dress. Blue accentuates the color of my eyes.

I entered without knocking. Mr. Jeffries rose immediately. He had been sitting with his hat in his lap; it fell to the floor when he stood. He picked it up and tossed it into the chair. He was wearing a black suit ten years out of style, his thinning black hair swept straight back from his high forehead. Daddy introduced us.

"Mavis, this is the Reverend Ned Jeffries."

"How do you do?" I asked. His hand was freezing cold, his grip loose.

"It is my pleasure," he said, and again that look came over his face, the same expression he wore the day I first laid eyes on him, as if he were about to burst into uncontrollable tears.

"Pastor Jeffries has come to start a church here in Homeland," Daddy said. "Although I've assured him, repeatedly, that we already have more than our fair share of Baptists."

"One can't have too many," he said. He smiled painfully. He looked so awkward standing there, his long, thin arms hanging loosely at his sides, that I insisted he sit. He did—upon his hat. He pulled it out and began to reshape it. He seemed pleased: Now he had something to do with his hands.

"He keeps hittin' me up for money," Daddy said. "An' I keep tellin' him we're poor as damn Irishmen." Although his face still had that washed-out, fleshy quality, Daddy's eyes sparkled and he sounded like his old self. Clearly this Ned Jeffries did something for his spirits.

He was just as you described him, Halley. Slight, with a narrow nose and very small eyes. There was, as you said, a "twitchiness" to him, an impression that at any moment he would completely fall to pieces. I found it endearing.

"My father is not what one would call a church-goer, Mr. Jeffries," I said.

"I ain't what *anyone* would call a church-goer. I don't cotton toward no Bible-thumpers, that's for sure. But Ned here ain't no Bible-thumper, are you, Ned?"

"More of a tapper."

Daddy laughed and slapped his thigh, something I had not seen for months. I felt grateful to Ned Jeffries for whatever magic this was he had worked on my father. And at the same time I was trying to think of a way to get him alone. Seated before me was the one person on earth whom I shared in common with you. The one *living* person.

"Ned's picked him and his mother a place out on Jefferson. Little lot which used to be ours, if you recall," Daddy said.

"The one on the hill," I said.

"Yes, that's it," Daddy said. "Where you planted that tree." He said to Ned Jeffries, "Mavis planted a remembrance tree at the start of the war, you know."

"Oh," Ned Jeffries said, his small eyes widening ever so slightly. "Yes, I seem to remember that. That tree. Seeing that tree. Is that the tree, then? Hmmmm." He bobbed his head up and down rapidly, still fussing with the brim of his hat. "It's a lovely spot . . . quite a . . . a . . . ."

"Commanding view," Daddy said.

"Yes, commanding view. Mother loves it here, you know. This warm weather does wonders for her joints. She has very poor joints."

"Where are you from, Mr. Jeffries?" I asked.

"Oh, a little town you've probably never heard of, up in Ohio. But I was raised, partially at least, here in Florida. Pensacola area."

"Alabama," Daddy said.

"I beg your pardon?"

"That ain't the real Florida," Daddy said. "Up there in the Panhandle. You want to find real crackers, you got to come down here."

"Oh, yes. Real crackers," Ned Jeffries said, and for some reason I laughed out loud. Both men stared at me, and I stopped.

"Ned asked to meet you," Daddy said.

"Oh?"

Ned Jeffries cleared his throat, lowered his head, and carefully brushed an invisible wrinkle from his pants.

"Why, yes. That I did. Your father has told me . . ." He glanced at Daddy. " . . . that you have a practical genius for organization."

"He has?" I was genuinely surprised. Daddy was smiling at me. "I've never organized anything."

"Every church needs a planning committee," Daddy said.

"I've never even been baptized," I said.

"Oh, that don't take no time at all," Daddy said, giving a little wave of his hand. "Pastor here'll dunk you."

"I didn't say I wanted to be dunked," I said. "Really, Mr. Jeffries, I am one of the most disorganized people in the—"

"Mavis is really very modest," Daddy said. "Why, did you know she single-handedly took over her cousin's wedding when her auntie took sick? Now, you want to talk about somethin' that needed organizing . . . !"

"My father has misled you," I said to Ned Jeffries. "I'm sorry."

"My only daughter impugns my honesty," Daddy said with mock sadness. "These are bitter dregs indeed! But if we must be frank, I was looking for something to occupy Mavis's time, something to get her mind off her troubles. Look at her, Ned! She's withered away to a stick! You could wrap one hand around her waist! Why, I don't think she's seen the sun in four months. It's her mother, you know. Terrible thing."

I was staring at him, shocked by his bluntness. What was he doing? Was this a way to save himself the humiliation of his daughter working at the drugstore? My father was never a religious man, and now it seemed he had taken as his dearest friend and confidant a Baptist preacher, and a Yankee to boot! I was flabbergasted.

"My father exaggerates," I told Ned Jeffries. "I am in perfect health."

"And you look it!" Ned Jeffries said, then turned a bright crimson. His head fell down again, and he spoke to his lap. "The truth is, there's plenty of people in this town who think there *are* enough churches."

It took everything in me not to laugh at that point, not because of anything he said, but because it suddenly occurred to me here was the perfect excuse to spend as much time as I wanted with Ned Jeffries with my father's full knowledge and approval. It was clear he had no idea that Ned Jeffries was connected in any way to Halley Martin.

"Of course, I will help you," I said. "If you think you can use someone like me."

"Oh," Ned Jeffries said, "I most certainly could."

I had to stop. Mother was calling me. Anyway, Ned Jeffries escorted me
to the front door at the end of his visit.

"Thank you," I said.

"For what?"

"For everything. The post office box, that first letter, saving his life,
everything." I spoke in a furious rush, standing very close to him by the
front door. "Are you going back there soon, to Starke?"

"Yes. Yes, in a week or so . . ."

"Ned, there's no time now, but will you come back tomorrow? I
have a thousand questions. I want to know everything. Everything. He
doesn't tell me everything; I know there are things he spares me, but I
don't want to be spared anything, not anything. Will you? Will you
tell me everything?"

"I—um, well, certainly, I—"

"He writes of you often."

He blinked. "He does?"

"You are a godsend," I told him, and impulsively kissed him on the
cheek. Again he looked as if he was about to cry.

"Good afternoon, Miss Mavis," he said hoarsely. "I shall call
tomorrow."

"Meet me in the garden at four."

"The garden?"

"The rose garden. Come in through the break in the hedgerow.
Daddy won't see you, and if he does, it won't matter. He'll assume it's
church business."

"Yes. Yes, church business. Exactly." And he scurried out the
door . . .

February 13, 1950

Dear Halley,

I'm afraid I can manage only a short note tonight, Mr. Martin. I am
exhausted. I have been up since five o'clock this morning and now it is
almost midnight. It was well after ten this evening when I finally had a

moment to myself. But Ned was still full of energy when we said good night. All in all, I think the fund-raising exceeds his wildest expectations. We signed the contract with the construction company today for the building of the church, which, as of this past Sunday, boasts over fifty members! And the construction on the parsonage is nearly completed. There was some grumbling among the parishioners: "Finishing the house before the church is even built!" But I pointed out to Miss Willifred Peters (the most vociferous critic) that we couldn't expect the shepherd of the flock, as well as his invalid mother, to live for the next four months in a decrepit old boardinghouse.

There has resulted a bit of a power struggle between Miss Willifred and myself. When she joined the congregation, she informed me she was going to *personally* assume responsibility for the various committees. "What committees?" I asked. She presented me with a list of committees that would be, in her words, "absolutely *essential*" for the establishment and maintenance of the new church. There were thirty-two. After intense negotiations, we had them whittled down to five. I have taken three and Miss Willifred has two, but I am fairly certain there are "Miss Willy spies" within at least two of mine.

Tomorrow I shall have my first "proper" meeting with Ned's mother. I'm a bit nervous. Several people have told me she is one of those "brash, loud-mouthed, know-it-all" Yankees, and add that Sherman was also from Ohio. She has come to a service or two (we have moved again, to the social hall at the VFW), but I have yet to speak to her at any length.

Daddy is feeling a bit better, and the doctor said he should be out of bed in two or three days—just in time to meet with the auction company. It has been painful, picking those items especially dear to me and Mother to sell to strangers just so we can eat and pay the bills. The doctor told me in private Daddy's ills owe as much to his depression as to his drinking. "I'm afraid I'm powerless to do anything about either," I told him.

In your last letter you vowed never again to ask me to write or come see you. I shall always write to you, strange as this correspondence may be. To stop would be to let a part of me die.

March 15, 1950

Dear Halley,

Tonight I re-read all our letters; I haven't touched them in a month.
Oh, Halley, so many letters, yours to me, here in Homeland, and mine
to you, the you inside me, the Halley Martin in my heart. So many
letters . . . for years now I have imagined our wedding day (dare I admit
this?), when I give you our letters, bundled together in alternating
order, one of yours, one of mine, tied in pink and blue ribbon, as a
present on our wedding night . . . oh, I pray to God that the heart can
redeem what time and cruel circumstance have stolen! You write how
this is the only thing that keeps you going: not the promise of love
fulfilled, but the chance to fulfill it. How often I have pictured meeting
you at the train station, wearing the white dress you envisioned on the
day you expected to run away with me. Halley, why didn't you come
find me? Why did you throw Daddy's money into the fire? Why didn't
you break into the house and spirit me away, like a hero in one of those
horrid romance novels my mother used to read? If you had, we would
be together and Walter would be alive. Sometimes I wonder if it is real
love you long for, or merely the dream of love, whether it is me, or a
vision of me.

I haven't written lately because I have been angry with you. I
became intimately familiar with your "vision" of me last month, when
I saw the indecent drawings you made in the Homeland County Jail. I
suppose it wasn't the drawings themselves that made me so angry
(though they did cause great embarrassment and shame). It was that
you gave them away; you let them fall into the hands of a stranger, and
if I had had my senses about me at the time I would have taken those
drawings and destroyed them, or at least have hidden them from
human eyes.

Halley, those drawings! My first reaction was, "But I'm not that
beautiful!" Then the horrible thought that you had spied on me in
places other than the rose garden. Did you sneak into this house? Were
you in my closet while I changed? I felt violated, betrayed by a man
whom I consider a dear friend. You see, they were presented to me by

none other than Mother Jeffries on the very day we met for the first time.

It was after a modest but pleasant dinner with Ned and his mother in their room at the Granger boardinghouse. Ned had stepped out to visit an ailing parishioner (Mrs. Beverly Wilt, whose hip has gone out again). I offered to go with him, but Mother Jeffries insisted I stay.

"It will give us the opportunity to become better acquainted, dear."

I really wasn't looking for that sort of opportunity. There is a kernel of truth in the gossip that Mother Jeffries is a brash, loud-mouthed Yankee.

Ned was barely out the door when she turned to me and said, "He is in love with you, you know."

"Who?" I asked. It never occurred to me she might be talking about Ned.

"My son, Ned! I keep telling him he's got to tell you, but he doesn't listen. Scared out of his mind! Thinks you're too sophisticated and pretty." She spat out these two adjectives derisively. "Out of his league. I tell him, 'She's not out of your league. She's practically a spinster; her daddy's dead broke and her mother's off her nut. Got a scandal in her past and a madman waiting in the wings. She needs a good man to rescue her from certain destruction!'" She took a deep breath and sipped at her coffee. I should have left at that point, I know, but I was strangely intrigued. Insulted, certainly, but also impressed by her candor. "I didn't say that last part," she confessed. "About certain destruction. Of course, even a shut-in like me hears things about you, dear. How your last boyfriend dumped you because you're damaged goods." Listening to her, it was hard to imagine she was the wife of one preacher and the mother of another. Ned had told me her illness required massive doses of a chemical that affected her brain. "It has loosened her tongue," as he politely put it.

"I am going to smoke. You mind?" She lit a cigarette and let the smoke billow out her nose. "Don't tell Ned." She tapped the ash in her saucer.

"What else do people say?" I asked.

"Oh Christ! Where do I start? Well, they say your mother's dead . . ."

"Dead!"

"Yep! Dead as a doornail, only nobody's supposed to know. Your father has her buried under the rosebushes, and that's why one white bush blooms crimson on the full moon." She nodded with satisfaction at the look of sick wonder on my face. "I don't believe that one. They say your father offered that Halley Martin ten thousand dollars to kill Walter Hughes for despoiling you. And then testified against him at the trial to cover his tracks! There are not too many in this little town who like your father."

"Or any of us," I said weakly. She passed me a paper napkin.

"Oh, don't cry now, honey. People are going to talk."

"People are cruel."

"Hell yes, they are. Where have you been? Ned tells me what you know about life comes out of books, and that's your first mistake. But Ned's just the same. Probably why he loves you."

"He doesn't love me . . ."

She laughed. It was a harsh, braying sound. "Oh, he's not going to admit it. Doesn't have the nerve. Won't even admit it to himself, and never will, unless something—or *someone*—pushes him into it. He's kind of a pansy, my son. You know what a pansy is?" She didn't wait for my answer. "You know the only reason he came to Homeland was to be close to you."

"But he doesn't—he didn't even know me when he first came . . ."

"He knew you well enough! That's all he talked about up in Starke. It drove him crazy, hearing day in and day out from that Halley Martin how beautiful you were, and it excited his mind, the way you inspire lust and murder and all sorts of mayhem. Ned is very naive and impressionable. From all the damn books. You became what Halley Martin drew."

"What he drew?" My voice was softening, growing weaker as hers grew louder and louder. I'm sure she could be heard through the thin walls.

"He thinks I don't know, but I'm his mother. He thinks he can hide things from me, but I'm a snoop. It's a particular curse, Mavis, to have a snoop for a mother."

She dropped her cigarette into the dregs of her coffee. It gave an angry hiss as she rose and went into the back room. She came out after a moment carrying the sketch pad.

"He's been hiding this under his mattress."

She placed it in front of me. She stood behind me, leaning over so her foul breath spread around my head like a fog.

"Go on," she whispered. "Open it."

And I did . . . at first my mind refused to register what I was seeing. "Look! There's dozens!" she said.

I slapped the pad closed, while she laughed that hideous, barking laugh.

"Naked as a jaybird! God knows what Neddy does with this when I'm asleep!"

"Please," I said. "Please, don't . . ."

"That's where he's one up on that Halley Martin," she said. "Ned's been in love with you *before* he even laid eyes on you!"

The next day I told Ned I was resigning from the committees.

"But why?" he asked. He looked absolutely panicked at the thought.

"Daddy is getting worse. I simply can't spare the time," I answered.

"But, Mavis . . . please, I can't do this without you."

"You have Miss Willifred."

"That woman's a worthless busybody."

"And your most devoted follower. You're taking a most un-Christian attitude."

"It's my mother, isn't it?" he asked bitterly. "I never should have let you meet her."

"Oh no, I'm glad you did."

"She's not quite right, Mavis," he said. "You know that." He begged me not to leave him, insisting that whatever offense she had given me he would make good. I assured him I had enjoyed working with him to see his dream to reality, but my family business was simply too pressing to neglect any longer.

"Besides," I said, "I'm not even a member. People are talking about that."

"Then you can join. You accept the Lord this Sunday and I'll baptize you."

"I don't want to be baptized, Ned."

"Whatever you like!" he cried. "I wouldn't care if you joined a coven and worshiped the Devil, only don't abandon me, Mavis! Not now, not while I'm so close . . ."

"Close to what, Ned?" I asked him directly.

He answered meekly, "Finishing my church."

"I will consider your request if you'll answer a question for me."

"Yes, ask it. Anything, Mavis. Absolutely anything!"

"Why do you have Halley's drawings and what are you planning to do with them?"

It took him a moment to absorb what I said. He wrung his hands and looked away. "I hate her," he said. He raised his eyes, and for just a moment I felt sorry for him. "They were given to me."

"Halley gave them to you?"

"He said . . . he said they only gave him pain—to look at them—so he gave them to me."

"I don't believe you."

"He was afraid something might happen to them there, in Starke. He entrusted them to me, for safekeeping. I haven't looked at them . . . all right, that is a lie. A stupid lie, really; of course I looked at them. Can you blame me? But you shouldn't be ashamed, Mavis. They are the most beautiful . . ."

I slapped him across the cheek. His lower lip came forward, and he dropped his head.

"I have no defense," he said.

I might have told him he did: the same as yours, Halley. He was in love.

September 21, 1950

Dear Halley,

My father is dead. Even as I write these words, I can hardly believe it. My father, Lester Alton Howell, is dead. We buried him today in the family plot. Mother did not attend. Mother still believes he is alive and playing a cruel joke. In a way, he is, of course, the last and cruelest: My father has taken his own life.

We were sitting on the porch, Ned and I. A heavy rain had fallen throughout dinner, so heavy we had to practically shout to be heard over the pounding upon the eaves and the explosions of thunder. Daddy was positively giddy, telling off-color jokes that he knew would embarrass Ned. "Look at that! Look at ol' Neddy's face!" Pounding his fist on the table. Only Elias seemed to realize something was amiss. He hovered over Daddy like a mother hen, never more than a few feet from him all day. The rain moved out after an hour or so, and Ned and I took our coffee on the porch, which had become our favorite place to talk. It is cooler outside this time of year, especially after a storm, in the early evening, when a nice breeze chases after the departing thunderheads. Ned and I sat in matching white rocking chairs, on this, the same porch where, years ago, Daddy stood that day you broke his cane across your back. We made small talk about the weather, how the rains had come early this year; we talked about his house-warming party; how, after months in the boardinghouse, it felt as if they had moved into a mansion. We laughed over the rumors in town that we were an "item."

"But that troubles me, Mavis," he said, growing somber all at once.

"Oh, please, Ned, we were having such a nice time. Must you get that dark, poetical look of yours? What a brooder you are!" And I laughed. I wanted to keep the mood light. Since our fight over your drawings, the subject had not come up, nor did I want it to.

"I'm serious, Mavis. And I'll tell you why it troubles me: As long as people think we are . . . romantically entangled, men may shy away."

"Oh, yes," I said gaily. "Before that rumor came along I had to beat them off with a stick!"

"Don't you want to marry . . . someday?"

"To be honest, Ned, I don't give it much thought. Anyway, aren't you the one who always says such things are in God's hands?"

"I thought you didn't believe in God."

"Whatever made you think that? What, because I don't wave my arms in the air in church and shake my body like an epileptic? Because I don't mouth platitudes like 'Love thy neighbor' and then spread gossip about them? Because I don't believe dunking myself in a tub of water might do anything for me but give me an ear infection? The truth is, I certainly do believe in God. In fact, I can hear him right now. Listen!"

He stared at me, then out into the night. The remnants of the evening's rain dripped from the eaves and spattered upon the upturned leaves of the grape bushes. His whole body strained forward as he listened. His face twisted with his desperate desire to hear the voice of God. Finally, with a heavy sigh, he shook his head. "I don't hear anything."

"Well, then." I patted his hand. "Don't worry about me, Ned. You should never worry about me."

"But I do. You more than anyone." He sounded absolutely miserable. "You are . . . dear to me, Mavis."

"Stop this, Ned," I was beginning to lose my temper. He should have known better than to broach this subject.

"Whatever you like, Mavis," he answered. He reached over and took my hand. I allowed him to hold it. His hand was cold, as cold as death, and a small shudder went through me.

We were quiet for a few moments. Miles away the thunder rumbled, then, as if in answer, an explosion behind us, inside the house. I heard Elias cry out, and the heavy thud of footsteps inside: someone running. We jumped to our feet and I followed Ned into the front hall. Then Elias's voice, from the study: "Mistah Lester! Mistah Lester, *goddamn you!*"

We raced down the hallway, still holding hands. Ned reached the door first, just as Elias came out. I have never seen such a look on a man's face and, God willing, never will again. Ned looked over his shoulder into the room, then turned quickly and embraced me, forcing me backward. "Close it, Elias!" he shouted. "Close the door!" Elias slammed the door.

"What is it?" I cried. "What has happened?" But I knew. I did not need to see what was in the study to know. Daddy laughed and joked at dinner as if he hadn't a care in the world, his gaiety bordering on hysteria, and I knew: The world held no cares for him anymore; he had made his decision.

He left no note. Yesterday, as I was going through his papers, I found the foreclosure notice from the bank, the lone sheet of paper on his desk. I made a call to Mr. Haroldson at the bank, but he explained it was out of his hands. If we do not move by the end of this month, Sheriff Trimbul will come and make us move. I tried to explain this to Mother, but she either does not understand or refuses to. "Tell your father, dear," she said. "He handles all those matters." Elias walks about in stunned silence, dropping his eyes at my approach and hurrying away. Only Vera seems to have accepted our change in fortune; she is hysterical. I have put her to work packing Mother's clothing.

"But what we gonna do, Miss Mavis?" she asked. "Where we gonna go?"

"I'm putting you and Mother on a train to Inverness," I told her.

"Puttin' us on a train? Where you goin'?"

"I am going to Starke."

We were standing in my bedroom. It was the eve of Daddy's funeral. My suitcase lay open on the bed, and beside it a small mountain of paper: our letters.

"You goin' *where*?" She could not have been more surprised if I had announced I was taking a trip to the moon.

"I am going to see him. I am going to see Halley. And I am going to deliver these letters."

"But Miss Mavis . . ."

"I did not know . . . I never understood why I couldn't send them. I was clinging to something or something was clinging to me, but now I can go, Vera. Now I *will* go." I was giddy, my mind reeling. I had been cut free from the mooring, and a powerful tide was sweeping me out to sea. And the shore: you.

"Miss Mavis, you ain't makin' no sense. What you gonna do up there in Starke?"

"I just told you."

"Yeah-a, but *then* what you gonna do? Pitch a tent outside the gates till he goes free? You don't know nobody up there."

"I know the only person I need to know. Don't you see, Vera? I'm free. I'm finally free."

"How're you free?"

"I don't know what I'll do," I said, answering her first question, because the second was impossible to answer. "And I don't know what I'll say. But I'm going to see him. I'm going to sit across from him, and I'm going to touch his broken hands, and I'm going to touch his face, if that's allowed, and if it isn't allowed I'm going to do it anyway; and I'm going to deliver these letters, and I'm going to redeem the time, and I will not consider what I will do; I will redeem the time . . ."

"Lord, chil', you out of your head!"

"I am all the way in my head," I echoed your words. "Now go tell Elias to pull the car around. We're leaving in thirty minutes."

She lingered in the doorway. I screamed for her to go and she backed quickly out of the room. I heard her in the hall saying, "Oh, Lordy, Lordy, we all gone mad. We all gone plumb out of our heads. Elias! Elias Johnson!"

I sat on the bed and carefully stacked my letters, tied them with a pink ribbon. I was laughing even as tears streamed down my face.

And now Elias was at the door, still wearing that dumbfounded look, his hat in his hand.

"We goin' somewhere, Miss Mavis?"

Downstairs, Vera was standing by the front door, holding my wrap and my hat.

"Do not tell Mother I've gone," I said. "No; tell her I have gone to Inverness, to prepare for her arrival."

"Miss Mavis, you ain't . . ."

"Do you understand me, Vera?"

"Yes'm. I'll tell her."

Elias was silent as we drove to the station. It was a lovely, cloudless night. The whole canopy of the heavens opened above us. *Our hearts are like stars,* I had written. I could see Elias's eyes in the rearview mirror, looking at me or past me.

"What is it?" I asked.

"Nothin', Miss Mavis," he muttered, and we spent the rest of the drive in silence.

"Miss Mavis!" Mr. Phillips, the stationmaster, cried when he saw me mount the platform. "Why you're the last person I . . ." He stopped when Elias came into view, carrying my luggage.

"I desire a one-way ticket to Starke," I told Mr. Phillips.

"There ain't such a thing," he answered. "Train don't go to Starke. Next train through goin' to Tampa."

"I do not wish to go to Tampa."

"Well, you can pick up the three-twenty for Jacksonville, and from there a bus goes down."

"Why don't I just drive you, Miss Mavis?" Elias asked. "I don't mind."

I ignored him. "Then give me the ticket to Jacksonville, Mr. Phillips."

"There ain't no train to Jacksonville."

"You just said there was."

"From Tampa. There's a train to Tampa, and in Tampa you can—"

"To Tampa, then," I snapped. "When does the train arrive?"

He checked his pocket watch. "Ten minutes. Here, set those bags right over here, boy." He eyed me curiously. A cigarette was dangling from his mouth, its ash half its length. "Goin' to Starke, are you?"

"Yes," I said. "And giving you a juicy bit of gossip in the bargain."

He dropped his head and shuffled away, ashamed, but not so ashamed he wouldn't spread the news. By dawn it would be all over town, but I didn't care. I would not be in Homeland; I would be in a different country entirely. Now, there was nothing to do but wait for the train. I told Elias to go home.

"Oh, Miss Mavis, I can't leave you here all by yourself . . ."

"I'll be all right. Mr. Phillips is here."

"I 'spect I'll wait with you, just the same."

It was as if he knew I would not be boarding the train and I would need a ride home.

"Elias, you're being ridiculous. Mother and Vera need you more than I now. They are all alone."

"Just the same . . ."

And at that moment a shadow appeared behind him; I saw it rise into the lights of the platform, as a ghost from the dark ground. The face was lost in shadow, but I knew who it was.

"Mavis . . ." Ned Jeffries said.

"Oh my Lordy," Elias said, backing away.

"Mavis, why are you here?"

"Why are *you* here?" I asked.

"Vera called me."

"Of course she did. I knew she would call someone. I just never thought it would be you."

"Don't go, Mavis. Please don't go," he glanced toward Elias, expecting some support, I suppose, but Elias had walked to the other end of the platform and was staring into the distance, down the long dark ribbon of track.

"You are being rash," Ned Jeffries said. "You're not thinking things through."

"Oh, yes, thinking things through, that's always necessary, isn't it? One must always think things through, take the safe course, the practical way."

"Think of your mother. What is she going to do without you?"

"She has Vera."

"And neither of them have any money."

"Neither have I," I laughed. "Really, Ned, this is pitiful."

"They can't stay in Inverness. You know that. Your aunt and uncle don't have the resources or the desire to—"

"Then I suppose they'll have to go to the poorhouse! Or perhaps the good Christian ladies of your church will care for them! Don't you understand, Ned? I don't care anymore! I don't care what happens to them or what happens to me or to anyone. I am where Daddy was, only

I'm not ready to die. Not yet. There are dues that need paying. Daddy had his debt and I have mine, and I will not cheat my creditor—"

"Mavis, Mavis, you're not making sense . . ." He reached for me.

"Don't touch me!" I stepped back, toward the six-foot drop to the tracks below.

His face contorted in anger. "Oh, no, why should I touch you? There's only one man's touch you want, and it isn't mine. I am not the one, though I am the *only* one who can save you."

"What do you mean?"

"Marry me, Mavis. Marry me. You and your mother can live with us. We can build a life together. A normal life, and you can turn your back on this madness once and for all. You'll be out of his reach, Mavis. It's not what you want, but it's what you need . . ."

"You have no idea what I need."

The train's whistle shrieked in the distance. He shouted over the noise but did not come closer. I noticed for the first time he was barefoot; he had not stopped to put anything on his feet.

"I love you, Mavis. I have loved you since the moment I laid eyes on you. I loved you the moment I saw you, and you know the moment I saw you. I loved you before I even knew the sound of your voice, before I felt the touch of your hand. I cannot bear the thought of life without you. It would be like someone telling me I must live without breathing. Let me show you. Let me show you how much I love you." And then Ned Jeffries fell to his knees. "Marry me! Marry me and I'll make this promise to you. I promise if he ever comes home, I will release you. I will let you go, if that's what you want. For to be with you for just a short time is better than for no time at all. Even if he kills me for this, I will gladly pay the price."

The platform began to shake with the force of the coming train. Its great light pierced the darkness all around us. The station lights flickered, throwing harsh shadow across his vulpine features. He was like some figure from a dream, calling me to follow him. I looked over my shoulder, to the approaching train.

"If you get on that train, Mavis, I swear before all that's holy I'll throw myself in front of it!"

"Ned, it won't be moving."

He held out his arms as the train screamed into the station, and the air shook with the demon cry of its brakes and the howling whistle. Ned's hands were long and thin and cold as death.

I went home.

SIX

Pastor and Miss Mavis were gone when we got up. At breakfast Sharon-Rose sat across the table from me and kept darting her eyes at me. I tried to keep my eyes down at my plate, but I'd peek up every now and then, and there'd be her eyes, dart, dart. Her momma must have dressed her before breakfast; she came to the table in a pink dress with a big pink bow in her hair. Sharon-Rose didn't look more girl-like in a dress, just less Sharon-Rose-like. Nobody said much, except Bertram started in on his tummy and how it hurt so bad he couldn't go to church. Everybody ignored him. We went to our room to change. Bertram closed the door and said, "Don't know why she's still here. Why couldn't she go in with her momma and daddy?" He dressed by the closet. "Here's your shoes," he said, and threw them across the room at my head.

In the car I was smushed in the middle of the back seat between Sharon-Rose and Bertram. I could smell her hair. She was wearing white stockings with her pink dress, and pink shoes with white straps and a pink buckle.

"How's your head?" she whispered to me.

I didn't say anything.

Daddy could hardly find a place to park near the church. I had never seen so many cars there, not even at Christmas or Easter. We stepped out of the car, and the sun was hot against my scalp. There wasn't even a breath of breeze. We walked between the cars and the gravel crunched under our feet. The church bells rang and Daddy went ahead of us to clear a path through the knot of people around the door. All the chattering and laughing stopped when they saw Sharon-Rose with us. They said, "Good morning, sweetie," and, "We're all so proud of your daddy," and, "God bless you, honey." We walked in, and I had never seen the church so full. Every pew was packed, and people were standing in the side aisles and shoulder to shoulder in the middle aisle. Miss Mavis had saved us a place down front, the worst place of all to be. Everybody could see you there, especially the choir and Miss Nadine on the piano and, worst of all, Pastor, when his turn came. Bertram sometimes got the pew-neck, where you start to fall asleep and your head falls forward and you catch yourself, snapping your head back fast. Pastor never gave good sermons. He spoke real slow and soft so the back rows never heard all he said, and after about twenty minutes most folks got so bored they started to talk or fell asleep. One time even Daddy fell asleep, though he swore to Momma he didn't.

We slid into the pew. It was Miss Mavis on the end, then Sharon-Rose, me, Bertram, Momma, and Daddy last of all, by the center aisle. Miss Nadine was playing "Lord Lifted Me." The choir stood up when she was done, and we all sang "Amazing Grace." The side door flung open and Pastor kind of lunged in, wearing a black robe with a deep purple sash. He was carrying his cane but walking without anyone's help. He lowered himself into the wooden chair by the podium, and I got my first real good look at him. He did look a little like a turtle, with a long stringy kind of neck and the skin pulled into folds along his face. His hair was just a halo of black fuzz around his head, and his nose a little bump in the middle of his face. His skin was the color of red clay, like he had a terrible sunburn. I wondered why he was sitting there with his mouth open, showing his upper teeth, until I realized he didn't have any lips left. That made me feel a little sick, and I looked away.

I looked the wrong way, toward Sharon-Rose. She was looking at me, and when I looked at her a bright smile spread over her face. I felt myself go hot all over, and I looked away.

We sat down after the hymn. Then Miss Willifred stood up at the podium and gave a speech. She talked about the wonderful welcome-home extravaganza put on by Bertram and Annie Parker. Everybody clapped. Then she thanked all the committees. Then she said there was much work to be done, but we all praised God for his manifold blessings in bringing the pastor back to his flock. "Our prayers are with you,

Pastor, and your family," she said to him. He looked at her like he didn't know what she was talking about. We stood up and said the Doxology. We sang "Onward Christian Soldiers" as the plate was passed. We said the Lord's Prayer. Then we sat down and waited for the sermon.

For a long time, Pastor did not move. He sat with his head bowed; you could see his scarred scalp beneath the black fuzz of hair. Finally he pushed himself to his feet using the cane for support and took about ten minutes getting to the podium. It hurt, it actually hurt to watch him get there. He grasped both sides of the podium, bent his head again, then stretched forth his neck, reminding me more than anything of a turtle poking its head from its shell. Pastor opened his mouth and spoke, and this is what he said: "In the beginning, God created the heavens and the earth. And the earth was without form, and void . . . Uncounted eons ago, all that was—or ever will be—was contained in a single ball of matter . . ."

He slapped his hands together, clenching them into a fist. The clap was so loud we all jumped. His arms shook with the pressure of holding his hands together like that.

"And there was nothing else. All that was. All that ever will be, in one place, in one time, which had no Time at all, packed tight, straining for release. Straining for birth. And surrounding it, an infinity of Nothing. No light. No sound. Simply, nothing. And then, at some point, nobody really knows when or why, the ball could contain itself no longer and EXPLODED INTO THE NOTHINGNESS!"

He flung his hands apart as he yelled, flung them so hard I expected them to come flying off his wrists into our laps. "Astronomers call it the Big Bang; God called it the Light, and God called the Light good, and he separated it from the darkness, and the matter flung itself out into the Nothingness, and the stars were born, and about them planets and about them moons and asteroids and comets. And great spinning galaxies whipped through the Nothingness, traveling at speeds beyond human imagining, and God said, Let there be a firmament in the midst of the waters, and the earth was born. He raised the mountains and pushed down the valleys and spat out the great waters of the earth, and when he was done, he took what little was left . . . and he made a man."

Pastor took a breath, the first breath he'd taken since he started. His voice had changed since the fire, and it didn't sound like the high, thin voice from the night before. It was deep and booming and loud, as if thunder had been given a voice.

"Because God was lonely. God himself was lonely. He scooped man out of the wet clay; he breathed life into him. He said, Walk with me, the man who was made of the same stuff as the mountains and the valleys and the great waters of the earth; the same stuff as the spinning galaxies, the suns, the asteroids, the comets—random, spinning matter given spirit, given con-scious-ness. And of all the teeming, living things he had created, man was God's favorite. He blessed him not only in the form of God, but in the spirit of God. Able to reason, able to love.

"And it is love that brings me here today, stripped to my bones. Burned to my marrow. For I was not sent to this place to confess to crimes or to the failings of the human heart, though, Lord, they are many. No, I was sent to this place, in this moment, to speak of love.

"And empty-handed I come. I have nothing to offer and I have nothing to gain. For I am damned already. Oh, yes! I have witnessed my own damnation; I have heard it declared within the inferno.

"I . . . am . . . the . . . dead. I left the fire, yet the fire would not leave me. For you all have heard. You all do know what I saw in the fire, and we all know, even we here know, that no one can look at the face of God and live. See my face; this is the face born in the primal furnace. This is the face of damnation. This is the face of despair. This is the face of love. This is the voice of one who cries out in the wilderness. Make straight the way! Gird your loins! Unsheathe your blades! Love's fulfillment comes. And it comes in flames! And there is not enough water in this whole damned universe to quench its insatiable thirst. 'Many waters cannot quench love, neither can the floods drown it. If a man would give all the substance of his house to love, it would utterly be contemned.'

"That is my report and my prophecy: The sun rises upon what we plan and sets upon what we've done. And what have we done? What have we done? What have we done that men will speak of us? Surely, surely, life is more than a procession of days. More than the sum of thirty thousand sunrises. More than the putting on and taking off. More than

the sleeping and more than the waking. My eyes were closed, until they were opened by fire. My heart slept, until the heat of a thousand suns awoke it. My heart awoke to the greatest of truths, that our sin arises not from hate or jealousy or fear or anger or despair. No, all our sin comes from *love.*

"For out of this longing for love comes evil thoughts—murder, adultery, unchastity, theft, false witness, blasphemy. This is our fatal flaw: that God so loved the world that he gave love to the world. That he placed in man's heart the need for love, the desire for love, the hunger for love.

"For our lonely God took pity on his lonely creation, and gave him a companion, meant to be a complement and a virtue, but which proved to be his fatal flaw, and this fatal flaw we call—*Woman.*"

A man behind us laughed out loud. "Amen!" another man shouted. Someone else gave a little gasp, and I heard a couple of "oohs!" from the old ladies.

"Now she was made of the same stuff. The same ancient atoms there in that Great Ball of Life, so she too was cosmic effluvia, the residue of brilliant white light. Yet she had something man did not have, but wanted very much, more than shelter over his naked head, more than food for his empty belly, and that something scientists call a *vagina.*"

"Oh my!" someone behind me cried out, and now the pews were creaking and the floor shaking as some people got up and started pushing their way toward the door. Momma and Daddy had their heads together, whispering. Sharon-Rose leaned over and put her mouth against my ear.

"*I* have a vagina," she said.

"And man hungered for this vagina," Pastor cried. "He fought for it, stole for it, even killed for it, and God in his heaven must have wondered what the hell he had done."

Now the whole church was shaking and grumbling, and Pastor ⱨ to shout over the noise.

"What shocks you, that I speak the word vagina or that I spe⸝ truth?! Verily I say to you, you will hear more shocking things th⸝ in the days to come!"

Momma turned to us and said, "Come, boys, it's time to g

Bertram said, "But I want to hear more about the vagin⸝

"What is a vagina?" I asked.

"Vagina! Vagina, from the Latin, meaning 'sheath!'" Pastor was shouting now. "My dictionary calls a sheath 'a case for a blade, as for a knife.' A knife! To sheath your blade means to put it away; put it somewhere where it will be safe and protected against damage. A sheath is sanctuary. A sheath is home."

Momma stood up and pulled Bertram to his feet. She looked at Sharon-Rose.

Miss Mavis said, "I will stay."

Momma nodded and herded us into the aisle, which was clear now of people.

"Yes! Leave now! Go home to your safe little beds, snuggle down in your covers tonight and take comfort. Wives, take comfort in your blades and husbands in your sheaths!"

Half the church was empty, and angry voices were going on beyond the doors. Daddy was already gone. Momma pushed us down the aisle, her lips tight and her eyes straight ahead.

"Do you think I do not know your minds? You will chase me into the wilderness; you will drive me into exile, but my voice will cry unto heaven, and I will be heard!"

Daddy was standing next to Mr. Fredericks at the bottom of the steps. They were having a fight.

" . . . defiling the house of God!" Mr. Fredericks boomed. There was a knot of people around him and Daddy, listening.

"What would you have me do about it?" Daddy asked.

"Remove him!"

"I think we should remember what he's gone through."

"Dear Jesus, Bertram, the man is on the pulpit talking about vaginas! In front of children! I didn't even know what a vagina was until I was twenty-five!"

"I'm sorry to hear that, Bob."

"As deacons of this church we have an obligation—"

"I agree," said Daddy. "But we also have an obligation to Ned. He is our pastor. I say we wait him out."

"What's that mean, 'wait him out'?"

"He'll tire himself out—" Daddy glanced behind him at the people pouring out of the church. "Or get tired of speaking to an empty room."

"This was a terrible mistake," Mr. Fredericks said. "We all heard the kind of things he was saying at the party. We should have known. The man's out of his senses."

"All the more reason for understanding," Daddy said.

Miss Willifred came out of the church and said, "I have never in my life . . . I want that man prosecuted . . . I want him run out of town . . . I want his head on a platter!" She stopped and shouted to no one in particular, "I want the committees immediately dissolved and the money remaining used to find a new pastor!" She swayed at the bottom of the stairs and Mr. Fredericks grabbed her elbow.

"Steady there, Miss Willie," he said. "Steady."

"Oh, the treachery," she said. "The betrayal."

"I'll call you this afternoon," Mr. Fredericks called over his shoulder to Daddy as he led Miss Willifred to her car.

"What's gonna happen now?" Bertram asked Daddy. "They gonna arrest Pastor?"

Just then Sheriff Trimbul pulled up in his patrol car and got out. He hitched up his pants and came to the steps. He shook Daddy's hand. "Got a disturbing the peace call," he said, with a little smile.

Daddy said, "Most everyone's left."

"But Mavis," Sheriff Trimbul said.

"Yes," Daddy said. "She's still in there."

"I'll go talk to him," Trimbul said. "See if I can get him to come on home. Ain't no one goin' to listen now."

"I'm not sure that matters," Daddy said.

We went to our car. I looked down at the foot of the hill, and standing there was a black man in a white jacket with black pants, black and white against the yellowish-tan ribbon of the dirt road. He was watching us.

Sharon-Rose slipped her shoes off in the hot car. I could see her red-painted toenails through the white stockings. She sat right beside me, her arm brushing my shoulder. I looked straight ahead. Nobody said anything. I had figured a vagina was what you stuck a knife into, but that's about as far as I got. Something told me not to ask about it. Mostly it was the stiff look to the back of Momma's head. I had never heard a sermon like that. I had never heard *anything* like that. You expect a preacher to talk about God and Jesus and maybe some about Moses and the prophets; sometimes they throw in a joke or a little story that shows you how good people can be. But you don't go into church expecting to hear about Big Bangs and suns and planets and comets and people made of star dust. I looked at my hands. The same stuff as great mountains and valleys and flowing waters, Pastor had said. When I was little I asked Momma where I had come from, and she said from God. That God had given me to her as a present, because that's what God does, he gives presents to people. "And life is the greatest one," she said. I guessed Pastor was saying before I came to Momma I was in that Big Ball of Stuff out in the middle of Nothing, waiting to be flung out. And of all places I'd landed right here, stuck in a car with Sharon-Rose's shoulder rubbing mine.

We went to our room to change. Daddy came in, his tie hanging loose around his neck. He shut the door.

"Daddy," Bertram said, "is Pastor going to prison for talking dirty in church?"

"No," Daddy said. "Pastor is going to get the help he needs."

He sat beside me on the bed and put his arm around my shoulder.

"And you, Robert Lee," he said. "What do you think of all this?"

"I don't want them here, Daddy," I said.

He nodded. He didn't answer, but he nodded.

"I have to go back to the church," he said. "To meet with the deacons."

"You gonna put him in a home for the mentally insane?" Bertram asked.

"What makes you think he's insane?" Daddy asked him.

"Because he's crazy."

"You shouldn't form opinions without having all the facts, Bertram," Daddy said. He patted me on the head and stood up.

"You boys help your mother today," he said. "I don't know how long I'll be."

"Can I go with you?" Bertram asked.

"No. I need you to stay home, with your mother," he said.

He left us alone. Bertram said, "Halley Martin's coming."

"How do you know?" I asked.

"That's why Daddy wanted me to stay here. I got to guard the house. I know where he keeps the shotgun."

He marched out of the room, leaving the door open and here I was, still in my underwear. I closed the door and sat for a minute on my bed. I was more afraid of Sharon-Rose right then than Halley Martin. Momma told me if I couldn't get along with Sharon-Rose I should stay in my room, away from her. But it wasn't getting along with her I was worried about, it was the night before, and her stepping out of the tub naked. All morning there were those little darty looks, and what she said to me in church, and her asking me how my head was. I got off the bed and got dressed, and then I sat down again. You never want out of your room more than when you have to stay in there.

The door opened without a knock. I didn't even have to look to know who it was. I didn't move. There was no point to it. I could run, but where would I run to? She was bigger and faster, and she'd just chase me down like a dog. She came and sat beside me and said, "Well, now you know we got to get married."

I didn't answer her or look at her.

She said, "Don't be stupid, Shiny. You got to marry me."

"Why?" I asked softly.

"Because I'm pregnant."

"What?"

"Pregnant. Pregnant. Everybody knows when a boy sees a girl without no clothes on she gets pregnant."

"I didn't know that," I said.

"Well, that's just your fat bad luck."

"It was an accident," I said.

"Ain't nothin' an accident," she said. She sounded very sure of herself. "So now, tell me a secret."

"What?"

"Tell me a secret. See, a husband and wife got to share their secrets, else their union ain't holy in the eyes of God."

"I don't know any secrets, Sharon-Rose."

"That's a lie. Everybody's got secrets."

"Well," I said, then I thought and thought, trying to think of a secret. "I cheated on a test, once."

"So what? Come on, Shiny, some dark, dirty secret you'd cry about if anybody knew."

"Well—I bite my toenails, sometimes, when nobody's looking."

"Everybody does that. Okay, I'll tell my secret first. And my secret isn't about cheating on some stupid test or biting toenails. My secret's about a crime."

"You're a criminal?"

"I'm a witness."

And then she told the story of how her house burned. Miss Mavis had fried some fish for dinner. Catfish and hush puppies and fried okra and fresh iced tea with squeezed lemon. "Momma's not a very good cook," she said, "but she knows how to fry fish." Pastor led them in the evening Bible study, and Sharon-Rose was sent to bed. She was sleeping, sleeping like a dead person, she said, having a dream about the circus, which was funny because she had never been to the circus, when their shouting woke her up. "They were going at it so loud the walls were shaking," she said. She snuck down the hallway to the kitchen door and stood outside against the wall, listening. "They fight all the time," she said. "Least they did before the fire. Now they don't hardly talk at all." Pastor was going on and on to her about her "wifely duty," whatever that was, and Miss Mavis was saying, "You knew, you knew what you were getting into. I made no secret of that," and Pastor said, "But there are other secrets." And Miss Mavis said, "There are no secrets you don't know about." And Pastor told her in marriage there can be no secrets, otherwise the union could not be holy in the eyes of God. And he told her he knew Sheriff Trimbul had been by that day and he knew what his news was. He knew Halley Martin was coming home. "Halley Martin killed a man for my momma," Sharon-Rose said. "And they sent him to prison for it and now he's out." Pastor told Miss Mavis he knew and she still hadn't told him, and Miss Mavis said, "You know already, why should I tell you?" And Pastor kept saying, "What does he want, Mavis? What does he want?" And Miss Mavis said, "I don't know; why don't you ask him when he gets here?" And then Sharon-Rose heard a sound like a slap, and Pastor cried, "No secrets, Mavis! Tell me there are no secrets!" And she heard her momma whimper, "No. No secrets. No more secrets." And Pastor yelled, "No more! Tell me there's no more!" And Miss Mavis raised her voice and yelled, "She is dead!" And Pastor said, "Who is? Who is dead?" And Miss Mavis said, "The woman who loved him." And then Sharon-Rose had to duck behind the grandfather clock because her daddy came rushing out of the kitchen and down the hall to their bedroom, and Miss Mavis after him, crying, "Ned! Ned, where are you going?" And then here came Pastor, dragging their mattress down the hall, and Miss Mavis backed into the kitchen out of sight. Pastor pushed and yanked that mattress into the kitchen, and Sharon-Rose heard him say, "She's dead, is she? The woman who loved Halley Martin is dead?!" Sharon-Rose peeked into the room, and there was Pastor with a long knife in his hand, the mattress on its side between him and Miss Mavis. And he took that knife and stabbed the mattress and cut it down its center. "And a million envelopes fell out, letter after letter after letter. I guess there might've been more'n a million. I never seen so many letters," Sharon-Rose said. Pastor yelled, "Then I suppose you would call these missives to the dead!" And Miss Mavis burst into tears and hit him as hard as she could in the face. "I don't love him!" she yelled. And Pastor right back at her, "No, you just hide his letters in our marital bed!" And Miss Mavis, "I never answered them. I never answered one of them!" And Pastor, "Dear God, Mavis, don't you see you don't have to? *This is the answer.*" And Miss Mavis fell to her knees; she fell to her knees and scooped up a handful of letters; she filled her arms with the letters and she carried them to the sink, where the dishes were still piled high. She dumped them into the sink, and she was saying, "All right, all right, I'll burn them all. If that's what you want, I shall burn them all." And she grabbed the kitchen matches and lit one, and Pastor cried, "No!" But it was too late: She dropped the lit match onto the paper. But she had dropped them in the crowded sink, and in the crowded sink was the frying pan still full of cooking oil, and the whole sink exploded in fire. The fire leapt up, Sharon-Rose said, like something alive, and gobbled at the kitchen curtains. She stepped out of her hiding place then, standing in the doorway, and Pastor shoved her out of the way and went down the hall. He came back with a blanket and swatted it at the burning curtains, but the blanket caught fire too, and he shouted for Miss Mavis to get Sharon-Rose out of the house, get her out of the house *now*. He dropped the burning blanket on the pile of letters and the mattress, and they caught fire too. Miss Mavis grabbed Sharon-Rose, and the last thing Sharon-Rose saw before her momma shoved her out into the night was her daddy, dancing like an Indian around a say-ounce fire, stomping on the burning letters.

"Why didn't your daddy come out then too?" I asked.

"I don't know," she said. She looked sad again. "I begged Momma to let me back inside. I wanted my dolls and my shoes. I could have lived without everything else, but I had to have my dolls and shoes."

She stood up and turned to me. She held out her hand, and when I didn't move she grabbed my wrist and pulled me to my feet. "It's time," she said.

"Time for what?"

"Time for us to finish getting married."

She started to unbutton her shirt.

"See, we both get naked and then we roll around on the bed, and then we're married."

"I ain't gettin' naked and rollin' around on the bed with you, Sharon-Rose."

"You don't got no choice now."

Just then the door came open and Bertram was standing there, his mouth open, staring at Sharon-Rose. Seeing her in our room was like seeing a big-mouth bass walking down the road. It was something that just shouldn't happen. She turned her back to him fast and buttoned up her shirt.

"Get out," he said.

"That's no way to talk to your little brother's intended," she told him.

"My little brother's what?"

"Oh, Bertram Parker, you sad, sad, sad boy," she said. Then she

smiled and skipped out of the room. He slammed the door behind her
and flicked the lock.

"What's she talking about, Shiny?"

I didn't say anything at first. I was shaking like a leaf.

"I know who set Pastor's house on fire," I said.

Daddy came home around supper time. His tie was loose and his shirt
baggy around his waist. He looked tired. He sank into his chair at the
head of the table and said, "I'm tired."

Momma brought him a glass of water. It was just the four of us; I
didn't know where Sharon-Rose was. Bertram and me had stayed in our
room all afternoon, playing checkers. I don't know why I kept playing
checkers with Bertram, because he always beat me. And he would say
things like, "Whoa! That's a sharp move!" mocking me, and, "This ain't
no challenge, playing with you."

Momma said, "Boys, fetch Sharon-Rose for supper. I want to talk to
your father."

And Daddy said, "No, Annie. I think they should hear this."

So he told us Pastor was still preaching. Momma couldn't believe her
ears. She asked Daddy if he meant to tell her Pastor Ned had been
preaching since eleven-twenty that morning, and now here it was almost
six o'clock? And Daddy said, Yes, he was still preaching, and people were
starting to come back now. Word had gotten out. He and Mr. Fredericks
had gone inside and Pastor told them he was not coming out. He was not
coming out and he was not through talking, because he had an
Announcement to make, a very important Announcement, and he would
be making it at midnight tonight, and he intended to man his pulpit
though the fires of Hell itself beat upon the door.

"What Announcement?" Momma asked.

Daddy said he didn't know, but word had spread all over town, and
now everybody was coming back to the church or were planning to after
supper.

"You know, I listened for a while, and although I can't say I understood all of it, some of what he said was actually beautiful," Daddy said.

"I find that very difficult to believe," Momma said, and Daddy gave a little shrug.

"Are we going, Momma?" Bertram asked. I had never seen him so excited about going to church before.

"No, we are not. Your father will go."

"But I want to hear the Announcement!"

"Midnight is well past your bedtime."

"But it's summer!"

"I think he should come," Daddy said quietly. "He's old enough. You can stay here with Robert Lee and Sharon-Rose."

"You should remove him before things get worse," Momma said. Her lips had gone thin.

"That's what Bob says, but I just can't see what harm he can do. He's probably found the safest place on earth."

I lay in my bed that night, in my room, which up to then I had always thought the safest place on earth. After Momma left, I tiptoed to the door and flipped the lock. I didn't want Sharon-Rose sneaking in with any thoughts of stripping us down. Bertram and Daddy had left just before my bedtime. Bertram was practically dancing from foot to foot with excitement. I asked him what he thought Pastor's Announcement was.

"I don't know," he said. "But I bet it's got somethin' to do with a certain knife-carryin' murderer."

As I lay in my bed I heard Momma moving through the house, checking the doors and windows. She and Daddy had snuck off after supper for a Talk, and Bertram said they were discussing what Momma should do if Halley Martin showed up on our doorstep, looking for Miss Mavis.

"If I was her," he said, "I'd just open that door and let him have it with both barrels."

"Why would Halley Martin hurt us, Bertram?" I asked.

"Okay, you're right. We should invite him in for some cake and ice cream. You are an idiot."

Bertram and Daddy changed clothes. Momma kissed them both on the porch and stood there watching until the car was out of sight. We came inside and there was Sharon-Rose standing in the middle of the living room, and she said, "I want my momma." She was crying. Momma hugged her and I went to my room. It felt hollowed out without Bertram in it. I couldn't remember when Bertram wasn't in his bed next to me at night, breathing heavy while the leaf-shadows danced me to sleep. I thought about what he said, about Halley Martin sneaking through the open window. I slid it closed and flipped the lock, but I didn't really believe that would stop a big man with a Purpose. When Momma came in for my prayer I asked her if I could sleep with her, and she asked Why, because now I was a big boy. But she knew why, and before I could answer, she said, "I want to tell you a story." And she told me how when he was in prison some men fell upon Halley Martin and smashed his hands. They took a big hammer and crushed every bone in his hands and now he couldn't use them. So there was no way he could get through my window. "Why did they do that to him, Momma?" I asked.

"I don't know, Shiny," she said. "I don't know why there's such ugliness in the world."

I didn't either, so I tucked the baseball bat under the covers with me for extra protection. I don't know if it was protection from Halley Martin or from Sharon-Rose, but it made me feel better. Down the road and up the hill in the little white church Pastor was still preaching. He'd been preaching since eleven o'clock and now it was about nine o'clock. I counted the hours on my fingers. I couldn't imagine anyone with so much to say it took them ten hours to say it. And he still had three hours to go. I couldn't figure how he was doing it. He must be hungry and tired and must have to go to the bathroom really bad. I was sure I knew what the Announcement was, but I didn't tell anybody, because I knew they might laugh at me, except Bertram, who I knew would laugh at me. I thought Pastor was going to announce what happened in the fire.

I was wrong.

"Bertram?"

"What?"

"I'm awake," I said.

"Really? Thanks for telling me."

"What did he say, Bertram? What was the Announcement?"

He had woke me banging on the locked door. I opened it with the baseball bat in my hand. He grabbed it from me when he came in and acted like he was going to hit me with it. I expected that, so I didn't even flinch. He told me to stop acting stupid and go back to sleep. He said it was after one o'clock. I got back into bed and Bertram turned on the light to change. He threw his shoes against the back wall of the closet and slammed the dresser drawers. He huffed and grunted and fussed with his covers. He got all settled, then cursed and flung back his covers and went back to the light switch to turn off the overhead light. He banged his toe on the end of his bed and hopped about in the dark, yipping like a little dog. His bed creaked and groaned, and the covers snapped in the darkness as Bertram fussed with them again.

"Bertram, what was Pastor's Announcement?" I asked again.

"Oh." Bertram yawned. "The world's going to end."

"The world?"

"In three days. And on the third day, Jesus is going to come with all the hordes of heaven and take us home."

SEVEN

Wiley follows Elias into the study. Wiley stands for a moment, his hat in his hands more from force of habit than a concern for etiquette. Elias gently pries it from his fingers and eases from the room, closing the wide doors behind him.

Twenty years have made Wiley thinner, except for a paunch that hangs over his belt. With that bulging belly and spindly arms and legs, he reminds me of a spider.

"Well, Jesus Christ," he says. "Look at you."

I come around the desk. He does not offer me his hand, but places both of his upon my shoulders and looks into my eyes.

"You son of a bitch," he says. There is a knock on the door and Elias comes back with a tray. He places a glass of water on the desk and hands Wiley a bottle of beer. He plops a straw into my drink before he leaves.

"When I heard this ol' place finally sold, I never dreamed—"

"You never kept in touch," I say.

"I know; I know, now, Halley, I know that was my fault. That was all my fault. I kept telling Lorraine, you know, we ought to get up to Starke and see Halley. We got to do that. But what with the kids and me out of work, you know, it was—"

"Tough," I say.

He is relieved. "Yeah. Yeah, that's it, tough."

"You still out of work?"

"Oh, I pick up some work, here and there. Ain't been easy, but Jeremiah, he helps out. Got his wife and kids with us, you know."

"How is Jeremiah?"

"He's good. He's doin' real good, Halley."

He drops his eyes. There is a silence between us. Too many years gone by. We are no longer friends.

"Lookin' for work now, though," he says softly.

"Something will turn up," I say. I say no more about it. He gives a little nod. He understands.

"Damn, Halley, what happened to you up there? You don't even sound like you used to."

"Read too many goddamned books."

He nods as if that made perfect sense to him and takes a long pull from his bottle.

"I suppose you got some big plans now you're home," he says.

"I'm going to see what develops."

"Lotta folks talkin'. Guess you know things've been a little crazy around here."

"I've heard some stories," I say.

"That man she married, that preacher." He will not say your name. "They say he's plumb out of his head crazy. They say the heat from that house-fire fried his brain."

"Wiley," I say, "before all this is over, I might need your help."

"Before all what's over? Like to know what I'm getting into before I say yes, Halley."

"There's money in it."

"All right," he says. "I'll help."

Trimbul comes to see me the next night. I wonder if you know he's coming. I stand on the front porch as he rolls his enormous bulk up the gravel path. Elias is behind me, ever watchful. I tell him to go inside. As Wiley shrank, Trimbul grew. I find myself watching his mouth as we speak, remembering the endless lectures on tooth decay.

"Halley Martin," he says.

"Sheriff Trimbul. How's your teeth?"

He laughs. He reaches into his mouth and removes his upper plate, holding it out in his hand like an offering.

"Sorry," I say. "It's not teeth I need."

He nods quickly, suddenly embarrassed. He fumbles getting the teeth back in. I invite him onto the porch, and we sit in the matching rocking chairs, as the stars begin to come out. Every night since my return I have come onto the porch to look at the stars. I scan the sky, looking for something, a sign, maybe, but no sign is given me. Usually Elias joins me and sits with his hunting rifle in his lap. "Been a lot of crazy talk about town," he told me on the first night.

"You want a drink?" I ask Trimbul.

"No thanks, Halley. I can't stay long."

"On your way to the party?"

He gives me a sideways glance. His eyes stop briefly on my hands, resting uselessly in my lap.

"So you know about Pastor Jeffries."

I nod. "Elias keeps me informed."

He smiles in spite of himself. "Elias keeps you informed? You become a college professor in prison?"

"I knew Ned Jeffries in prison," I say.

"That's what he told me."

"Will he live?" I ask.

"Maybe I should ask you the same question."

I laugh. "You find what caused that fire, Sheriff?"

"It was an accident."

"An act of God," I say. He nods seriously. "His preachin' days over?"

"You thinkin' of joining the church?"

"Sheriff, I haven't been to church in twenty-five years. I have no intention of starting now."

"Well," he clears his throat. "That sort of brings me to why I come. Your, uh, intentions."

"My intentions? My intentions. What business of yours are my intentions, Sheriff?"

"Ah, Halley, there ain't no need for this. I always liked you. You gotta know that. If you're still mad about me testifying at your trial—"

"Oh, no, Sheriff. I don't worry about the past anymore. I am a forward-thinking man."

"Good," he says. "Good." But with a sideways glance.

I find I'm enjoying myself more than I probably should. "You want to know my intentions? Been thinking about taking up the guitar. Seriously, I intend to buy some land, put in some orange groves. I think I'm going to buy back all the land Lester Howell had, and rebuild the kingdom he lost. Or I've been thinking about moving farther south, maybe Mexico. Buy a little hacienda by the sea and raise ponies. I've always wanted to see the ocean. And I think I shall marry. I am thirty-eight years old and in a few years it'll be too late to start a family. Do you know, Sheriff Trimbul, that I am thirty-eight years old and have never even laid with a woman? What do you think about that?"

His face grows crimson. It never ceases to surprise me, how this man who must see so many mortifying things is so easily embarrassed. He hangs his large head.

"I just—I just don't want to—I don't want anyone taking things—into their own hands."

"That would be extremely difficult for me to do, Sheriff."

"You know, some parties, certain people, they have rights. I mean to say, sometimes you need to involve others in your decision-making process."

"No one ever involved me in theirs."

"You said you were a forward-thinking man. There's been a hell of a lot of water under the bridge since you left, Halley, since all that happened. Certain things have happened, and it's nobody's fault, really. A lot of suffering. You've suffered, Ned's suffered, she's suffered. In some ways, she's suffered more than anyone. My point is, the reason I've come, at some point it's got to end. You got to let it go. There's nothing left to be done. You should see him, Halley, you should see what's become of Ned Jeffries—"

"Oh, I intend to."

"You can't blame him for doing something you yourself did."

"What would that be?"

"Falling in love."

I laugh. "I have nothing personal against Ned Jeffries, Sheriff."

"Funny, I seem to recall you saying the same thing about Walter Hughes."

He stands. There is that familiar awkward moment between grown men when they part and shaking hands is not an option open to them. He starts down the steps.

"Sheriff," I say.

He turns. "Yes, Halley?"

"Has she suffered?"

"Yes, Halley. Not in the way that you have, or Ned, or any man does, I guess. But she has. She has suffered."

Elias comes outside as Trimbul backs his cruiser down the long gravel drive.

"He ain't a bad man," Elias says.

"Too much fear in him," I say. "Blinds a man."

"Not the only thing that do."

He opens the door for me and follows me up the grand staircase to my bedroom. I have taken the one in the far west corner of the house, the one Elias tells me is the old guest room. I will not sleep in your father's old room and wouldn't dream of sleeping in yours. After my first week home I asked him to show me your room. But whatever I had expected to find, I was doomed to be disappointed: The room had been stripped bare. Even the furniture had been packed up and carted away. There was nothing of you left inside, not in the whole house.

In my room, Elias undresses me. I fought with him about that the first few nights, but the simple act of putting on or taking off clothes can take me a good hour, and by the end my hands sing with agony. He works quickly, keeping his eyes down. I stare straight ahead, my arms extended like a dime-store mannequin.

"Ned Jeffries is preaching tomorrow," I said.

"Yessah."

"You going to church tomorrow, Elias?"

"Go ev'ry Sunday, Mistah Halley. Not that same church, though."

"I need word sent to her."

He doesn't say anything. He is pulling down the covers, fluffing the pillows. His mouth is set in a tight, disapproving line.

"You know what word I want sent," I say.

He nods quickly, two short jerks of his head.

"I trust you, Elias."

I lie back in bed. He covers me to the waist.

"Open the other window, Elias. It's stuffy in here."

"That better now, Mistah Halley?"

"Yes. Thank you, Elias."

"You want anything else? You want to read tonight?"

"No."

"You want some ice for your hands?"

"No."

He turns off the light.

"No. Leave the light on. Thank you."

"Good night, Mistah Halley."

"Good night, Elias."

I must lie with my hands above the level of my heart, or my own blood makes me squirm in pain. Corrigan had worried about nerve damage, but it seems to me my nerves are working just fine. I lie in the middle of the bed with my hands resting on pillows on either side of my head. The pillows are very soft; the bed very hard. I have trouble sleeping in this house. I can't get used to so much space around me, after twenty years of having hardly any. I feel like a dust mote, floating in a vast, black emptiness.

"Elias!" I cry, and he is immediately in the room. He has been waiting by the door, ready for my call. He carries a glass of water with a straw and one of my pills. He lifts my head from the pillow and drops the pill on my tongue. I sip some water.

"Leave the water," I say, and he does.

The sewing room door was closed the next morning. Momma told us children to be still and not make any noise whatsoever. Miss Mavis was resting. We went outside because we knew it wasn't in us to make no noise whatsoever. Outside looked like the same outside as yesterday. It smelled the same, had the same feel and taste. It didn't feel like the world was going to end. Bertram said Pastor was going to wait in the church until the End came. He was going to preach until the world blew apart and Jesus came down in swirling fire with all the choirs of angels singing. He said the church was so full now people were hanging outside the doors, climbing into the crawlspace above the church to listen to Pastor through the eaves.

"What's he talk about?" I asked. I didn't know there were so many words in the world.

"All kinds of stuff. Sometimes you can understand him, and sometimes I don't know what the hell he's talking about. Sometimes he just flips the Bible open and starts reading, then he looks at you like, You dummy, don't you get it? He talked about what he saw in the fire."

"What did he see, Bertram?"

He started to say something, then he shrugged and said, "God."

We walked down the dirt road until we could see the church standing at the top of the hill. There were cars everywhere, on the hillside and the road and the little gravel parking lot. People were sitting beneath the oak tree, having breakfast, and more people were gathered in the lot and on the road. I didn't want to go up there and hear anything about fire-raining skies or the hordes of heaven, so I stopped walking. Bertram stopped too, and gave me an eye.

"You ain't comin'?" he asked.

I shook my head no. He gave me a little wave and kept going, toward the church.

I called after him, "It ain't really gonna end, is it, Bertram?" meaning the world, but either he didn't hear me or decided not to answer. I watched him go until he reached the parking lot of the church, and then I turned and walked home. I crawled up under the porch and fell right to sleep. I hadn't slept good after Bertram's waking me up and the news about Jesus and the hordes. I didn't know exactly what a horde was, but it didn't sound good.

I woke up to someone knocking at the front door. I rubbed my eyes. It must have been late, because the wind was coming through the latticework and the light had gone gray. I heard the screen door creak and Momma said, "Yes?"

"Afternoon, ma'am," a voice said. It sounded familiar and strange at the same time. "You know who I am?"

"Yes, I know who you are, Mr. Johnson," Momma said. "I also know who you work for, and you are not welcome here."

The door creaked again as she started to close it.

"I come with a message for Miss Mavis," the man said. He had a nice voice, low and sing-songy. "Won't take more'n two minutes, Miss Parker."

"Miss Mavis is resting and cannot be disturbed. I'm sorry."

Then I heard Miss Mavis's voice. "It's all right, Annie. Hello, Elias."

"Hello, Miss Mavis."

"Won't you come in? It's all right, Annie. Isn't it, Elias?"

"Yes'm, Miss Mavis. It's all right."

"My husband," Momma said, her voice rising, "is not home. I think he should wait until Bertram gets home."

"I can wait long as you want," Elias said.

"No, no. There's a storm coming," Miss Mavis said. "It will be all right, Annie."

I heard some shuffling of feet, the screen door creaking, and then nothing at all. He had gone inside.

I wait for you in your father's study. No matter what changes Elias makes or how long I stay here, in my mind it will always be your father's study. I wait here because I can think of no other place to wait. Here in this fireplace my first drawing of you burned. It occurs to me how fire follows you: from the burning fields of your father's groves twenty years ago to your house with Ned Jeffries. Elias made a fire before he left to gather you to me, and now it burns brightly, the only light in the room, while outside thunder calls to thunder, softly, still far to the west. A breeze ruffles the white curtains and makes the fire snap. I am dressed in dark pants and a white shirt. The burgundy tie with the silver tiepin is Elias's idea. He has bathed and shaved me and fixed my French cuffs with gold links he claims belonged to his father. He was brimming with advice but would not give it unless I asked, which I did not.

"Don't come back without her," I told him.

I cannot stand still. The windows overlook the weed-tangled fields of what used to be your father's groves, offering no view of the drive; I will not see you coming. I sit in the fat-backed leather chair for a while, watching the fire, then I can't take that anymore, and I pace the room. Without his knickknacks of sculpted ivory and leering heads of dead animals, your father's study has lost all its character. There is nothing here that makes it mine. I practice walking while holding my hands behind my back. I sit in each chair in the room, trying to decide the best position to be in when you finally come. I wonder what I will say. I wonder if I will be able to speak at all.

I am standing behind the desk, looking at the fire, when I hear Elias come in. I close my eyes. He is at the door.

"Mistah Halley," he says. "Miss Mavis come."

And so, you have come.

Elias takes your coat. You walk slowly into the room, a few steps ahead of him. Your hair is pulled back from your face, but a few dark strands fall forward, curving around your cheeks. You do not look at me. I stand with my hands behind my back. I am waiting. I don't know what I'm waiting for. I have waited so long I don't know how to do anything else.

"Can I bring you somethin', Miss Mavis?" he asks.

You shake your head no. He stands by the open door, your coat over one arm. I can feel his nervousness from across the room.

"Elias," I say. He steps forward, and you raise your eyes.

"I don't believe we've ever been properly introduced," I say to you.

"Elias."

He is expecting this. He stands between us. "Miss Mavis Howell Jeffries, it is my pleasure to introduce you to Mistah Halley Martin."

And he hangs there: I never told him what to do next.

"Thank you, Elias," I say, looking at you. Finally, you.

He nods at me, then smiles at you. He goes.

We are alone now, you and I.

You speak: "This was the last place I ever expected to see you."

You see something in my eyes and ask, "What is it?"

"I'm sorry," I say. "This is the first time I've ever heard your voice. It's a nice voice. Would you like to go for a walk with me?"

I offer the crook of my arm, keeping my hands behind my back, out of sight. You slip your hand through, resting it lightly on my forearm. The first touch. We walk through the kitchen into the garden, under a gray sky. The air is heavy with the weight of the coming storm. We stop at the edge of the path, and I watch as you bring a hand to your mouth.

"Don't cry, Mavis," I say. "I wanted to make you happy."

"There must be hundreds of them."

"You can thank Elias for it. I told him I'd hire a gardener, but he insisted on doing it himself."

In the breeze of the coming storm a thousand blooms sway and dip their heads, nodding to us. Yes, yes.

"It looks—" you say. "It looks exactly like it used to."

"Then you like it?"

You nod and wipe your cheeks with the back of your hands.

"Oh, Halley," you say, but leave the thought unspoken.

"Look over here, right over here," I say. "That's the spot. That's where I used to hide, to watch you. Sometimes I wondered if you knew I was there, knew I was there the whole time, and just . . . let me watch."

"I never knew," you say.

And with that, the sky opens up with a crash and we run for the sanctuary of the gazebo. Water runs the length of the thick strands framing your face and drips from the dark ends, rivulets tracing down your neck. The rain falls straight and hard; the rosebuds bob frantically in the downpour.

"We're trapped," you say.

After twenty years to prepare, I still don't know where to begin. It is as if we are strangers. The feeling is almost unbearable, as if I am a ferocious theologian who has discovered there is no God.

"You never wrote me," I finally say.

"You know I did—"

"You never sent them."

"I did . . ."

"A little late. Why didn't you get on the train that night?"

"I was a child, Halley. Does a child understand what she really wants?"

"I thought I did."

"And what is that, Halley? What did you want?"

"You said in that letter, that one letter, that you would wait for me." You do not answer.

" 'As long as this tree lives and grows, I will wait for you.' "

"Have you kept every promise you ever made?"

"Yes."

I swallow hard. I have re-created the garden of my youth, and suddenly I am eighteen again, stuttering, *This is for you.* "I just took what you said at—at your word. I took what you said to mean that—that you loved me."

You laugh so softly the pounding rain drowns out the sound. "Oh, Halley, when did it ever matter whether or not I loved you?"

"It matters now."

"And now it's too late."

"It's not too late for me."

"But it is too late for us." You turn and level your eyes at me, speaking urgently. "Show me your hands, Halley. You've been hiding them, but you know I have to see. I have to see what they did to you."

I bring my hands from behind my back. I hold them up, thinking of those dead, tormented rosebushes that greeted me when I came home to this garden. You do not say a word, but press your hand against your mouth and close your eyes.

"I'm sorry," you whisper. "Dear God, I'm sorry."

"It looks worse than it feels," I lie.

You sink onto the wet bench. The windblown water splashes against your back. You begin to rock back and forth, whispering something I can't hear. I sit beside you, feeling the water soak into my freshly pressed trousers.

"It's all right, Mavis," I say. "It's all right."

"You don't understand."

"Then help me, Mavis. Help me to understand. I don't pretend to understand much, I never did, even after I went to prison and learned to read and read every damned book I could get my hands on. See, I just said a cuss word. I can't even speak civil to you. I don't know how to talk to women. I never had a real conversation with a woman my whole life, except kin, which doesn't count. Please, Mavis, please, help me. Complete my education."

"He never raped me." You glance at me, expecting an answer. And, when no answer comes, "Daddy arranged everything, and you know my father always had what he arranged. I didn't know how to stop it; I didn't know how to stop *him*. So that night after Walter left I told Daddy he raped me, to stop the marriage, to stop him. I couldn't tell him the truth; I couldn't tell anyone. I sent Elias to you to tell you everything was all right. I was going to wait until I could see you again to tell you the truth, but Daddy put me on the first train to Inverness, and I never had the chance. I was a child. I thought as a child. I just wanted it to go away. I never thought, I never dreamed you would kill him. That's what I've had to live with for the past twenty years. That's what I've kept from everyone, had to keep from everyone, especially you, especially you, Halley, because I knew, I knew what the truth would do to you. Walter is dead for something he didn't do, and you went to prison for twenty years for killing an innocent man. I've had to live with that and I always promised myself I would not make you live with that. But I am a breaker of promises, Halley. I am a breaker of promises, and you should go away from me."

I am not looking at you now. I am looking out into the garden. The way of life is simple, really. The earth turns around the sun. The green, growing things feed. The rains come. The earth is washed clean.

You run. I watch you duck your head and stumble onto the path, and in an instant I am struck by the ridiculousness of it, the absurdity of my position. My position had always been absurd; until this moment, though, I was not aware of the height to which my absurdity reached. I have a strange feeling I have somehow landed in one of those tear-jerker novels by some dead Englishwoman. If there was a cliff, you'd find it and throw yourself off it. And I would mope in my chambers. If you had a sister, I'd take up with her and live the rest of my days in melancholic dreariness. I cry your name. That's what you do in dead Englishwomen's novels, against the howling wind, the lashing rain. I run after you, catching you by the edge of the path, throwing my arms around you, my momentum carrying us both down, into the young rosebushes, thorns tearing our clothes, penetrating our exposed flesh. I scream as my withered hands smack hard against the ground, your body on top of them. If this was the novel I imagine, you would roll over and we would kiss, a redemptive embrace, and you would realize with a stunning burst of white-hot revelation that you did love me after all, and I, I would forgive you, my darling, my one, my all.

"Bertram?"

"Don't start on me, Shiny."

I watched the leaf-shadows dance on the ceiling. I worked hard on not starting on him. It had been a bad storm, the worst that summer. The wind still brushed against the window. I pressed my hand against the wall. There, right there, on the other side, was Momma and Daddy. That thought usually let me rest, kept me from starting on Bertram, but it wasn't every night that soon the world would end. In the end, I couldn't help it.

"Bertram, I saw her. I saw Sharon-Rose naked and then we told secrets and then we were married, sort of, I think. And now she says she's pregnant and I don't even know what that means but I don't think it's good, 'cause I saw her naked and now when Jesus comes he's gonna send me straight to hell."

Bertram said, "You saw her what?"

"Naked," I whispered.

"You saw Sharon-Rose Jeffries naked?"

"Yeah-a."

"On purpose?"

"No! I had to pee. I had to pee and I went into the bathroom and she was there; I mean, she was coming out of the tub. I didn't mean to. I swear I didn't mean to."

Bertram laughed. He curled himself into a ball on his bed and laughed until tears shone in his eyes.

"You ain't married, Shiny."

"But Sharon-Rose said—"

"Sharon-Rose said? Jesus, Shiny, I told you to stay away from her. What's the matter with you? Ain't I told you over and over to stay away from her and what's the first thing you do? Waltz in on her naked!"

"I didn't waltz . . ."

"Shiny, her daddy says Jesus burned him in his kitchen, you think that makes it so? You can't believe everything somebody tells you."

"Why not?"

"Because that's stupid."

"Why?"

"Because people lie."

"Why?"

"Lots of reasons. Sharon-Rose lies because she thinks it's fun. You really think she's got a tumor?"

"But why would she—?"

"For attention, stupid! She's jealous of her daddy."

"So Pastor's lying too?"

"No. Well, a different kind of lie, maybe. Some people lie 'cause they just can't take the truth."

"What truth?" The more he tried to explain, the more confused I got.

"The truth that it was just an accident. Just a fire. And Pastor got all burned up to no purpose."

"I don't understand."

"Me either, much. Daddy tried to explain it to me."

"So Pastor really didn't see God in the fire?"

"Daddy said it don't matter much whether he did or not. He says what matters is, Pastor thinks he did."

"And the world ain't gonna end?"

Bertram yawned. "Some day, I s'pose. But it ain't ending any time soon."

"But what if it does? What if it's all true, about God in the fire and Jesus and the heavenly hordes and the world falling back into the Big Bang Ball?"

"Then," Bertram said, "I'll see you in hell."

"I lied to Ned. I told him I closed the post office box. He believed me. He believed me because he had to believe me. I left it open for two years after the letters stopped coming. I couldn't bring myself to close it. It was like admitting something, something I couldn't admit to."

"What?" I ask.

We are sitting in the study. Elias has made you a cup of hot tea, with a slice of orange, the way you like it. Elias never forgets. You are wearing one of my robes while Elias washes and dries your dress. Your hair is down, flowing over your shoulders, dark against the white terry cloth. I do not sit in Lester's chair. I sit across the room, by the window. While you were in the shower, I had Elias push the desk away from the fireplace and roll the chair into the hallway. He threw more logs on the fire, and now your skin shines golden in the flickering light.

You don't answer. You hold the cup with both hands, your bare legs drawn under you. I feel large, as if I'm taking up too much space. The air is moist from the storm, and hothouse warm.

"I should have got on that train," you say finally.

"Why didn't you?"

"I thought . . . I thought that the time for the truth had passed, and it was just easier, for everyone, to live without it."

"You didn't."

"I didn't have a choice."

I clear my throat. "Don't cry, Mavis."

"Can you let it go now, Halley? Now can you finally let it be over?"

"I don't understand your question."

"Let us go," you say, "Ned and me and my little girl." As if I have them trussed up in the basement. "Can't you do that now?"

It takes time to find my answer. When I have it, I rise from my chair. You lift your face. I touch your wet cheek with one twisted finger. You close your eyes and reach up, running your fingertips along the inside of my arm, to my wrist, and you bring my finger to your lips. You reach for my other hand. You press your warm lips against my wasted hands as I stand before you.

"It hurts, Mavis. It hurts."

You release me. I step back. You rise. The robe falls to the floor. For the first time in my life, I have no need for my imagination.

I touch. But each touch brings fire. Flame dances inside my skin, races along my nerves, swims in my veins. You close your eyes, your head tilted back slightly. Your eyes are closed and your mouth, slightly open. Your breath is warmer than the warm air around us. Your shoulders are back, your arms loose at your sides. You are shamelessly pure. You are in the light, the golden light I pictured as I raced to your house after killing Walter. It skitters along the length of your lashes and glimmers upon your moist lips. I trace the back of my hand along your neck, down your chest, across your stomach. My hand aches with the pain. Your mouth opens wider as you cry out, a whispered call, *Halley.*

"Mistah Halley?"

"Yes, Elias. I'm awake."

He steps into my bedroom, a darker shadow among the grays. I think of Preacher suddenly, another victim in my wake. If Elias has any sense, he will make tracks soon. A strong breeze billows the curtains, and he crosses over to the window to close it.

"Lord, Mistah Halley, ain't you cold?"

"It feels good. Leave it."

I lie on my back, naked on the bed, my hands resting beside my face.

"She get back all right?" I ask.

"Yessah, Mistah Halley. She fine. Snuck in through the window."

"You are an excellent man, Elias. Very discreet."

"What's that, Mistah Halley?"

"Nothing."

"She tol' me in the car her husband waiting for the world to end. Half the town over in that church with him, waiting too."

I laugh. "Anybody know when?"

"Pastor Ned say day after tomorrow. He a sad case, Mistah Halley. Out of his head, they say. Burned up so bad he don't hardly look human no more."

"Why did she marry him, Elias?"

He studies me before answering. "What Miss Mavis say?"

"I didn't ask her."

"Be the first thing I ask."

"There was a lot of ground to cover."

"Well, Mistah Halley, you know I never been married. Got ten chillen and twenty-five granchillen, but I ain't never worn a ring on my finger. I s'pose she didn't want to be an old maid, maybe. And he was awful sweet on her, in the beginning. Took good care of her momma till she died. I don't know, Mistah Halley. I don't understand half the things people do and not one thing a woman does."

"She should have waited for me."

"Oh, now, Mistah Halley, 'pears to me, she has."

Afterward, as you dressed me, I said, "Stay with me tonight."

"I can't. I have to get back to my daughter."

"Bring her here."

"Halley, the child has been through a great deal. I don't think meeting you is going to help speed her recovery."

"I was thinking more of my own," I said.

"Life, Halley . . ." you paused as you struggled with a button. There was a motherly tone to your voice that probably had something to do with you dressing me. "Life is a compromise between desire and necessity."

"I never compromised."

"And look what happened." You let go of my shirt and turned away. "I'm sorry."

"I'm going to leave here," I said. You nodded, as if you were expecting this. You went to the fireplace; you were still naked, and I marveled at you, the deep shadow in the crevice of your lower back, the curve of your hips, the sweep of your hair on your shoulders. I never knew there was such beauty in the world. I always assumed that after I possessed you the longing would go away, that part of it at least would be finished, would finally perish. But I didn't understand possession. You didn't belong to me now. I belonged to you.

"Come with me, Mavis."

You didn't answer, but I saw you stiffen. You folded your arms over your chest. I took that as a no. I came up behind you and brought my mouth close to your neck. My warm breath brushed your flesh.

"Come away with me," I whispered.

You said, "That is the ending, isn't it? Our love overwhelms us and I abandon everything to be with you." You were speaking so softly that even this close I could barely hear you. "My home, my friends, my husband, my daughter. And we ride off into the sunset to . . ."

"Mexico," I said.

You laughed. "Mexico. Of course, it's perfect. The perfect ending."

"Yes," I said.

"For me, because now I can have the life I thought I was meant to have. For you, because it's the only reason you . . . endured."

"Yes."

"And for Ned?"

"Justice."

"Is that what you call it?"

"It's what I call it."

"And my daughter. My baby girl."

"She'll come with us."

"You might not like her, Halley. Not many people do."

"It doesn't matter."

"To you or to Sharon-Rose? I don't understand. I don't understand any of this."

"You don't have to understand it."

I pressed my body against yours. You arched your back, pushing yourself against me, hard.

"What is that supposed to mean?" you asked. The frustration and anger in your voice somehow made our touching more exciting. I watched the firelight shimmer in the sweat-slick skin of your belly.

"You don't have to understand it."

"You should hate me."

"How could I hate you, Mavis? It would be useless, like hating the sun."

"No, it's better—everything would be better if you hated me. I want you to hate me."

"You have a strange way of showing it."

You stepped away. The loss of my hands gave you that freedom to step away and walk back to the chair. You picked up the robe, and instead of slipping back into it as I expected, you reached into the pocket and drew out a rain-soaked envelope.

"What's that?" I asked.

"A present from a mutual acquaintance. Two train tickets to Atlanta. I brought them here tonight . . ." You shrugged helplessly. "Because I was thinking like you. I was thinking I didn't have to understand this. But I can't do that. I'm not like you, Halley. I don't see things, the world, like you do."

You came back to me and, looking into my face, tossed the envelope into the fire. The acrid smell of the wet paper burning. The moisture shining at the edges of your eyes. The finality in your voice: "For all that he is, he is still my husband."

And I said, "If he's still your husband, why are you standing there, like that, in front of me?"

Farley Wells drops off the papers the next morning. He is distracted and seems in a hurry to leave.

"Best thing all around," he says. "I never thought you should come back here."

"I had nowhere else to go."

"Well, now you do."

He shuffles on his little feet. His hairpiece is an enormous affair, a tortured drama being played out on his head.

"Look me up before you go," he says, without much conviction.

He pats me on the shoulder. "Don't linger, Halley. Break clean and get out fast: World's ending tomorrow, you know."

He gives me a wink and follows Elias out the door. Elias comes back, a question in his eyes. We understand each other so well that he does not have to ask it. I motion toward the envelope Farley left on the desk.

"Open it, Elias."

He gives me a wary glance, then gingerly picks up the envelope and opens it. He frowns at the document inside.

"What is this, Mistah Halley?"

"The deed to this house. I've signed it over to you."

He stares at me, then at the paper, then back at me.

"A reward for your years of faithful service," I say.

"But I already got a house, Mistah Halley."

"Now you have two. Farley is the trustee of my estate; anything you need from now on, you can call him."

"I don't understand, Mistah Halley. I don't understand why you doin' this."

"I'm leaving, Elias."

"Where you goin'?"

"Farley's found me a place, a little cottage by the sea, in Mexico."

"You goin' to Mexico, Mistah Halley?" It is too much for him. He sinks into a chair, the deed still in his hand.

"There are no strings attached to this, Elias. There's no catch. But there is one more service you must perform for me."

He looks up at me, tears in his eyes. It occurs to me my leaving has hit him hard. He has been lonely these past few years, after Lester died and you married Ned and moved away.

"I do anything for you, Mistah Halley, anything at all, you know that."

I tell him what it is.

"I do anything but that, Mistah Halley."

"I didn't tell you what I intend to do with it, Elias."

"I ain't stupid, Mistah Halley. I know what you fixin' to do with it. No string attached! Mighty heavy string, you ask me."

"There must be a reckoning," I say.

"Reckoning for what? Pastor Ned ain't no Walter Hughes."

"No. Pastor Ned is no Walter Hughes. Walter Hughes was innocent; Pastor Ned is not."

He stares at me for a long moment. He bows his head and scuffs his immaculately shined shoes against the Persian rug. He slowly shakes his head back and forth, crumpling the deed in his hands.

"I can't do it, Mistah Halley," he says finally. "I just can't."

"Why, Elias? Who is Ned Jeffries to you?"

"He ain't nothin' to me, but you are. Last time I tried to help you, you went to prison for twenty years. I help you like this an' likely I'm goin' with you."

"No one will know."

"I will know."

I sigh. I sit in my chair behind the desk. I no longer think of it as Lester's. Now, it is mine.

"Have you ever wanted anything so badly, Elias Johnson, that you would stop at nothing to get it?"

He doesn't answer for a moment. His eyes narrow at me from across the room, and now there is something hard in his voice, a tone I've never heard from him. It is as if he too has realized who owns the chair in which I sit.

"And what do you want so bad, Mistah Halley? What do you want? You want Miss Mavis, that what you want?" He shakes his head, his voice rising. "That ain't what you want; that's just what you think you want. What you really want is a reason, a reason you spent twenty years i prison, a reason you lost your hands, a reason Walter Hughes is dead, reason you landed after all these years in that chair. Why, you ain't better'n that pastor out there, findin' the end of the whole goddam world in the burning down of his house. You think havin' Miss M gonna make sense of it? You think havin' her's gonna give you any p You had her last night—you at peace now, Mistah Halley?"

I take my time answering. "Is that a no?

"Mistah Halley, I hated Lester Howell. I hated that man witl heart and soul, and when he took sick, who you think was wi Who you think holdin' his head when he pukin' in the comr who you think feed and dress him like now I feed an' dress you you think on his hands and knees with a slop bucket cleanin' when he blowed his goddamn head off? But I did it; I didn't wishing for this and hoping for that. I didn't look up and sა me? I didn't look for no reason where there was no reason. Y looks for reasons, Mistah Halley? A child. A child hun Little child, he wants to know the why behind everyt scared. He want the world to make sense. He want to kn we men now, Mistah Halley. We men now."

He stands. He is shaking slightly. The deed in his snapping noises.

"You search your heart, Mistah Halley," he tells me. "You search it good. You know what the truth is. You know."

Bertram shook me awake, his face low to mine. He hadn't brushed his teeth yet, and it smelled like something had crawled into his mouth and died.

"Shiny, come on, get up, wanna show you somethin'." He pulled me out of bed and stood by the door while I got dressed. I was moving too slow for him; he had his arms folded over his chest and was drumming his thick fingers on his arms. It's hard to move fast when somebody's waiting on you and that somebody is someone who beats you up regularly. I put my shirt on backward, and he gave a disgusted grunt while I pulled my arms out of the holes and yanked the shirt around the right way. I followed him down the hall. I could hear Momma in the kitchen cooking breakfast and could smell the bacon frying.

"What is it, Bertram?" I whispered.

He put a finger to his lips and led me to the window by the front door. He pulled aside the curtain and said, "Look."

I looked. I didn't see anything at first except the long morning shadows of the trees on the dew-damp grass, stretching to touch the edge of the dirt road.

Then I saw Sharon-Rose. She was standing in the middle of the road, her arms spread wide, turning slowly, her face lifted up to the cloudless sky. She turned around and around, like one of those porcelain ballerinas on a music box, her eyes closed, her long hair falling straight down behind her back. It reminded me of how Pastor came out of his burning house with his arms spread wide like he was saying, "Here I am. Here I am; come and get me."

"She's been out there for the last half-hour," Bertram said.

"Why's she doin' that, Bertram?"

"'Cause she's crazy. Before she was a little crazy. Now she's all the way azy. I been thinkin' maybe that tumor story's true after all, and it's own up in her head."

We watched her turn until Momma called that breakfast was ready. I n't know how she heard, but Sharon-Rose dropped her arms and came

running toward us. We headed for the kitchen where Momma had laid out eggs and bacon and cinnamon rolls and fresh biscuits and fried potatoes.

Sharon-Rose slid into her chair beside me and said, "Where's my momma?"

"Still asleep, poor dear," Momma said. "Your mother is a brave woman, Sharon-Rose. I don't know how she endures."

"I want to see my daddy," Sharon-Rose said.

"And you will, dear. Very soon, now."

"I want to see my daddy today. I'm goin' to the church to see him."

"Now, Sharon-Rose, dear, I don't believe that's—"

"He's my daddy and I got a right to see him. Tomorrow the world's gonna end and I want to see him before Jesus comes to take him away."

"Jesus isn't going to take anyone away," Momma said.

Sharon-Rose said, "You callin' my daddy a liar?" Momma opened her mouth, then just let it stay open. I'd never seen Momma with nothing to say. Sharon-Rose was looking up at her, her chin stuck out, her lower lip poking up.

"I have nothing," Momma finally said, "nothing but the utmost admiration and pity for your father, Sharon-Rose."

"No, you don't," Sharon-Rose said. "No you don't. None of you do. None of you believe him; none of you got faith in what he says. You all think he's crazy."

Momma said calmly, "We do not."

"I do," Bertram said.

"Bertram!" Momma said.

"See!" Sharon-Rose yelled. "You make fun of him, I hear you; you all make fun and laugh at him; well, we'll see who's laughing tomorrow when the fire rains down from the sky and the earth cracks and spits up all the blood of everyone who's ever died in the whole history of time. We'll see who's crazy then!"

"Sharon-Rose, honey . . ."

"And I hope . . . I hope . . ." She was gulping for air, like she had just run up a hill. "I hope when it comes you all go to *hell*."

She jumped up and ran from the room. Momma lowered herself into her chair and ran her hand over her forehead. "Well," she said. That's all. Just "Well."

Me and Bertram left the table and went to our room. The door was open to the sewing room, and when I looked inside I saw Sharon-Rose cuddled up against Miss Mavis, her head tucked just under her momma's chin, and Miss Mavis was saying in a sleepy way, "Hush, now, hush, my sweet thing, my Rose of Sharon," and she was stroking Sharon-Rose's hair as they lay curled against each other on the little bed.

Daddy came home that afternoon with Mr. Fredericks and Mr. Peterson and Mr. Carlson and Mr. Crawley. He told Momma it was time for the final vote of the Board of Deacons. Momma made coffee and set out a plate of oatmeal cookies on the kitchen table, and the deacon-men sat with my daddy at the table and they talked about Pastor.

"Crawley, the papers," Mr. Fredericks said.

Mr. Crawley opened his briefcase and took out a stack of papers. He slid them across the table to Daddy. Daddy took out his black glasses and set them on his nose and studied the papers while the other deacon-men talked. They all wore short-sleeved white dress shirts and dark ties.

"You been out to the church this morning, Bob?" Mr. Carlson asked.

Mr. Fredericks nodded.

"How's he holding up?"

Mr. Fredericks said, "So hoarse you can't hardly hear him. Some damn fool was worried 'bout him fallin' over, so they got some rope and tied him to the pulpit."

The deacon-men shook their heads. Mr. Crawley sucked air hard through his nose and made a gargley sound deep in his throat.

"This is quickly turning from a spiritual emergency to a medical emergency," Mr. Peterson said.

"What's he sayin' now?" Mr. Carlson asked.

"Some damn fool nonsense about the reproductive cycle of the seven-year locust."

"The what?" Mr. Crawley asked.

"What's that got to do with the price of rice in China?" Mr. Carlson demanded.

"Does it really matter, Vern?" Mr. Peterson said.

Mr. Crawley said, "Yesterday he said he wanted to kiss God full on the mouth. Said he wanted to grab God by the ears and kiss him full on the mouth."

"Never seen the like," Mr. Carlson said, and all the deacon-men nodded their heads and said they had never seen the like either.

Then they all started talking at once, repeating stuff the pastor had said or stuff somebody said he said. They started arguing whether he really said this or that, and then Mr. Carlson said some folks from the Methodist church had showed up and they were taking notes. That got them all going on about what in the world the Methodists were up to taking notes like that, and Mr. Fredericks got all upset because Mrs. Fredericks used to be a Methodist and her family still was, so it was like they were attacking his own family. Mr. Crawley said he caught two or three teenagers outside the church trying to charge two dollars a head to get a peek at the pastor, like this was some kind of freak show, and Mr. Fredericks said, It *is* a damn freak show. And Mr. Peterson said he met two or three folks who claimed they touched Pastor's robe and were healed of their cancer. No, one had cancer and the other sciatica, though it may have been shingles. That'll start a frenzy for sure, Mr. Fredericks said, and all the deacon-men agreed they ought to find a way to keep people from touching Pastor till they got the asylum people there to cart him off.

Daddy set down the papers, took off his glasses, and rubbed his eyes.

"So what you think, Bertram?" Mr. Peterson asked.

"We think it oughtta be you who talks to her," Mr. Fredericks said. "You're closer to her than any of us."

"I'm not close to her," Daddy said. He sounded sad. "I'm not sure anyone's close to her."

"Annie, then," Mr. Fredericks said. "Annie can get her to sign it."

"Aren't we putting the cart before the horse here?" Daddy asked. "We haven't voted yet."

Mr. Fredericks said, "All those in favor of removing Ned Jeffries from the pastorship of the First Baptist Church of Homeland . . ."

"Bob," Daddy said. "Bob, the bylaws state the vote must be by secret ballot."

"I don't recall the bylaws saying that," Mr. Fredericks said.

Mr. Crawley said, "Bertram's right, Bob. Got to be a secret ballot."

Mr. Peterson and Mr. Carlson nodded, and Mr. Fredericks shut his mouth and sat back with his arms across his chest and gave a little wave of his hand. "All right, let's get this over with."

So Daddy took a piece of paper and tore it into five strips, and each deacon-man wrote down his vote. Then Daddy gathered up the papers and dropped them into Mr. Crawley's straw hat. He set the hat on the table and said, "Why don't you do the honors, Vern."

Mr. Carlson drew the first piece of paper and read, "Yes."

"What's that mean?" Mr. Peterson said. "Does it mean 'yes' he goes or 'yes' he stays?"

"That's my handwriting," Mr. Crawley said. "Means 'yes' he goes."

"I wrote mine the other way," Mr. Peterson said. " 'No' he goes."

"No he goes?" Mr. Fredericks said to him, his bushy eyebrows coming together so it looked like he had just one big, fat eyebrow.

"We're gonna have to do this again," Mr. Carlson said. "We didn't get it right and besides it ain't secret now."

Mr. Fredericks said in a loud voice, "Here's the question! Should Pastor Ned Jeffries be stripped of his pastorship of our church! Write Yes, strip him; No, leave him. Now let's get this damn thing over with so we can go home!"

So they flipped the papers over and everyone wrote down their vote. Mr. Carlson drew the papers out of the hat, one by one.

"First vote, Yes. Second vote, Yes. Third vote, No. Fourth vote, Yes. And the fifth vote is, Yes. That's four for and one against."

"Who the hell voted against?" Mr. Peterson shouted.

"It's a secret ballot, Bob," Daddy said quietly, and they all looked at him for a long, silent time. Daddy said, "There is one thing we haven't considered, in all our debate on the church's future."

Daddy folded his hands in front of him and pressed his thumbs together. He always pressed his thumbs together when a Talk was coming.

"What if he's right?"

Nobody said anything at first, then Mr. Fredericks busted out laughing and one by one they joined in until everyone was laughing except Daddy, who was smiling a little, looking at his thumbs go white at the spot where they pressed together.

"No, no, no, now listen. Hear me out," Daddy said.

"Maybe we drew up papers on the wrong man!" Mr. Peterson said, and that got them tickled again.

"Maybe, maybe, but think about this. We should think about this," Daddy said. "Seems to me I recall another man a couple thousand years ago, another homeless man who went about preaching 'bout the last being first and the first last and shocking everybody with the things he said, shocking 'em so bad they took a vote and voted him out of his ministry. Voted him clean out of life."

They weren't laughing now. Mr. Fredericks had that one big, bushy eyebrow again.

"Now I ain't sayin' we got the Second Coming in the form of Ned Jeffries. I ain't even saying we definitely got the Second Coming coming. What I am saying is, if we accept the proposition that we are men of faith, then we should remember what our faith teaches us."

Mr. Fredericks said, "And what would that be, Bertram?" His voice was so low and deep in his throat he reminded me of a dog growling.

"That he will come again," Daddy said.

They all started talking at once, trying to shout over each other. I heard Mr. Fredericks yell, "The Bible says no one will know when the end cometh!" And Mr. Carlson shouted over and over, "Only God! Only God! Only God!" Daddy let them go on, the way he sometimes lets Bertram go on, to get the steam out of his engine, then he held up his hand.

"All I'm saying is perhaps this *is* a test of faith! Not Ned Jeffries's faith; *our* faith. Maybe we ought to be questioning what *we* believe, not what *he* believes!"

"That don't matter one goddamned bit!" Mr. Fredericks said. "It's a moot point now, Bertram Parker! Because that man is *out*."

"She hasn't agreed to sign these papers . . ."

Mr. Fredericks stood up. He jabbed his finger on the tabletop. "That don't matter one damn bit either! The vote is to remove him from our pulpit, and by God that's what we're going to do, whether he's in a strait-jacket or the paddy wagon I don't care!"

Daddy stood up. He was a good head taller than Mr. Fredericks. He squared his shoulders and looked Mr. Fredericks right in the eye.

"If you do that, Bob," Daddy said quietly. "If you do that, you can rest assured I will not be part of it. You can bank on me being there with him, by his side, holding him down, if that's what it takes."

"Oh, Lord, Bertram, I never took you for a fool, but you sure are acting like one. It ever occur to you the real reason Ned Jeffries won't leave that church has nothing to do with the end of the world?"

Mr. Carlson said, "End of him more than likely!"

Mr. Crawley said, "Like as not he cooked up the whole thing from the get-go!"

"Ned Jeffries set himself on fire, Wynn?" Daddy asked. "Ned Jeffries endangered the lives of his wife and little girl?"

"I'm not talking about that, I'm talking about—"

"We all know what you're talking about," Daddy said. "And I will tell you I have it from reliable sources Halley Martin has no intention—"

"Yeah, like Ned Jeffries would know that, and if he did, would trust it! You know what that man is capable of!"

"The man was a damn fool to marry her in the first place!" Mr. Peterson said.

"Had a death wish since he come here," Mr. Carlson said.

"I don't think this has anything to do with Halley Martin," Daddy said. "You may feel differently. You all know what happened to Halley Martin in prison. You know it, and so does Ned. Ned was there, remember."

"Just 'cause he's a cripple don't mean nothing," Mr. Fredericks said. "We're wasting our time here. The vote's been taken, and the bylaws state"—he sneered the word "bylaws" at Daddy—"the bylaws state that once taken, the vote is final."

He stuck his chin out in Daddy's direction, like Sharon-Rose had done to Momma. Daddy left the table and went to the sink.

"What you doin'?" Mr. Fredericks said.

"Washing my hands."

"Well, it's all one big joke to him," Mr. Crawley said.

"No!" Daddy turned from the sink, water dripping from his hands. "No, it is not a joke to me. This is the sorriest thing that's ever happened to this town. Worse than what happened in nineteen forty, because this time there are four lives at stake. And if there is any human decency in any of you, you will stay the execution of your sentence until Mavis has an opportunity to make her decision."

Mr. Fredericks said he was going to fetch Sheriff Trimbul in case Miss Mavis refused to sign the papers to put Pastor in a Home for the Mentally Deranged. If she refused, the deacon-men would have Pastor arrested for trespassing. By the time the deacon-men left our house on the afternoon of that Last Day, Pastor wasn't Pastor anymore.

In the afternoon, Elias washes me. I lie in the gleaming, claw-footed porcelain tub as he pours a pitcher of water over my head and works the suds into my hair. He works his slender fingers through my hair, gently massaging my scalp. He pours the warm water over my head a second time, and I think of Wiley twenty years ago, washing me down with ice-cold well water, water and blood soaking into the earth at my feet. Elias does not speak as he bathes me. I throw my left arm over his shoulder, and he heaves my naked body out of the tub and dries me with a fresh towel, still warm from the line. He holds my robe for me, the same robe you wore, and follows me into my room. It is time to dress for the party.

I stand before the full-length mirror as Elias dresses me, leaning my forearm on his shoulder to step into the white pants. He stands behind me with the shirt. Once my arms are through, he steps in front and buttons me up. I look over his shoulder at my face in the mirror. My shirt is white silk, with gold cuff links in the shape of diamonds. A single diamond stud is set in the middle of each link. He selects a white dinner jacket from the closet, then carefully brushes the shoulders and the sleeves, frowning in concentration. He runs a comb through my hair, now humming softly a tune that sounds vaguely familiar, like a lullaby floating at the edge of memory.

"What is that, Elias?" I ask.

"What, Mistah Halley?"

"That song."

"Oh, Mistah Halley, just an old song we used to sing years ago. Call it 'Gloryland.'"

"I know that song."

He steps back to inspect his handiwork. "Looks like it might rain tonight, Mistah Halley," he says, and I tell him to bring the white duster, but no hat. I never liked hats.

I follow him out to the garage. The night is cool; the clouds had never left after yesterday's rain, and there is little heat for the earth to give back. I catch my reflection in the bay windows as we cross the walkway to the garage and hardly recognize myself. Now, like Richard Cory, I glitter as I walk.

Elias must negotiate the long black Cadillac through the people crowding the road leading to Wiley's. The news has got out of my homecoming, and the portion of Homeland not in the church waiting for the end of the world has come here, to the ends of the earth, to catch a glimpse of this errant comet's return. Children of the children I left behind pound on the hood of the car and try to jump onto the bumper. Elias lays on the horn until I tell him to stop. He parks the car on the edge of Wiley's yard. I can see the tension in his hands, the sweat glistening on the back of his neck. His rifle rests in the seat beside him. "You leave that in the car," I say. "You understand?" He nods, but I can tell he isn't happy about it. He opens the door for me and helps me out, pulling on my elbow to heave me out of the seat. I have hidden my hands in the wide pockets of the duster. Someone has lit a bonfire in the middle of Wiley's front yard, and little children caper around it, twisting and cavorting like the shades of demons in a dream. Elias leads me through the pressing crowd, and voices cry to me, "Halley! Halley Martin!" and faces come toward me in the gloom, firelight reflecting in their eyes. Large hands slap at my back and little hands pull at my legs. On the porch stands my mother, with two children on either side of her I do not know. Wiley and Lorraine come off the porch. A few paces behind them is a tall boy of about twenty, stronger and taller than Wiley; clearly he took after his momma's side. Jeremiah. Someone strikes up a tune on their banjo, and I barely hear Wiley as he leans forward to shout in my ear: "Welcome home, Halley Martin!"

"Wiley, I think I got a job for you."

We are sitting on the back porch, the small house behind us practically shaking with the revelry inside. We have snuck out here to talk. I know I don't have much time before someone discovers us. Elias has hovered close all night. He knows, but doesn't know how to stop me or if he can stop me or even if what he knows is true. Across the yard the cypress trees look as young and lithe and beautiful as they did twenty years ago, when I first met Elias, sitting on this porch, Jeremiah in my arms. These cypresses too are shamelessly pure.

I sit with my hands in my lap. I have developed a twitch in them, a quivering, as if too much force has been bottled up, and now it is leaking out. Wiley is drunk. His eyes seem huge in the light from the kerosene lamps set on either side of the porch.

"Oh, that's a blessing, Halley. I can't tell you. But it's real work, ain't it? I ain't lookin' for no handout."

"No, it's real work. That old house of Lester's is falling apart. Literally. I catch myself tiptoeing around upstairs because I'm afraid the whole ceiling's gonna come crashing down. Needs electric work, some plumbing, carpentry. Elias is working on a list."

"I'll start tomorrow, if tomorrow comes." He laughs at this. As if in answer, thunder rolls in the distance. Another hard rain is coming.

"Thank you, Halley," he says quietly, and I shrug.

"You're kin," I say.

I feel time pressing on me; I actually feel it on my shoulders, squeezing.

"It's good having you home, finally. It truly is. Lorraine and I were just talking about it. Place felt a little less . . . alive while you was gone."

"You know what I missed most, Wiley?"

"What's that?"

"The times I'd sneak off into the cypress stands, into the swamp, all by myself, with nothing but my knife with me. And I'd find a nice high spot of ground and lay there all night, thinking and whittling. Most peaceful I'd ever been. I used to lie in my bunk in prison and think about that, think about it for hours. Of course, now that'd be kind of difficult to do."

I look down at my hands, twitching in my lap. He follows my gaze, then looks away.

"Yeah-a," he says softly.

"But I got to thinking," I say. "I still could do it, with some help."

"How's that, Halley?"

I explain it to him. If he fully understands me, he doesn't let on.

"You mean, right now?"

"Yes, right now. I got the feeling in me bad right now, Wiley. I never liked crowds, and I can't hardly take it, them treating me like the god-damned prodigal son. I'm ready right now."

He hears the urgency in my voice, and suspicion must stir like the distant thunder in his alcohol-clouded brain.

"We all missed you, Halley," he says. "They all came to see you. Maybe tomorrow . . ."

"Where were they when I was in Starke for twenty years, Wiley? Where were *you?* Nobody gave a shit about me until I came home rich. Now I got more goddamned friends and family than I know what to do with. You know what it feels like to come home and be treated like the conquering hero by the likes of you? You people are torturing me. You're making it worse."

"All right, now, all right," he says, a little panicked.

"I never should have come back here. Farley told me not to. Told me there was nothing for me here anymore. Oh, plenty for all of *you,* but nothing for me."

"Okay, Halley, okay . . ."

"I had nowhere else to go. I cut off all my choices a long time ago, and I didn't ask for that. I didn't ask for it, Wiley. I didn't choose. And once I was there, how could I turn my back? This is important; listen to me, Wiley. In Starke I'd lie in my bunk and turn it over and over in my head; I looked over it from every angle, and no matter how I turned it, it turned out the same. Everything came out of it, and everything out of it came into me. There's nowhere else to go. There was never anywhere else to go. It's like arguing about gravity. It's like deciding I'm going to jump off this porch and fly to the moon. I found it in myself to break practically every law but that one."

"Well!" Wiley says. He hasn't understood a word I've said.

"I'm leaving Homeland," I tell him.

He is shocked. "You're—where you goin'?"

Without thinking, I say, "Gloryland."

"That near Tampa?"

"But before I leave," I say, "before I leave, I want to go into those woods; I want to go back there and I want to remember. I want to remember what brought me here. I want to reckon with the past. There are dues need paying; one more bill come due, and then, I'm gone."

I was sitting by the window, watching the light die outside while the rain came down hard, slamming into the ground and bending the tree limbs and hitting the tin roof of the porch so hard it sounded like the rain was laughing, hahahahahaha. Daddy and Bertram were gone to church with Miss Mavis. Momma was in the kitchen, baking cookies. Momma baked when she was upset. She baked the way some people cried, a lot and to no real purpose. Sharon-Rose had pitched a fit before Daddy left. She wanted to go to church too and wait for the hordes of heaven with her daddy. She cried and begged and screamed, and when she told her momma if they left her she'd cut her wrists open with a butcher knife Miss Mavis hauled off and slapped her in the face. Sharon-Rose busted out screaming and locked herself in the sewing room. Momma told Miss Mavis, "Go on, I'll watch her," and Miss Mavis left. Momma kissed Daddy at the door and fussed at him for almost walking out without his umbrella, look at that sky, and she asked him if Miss Mavis signed the crazy papers. Daddy shook his head no, and I wondered if he was going to stick to his promise to take any man who tried to take Pastor. I think that's why Bertram wanted to go so bad, because whether the world ended tonight or Pastor got arrested, either way it was bound to be interesting. "'Bye, stupid," he called to me, which isn't something you should say to someone you might never see again.

Behind me, Sharon-Rose said, "Maybe God changed his mind about the fire." She sounded sad. She sat beside me and pressed her face against the glass, so a little circle of fog grew around her nose. When she leaned back there was a greasy spot left on the glass.

"You ain't scared, Sharon-Rose?" I asked.

"No, I ain't scared. I'm gonna die anyway, on account of my tumor."

I didn't say anything, and she said, "You don't believe in my tumor."

The thunder popped right over our heads and I jumped a little. Sharon-Rose laughed. I don't know if she was laughing at the thunder or at me.

"You know why you're so scared all the time, Mr. Shiny Robert Lee Parker? You ain't got no faith. You got to have faith or you ain't no better than a rabbit in a hole. That what you want to be, a rabbit in a hole?"

"I just don't want to die, Sharon-Rose. I was going to start Little League this fall."

"Well, you're a big dreamer, ain't you?"

She stood up. "Come on, Shiny, let's you and me walk in the rain."

"Momma don't let us outside in thunderstorms. Lightning is the number one cause of death in—"

"Your momma ain't my momma. And besides, I for one ain't gonna spend my last day on earth sittin' inside like a lump of something. You come if you want, scaredy-cat."

She flung open the front door and raced off the porch, right into the rain-smacked yard. I grabbed the door because the wind was pushing it back and Momma would kill me if I let water get on the rug. The wind was pushing so fierce against the door I had trouble closing it. I should have closed it with me on the inside, but instead I stepped onto the porch and pulled it shut. I still don't know why I went out there. Sharon-Rose was in the middle of the yard with her face up at the sky, turning around in circles, her shoes caked in mud, her shirt clinging to her body, her long hair dark in its wetness hanging down her back.

"Come on, Shiny!" she shouted over the drumming of the rain. "It's wonderful!" She stopped spinning and clapped her hands over and over, slapping the raindrops between them. "Whoop! Whoop! Whoop!" she shouted. "Come on!" Thunder cracked in the sky, and the lightning popped so bright it was like God was taking a picture of her. Inside my house Momma was pulling a sheet of fresh oatmeal cookies from the oven. The kitchen would be warm and smell like cookies, and Momma would slide a cookie onto a plate, hand it to me, and say, "Here you are, my Robert Lee," and I would eat the cookie with a tall glass of milk, sitting at the kitchen table while Momma dropped another batch of cookie dough onto the sheet. I could go inside and leave Sharon-Rose out here with the hateful rain and the thunder and lightning and God, or I could stay. I could jump off the porch and spin with Sharon-Rose under the black sky.

"I ain't no rabbit in a hole!" I yelled, and jumped off the porch. I ran to Sharon-Rose and she grabbed my arms and spun me around, and I was wet all the way through, and her mouth was open wide and her breath smelled like chocolate, and the rain was so loud I couldn't hear her laughing but felt the breath of it against my face as we turned.

"Can't you hold still?"

Wiley must shout over the roar of the rain pounding the tin roof. I grind my teeth and manage a nod as he forces the fingers of my right hand apart. It feels as if he is tearing my fingers out by the roots. Black spots swim before my eyes and I'm afraid I'm going to pass out. He lays the handle of the hunting knife into my jerking palm and pushes the fingers down over it. I am shaking violently now from the pain. It is too much. I don't know how I will be able to get up from this chair, much less hike three miles through a cypress swamp. He holds my hand closed and struggles with the roll of duct tape; he's having trouble getting the end to stick to my wet flesh.

"You okay?" he shouts, and I give him another nod. "Seems like a helluva lot to go through just to whittle!"

He presses the end of the tape against the knife handle, then quickly wraps it around my hand. He rolls three layers around it, and I shout, "More!" So he gives it five more, and by this point my hand is shaking so violently I'm afraid I will slice his wrist open.

"Wiley!" I shout. "In my pocket!"

He doesn't react at first; he is staring at the knife twitching like something alive on the arm of the chair. The black spots have blossomed into dark, shimmering stars. He fumbles in the pockets of my white duster until he finds the pill bottle. "Two!" I yell. He drops two pills on my tongue, and I swallow them dry.

"Help me!" I shout.

He pulls me up. I stumble forward, then go down to one knee. I am close enough to the edge that the curtain of falling water spits in my face. Wiley goes down beside me.

"You ain't gonna make it! Let's go inside till the rain stops!"

I shake my head. "Pull me up!"

Now on my feet, the black stars begin to fade. My hand still shakes and twists slightly to the right, and I worry that when the time comes I will not be able to put enough force behind the thrust. I lean on Wiley as we step through the curtain of water, into the driving rain on the other side.

"Wait for the rain to stop!" he yells.

"I'm done waiting!" I shout back, and anything else he might have said is drowned out by the hateful rain as I walk into the waiting arms of the cypresses. I turn before stepping into the trees. Someone has joined Wiley on the porch: Elias.

She yelled, "Come on, Shiny, let's go!"

And Sharon-Rose pulled on my arm, dragging me onto the yellow slop of the muddy dirt road, to the barbed-wire fence bordering Mr. Newton's field.

"Where we goin', Sharon-Rose?"

She didn't answer. She slipped through the wire and stood on the other side. Her face was wet and red, and her lips looked puffy.

"What you waitin' for, boy?" she asked.

Then she turned and ran, straight for the cypresses across the field. Mr. Newton's herd was standing between her and the trees, their heads down in the driving rain. They saw her coming and the cows took off, skittering around in that panicky way cows have, butting each other and generally fighting because they're scared. I looked back at my house, where the lights glowed yellow and warm. Bertram's voice was in my head, saying, "Stay away from that girl, Shiny." But the same voice was saying, "Snakes . . . the rains bring 'em out . . ." I watched the cows bolting across the pasture, clods of mud flying from their hooves into the air, their eyes rolling back in their heads, and thought I was no better than them, no better than a scared ol' cow, and then I slipped through the fence and followed her down the long slope of land, to the waiting arms of the slender cypress trees.

The rain has slackened by the time I reach the church. I climb the hill in a swirl of gray mist. To the west, lightning flickers in the vast darkness of the retreating thunderheads. I lean against the live-oak tree that you planted as a promise and a beacon to rest. The church is surrounded by cars and more are parked willy-nilly on the road. Above me, a mocking-bird fusses in his nest. I have no real plan, except to wait, which has been my plan from the beginning. We stick to what we know. He can't stay in there forever, unless he is right and Forever has come, which would make my being here pointless. That's what I think as I lean against the tree, my right hand twitching, my mind foggy with morphine: Dear Lord, let this not be pointless.

There is a gathering of people around the door of the church. They all are straining to peer inside, except one, who is facing toward the road, as if waiting for something. In the darkness I cannot make out his face, but I recognize the brown Stetson. Trimbul. Another man with thick, dark eyebrows joins him, and together they come down the steps and stand amid the parked cars, conferring with heads bowed. The man hands Trimbul some papers. They are still talking when an ambulance comes down the road and pulls up the hill, wheels spinning on the wet grass. Two men in white jump out, and Trimbul flags them down. They join the conference between Trimbul and Bushy-Brows. Now the people around the doors are conflicted: They don't know which drama to watch. Bushy-Brows is jabbing his finger in the direction of Trimbul's chest and Trimbul is nodding. He says something to the white-coated men, then lumbers up the church steps. He speaks to the people at the door. Some kind of argument ensues that Bushy-Brows can't resist joining. The people on the steps reluctantly pull back and Trimbul disappears inside, Bushy-Brows in his wake.

I realize I am too late. Trimbul and Bushy-Brows will emerge from the church with Ned in tow, and the ambulance will take him away. As plans go, mine lacks a certain logic. In fact, there is no logic in it at all. Logic and common sense were never my strong suits. When I arrived at your house after killing Walter, I asked Trimbul how he knew where to find me. "Where else would you go?" he had answered. Unlike me, Trimbul is a man who thinks things through. There is no way he will let Ned Jeffries out of his sight, and it is not in me to go through Trimbul to get to Ned, something else Trimbul understands. This excruciating pain in my hand, this return to Homeland, this tree I'm leaning against, all a colossal waste of time. I decide Preacher was wrong about compensation. For all that I had lost, what was given to me? And the first thing that pops into my mind is, *Lester's chair.* That's what's been given to me.

The doors to the church are flung open and people begin to pour out. They are not happy people as they stream toward their cars. I realize Trimbul wants them out first, in case they have to get rough with Ned. I am almost glad to see he has lost none of his tenacity. In his own way, he was almost as tenacious as me. He had, after all, succeeded completely where I had failed miserably. I can see Trimbul's silhouette just inside the door as he fusses with the crowd, hurrying them along, engaging in a rolling argument with each person as they squeeze out the door. The air vibrates with the sound of a dozen cars starting at once. The ambulance driver lights a cigarette and passes it to his partner. I hear Trimbul shouting, "Move along now! Move along! Stop pushing; we're all friends here, ain't we?"

A movement at the southwest wall of the church catches my eye. A side door is opened and a figure dressed in a black robe stumbles out and disappears behind the building. I leave my post beside the tree and run doubled over, keeping the cars between me and the line of sight from the church steps. When I reach the southwest corner I stop and peer around the back. The black-robed figure is scampering down the hill; I catch sight of the top of his head before he is out of sight again. I edge along the wall until I reach the southeast corner. The figure is already across the road and heading straight for the cypresses on the other side.

"Compensation," I whisper, a true believer, again.

The rain was done, the clouds gone, and the stars shone over us in a moonless sky. The stars were brighter this time of year; they looked bright and right over your head, like you could reach up and touch them if you wanted. Sharon-Rose and me laid on our backs beside the fort and she proceeded to name all the stars. She did seem to know a lot about them, and I wondered if she did have a larger than normal brainpan from a tumor, no matter what Bertram said. I tried to picture all that brightness in one big ball, the way Pastor said it used to be before God decided to make everything. I wondered why God decided one day to make a world and make people. Pastor said it was because God was lonely. He wanted somebody to talk to, and now there are so many people you wondered how God had time for us all. How could he listen to everyone all at once? Maybe that's why some people get killed or burned up bad like Pastor; maybe God was busy listening to somebody else. It's hard to think God doesn't have time for you. Momma said God hears everything, even things you think, and God sees everything. That would give me a headache. When I thought about God, I pictured him with his head full of a million billion voices, all talking at once, high voices and low voices and grown-up voices and little voices, like mine. God must have a huge head. All these voices, all at once, all at the same time, and when I asked Momma about it she said maybe that's so, but what to us might be a bunch of crazy noise was to God like music. Like the sound of a stream, she said, running over rocks, each little drop making a splashing noise, but you hear all the splashes at once, and it's a nice sound, a peaceful sound.

When she was done naming the stars, Sharon-Rose rolled her head to the side and grabbed my hand. I stiffened up. I think I knew what was coming before it came.

"I love you, Shiny," she said.

I didn't say anything. She let go of my hand and stood up.

"We might as well finish it," she said.

"Finish what, Sharon-Rose?"

"Gettin' married."

She pulled off her shirt.

"Sharon-Rose," I said, "stop that."

She unzipped her jeans and kicked them off, and now she was standing in front of me in just her underwear, which was white, except there was a tiny pink bow on the waistband of her panties.

"See, we get naked and roll around, and then we're married," she said.

"You gotta have a preacher and flowers and rings and stuff like that," I said.

She ignored me. She held out her hand. "Come on, Shiny. Don't you love me?"

That was a question I didn't have an answer to, or if I did have one, it would probably get me beaten up. She grabbed my wrist and pulled me to my feet.

"Look, we're gettin' married whether you like it or not," she hissed at me. "Now take off your clothes."

I yanked my hand away, lost my balance, and fell flat on my butt. I scrambled to my feet and did the only thing I could do right then. I ran.

She yelled after me as I plunged into the cypresses, her voice high and sing-songy, and I heard the wet earth sucking at her feet and the fallen branches creak under her weight as she came running behind me, "Shiny . . . oh, Shineeeeeee!"

I tore through the swamp, branches with sharp little fingernails scratching at my face, long twisting vines curling around my feet. I had lost the trail and was just running blind in the darkness, in the close, sweet-smelling rot of the cypress stand. Behind me Sharon-Rose came crashing through the brush like a bull, bellowing my name. I prayed,

Dear God, out of all the voices right now, please, please hear mine and lead me home. I just want to be back home with Momma, and let Bertram and Daddy be there and let me be safe, God, let me be home and safe. I want to be home in my bed where it's dark, but a good kind of dark, not outside dark but dark laced with light, from our hallway, and just on the other side of the wall Momma and Daddy asleep, close to me.

I ran with my hands in front of me to clear the hanging vines and scratchy branches. Twice I tripped over the bulging cypress knees, falling smack down face first in the mud and coming up spitting dirt. Then suddenly there was nothing in front of me and I was standing in the open under the stars. I was at the fort. I had come full circle back to where I started. And sitting near the mouth of the fort was a little man in a black robe. Pastor stood up when he saw me, and he swayed a little on his feet, as if the ground below him was rocking. I turned back to the woods and he cried, "Child! Child!" I couldn't hear Sharon-Rose anymore. She was still lost somewhere in the swamp dressed in nothing but her underwear. Pastor called softly, "Come here, child. Come and sit with me." I walked to him. He was holding one withered, red hand out to me. I didn't take his hand. I just sat beside him. I was too tired to be scared anymore. I suppose that's what happens when you get tired enough.

We didn't say much. We were both pretty distracted, I guess. He was waiting for Jesus to come in all his naked glory, and I was waiting for his daughter in all of hers. There was a rattly sound deep in Pastor's chest. His voice was very hoarse, probably from talking three days straight without a break. He kept saying, This is beautiful, this is beautiful, which I supposed meant the stars over our heads, though he wasn't looking up there or at anything really, so I don't know what he thought was so beautiful. I decided to ask him what I'd been wondering since the night his house burned down.

"Pastor," I said. "Did you really see Jesus in the fire?"

"Yes, child," he said. "The problem is, I don't think that he saw me."

I couldn't bring myself to look at his face, not this close up. He wasn't a scary man. Just there was something so lost and sad about him it was almost scary. I wondered if he still thought the world was going to end tonight. The rain had cooled everything off. It felt cool and moist and nice sitting out in the night. It was hard to believe any fire would come raining from the sky.

And then a man came into the ring of trees, a man in white with dark hair, his face in shadow. He came into the clearing and stopped, his hands behind his back, and Pastor stood up and then I stood up, and so the three of us were standing looking at one another. I heard Pastor whisper real low, so low that the man in white couldn't have heard him: "You're late."

"Get out of here," the tall man in white said to me. "Go."

And Pastor went to the man in white. He walked with his legs kind of bowed, his arms slowly coming up, hands shaking at the ends of his wrists.

"Here he is, he is come," he said.

Pastor fell into the man in white. He fell straight into his tall body, and the man's arms flew from behind his back. Something silvery flashed in one of his hands. Pastor's face crushed into the man's chest, and the man brought his arms around Pastor's back to catch him. The man looked at me and was still looking at me when Sharon-Rose busted into the clearing, naked but for the underwear, covered in mud, with moss clinging to her wet hair. She didn't see her daddy and the big man hugging at first. She looked at me and yelled, "Shiny!" and then she stopped.

Ned lifts up his face. He pushes against me. My arms loosen. He grips my hips as he straightens himself. His face is unrecognizable.

He grabs my right wrist and before I can react he has the knife's point against his chest, and he is whispering, "I am glad, I am glad you've come." And he pulls on my wrist so the tip punctures his robe and sinks into his flesh. I am fighting him now, pulling back as he drives his body forward, and twenty years fall away: I am in Starke, dreaming on the first night of my sentence, and you are naked before me, whispering *deeper, deeper.*

"Dear Jesus, it's Jesus!" Sharon-Rose shrieked, and she fainted right there on the spot. She fell over and lay still as the dead. But I knew it wasn't

EIGHT

Sharon-Rose was on her way to Inverness with Miss Mavis, or maybe she was already there; I didn't know how long a train ride to Inverness took or even how far away Inverness was. But the smell of her still hung in the house and little pieces of her too, lying around, here and there, that her momma had forgotten to pack. A comb with little pink flowers on the handle. A pink sock with the hole where her big toe went. A doll Daddy had bought for her from the hospital gift shop. Momma said she would pack them up and mail them to her in Inverness, when she had the chance. I wished she could pack up everything else too. Her loud laugh. Her sad and angry eyes. And especially the sight of her naked and that mud-caked underwear and moss-dangly hair.

"Bertram?"

"What?"

"Are you asleep?"

"No, I was just lying here wondering if I should come over there and smother you with my pillow."

"Bertram, if you make a promise to someone that they made you make, is that really a promise like the kind you have to keep?"

"What?"

"If someone makes you swear you'll do something, do you have to do it?"

"Who?"

"Sharon-Rose."

"Was it a blood swear?"

"What's a blood swear?"

"A blood swear is when you seal the swear in blood. You prick your fingers and press your blood together."

"We didn't prick our fingers."

"Pinky swear?"

"No," I said.

"What'd you swear to?"

I didn't answer him. I was afraid he'd laugh at me or call me stupid or come over and smother me with his pillow. It's a sad thing, being afraid your only big brother will smother you with a pillow. I watched the leaf-shadows dance on the ceiling and thought, if I wanted to, I could get up and go to the bathroom and there'd be no chance of walking in on a naked girl. Sharon-Rose was gone.

On the last day I saw her, she wore the same white dress with pink bow she wore the day Pastor came home from the hospital. That whole morning she didn't say more than two words to me. She stayed close to Miss Mavis, and that morning she was angry and crying and saying it wasn't fair, everyone else was wearing black, so why couldn't she? Miss Mavis never told her why, not so I heard, but, "Hush, Sharon-Rose. Peace, please, give me a little peace," stuff like that, never looking at her but at some spot over her head, like she really wasn't at the place she should be.

By noon the big table was back in our living room, and Momma had most of the cooking done and the plates laid out and was fussing at Daddy that she hardly had time to get herself ready, much less the house and children, though me and Bertram had been ready since ten and waiting for them on the porch as we watched the cars go up the dirt road toward the church. Across the pasture the cypresses glowed green and wriggled in the heat. Those trees looked the same, but different, like something you dream about but in real life don't look that way at all.

"I'm never going back to that swamp again," I told Bertram.

"You're stupid," he said.

I sat in the backseat, next to Sharon-Rose, on our last ride together to the church. She was still angry about the dress and was making snuffling sounds in her throat and sitting with both fists balled tight in her lap. She had some gum in her mouth and was smacking it hard. Nobody said anything to her about it, though if me and Bertram smacked gum Momma would pinch our earlobes and make us spit it out.

All the deacons were outside the church when we got there, and they made a circle around Daddy and led him around back, away from us. There had been a true panic until the deacons got together and decided Daddy should be the substitute pastor until the next pastor could be found; they put an ad in three newspapers, but so far nobody had answered it. Daddy said they were all waiting for Pastor to get cold in the ground; otherwise, they would seem overanxious, and for some reason nobody wanted an overanxious preacher in the house. That made me wonder how long you stayed warm in the ground. I'd never touched a fresh grave, but that was scary to think about, feeling the warmth of a dead person coming up from the ground. After the funeral, Bertram told me a person's fingernails and hair keep growing, even after they're dead and the rest of their body rotted all to nothing, so the earth was full of skeletons with five-inch fingernails and toenails and hair down to their ankles.

Daddy didn't want to be the substitute pastor, but Mr. Fredericks said they had to have *somebody* to lead the prayers and singing and give a *little* sermon. Daddy said they should ask Reverend Baker, but Mr. Carlson said Reverend Baker was a Methodist and that wouldn't do *at all*, and Mr. Fredericks got mad at that because, like I said, his wife was a Methodist and so was all her family, and that started a big fight about who came the closest, the Methodists or the Nazarenes or the Presbyterians or the Church of God or the Church of Christ, until Daddy held up his hand and said, Yes, he would do it, but only for the funeral. "I'm not getting into the God business," he said, which made Momma laugh out loud, I don't know why.

There was a good many people in the church that morning, though not as many as in those days when Pastor, tied to the pulpit with big, thick ropes, talked about the world ending. I guess the ending of just one person isn't as interesting. All the people who normally went were there, and those people who came just on Christmas and Easter, and some people I'd never seen before, including some black people, who sat in the back pews, the women in big hats and long black veils and the men in crisp suits and wide straw hats that they held on their laps. One of them was Jasper Johnson, the guard at Daddy's bank. He gave me a big wink when I came in. Next to him was another black man I had seen somewhere before, but I couldn't remember where. He was looking down when we came in, but he brought his eyes up just as Miss Mavis walked in.

The big black casket was set right before the podium. It was closed. They put us right up front, so I got to stare at that big casket during the whole service. Right in the middle of it, while Daddy was giving his speech, Sharon-Rose reached over and grabbed my hand. I tried to pull it away, but she held on tight. Her hand was hot and sticky. I gave up trying to get my hand back and just let her hold it.

After Daddy was done talking, all the deacons came up, one by one, and each told how much he loved Pastor and thought so much of him as a preacher and a Man of God, and all I could think of was each and every one of them sitting at our kitchen table trying to figure out ways to get rid of him, calling him all sorts of names and pounding the table with their fists. Then Miss Willifred got up and talked about how much Pastor had done for our community, and didn't mention once how she swore to have his head on a platter. She busted out screaming and crying, and Miss Nadine and Miss Rachel had to help her down to her seat while she softly moaned, "What shall we do? What shall we do without him?" Then we all stood up and sang "Amazing Grace," and after we sang Daddy stepped down to the casket and five other men joined him, and we followed the group of them carrying the casket outside, into the hot, pressing air. They brought it under the tent in the graveyard behind the church. Miss Mavis fell then, just fell straight down to the ground, and she cried out in a loud voice, and people reached for her, to pull her up, but she flung her arms at them and screamed for them to leave her alone, and nobody knew what to do. Sharon-Rose bent down beside her, and now she was crying too, pulling on her shoulder, saying, "Please, Momma, please get up. Please, Momma." And Miss Mavis was whispering, not to her, not to Sharon-Rose, I don't know who she was whispering to, but she was whispering, "Like stars, forever shining! Like stars!"

They put Pastor in the ground right next to Halley Martin, and both their stones had the same ending date, and somebody afterward said there was a story there that would be told long after we were all gone, though I don't know what they meant by that, since a whole town can't just up and go, except some of those you hear about in the Bible that God smote on.

Miss Mavis stood long by their graves, and the black man who looked at her in the church came up and said, "It was a misunderstanding, Miss Mavis. It all was."

And Miss Mavis said to him, "Yes, Elias. It was a misunderstanding." And she put a hand on his arm and he walked her back to our car.

"You gonna be all right, Miss Mavis," he told her, and Miss Mavis laughed like he was a child and had said something very silly.

We drove home. I looked through the back window and he was standing in the middle of the road, his hat in his hand, and he was watching our car, and just before he was too far away to see, I saw him put his hat on his head and turn away.

Everyone came to our house for the food and to stand around and look at one another and not say much, except the deacon-men, who stood in one corner and argued about what *really* happened that night in the swamp, though I was there and saw it all except the last part and had told Sheriff Trimbul everything I saw and at the end of it he patted me on the head and said one day I would make a fine young man. He didn't say what he thought I was now. And the deacon-men fought over who attacked which one, whether Halley came at Pastor or Pastor came at Halley, and Mr. Crawley said it was his theory that Pastor was in cahoots with Elias Johnson, whatever that meant, and the whole thing was planned to lure Halley Martin into the swamp so Elias could shoot him. But Elias was delayed, and Halley had his knife in Pastor before Elias got there. But Mr. Carlson said Elias would never shoot Halley; he was aiming for Pastor, and missed. Then Mr. Fredericks said Elias wasn't in cahoots with anyone: He wanted to kill Halley so he could have all his lands and the big house and all, but Mr. Crawley said Elias already had those things so he wouldn't have to kill Halley for them. Then they decided that most likely Elias and Halley were in it together, with the plan for Halley to hold Pastor still while Elias shot him, but Elias shot Halley instead. "It's the only thing that makes sense," they said. Mr. Carlson said in the end nobody would ever know what really happened out there, because deep in the human heart there were mysteries beyond our reckoning. And Mr. Fredericks said, "Oh, what the hell do you know about the human heart?"

Miss Mavis went into the sewing room and nobody could get her out, not even Momma, who went in there for a long time, and when she came out it looked like she had been crying; her eyes were all dark from where the makeup ran. I heard her tell Daddy that Sharon-Rose was the only thing that kept Miss Mavis from doing something bad to herself, and that made me think that maybe everybody does serve a purpose, even someone like Sharon-Rose.

"We're going to live in Inverness with my second cousin," Sharon-Rose told me. She had caught me out on the porch. I was just about to crawl underneath it to get away from all the noise and, because it bothered me, away from seeing Momma cry like that.

"That's a long way from here," she said, very serious, looking right into my eyes. "You know how far that is, Shiny?"

I shook my head no.

"Well," she said. "It's too far to walk in a day. You'll have to write me."

"Why?" I asked.

"Every day," she said. "And I'll write you. And someday I'll come back for you."

"Why would you do that, Sharon-Rose?"

"Because that's what true lovers do."

"Sharon-Rose, I don't love you."

"You don't understand nothin' about love," she said. "Swear it."

"I swear I don't know nothin' about love."

"No, dummy! Swear you'll wait for me. Swear you'll wait for me if it takes twenty years. If it takes forever. Swear you'll wait for me until the end of time."

"I . . . I just can't do that, Sharon-Rose."

"Swear or I'll break your thumb."

She grabbed my hand and commenced to pulling on my thumb.

"Okay! Okay, I will, I will!"

She let me go, and then she said, "When I woke up in that swamp they were hugging each other, my daddy and Halley Martin, just hugging like the best of friends. My daddy's in heaven, waiting for me. That's why I'm not sad. I'm not sad at all. He's up there waiting for me—and Momma. Only I don't know what's going to happen when she gets there. Ol' Halley Martin'll be there too, and then I suppose she'll have to finally choose."

The next day they left us, and the house seemed all hollow somehow and didn't feel right again for months after they left.

And in November of that same year, when the air at last began to cool and the season had gone dry, the oak tree Miss Mavis planted twenty years ago was cut down and burned at the top of the green hill, and they say you could see the smoke from that fire from every house in Homeland as it rose to heaven in a cloudless sky, a column of gray and black against the blue, rising straight up until the wind tore it apart and it was gone.

INDEX